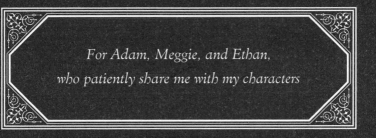

For Adam, Meggie, and Ethan,
who patiently share me with my characters

A NOVEL BY
CAT WINTERS

IN THE SHADOW OF BLACKBIRDS

AMULET BOOKS
NEW YORK

Image Credits
Page vi: Library of Congress, Prints and Photographs Division, LC-DIG-ds-01290;
Page 26: Library of Congress, Prints & Photographs Division, WWI Posters,
LC-USZ62-8278; Page 50: National Media Museum / Science & Society Picture Library;
Page 99: Wm. B. Becker Collection/PhotographyMuseum.com, © 2013 The American
Photography Museum, Inc.; Pages 113, 193, 234, 291: Courtesy U.S. National Library of
Medicine; Page 149: National Media Museum / Science & Society Picture Library;
Page 337: National Archives (165-WW-269B-25)

Library of Congress Cataloging-in-Publication Data

Winters, Cat.
In the shadow of blackbirds / Cat Winters.
p. cm.
Summary: In San Diego in 1918, as deadly influenza and World War I take their toll,
sixteen-year-old Mary Shelley Black watches desperate mourners flock to séances and spirit
photographers for comfort and, despite her scientific leanings, must consider if ghosts are real
when her first love, killed in battle, returns.
ISBN 978-1-4197-0530-4
[1. Spiritualism—Fiction. 2. Ghosts—Fiction. 3. Influenza Epidemic, 1918–1919—Fiction.
4. World War, 1914–1918—Fiction. 5. San Diego (Calif.)—History—20th century—
Fiction.] I. Title.
PZ7.W76673In 2013
[Fic]—dc23
2012039262

Text copyright © 2013 Catherine Karp
Book design by Maria T. Middleton

Printed and bound in U.S.A.
10 9 8 7 6 5 4 3 2 1

THE ART OF BOOKS SINCE 1949
115 West 18th Street
New York, NY 10011
www.abramsbooks.com

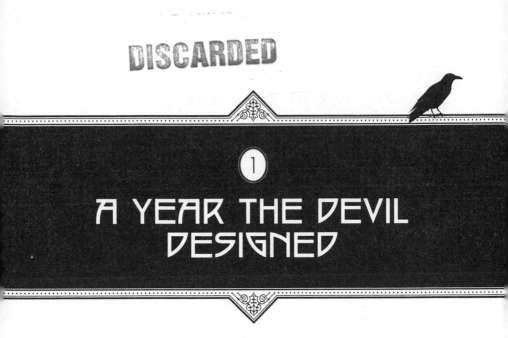

1
A YEAR THE DEVIL DESIGNED

· *Portland, Oregon—October 16, 1918* ·

I STEPPED INSIDE THE RAILROAD CAR, AND THREE DOZEN pairs of eyes peered my way. Gauze masks concealed the passengers' mouths and noses. The train smelled of my own mask's cotton, boiling onions, and a whiff of something clammy and sour I took to be fear.

Keep moving, I told myself.

My legs shook and threatened to buckle, but I managed to clomp down the aisle in the brown Boy Scout boots I wore in case I ever needed to run at a moment's notice. The heavy tread drew unwanted glances and at least one raised eyebrow, but nobody uttered a word.

"Good morning," I said to a woman with a puff of black poodle curls crowning her head.

"Morning," the woman grunted into her gauze.

As I had hoped, all eyes soon lost interest in me and drifted back to their own concerns. I was merely a healthy-sounding sixteen-year-old girl in a navy-blue dress. I didn't talk like a foreign spy, and I wasn't sick with the flu. No harm there.

Coal-colored traveling suits paired with fresh cotton masks gave the compartment a surreal black-and-white appearance, blurred slightly by the onion scent snaking in from the dining car. I imagined the cooks dicing up the pungent bulbs in a mad scramble to keep the flu from overtaking the train, their eyes watering, their foreheads dripping with sweat. I blinked away the sting of the air and took the sole empty seat, beside a woman of middle age and stout build, with thick arms and thicker eyebrows. An anti-influenza pouch reeking of medicine dangled from her neck, overpowering even the onions.

"Hello." She rubbed the pouch and looked me over. "I'm Mrs. Peters."

"I'm . . ." I hoisted my black leather bag onto my lap and answered with a shortened version of my name: "Mary." The newspapers rustling around me more than likely carried an article about my father, and I envisioned a mention of me: *Also present at the house during the arrest last night was Mr. Black's daughter, Mary Shelley. The girl seems to have been named after the author of a certain horror novel with an extremely German-sounding title:* Frankenstein.

"Is that a doctor's bag?" asked Mrs. Peters.

"Yes." I squeezed the handles tighter. "It was my mother's."

"Your mother was a doctor?"

"The best one around."

"I'm sorry she's not on this train with us." Mrs. Peters eyeballed the other passengers. "I don't know what will happen if anyone collapses while we're en route. No one will be able to save us."

"If we get sick, we'll probably just get dumped off at the next stop."

She wrinkled her forehead and gasped. "What a highly unpleasant thing to say."

I shifted my knees away from her. "If you don't mind, I'd rather not talk about the flu."

Mrs. Peters gasped again. "How can you not talk about it? We're speaking through gauze masks, for heaven's sake. We're crammed together like helpless—"

"Ma'am, please—stop talking about it. I've got enough other worries."

She scooted an inch away. "I hope you aren't riddled with germs."

"I hope you aren't, either." I leaned back against the wood and tried to get comfortable, despite my surroundings and the nausea that had been haunting me ever since my father's arrest. Images of government officials punching Dad in the gut and calling him a traitor flickered though my head like grotesque scenes on a movie screen.

Steam hissed from all sides of the car. The floor vibrated against my boots. My hands and knees trembled, and my teeth chattered with the frantic intensity of a Morse code distress signal: *tap tap tap TAP TAP TAP tap tap tap.*

To escape, I undid my satchel's metal clasp and pulled out a bundle of letters six inches thick, bound together by a blue hair ribbon with fraying edges. I slid a crisp cream-colored envelope out from the top of the pile, opened the flap, and lost myself in the letter.

June 29, 1918

My Dearest Mary Shelley,

I arrived overseas four days ago. Our letters are censored, so I need to keep this message uneventful. The army will black out any phrases that indicate where I am, which makes me sound like an operative in a Sherlock Holmes novel. For example: I am in ███████████████ *and soon we'll be going to* ████████ ███. *Mysterious, no?*

I received your letter, and as much as seeing your words on paper sent my heart racing, I hated reading that my package never reached you. It should have arrived at your house nearly two months ago. I blame my brother. But I'll write to my mother and see if she knows when and if it was sent.

I also received your photograph. Thank you so much, Shell. That picture means the world to me. I look at your face all the time and still find it hard to believe that little Mary Shelley Black, my funny childhood friend and devoted letter-writing companion, grew up to be such a beauty. I would give anything to travel back in time to your visit in April and still be with you. If I close my eyes, I can almost taste your lips and feel your long brown hair brushing against my skin. I want so badly to hold you close again.

Sometimes I can't help imagining what would have happened if I hadn't moved away at fourteen. What if my grandfather hadn't died and my parents hadn't rushed us down to live in his house on the island? Would you and I still be as close? Would we have grown more intimate . . . or drifted apart? Whatever the case, I feel robbed of your presence every day of my life.

Never worry about me, Shell. I chose to be here, so anything that happens to me is my own fault. You told me in your letter you wished you could have stopped me from leaving for the war when we were together in April. I was determined to go, and you know better than anyone else I can be as stubborn as you sometimes.

Write soon. Send me a book or two if you can.

I miss you.

Yours with all my love,
Stephen

A sneeze erupted in the seat in front of me.

My eyes flew wide open, and Stephen's letter fell to my lap. All heads whipped toward a skinny redheaded woman, who sneezed again. My lips parted to utter a taboo word—*gesund-heit*—but I quickly clamped them together.

"My wife has allergies!" said the woman's companion, a man with thick, mashed-potato swirls of white hair. He scooted closer to his wife and tightened her mask. "It's not the flu. Stop looking at her that way."

The watchful stares continued.

At that moment, the train jerked into motion, knocking us all off balance. The whistle's cry evaporated into the October mist. I tucked Stephen's letter into my bag and gazed at the brick buildings passing by, followed by bursts of red and amber trees that offered small reminders of what I'd miss most about Portland. Autumn had always been my favorite season, with the smells of burning leaves and mulling spices and the arrival of bright orange pumpkins in my father's grocery store.

Rain soon drummed against the window.

Everything outside turned to gray.

Beside me Mrs. Peters knitted her furry eyebrows at the lady who had sneezed. "We're all going to be dead by the time we get off this train, thanks to that woman."

I nearly replied that if we were dead, we wouldn't be getting off the train, would we? But, again, I clamped my jaw shut—something that had never been easy for me.

Everyone around me sat stone-still with straight backs, stinking of folk remedies. The stench of my neighbor's medicine pouch and someone's garlic-scented gum was strong enough for me to taste through the four-ply barrier of my mask. The wheels of the train *click-clacked, click-clacked, click-clacked* over the lack of conversation.

Was I dreaming? Could it all just be a terrible, terrible nightmare that would end if I pried my eyes open? I dug my nails into my palms with high hopes of stirring myself out of sleep, but pain and half-moon marks emerged. I was wide awake.

Surely, though, I must have stolen into the future and landed in an H. G. Wells–style world—a horrific, fantastical society in which people's faces contained only eyes, millions of healthy young adults and children dropped dead from the flu, boys got transported out of the country to be blown to bits, and the government arrested citizens for speaking the wrong words. Such a place couldn't be real. And it couldn't be the United States of America, "the land of the free and the home of the brave."

But it was.

I was on a train in my own country, in a year the devil designed.

1918.

2

AUNT EVA
AND THE SPIRITS

· *San Diego, California—October 18, 1918* ·

AUNT EVA DIDN'T GREET ME ON THE RAILROAD PLATFORM when I arrived, which meant one of three things: she was running late, she hadn't received my telegram, or she had been stricken by the flu. The third possibility made me shake with both dread and loneliness, so I refused to dwell on it.

I slouched on a hard, uncomfortable bench in San Diego's Santa Fe Depot and stared up at the white plaster arches that spanned the ceiling like rainbows leeched of color. Great wagon wheels that held electric bulbs also loomed above me, so heavy they required a battalion of metal chains to keep them fastened to the arches. Sea air breezed through the open entryway—a mixture of salt and fish smells that made my empty stomach growl. My back ached and my brain longed for sleep after traveling more than a thousand miles. All I could do was sit and wait.

The posters hanging on the blue and gold mosaic walls had changed since my visit six months earlier. Back in April, signs in vivid red, white, and blue had screamed fear-inspiring slogans meant to rally us around the fight against the Germans:

BEAT BACK THE HUN WITH LIBERTY BONDS!
GIVE TILL IT HURTS—THEY GAVE TILL THEY DIED!
ARE YOU 100% AMERICAN? PROVE IT!
DON'T READ AMERICAN HISTORY—MAKE IT!

I remembered Aunt Eva grumbling about "questionable taste" when she steered me past an illustration of a slobbering German gorilla clutching a golden-haired maiden with bare breasts. DESTROY THIS MAD BRUTE. ENLIST. U.S. ARMY! barked that particular poster.

Aside from one navy recruitment notice, the propaganda signs were now gone, replaced by stark white warnings against coughing, sneezing, and spitting in public. The words INFLU-ENZA and EPIDEMIC watched over me from all directions in bold black letters—as if we all needed reminders we were living amid a plague.

A half hour after Aunt Eva was supposed to fetch me, a new train arrived, and it was full of U.S. Army recruits on their way to Camp Kearny, on the northern outskirts of San Diego. After a great deal of fuss and shouted orders, officers in olive-green tunics and flared-hip pants marched through the station, accompanied by a silent herd of young men out-fitted in flu masks and Sunday-best clothing. The boys were young—most of them not much older than eighteen, now that the draft age had dropped from twenty-one. Some of them saw me, and their eyes lit up above their gauze, even though I must have looked like a sack of potatoes slumped there on the bench and wearing my ugly mask.

"Hello, dollface," said a burly one with light brown hair.

"Hey there, beautiful," cooed a scrawny one in black trousers too long for his legs. "Got a kiss for a soldier?"

Others whistled until the officers snapped at them and told them to remember they were respectable members of the U.S. Army.

I felt neither flattered nor offended by the boys' attention. Mainly, they reminded me of the way Stephen had looked the last time I saw him, with that strange mixture of bravery and terror in his brown eyes.

Through the windows, I watched the boys proceed to a line of green military trucks that waited, rumbling, alongside the curb. The recruits climbed one by one beneath the vehicles' canvas coverings with the precision of shiny bullets being loaded into a gun. The trucks would cart them off to their training camp, which was no doubt overrun with feverish, shivering flu victims. The boys who didn't fall ill would learn how to kill other young men who were probably arriving at a German train station in their Sunday-best clothing at that very moment.

Don't think like that, I scolded myself. *That's why they took Dad away. You can't afford to think like him.*

I curled up my legs on the bench and leaned my head against my mother's black bag. The depot grew empty and silent around me, save for the high-pitched wail of an ambulance screaming through the city streets.

I let myself doze.

A hazy dream about Dad cooking up a soup that smelled like San Diego tuna canneries flitted through my brain, and then I heard Aunt Eva call my name. I opened my eyes and saw a short youngish man in gray work clothes tromping across the tiles in grease-stained boots. No Aunt Eva. Her voice must have been part of my dream.

My eyes drifted shut, but again someone said, "Mary Shelley."

I propped myself up on my elbows and blinked away my grogginess. The short man approached me with steps that echoed across the empty depot. He wore a familiar pair of bottle-cap glasses above his flu mask. Short blond hair peeked out from beneath his cap.

I jumped to my feet. "Aunt Eva?"

"I'm sorry I'm so late. They wouldn't let me leave as early as I hoped." She stopped a few feet away from me and wiped her grubby hands on her trousers. "I'm not going to hug you, because I'm filthy. Plus you've been crammed together with all those people on the train. As soon as we get you home, we'll put you in a boiling bath to scrub any flu germs off you."

"What are you doing dressed like that?"

"What? Didn't I tell you I've been working in the shipyard since Wilfred died?"

"No. You didn't say a word about that in your letters. Holy smoke!" I burst out laughing. "Dainty Aunt Eva is building battleships."

"Don't laugh—it's good work. Clears your mind of troubles. The men all left for the war, so they rounded up us women to take over." She hoisted my iron-bottomed trunk with such ease that there must have been some mighty biceps inside those bony arms of hers. "I hope you're feeling fit enough to walk to my house. I'm avoiding the germy air on public transportation."

"Don't you breathe germy factory air?"

"I mainly work outside. Now come along. Pick up your other bag so we can leave this place and get home."

I grabbed my black bag of treasures. "I like your hair."

She growled through her gauze. "Don't mention the hair. I cut it short only because the other girls said it's easier for working. I haven't had a single man give me a second glance since I chopped it off." She walked ahead of me, lugging my trunk with her new brute strength.

I didn't have the heart to tell her the lack of male attention probably had more to do with her greasy boots and sweat stink than the short hair. I plodded after her in my own boots, knowing we made quite a pair—two young women, only ten years apart in age, whose femininity had become yet another casualty of war.

Hardly a soul lingered on the streets outside the station now that the recruits were gone, just a gray-haired man in a pinstripe suit shoving his luggage into the enclosed passenger section of a black taxi. The driver smoked a cigarette through a hole poked in his gauze mask, and wafts of the smoke intermingled with the sea salt and cannery odors in the breeze. Overhead, the spotless sky beamed in an innocent baby blue.

Aunt Eva led me northward. "They've closed down the city to try to keep the flu from spreading. They quarantined the soldiers sooner than the rest of us, but now it's the churches, theaters, moving-picture houses, bathhouses, and dance halls—all closed."

"Schools?" I asked with hope in my heart.

"Closed."

My shoulders fell. "Dad told me the flu wouldn't be as bad in San Diego because of the warmer weather. That's one of the reasons he wanted me here if anything happened to him."

"It's become catastrophic down here, too, I'm afraid. I'm sorry." She glanced my way. "I suppose it'll be boring for you, but it's better than being dead. Make sure you wear your mask at all times. They're strict here about keeping them on."

"I wonder if surgical gauze is really doing anything besides making us look like monsters from another planet. My science teacher, Mr. Wright, wore a mask, and he's just as dead as the people who didn't."

She didn't respond, so I trudged beside her with the words about my dead teacher echoing in my brain. Our boots marched in unison. We traded the trunk and the doctor's bag every two corners and broke the silence of the streets by huffing from the strain of my belongings. My nose and chin sweated beneath my mask. It was entirely too hot for October.

A few blocks north, we turned right on Beech Street. A horse *clip-clopped* behind us, and I smelled something so rotten I gagged.

"Don't look, Mary Shelley." Aunt Eva pulled a handkerchief out of a trouser pocket and pressed it over her mask. "Keep your eyes to the ground."

But, of course, Aunt Eva's words made me want to look at whatever horror she was trying to conceal. I peeked over my shoulder and saw a horse-drawn cart driven by a gaunt dark-skinned man who stared at the road with empty eyes. His sun-bleached wagon rattled closer, and in the back of the cart lay a pile of bodies covered in sheets. Five pairs of feet—a deep purplish black—dangled over the edge.

"I said don't look!" Aunt Eva thrust her handkerchief my way. "Breathe into this."

Instead, I pulled down my mask, bent over the gutter, and threw up the small snack I had eaten on the train.

Aunt Eva dropped the trunk. "Put your mask back on— quick."

"I need fresh air."

"There is no fresh air with this flu. Put your mask on *now*."

I yanked the gauze back over my nose and inhaled my own hot, sour breath.

We were quieter after the cart rolled by. We still switched turns carrying my trunk once my nausea passed, but our labored panting softened out of respect for the dead. In the distance, another ambulance shrieked.

Crepes in black, gray, and white marked flu fatalities on several front doors, just the way they did back home: a black piece of fabric for an adult, gray for an elderly person, and white for a child. The Brandywine twins down the street from my house in Portland had died three months shy of their eighteenth birthday, so their mother—unsure whether to call her girls children or grown-ups—had braided black and white crepes together. As we turned left and entered Aunt Eva's block of modest-sized clapboard homes, I worried about whether my aunt would one day need to hang a piece of cloth representing me on her front door. My stomach got queasy again.

"Somehow, we've managed to avoid the flu on this block." Aunt Eva navigated my trunk along her cement front path. "I don't know how, but I hope to God we stay immune."

She led me up the porch steps of her two-story Victorian, an oversized doll's house with scalloped yellow siding and wooden fixtures shaped like lace doilies above our heads. A tan card in the front window declared the household MEMBERS

OF THE UNITED STATES FOOD ADMINISTRATION and included the organization's official insignia—a red, white, and blue shield surrounded by heads of wheat. The pledge card ensured Aunt Eva would forgo meat, wheat, and sugar on the days the government requested, to save food for our soldiers and the starving in Europe. It also proved to her neighbors she wasn't a spy, a traitor, or a dangerous immigrant and should be left well enough alone.

I wondered what my life would have been like if my father had just gone along with Americanisms like that blasted pledge card and let the war progress around us.

Aunt Eva unlocked her door and led me inside the narrow front hall, which, once I tugged my mask down to my throat, smelled as pungent with onions as the train. A Swiss cuckoo clock announced the four o'clock hour from somewhere in the depths of her kitchen, in the back.

From around the corner, a childish voice murmured, "Who's there?"

Startled, I dropped my bag. "Who said that?"

"That's just Oberon." Aunt Eva plunked my suitcase onto the hall's scuffed floorboards. "He's a rescued yellow-billed magpie that belongs to my neighbor, a bachelor veterinarian off at the war. I'm taking care of the bird while he's gone."

I stepped inside her lavender living room, to the left, and encountered a beautiful black-and-white bird with tapered tail feathers twice as long as his body. He stood on a perch in a tall domed cage.

The bird lowered his dark head and studied me through the bronze wires. "Who's there?"

I smiled. "I'm Mary Shelley—your adopted cousin, I suppose. What else can you say?"

"He says his name and *Hello*, and he likes to whistle and squeak," Aunt Eva answered as she removed her work coat. "You can get to know him better later, but right now you should take your bath. Use water as hot as you can stand, so we can boil the germs off you. And wash your mask while you're at it."

"All right. He's a gorgeous bird. I love those white patches on his wings and belly." I went back out to the hall, picked up my trunk and black doctor's bag, and was just about to head upstairs when I caught sight of my own face staring at me from a pale purple wall across the living room.

The image was a photograph of me, taken in Stephen's older brother Julius's Spiritualism studio during my April visit to San Diego. I lowered my luggage back to the ground and crossed the room for a closer look.

"Mary Shelley?" asked my aunt from behind me.

My blue irises—almost hauntingly absent in the black-and-white photograph—stared back at me in a defiant gaze. I had been so skeptical about genuine spirits showing up in the developed photo and had done my best to look marvelously stubborn. A pair of silver-painted aviatrix goggles hung around my neck, even though Julius and Aunt Eva had wanted them off me, and I wore a breezy white blouse with a collar that dipped into a V.

Julius's words from the moment before he captured the image crept into my ears: *Stay still. Smile. And summon the dead.*

Beside me in the developed photograph knelt a hulking, transparent figure draped in a pale cloak that concealed every inch of its head and body. The creature clung to my chair and leaned its forehead against the armrest, as if it were either in immense pain or bowing to me in worship.

"What do you think of your photograph?" The floorboards behind me creaked from Aunt Eva's work boots. "We told you something amazing would emerge if you posed for him."

A shiver snaked down my spine. Instead of responding, I read the text below the photograph aloud: "'Miss Mary Shelley Black and an admiring spirit. Beauty resides within the sacred studio of Mr. Julius Embers, Spiritualist Photographer.'" I spun around to face my aunt. "Julius used me as an advertisement?"

"That advertisement has led a great deal of grieving individuals to solace in his studio. You look absolutely beautiful in that photograph. Look at the way he almost captured the chestnut hue of your hair."

"Who cares how I look? I'm sitting next to a fake spirit! That's probably a transposed image of Julius covered in a white sheet."

"That's not a fake, Mary Shelley. Julius thinks your visitor may be proof that you possess clairvoyance. I told him you always seem to be channeling your mother's scientific spirit."

"Channeling her spirit?" I said with a snort. "Are you out

of your head? My mother's love of science is probably in my blood, just like she gave me blue eyes and the shape of her mouth. Sir Francis Galton wrote papers on that very subject."

She heaved a sigh. "Did Sir Francis Gallon—"

"*Galton.*"

"Whatever his name is, did he write about sixteen-year-old girls—*sixteen-year-old girls!*—who invent improved versions of doorbells for their science fair projects?"

"He wrote about intelligence being inherited, and that's probably what happened with me. Why can't a girl be smart without it being explained away as a rare supernatural phenomenon?"

"I'm not saying you can't be smart. In fact, a scientific mind like yours should want to explore the communication between spirits and mortals. It's no different than the mystery behind telephone wires and electrical currents."

I turned back to the photograph and scrutinized the "ghost" through narrowed eyes.

Aunt Eva crept closer. "Julius Embers is a good man. He specializes in the spirits of fallen soldiers now. See?" She pointed to a neighboring picture frame that held an article from the *San Diego Evening Tribune.*

The article, dated September 22, included three photographs of dark-clothed people, probably parents and wives, behind whom posed transparent young men in U.S. Army uniforms. Ghostly hands rested on the peoples' shoulders. The supposed spirit faces disappeared into blurry mists.

"Do you still visit Julius?" I asked.

"I didn't at first." A chill iced her voice. "I was too humiliated after what happened between you and Stephen that day."

I flinched.

"But then Wilfred died," she continued before I could say a word. "Julius's photography helped me with my grief." She nodded toward a small photograph of herself and a hazy man with a slim build, who could have been my uncle if you looked at the image cross-eyed. "I felt guilty for not loving Wilfred enough when he suffered so deeply from his illness." She straightened the photograph with her thumb. "But Julius and his mother always welcomed me into their home with warm smiles. He's photographed Wilfred and me a few times now."

"For a large fee, of course," I muttered.

"Stop criticizing Julius. Here—look closely at the last paragraph in this *Tribune* article." She tapped the glass framing the story with a fingernail caked in shipyard grime. "There's a local photography expert, a man named Aloysius Darning, who exposes fake Spiritualist photographers across the country. He sent two men to jail up in Los Angeles, but he can't find a single trace of fraud in Julius's work. He attends my church, when it's not shut down for the quarantine, and I've heard him discuss Julius's spirits."

I leaned toward the article and silently read the line about the fraud catcher:

Mr. Aloysius P. Darning, renowned for his ability to catch crooks in the act of falsifying spirit images, still cannot find one shred of proof that Mr. Embers is a fraud—much to Mr. Darning's chagrin.

"It's still impossible to believe." I shook my head. "Stephen told me this is all the work of a drug addict and a cheat."

"Julius isn't an addict."

"Stephen mentioned opium."

"Maybe Stephen was the one who was lying. Did you ever think of that?" She plopped onto her sofa's flowery cushions and untied her boots, which unleashed the foul odor of her feet. "Stephen was always jealous of his brother's success."

My stomach lurched. "What do you mean *was*?"

"I mean . . . Stephen's battalion headed to France over the summer."

"I know. We still write to each other."

Her face blanched. "Oh, Mary Shelley." She uncrossed her legs. "You shouldn't be in contact with him. Does your father know?"

"He's seen me receive Stephen's letters."

"No," she said, "does he know what happened between the two of you when you were last down here?"

"He doesn't know the made-up version you heard from Julius."

"Why would Julius lie about what he saw?"

"I told you back in April, he and Stephen were having a fight."

She pulled off her right boot without looking me in the eye.

I sank into the rocking chair across from her. "What has Julius said about Stephen's whereabouts? Has their mother received any letters?"

"Only one since Stephen arrived overseas."

"When was that?"

"June or July, I think."

"My last letter from him was dated June twenty-ninth, right after he made it to France. Then he stopped writing." I clutched my stomach. "Why hasn't he written anyone since then? Does his family think he's all right?"

She yanked off her other boot with a grunt. "As far as I know."

"Why hasn't his brother gone to war?"

"The draft board turned Julius down. He suffers from flat feet."

"Oh, poor Julius." I rolled my eyes. "I'm sure he's suffering deeply because of those feet."

"I was sincerely hoping you would have calmed down about Julius Embers during these past six months. He invited you over for another free photograph tomorrow. And he has something for you from Stephen."

"The package?"

"You know about it?"

"Stephen kept saying he asked his mother to send me a

parcel right before he left, but it never arrived. Why didn't she ever mail it?"

Aunt Eva avoided my question by rubbing the sole of her foot. I could see a gaping hole in her black stocking. Oberon let out an angry squawk, no doubt to break the tension gripping the room.

"Why didn't she mail it, Aunt Eva?"

My aunt's face flushed pink. "Mrs. Embers probably felt the relationship wouldn't be good for either of you. You were both too young and too unmarried for that sort of intimacy, Mary Shelley. You should have never gone into that room alone with Stephen."

"We didn't—"

"It took me two months before I could show my face to the family, and it's only because Mrs. Embers reached out to me after she read Wilfred's obituary."

I shot out of the rocking chair with the intention of grabbing my belongings and escaping upstairs.

"Mary Shelley—"

"My dad never even let me near Stephen's brother when I was growing up." I picked up my bags. "But you act like Julius is a saint. He told a terrible tale about his brother and me, but you worship him."

"Stop. Please stop." She kept on massaging her smelly old foot. "I know you're upset about Stephen and your father, and I know I'm only ten years older than you—"

"I just want you to understand that what happened that

day was a thousand times more innocent than what Julius told you. Will you please start believing your own flesh and blood instead of this *friend* who's striking it rich off war deaths?"

She lowered her head.

"Please, Aunt Eva."

"Julius has been so good to me," she said. "You don't understand how hard it is to be alone when the world's unraveling around you."

"Yes, I do. I understand completely."

She met my eyes, and her expression softened. She dropped her foot and exhaled a sigh that told me she was dead tired of everything, including our conversation.

I took a calming breath. "Despite this problem with Julius, I am extremely grateful you and I can be together right now. And I appreciate you letting me live here without once mentioning the danger Dad has posed to the family members still up in Oregon."

She jutted her chin into the air with typical Aunt Eva pride. "Thank you. I've been worried about my brothers ever since we saw those people beat on that German man during your last trip. A Swiss German surname like Boschert doesn't sit well with some people these days."

"I know. The inability to see the truth about a person is a terrible thing."

She returned to fussing over her foot, choosing to ignore the fact that I was still talking about Julius. "Go change out of those clothes, Mary Shelley," she said without any fight left in her, which made me feel guilty. "I'll start running your bathwater. Look on the bedside table while you're up there. I've left you something that belonged to Wilfred."

"Thank you." I cleared my throat. "I'll go look for it." I climbed the stairs with my traveling trunk thumping against the wood.

The gift she had left for me in my room was Uncle Wilfred's weighted brass nautical compass, inherited from his seafaring grandfather and mounted in a mahogany case the size of a large jewelry box. A gorgeous device.

While my bathwater roared through the downstairs pipes, I wandered around my new room with the compass, checking to see whether the walls behind the gilded paper contained any metal strong enough to move the needle. And for a short while, the lure of scientific discovery blotted out the sea of masked faces on the train ride south, the purplish-black feet rattling in the back of that cart, my father getting punched in the gut in front of my eyes, and the first boy I'd ever loved fighting for his life in a trench in France.

3

MR. MUSE

I TWISTED AND TURNED, TRYING TO GET COMFORTABLE IN my new bed. The mattress springs whined with every restless movement I made. Ambulance sirens screamed in the distance. I couldn't sleep. I ached to see and touch Stephen again. The briny air I'd smelled all afternoon reminded me that we were last together only a few miles from Aunt Eva's house—before the flu, before my father's arrest, when Stephen still lived in his home across the bay.

I reached down to the black doctor's bag on the floor and fetched Stephen's second-to-last letter, dated May 30, 1918. The picture he had included fell out of the envelope—a portrait taken at a studio where all the Camp Kearny recruits had gone to get photographed in their army uniforms. He wore a tight-fitting tunic that buttoned up to his throat, narrow trousers that disappeared inside knee-high boots, and a ranger-style Montana peak hat that hid his short brown hair. I could tell from the stiff way he held his jaw that he was attempting to look serious and bold for the picture, but mainly he resembled a Boy Scout ready for camp.

His lovely handwriting on the letter shone in my oil lamp's steady light.

Dear Mary Shelley,

They're shipping us overseas soon, even though I've barely been in training. We're needed in Europe something desperate, I guess. I'll be on a train to the East Coast in the coming weeks and then boarding a ship to cross the Atlantic.

I've been wondering why you haven't responded to the package I prepared for you the morning I left. At first I worried that I somehow offended you with the gift . . . or that I offended you by kissing you. But if you were offended, you would have told me so directly, wouldn't you? You have never been shy or evasive. So I choose to believe the package never reached you.

If you aren't mad at me, I would love to hear how you are doing and to receive a recent picture of you. I'm including an Army Post Office address where you can write to me at any point, even when I'm overseas. The only photographs I have of you are from your days of mammoth hair bows—those giant loops of ribbon that looked like they would start flapping and fly off the top of your head. I'm trying so hard to remember the grown-up version of

*you, with your bewitching smile and those haunting blue eyes that
seemed to understand exactly what I was feeling.*

*If you would rather not attach yourself to someone heading off
to war, I understand. After your aunt hurried you out of my house
that day, after Julius told his vicious version of what happened,
my mother yelled at me and called me cruel. She reminded me
you have your whole life ahead of you and said the last thing an
intelligent girl like you needs is to ruin her life for a boy heading
off to war.*

*You don't need to wait for me, Shell. I'm aware you need to
live your life without worrying about me. If you do want to write,
however, if you do think of me, I would love to receive your letters.
I miss you so much.*

*Yours affectionately,
Stephen*

*P.S. I wish I had those goggles of yours that supposedly let you
see the future. I could really use them right now.*

I smiled at his last line and leaned over to my black bag
again. Down in the cloth-lined depths of one of the side
compartments were the coarse leather straps of my aviatrix
goggles—a gift from Aunt Eva, purchased to blot out the
memory of the crowd beating on the German man at the
Liberty Loan drive during my last visit. We had come across
the chaos just as the police were dragging the victim away in

handcuffs, his right eye swelling, his nose and mouth a mess of bright red blood. Men with angry blue veins bulging from their foreheads had shouted words like *Kraut bastard* and *goddamned Hun*, even with ladies and children present.

I shoved aside the memory of the violence, fastened the goggles over my face, and lay back against the cool sheets to stare through the bug-eyed lenses at the empty white ceiling. Stephen's letter rested against my stomach—an invisible weight, but there just the same. My mind opened to the possibility that the goggle salesman's promises of enchantment had been true, as preposterous as the idea was. I would see the fate of the world through the glass lenses.

Yet the future refused to emerge.

Only the past.

I saw myself getting off the train on April 26 to celebrate my sixteenth birthday in Stephen's new city . . . and to distract Aunt Eva from life with a husband wasting away in a home for tuberculosis patients. She and Uncle Wilfred had moved to San Diego for the healthier air, and I jumped at the opportunity to visit her—and perhaps see my old friend again. Faces didn't yet hide behind gauze masks. Soldiers and sailors arriving for training smiled up at the Southern California sunshine and smacked one another on the back as if they were on vacation, and the air rang out with laughter and war talk and the boisterous melody of a brass band playing "Over There."

Aunt Eva had met me on the train platform in a lacy white dress that fell halfway between her knees and ankles. Her hair, still long enough to reach her waist, was pinned to the back of her head in shimmering blond loops of girly curls.

As soon as we had escaped the bustle of recruits and music in the depot, I asked her, "Have you seen my friend Stephen Embers's family since you moved here?"

"Actually, yes." Her leg bumped into my swinging suitcase, which she did not offer to carry. "Julius now runs the family photography studio. He's a spirit photographer—he captures images of the dead who've returned to visit loved ones."

"I know." I squinted into the burning sunlight. "Stephen mentioned that in one of his letters. He didn't sound pleased about his brother's work. And I've only received one letter from him since their father passed away in January. I'm really worried about Stephen."

"I've posed for Julius."

"You have?"

"A couple of times." The sun glinted off her round spectacles, but I could see a funny little gleam dancing in her hazel eyes. "I recognized his name in the newspaper when he presented an exhibit of his work in February, and I was absolutely flabbergasted when I saw his photos. He's trying to summon your mother and Grandma Ernestine for me."

I stopped in my tracks. "My mother and Grandma Ernestine have shown up . . . in spirit photographs?"

"I think so." She glanced at me out of the corner of her eye. "On three separate occasions, Julius captured the images of two glowing figures hovering behind me, but their faces haven't yet fully materialized for us. I told him you're very much like your mother. I explained she named you after Mary Shelley because of her love of electricity and science, and he thinks you may be able to lure her into making a full spirit manifestation."

"What? No!" I slammed my suitcase to the ground. "Dad would hate it if I posed for Julius Embers. Julius always got caught drinking and smoking at school and wound up in all sorts of fights and trouble."

Aunt Eva sniffed. "He's straightened his ways. He's quite the gentleman now—so tall and handsome, with his dashing black hair. Barely twenty-two years old and already a gifted Spiritualist photographer."

I gaped at her. "You sound like you're in love with him."

"Don't say that, Mary Shelley. I'm a married woman with a deathly ill husband. I simply admire the man's work."

"You're blushing."

"Stop it." She swatted my shoulder with her white-gloved hand. "I scheduled a sitting for you at Julius's in-home studio in two days, and if you behave yourself, I'm sure you could see his brother directly afterward."

I rubbed my shoulder and felt an uncomfortable twinge course through my stomach at the thought of posing for wild Julius Embers in close quarters.

However . . . I possessed a ticket to Stephen's house— a ticket to Stephen himself—which was exactly what I had wanted when I stepped off that train.

Two mornings later, Aunt Eva whisked me across San Diego Bay to the Emberses' home on Coronado Island. In Portland, Stephen's family had lived in a neighborhood exactly like ours, with homes so squished together that if houses could breathe, their sides would knock against one another when they inhaled.

This new residence, though—Stephen's grandparents' summerhouse, which the family had inherited in 1914—was an enormous seaside cottage covered in vast windows and thousands of cocoa-brown shingles. The neighboring house, a towering brick monstrosity, could have been Thornfield Hall from *Jane Eyre*, or any other grand estate that ruled over the English moors. I felt like an insignificant speck of Stephen's former life entering this luxurious new world.

Julius greeted us and made jokes about how tiny and serious I used to look. He took my photograph in his chilly studio in the family's living room, and, afterward, Mrs. Embers—a robust woman with ink-black hair rolled into two thick sausages at the nape of her neck—served my aunt and me tea in a dining room awash in springtime sunlight. Through the open windows we could hear the crashing of waves from the Pacific Ocean. Thirteen different photographs of Coronado beaches dotted the dark paneled walls.

"Where's Stephen?" I asked, unable to take a single bite of Mrs. Embers's lemon cake. The anticipation of finally seeing him again had stolen my appetite.

"I was just wondering the same thing." Mrs. Embers leaned

back with a squeak of her chair and called toward the dining room's entrance. "Stephen? Come down and visit your friend, please. Stephen?"

I strained my ears but heard nothing. Sweat broke out across my neck. *Stephen is avoiding me,* I realized. *He hasn't been writing me since his father's death because he's tired of me.*

Mrs. Embers sighed and went back to stirring her Earl Grey. "He's probably upstairs, packing."

"Packing for what?" I asked.

"Didn't he tell you in one of his letters?"

"Tell me what?"

"He's leaving for the army tomorrow."

It felt as though someone had just socked me in the chest. I clutched the edge of the table.

Aunt Eva grabbed my arm. "Are you all right, Mary Shelley?"

I stared into the depths of my teacup and struggled to catch my breath while Mrs. Embers's sentence replayed over and over in my head.

He's leaving for the army tomorrow.

Back in Portland, one of my classmate's uncles had just lost half his body to a massive shell explosion on a battlefield in France. Only a week earlier, an eighteen-year-old neighbor from back home—Ben Langley—died of pneumonia at his Northern California training camp.

"Mary Shelley?"

I cleared my throat to find my voice. "I didn't know Stephen had enlisted. He won't even turn eighteen until June. What is he doing going over there?"

"About a month ago he started insisting he wanted to get out of this house." Mrs. Embers blotted a drop of tea before it could stain the tablecloth. "He'll be training at Camp Kearny, just up north, but he says he doesn't even want to come back home to visit if he gets a weekend pass. His father's death hit him hard."

"That's very sad to hear," said my aunt. "Hasn't Julius ever helped Stephen through his grief? Perhaps if their father's spirit showed up in a photograph—"

"No, that's never going to happen." Mrs. Embers smiled, but her brown eyes moistened. "My two boys couldn't be any more different from each other. They're like a volcanic eruption whenever they're together."

I couldn't keep my legs still. I had to hunt down Stephen. "May I use your washroom, Mrs. Embers?"

"Certainly. Go past the bottom of the staircase. It'll be the first door on your right before the study."

"Take those silly goggles off your neck first," said Aunt Eva, with a tug at my leather straps.

Mrs. Embers chuckled. "I was wondering about those goggles. It seems like you were always wearing some sort of new contraption whenever I saw you in the old days, Mary Shelley."

"I bought them for her yesterday at the Liberty Loan drive." Aunt Eva shook her head at me. "Some salesman with yellow mule teeth tried to convince her they'd let her see the future, and I think she half believes him."

"I'm hoping they'll be my good-luck charm." I rose with as much grace as a person defending quasi-magical goggles could muster. "You know I've always admired aviatrixes."

"But you don't need to wear them all the time." My aunt sighed. "Boys were giving her the oddest looks when she walked around Horton Plaza Park with those things over her eyes. You should have seen their faces."

"I wasn't trying to impress boys at a Liberty Loan drive." I gripped the back of my chair. "I was desperate to see if there's anything in my future besides a war. Thank you for the tea, Mrs. Embers."

"You're welcome, dear."

As I made my way to the heart of the house, I overheard Aunt Eva explaining my obsession with aviatrixes, electricity, anatomy, and machinery, as though I were some sort of bizarre species—the rare *Female scientificus, North American.* "I don't know if you remember, but my older sister, her mother, was a physician," she said in a voice she probably assumed I couldn't hear. "Mary Shelley seems to be channeling Amelia's love of exploration and technology. That girl has always been passionate and headstrong about everything."

Dark, knotty wood lined every wall, ceiling, and floor in the Emberses' entry hall—an immense space that reminded me of the belly of a ship. A brass lantern hung overhead. I almost expected the floor to roll with the swell of a wave.

The soles of my shoes pattered across the floorboards to the rhythm of a beast of a grandfather clock that rose to the ceiling at the opposite end of the hall. I slowed my pace, placed my goggles over my eyes, and approached the clock with interest. The minute hand ticked its shadowy finger toward the twelve on a face painted to look like the moon, with eyes and a mouth and pockmark craters. The metallic gears spun and clicked deep inside, all those shiny pieces fitting into just the precise positions to make the contraption work. The pendulum swung back and forth, back and forth, hypnotizing with its gleaming brass.

"The boys who gave you odd looks don't appreciate originality."

I jumped backward a foot at the unexpected voice.

Through my lenses, I viewed a stunning boy who looked to be an older version of the Stephen I remembered, with hair a rich brown and deep, dark eyes that watched me with interest. He sat toward the bottom of the staircase, a book in hand, with one of his long legs stretched down to the floor. A black band of mourning encircled his white shirtsleeve. A gray silken tie hung down to his stomach and made him look so grown up, so distinguished, compared to my Portland childhood friend.

I caught my breath. "The Stephen Embers I knew wasn't an eavesdropper."

"Did a man really try to convince you those goggles would let you see the future?" he asked.

"Yes."

"And what do you see?"

"Only a person who lurks in the backs of houses instead of coming to see his long-lost friend."

He grinned and revealed a dimple I'd long forgotten.

I smiled and pulled the goggles down below my chin. "You're not as gentlemanly as you used to be, Stephen. I remember you used to jump to your feet whenever a lady entered the room."

"I'm far too stunned by the fact that you are a lady now." He scanned me down to my toes. "You used to be so small and scrawny."

"And you used to wear short pants that showed off your knobby knees and drooping socks. Plus you always had that scuffed-up old camera satchel hanging off your shoulder."

He laughed. "I still have that satchel."

"Well, I'm glad to hear not everything's changed." I stepped closer to him, my heart beating at twice its normal rate. My skin burned as if with fever. "Why are you hiding back here instead of coming out to see me?"

"Because . . ." His dimple faded. "I got the impression you came to see my brother instead of me."

"That's a silly thing to assume. The only way my aunt would let me come over here was if I sat for a photograph. She's madly in love with your brother's work."

Stephen closed his book—Jules Verne's *The Mysterious Island*. "Julius is a fraud, Shell. He'll scam you out of your money faster than that goggles salesman. Did you let him take your picture?"

"I think he's working on developing it right now."

"Then you're hooked." He glanced over his shoulder, through the balusters of the stair rail, and then returned his attention to me. "Why'd you let him do that? I thought you of all people wouldn't be gullible."

"I didn't say I believed in his photos."

"You shouldn't."

"What makes you so certain he's a fraud?"

He sat up straighter. "My father told me how Julius is creating his ghosts—doctoring the plates, creating double exposures, damaging his brain with too much opium until he convinces himself the mistakes he makes while developing the plates are spirit images."

"Julius is an opium fiend?"

"Are you really that surprised?"

"Well . . ." I had heard tales of artists and depraved gentlemen who frequented dark opium dens, smoking the drug from long pipes until they hallucinated and passed out. But never in my life had I known anyone who tried it. I closed my gaping mouth. "I suppose your brother would enjoy something like that."

Stephen stretched out his other leg. "He also runs a fan over ice blocks in between sittings to cool the air in there. He tries to make everyone feel like phantoms are hovering around the studio."

"Really?"

"Yes, really. I've caught him doing it. And he leaves the windows open all night to capture the chill from the sea. He locks the doors to the studio to keep me from getting in, but I've crawled through the windows and closed the panes to save the equipment. He's contemplating installing bars to keep me out."

A lump of disappointment settled in my stomach, even though I had started off so skeptical about the spirit images. "My poor aunt. She's convinced Julius will find my mother and grandmother for her."

"Tell her the truth. I hate seeing people so desperate for proof of the afterlife they'll sacrifice just about anything to communicate with the dead." Stephen pursed his lips and rubbed his thumb across *The Mysterious Island*'s leather cover. "I hear them crying when they receive their finished photographs. It's heartbreaking. They react to Julius's photos like rummies chasing bottles."

I thought I heard a moan in a floorboard down the hall. My eyes darted toward the sunbeam-hazy front entrance to make sure no one was listening.

Aunt Eva and Mrs. Embers tittered over some shared anecdote in the dining room.

Nothing else stirred.

I turned back to Stephen and asked in a lowered voice, "Why is Julius doing this to people? I didn't think he ever wanted to have anything to do with photography."

"He didn't, but an odd, ghostly image appeared in one of Dad's photographs last Christmas, and Julius showed it around the hangouts of rich tourists. He claimed he was saving Dad's business by finally bringing some solid money to it. Dad hated having his studio turned into a theatrical exhibit. It could be one of the reasons his heart failed."

"I'm so sorry." I wrapped my arm around the slick newel post at the end of the stair rail, so close to Stephen that the citrus and spices of his bay rum aftershave filled my nose. "I know you were close to your dad."

He turned his head so I could see only the side of his face. His eyelashes fluttered like mad, and I could tell he was fighting off tears. "You always told me . . ." His voice cracked with emotion. "You always said you feel like a piece of you is permanently missing."

I bit my lip and nodded. I'd often told him part of me was missing because my mother died the day I was born. "Yes."

"Now I know what that feels like." He cleared his throat and regained control of his breathing. "It's agonizing."

"It'll get better over time. You'll always feel that missing piece, but it will get easier."

His eyes, now bloodshot, traveled back to mine. He took hold of the baluster closest to my hand. "It's really good seeing you again, Shell. I've missed you."

"I've missed you, too." A lump caught in my throat. "You know, you're still the only boy who hasn't ever made fun of my science experiments and machinery obsessions."

"I'm sure that's changed, now that you're looking"—a grin awakened in the corners of his mouth—"older."

I shook my head and felt my cheeks warm. "It's only gotten worse. They still call me names, like Monster Brain and Frankenstein, but now they also make obscene jokes about me and some lecherous old professor who lives near the high school. The girls can be terrible, too."

"I'm sure everyone's just intimidated by you. They're probably afraid of sounding stupid when they talk to you."

"That never stopped you from talking to me."

"What?" His mouth fell open. "Hey!" He chuckled, a new, deep laugh I didn't recognize, and nudged my arm.

I giggled and nudged him back, though what I wanted so badly was to wrap my arms around him and hold him close.

"Stephen?" called his mother from the dining room. "Are you back there? Did you find Mary Shelley?"

"Show me some of your new photographs before we have to go sit with the ladies," I whispered.

"They're going to wonder what's taking you so long."

"I don't care."

"All right." He put *The Mysterious Island* aside on the stairs and stood to his full height, about five inches taller than me but probably six inches shorter than his giant of a brother. I noticed his sturdy arms and lean stomach beneath his white shirt and found my blood burning fiery hot in my veins. I debated placing my goggles back over my eyes in an attempt to conceal my physical reaction to him.

He led me into a back sitting room wallpapered in peacock green. Chairs and a sofa upholstered in a pinkish hue that reminded me of the inside of a seashell formed a circle around the room's center. Vases of dried lavender sweetened the air. Framed photographs—nature scenes, family members, still lifes—formed a patchwork quilt of glossy sepia across the walls.

Stephen headed toward the corner behind the largest armchair, lifted one of the photos off its nail, and brought it to me. It was the image of a monarch butterfly drinking nectar from a rose. Even though the photograph was printed in brown and white, the clarity of the insect's shading made me feel as though I were looking at wings a vivid orange, a flower the softest whisper of yellow.

"This is one of my favorites," he said.

"It's gorgeous. How did you manage to catch a butterfly in a photo? They fly away so quickly."

"My father taught me how to stay extremely still and keep a camera pointed in the right direction. I had to sit in our backyard for an hour before I caught it."

"You're the most patient person I've ever known, Stephen. I wish some of that quality had rubbed off on me."

"You're patient when you work on a project you love."

"Not the way you are." I reached out and touched the frame, a couple of inches below his fingers. "What did you write down here at the bottom?" I squinted at two words in the lower right-hand corner. "*Mr. Muse?*"

"That's a fake title. Julius makes fun of the names I give my pictures, so I turn the real ones into anagrams to keep him from figuring them out."

"I wonder . . . let's see . . . *Mr. Muse* . . ." I examined the words, letting their letters unscramble and fit back together like puzzle pieces in my brain. "Ruse . . . rum . . . sum . . . *Summer*?"

"Cripes." He grinned. "You've gotten faster than when you were little."

"You taught me well."

"I'm going off to war, Shell." His words just flew out there, smacking me in the face like a stinging bucket of ice water.

"I know." I shrank back. "Your mother told me. Why on earth did you enlist when you're so close to finishing school? I thought you were going to college."

His eyes shifted toward the window to his right. "I need to get out of this house. Everyone on this island ends up spoiled or corrupt. There's so much wealth and pampering and self-ishness. I'm tired of being part of it."

"Are you running away?"

"I don't know." His fingers inched closer to mine on the frame. "Maybe."

"Be careful over there, Stephen."

He turned his attention to the floor.

"I've grown up looking at my father's Spanish-American War scar," I said. "Remember that pink line running down his left cheek?"

Stephen nodded. "I remember."

"He says it gives his face character, but it's always made me terrified of war."

"I'll be fine." He looked directly into my eyes with an expression that made me think he wasn't necessarily sure he would be all right. He held my gaze, and I almost felt he was about to lean forward and kiss me, even though we had never once kissed when we were younger. We stood close enough that I could smell spearmint on his breath, even over the aftershave.

I slid my fingers up the frame until I touched his hand. "Please stay safe. It's not everyone who has the patience to photograph a butterfly."

He gave me a smile that seemed both grateful and sad.

I swallowed, and he continued to search my eyes with his own, as if he were trying to say something he couldn't articulate with words. The space between us shrank. Our breathing accelerated until it became the only sound in the house. My heart pounded like I was about to leap off a cliff a hundred feet high.

Before I could say anything awkward to break the spell, he pulled my face toward his and kissed me. I lost my balance at first, but then I closed my eyes and held his smooth neck and enjoyed the warmth and hunger of his mouth. His hand moved to the small of my back and brought me closer. Our stomachs touched. Our chests pinned the photograph between us. He wrapped his arms around me and held me tight against him, as though he were kissing life itself good-bye.

A deafening *bong* rang out in the hallway. Our lips parted, and the grandfather clock chimed eleven times. Neither of us said a word—we simply panted and remained together, entangled, tipsy, our mouths hovering a few teasing inches apart. His hairline above his neck felt both soft and bristly against my fingertips, which intrigued me.

The clock fell silent.

"Stephen?" called his mother.

A palpable sense of urgency passed between us. Stephen took my hand, hurried me across the sitting room, and closed the door, sealing us inside. He kissed me again and knocked us both off balance until I found myself bumping against one of the peacock-green walls.

His mouth left mine and kissed its way down to my neck. "Your goggles are in the way," he whispered.

I snickered and struggled to yank the lenses over my chin, but they wouldn't budge. He helped me pull the straps to the top of my head and then dove back to my awaiting throat, where his lips sent delicious chills spilling down to the tips of my toes. I closed my eyes again and sighed in a way I never had before, losing myself in his dizzying scent, the pressure of his hands around my hips, the pulse-quickening intimacy of his mouth against my bare skin.

The door opened.

"Jesus, Stephen. Control yourself."

Stephen and I both jumped.

The spell shattered.

Julius clutched the brass doorknob with his paw of a hand and smirked at our entwined bodies and flushed faces. His hair was darker and wavier than Stephen's, his features more rugged. His six-and-a-half-foot form filled the doorway. "Is that what you used to do to her back when you were little kids? Back when I thought you'd grow up to be a fruit?"

"Leave us alone." Stephen drew me closer. "Give us five more minutes."

Julius snorted. "You think I'm going to close this door and let you ruin Eva Ottinger's niece when she's sitting right out there in the other room? Have you ever met Eva Ottinger?"

"For Christ's sake, Julius, I haven't seen Mary Shelley in four years. We might not ever see each other again. Give us five more minutes."

Julius pondered the request while running his tongue along the inside of his cheek. He cocked his head and parted his lips, and for a moment I thought he was about to give us one small, precious gift of time.

Instead, he pushed the door farther open with the tips of his fingers. "Mary Shelley, the ladies are waiting for you."

My heart sank.

Julius waved for me to leave. "Let her go, Stephen."

"You're an ass, Julius," said Stephen. "I'll never forgive you for this."

"Let her go. Don't tease the poor girl before you run clear across the world."

Stephen swallowed loud enough to hear. He cupped my cheek and studied my face as though he were creating a photograph of me in his mind. I followed his lead and memorized every single one of his features—his dark eyes and brows, the soft shade of his lips, the faded freckles on his cheeks from summer days when he forgot to wear his cap—sick with fear that he was right: this would be the last time I'd ever see him.

He gave me one last kiss. A small, tender one fit to be seen by a brother. "Keep *Mr. Muse*, Shell."

"Keep it?" I felt the picture frame dangling from my fingers against his back. "No—I couldn't."

"It's just going to disappear off the wall. Julius has destroyed my work before."

"Why?"

"Who knows?"

I glanced at Julius and saw his jaw tense. "But he's your brother."

"Half brother," Stephen reminded me. "Only half. We had different fathers."

"But still—"

"His father was a drunk who treated my mother terribly before she left him. And violent, thieving drunks often breed violent, thieving children."

Julius tugged Stephen away from me, straight out of my arms, and hurled him against the sharp wooden ridge running across the top of the sofa. The impact knocked the sofa askew, and Stephen landed on the floor with an awful thud.

"Why did you say that to her?" asked Julius with genuine hurt in his voice.

"Obviously, I'm not lying," Stephen said from the ground. "You just proved my point."

"Mary Shelley, go back out to the ladies."

I didn't budge.

Julius's eyes pierced me. "I said go back."

"What are you going to do to him?"

"Now!" Julius stormed toward me with enough anger and humiliation in his eyes to send me scrambling out of the room. I ran away, foolish coward that I was. I ran away and left Stephen on the floor, twisted in pain.

The door shut. Something slammed against the wall in there—once, twice. I could hear all those picture frames rattling from the force.

Silence followed.

The door opened, and Julius exited, alone.

Sincerely Yours Will Thomas

4

THE MYSTERIOUS ISLAND

· *October 19, 1918* ·

FOOTSTEPS WOKE ME AT SUNRISE.

I blinked my eyes and tried to reorient myself in the foreign landscape of my new bedroom, but the lingering shadows of night crouched in the corners and crept across the unfamiliar furniture. My traveling trunk and Boy Scout boots huddled together in a disheveled heap next to a pine wardrobe.

It was October, no longer spring. I now lived in Aunt Eva's house as a refugee in the middle of a pandemic. Stephen was long gone.

My aunt couldn't afford electricity, so her face and flu mask glowed in the flickering light of a candle next to my bed. "Why are you wearing your goggles?" she asked.

I pulled off the straps and felt indentations from where the rubber had pressed against my skin. "I must have fallen asleep with them on."

"Are you feeling all right?"

"Yes, why?" I lifted my head. "Do I look sick?"

"No. I just worried all night you'd wake up with the flu from the train."

"I feel fine." I rubbed my dry eyes.

"We need to leave for Julius's studio in two hours. Get dressed soon so we can eat breakfast. We also need to make sacks of camphor balls to wear around our necks so the stink can fight off germs on the ferry."

On that repulsive-sounding note, she left the room.

I curled beneath my covers and watched the sun rise behind the lace curtains of my new window. Portland felt impossibly far away. I wondered when my father would go to trial. After the authorities had locked his wrists in handcuffs and punched him in the gut, I grabbed my bags, headed out the back door, and ran to telegraph Aunt Eva from the Portland Union Depot, as Dad had instructed me to do. I spent the night on a bench at the station until the morning train took me away. No one came looking for Mr. Robert Black's sixteen-year-old daughter. There were too many other concerns in the world for anyone to bother with an accused traitor's grown child.

I shut my eyes and pushed back the memory, finding breathing painful.

My thoughts turned to Aunt Eva's troubles and poor, dead Uncle Wilfred. He had died in June in the tuberculosis home, but I wondered if his spirit had found its way back to his own house. Despite my skepticism of Julius's spirit photography, and of ghosts in general, the possibility of life after death never seemed entirely foolish when I lay in bed all alone, my imagination whirring. I actually convinced myself I heard Uncle Wilfred cough in the room next door, which sent me flying out from under my blankets to get dressed.

I lifted the lid of my traveling trunk and grimaced.

"Cripes. What a morbid wardrobe."

My dresses and skirts were either black or a navy blue so dark it was almost black. The lack of German dyes in the country drained every ounce of color from our clothing, ensuring we all looked as grim as the world around us. I pulled out a navy dress with a calf-length hem, a sailor-style collar, and a loose tie the same shade as the rest of the garment. In an attempt to brighten my appearance, I opened the wide mouth of my mother's leather bag, slid my fingers inside the same slippery pocket that had held my goggles, and pulled out a necklace my father had made me from a clockmaker friend's spare brass gear.

Even the gleaming metal looked dull against my drab, dark wool.

"You're not going to see Stephen at his house," I reminded my reflection in the mirror. "You can look dour. Who's going to care?"

I gathered my long hair in a white ribbon at the base of my neck and tucked my gauze mask into the sash around my waist for later. Fumes from Aunt Eva's onion omelets bombarded my nostrils.

"Are you almost ready for breakfast, Mary Shelley?" my aunt called from downstairs.

"Who's there?" squawked Oberon.

"I'm coming," I said.

I looked at another of my treasures nestled inside my mother's black bag—Stephen's butterfly photograph, *Mr. Muse*—before facing the rest of the day.

WE TRAVELED TO CORONADO ON THE SAME FERRY WE'D taken back in April—the *Ramona*—and leaned against the polished rails of the vessel's bow while the cool winds of San Diego Bay whipped through our hair. During the trip in April, the breeze had carried the sharp scent of tar from the slips where the ferries docked, but this time around I could only smell my own onion breath stinking up my mask, as well as the menthol-like pungency of the camphor pouches hanging around our necks. Steam whistled into the clear sky from the ferry's two black smokestacks. Side paddle wheels churned the waters into a salty white spray that flicked against my hands.

"Before our last trip, I always pictured the Emberses living on the Swiss Family Robinson's island," I admitted to Aunt Eva as we cruised toward the populated stretch of land no more than a half mile across the bay. A biplane from the Naval Air Station on North Coronado buzzed into the cloudless sky. "Stephen always wrote about living on an island, so I envisioned him swinging on vines and eating his dinner out of coconut shells. But it's not even an island, is it? It's a peninsula."

"No one calls it that," said Aunt Eva.

"Stephen said there's a narrow road connecting the island to the mainland for people who don't mind driving around the bay."

"I wonder if this is a terrible idea." My aunt picked at the rail with one of her freshly scrubbed fingernails.

"If what is a terrible idea? Sitting for another spirit photograph?"

"No, taking you back over there. Letting you have that package."

"What do you think is going to happen if I get that package? Stephen will magically appear and ravish me right there in his brother's studio?"

"Shh! Mind your mouth, Mary Shelley. Good heavens." Aunt Eva eyed two children eight feet away from us—two little girls with big blue eyes half hidden beneath their flu masks. They stretched their chubby arms over the rails and called out to seagulls circling over the water, "Come here. Come here, silly birds."

My aunt lowered her voice so I could scarcely hear. "You used to be as pure as those little girls."

"Let's not have this conversation again."

"At your age, you shouldn't even know what men and women do behind closed doors." She shook her head with a pained sigh. "You're sixteen years old, for pity's sake. I didn't know about those sorts of things until my wedding night."

"You should have read Gray's *Anatomy*, then."

"Well, there you have it." She held up her hand as if she had just solved the deepest mysteries of the universe. "You read too many books that encourage the loss of innocence."

"I lost my innocence on April sixth, 1917. And it had nothing to do with Gray's *Anatomy*."

"What?"

"The day this country declared war against Germany," I reminded her. "The day spying on neighbors became patriotic and boys turned into rifle targets. That's enough to take the sweetness out of a girl."

"Shh." She furrowed her brow. "Mary Shelley Black! Don't you dare publicly announce such things about the war."

"Don't publicly announce such things about me losing my innocence." I kicked the toe of my boot against the rail and felt the vibration shinny up to my fingers.

Ten minutes later, we arrived at the island that wasn't an island and disembarked.

A double-decker electric streetcar that looked like one railroad car had been squished on top of another transported us down Coronado's main road, Orange Avenue. We clacked down the tracks, past plaster bungalows and traditional clapboard houses that loomed larger than the average American home. Buicks and Cadillacs rumbled by the streetcar, belching clouds of exhaust that smelled of city life and wealth. No signs of poverty existed anywhere on the island, but still, black and white crepes marked the Spanish influenza's lethal path just the same.

For half the journey, a motorized hearse drove by our side, its cargo—a shiny mahogany casket topped with calla lilies—on full display through open scarlet drapes. I ground my teeth and clenched my fists and felt as though Death himself were riding along next to us, taunting us. He was a nasty schoolyard thug, bullying us with a killer flu when we were already worrying about a war, flaunting the fact that we couldn't do a thing about the disease.

Just go, I thought. *Leave us alone.*

I turned my eyes to the passing palm and magnolia trees, and like everyone else on the streetcar, I tried to pretend the hearse wasn't there.

After reaching a stretch of shops and a pharmacy, Aunt Eva and I climbed off the streetcar, walked two blocks southwest, and arrived at the familiar row of houses that ran alongside the beach, separated from the white sands by Ocean Boulevard and a seawall of boulders. Waves crashed against the shore with a roar, echoed by the cry of seagulls combing the sand for food at the water's edge.

"You're going to see a noticeable change in the Emberses' front yard," said Aunt Eva when we neared our destination.

"What?"

"Look."

The brick chimney and brown shingles of the Emberses' home rose into view, as well as a serpentine line of black-clad men, women, and children that wound from the side of the house to the wall of privets along the property's front edge. As on the train from Oregon, I saw only desperate eyes and ugly white patches of gauze where mouths and noses used to be.

I sucked in my breath. "What are all those people doing there?"

"I told you, Julius specializes in photos of fallen servicemen now. People have been traveling across the country to benefit from his work, and the flu has tripled demand." Aunt Eva quickened her pace and led me across the Emberses' front lawn, past the waiting customers.

"There's a line, lady," barked a short woman with squinting eyes.

"I know the family, thank you very much." Aunt Eva adjusted the wide-brimmed hat she wore to conceal her boyish hair and, with an air of pride, bypassed the crowd.

I gulped at all the glares shooting our way over the masks and slouched with embarrassment.

We made our way to a side entrance that led directly into the studio. In April a simple wooden sign bearing the words EMBERS PHOTO STUDIO had greeted us, but now a large oval plaque made of polished brass announced in bold-faced letters:

MR. JULIUS EMBERS
SPIRITUALIST PHOTOGRAPHER

"Excuse me." Aunt Eva hiked up the hem of her dress and climbed past a small group on the cement steps. "I know the family."

A heavyset woman shoved her back to the ground. "Then use the main entrance."

"Mr. Embers told me not to."

"Then you must not know the family well."

The side door opened, and out poked the masked face of a thickset girl no older than eighteen, with a nest of chaotic brown hair pinned to the back of her head. Her white blouse bunched at the waist of her wrinkled gray skirt, and she had the overall appearance of a melting ice-cream cone. "Please make room for the exiting customers," she said in a voice as frazzled as her hair.

A family of four—two malnourished-looking parents and a small boy and girl—filed out of the studio with wreaths of garlic strung around their necks, as if they were warding off vampires instead of the flu. Behind them blared John Philip Sousa's "Stars and Stripes Forever."

"Good afternoon, Gracie." Aunt Eva elbowed her way back up the steps to reach the girl at the door. "Tell Mr. Embers I've brought Mary Shelley Black for him."

A hush fell over the crowd when my aunt spoke my name. All masked faces turned my way.

"Mary Shelley Black?" Gracie sized me up with eyes as large as golf balls. "Oh, my—it is you. Come in." She grabbed my hand with cold fingers, yanked me and Aunt Eva inside, and shut the door on the crowd with a *thwack*.

A wall of frigid air hit my skin the moment we entered. I shivered and adjusted my eyes to the dimness of the long rectangular room. Meager shafts of natural light came through three windows shaped like portholes on the western wall. Candles burned on all sides of the room.

"I'm so happy to finally meet you," shouted Gracie over the patriotic music trumpeting out of a phonograph's black-horned speaker. "I'm Julius's cousin. My brother and I have been helping out as his assistants ever since the flu took our mother last month."

"Oh . . . I'm so sorry to hear about your loss." I squeezed her hand. "It's nice to meet you, too. Stephen mentioned you in his—" I froze, for on the wall to my right, from floor to ceiling just inside the doorway, hung a poster featuring an artist's rendition of my photograph with the kneeling, white-draped ghost. My own painted eyes stared me down, as if in challenge.

"Hello, Mary Shelley." Julius Embers stepped out of the shadows of his studio wearing a black suit, an emerald-green vest, and a smile that almost looked hesitant. No flu mask concealed his mouth and nose, as if he were unafraid of Death striking him down. "It's good to see you again."

"What do you mean *again*?" I dropped my hand from Gracie's. "It looks like you see me every second of the day on your wall over here."

"That's true." His smile broadened to his usual overconfidence, any hint of uncertainty banished.

I straightened my posture to feel taller around him. "Did you use me in this advertisement to make your brother mad?"

"Not at all. I used your image because of the impressive spirit you lured into the photograph. My customers enjoy how regal you look with your proud expression and your ethereal visitor kneeling by your side. You bring everyone comfort." He stopped directly in front of me. "I want to capture you again—see what else you can give me."

I studied his face and caught a similarity between his and Stephen's eyes that I hadn't ever noticed before. He was four years older and at least a half foot taller than his brother, but his eyes were the same shape and shade—the deep, inviting brown of dark, liquid chocolate. I glanced away from him, unsettled by the resemblance. The words he had used to describe the way he found Stephen and me the last time I was in that house burned in my brain:

I found them on the sofa. He had her skirts pulled up to her waist and was on her like an animal.

"It's really good to see you, Julius," said Aunt Eva with a tender squeeze of his arm. "You look like you're holding up well, considering all the work you're doing."

"I'd look even better if I hadn't just endured a difficult morning with Aloysius Darning."

"Oh no."

"Oh yes." Julius sighed and took his arm away from Aunt Eva's clutches. "That nincompoop is so determined to prove me a fraud that he hovered over my sittings from eight o'clock to nine thirty. He made some of my customers nervous with all his poking and prodding of my equipment."

"I'm sure he didn't find anything amiss, though," said my aunt.

"Of course not. Because nothing was amiss."

I lifted my eyes back to Julius's. "Aunt Eva said you're finally going to give me Stephen's package."

"Yes." He took my hand and pressed it between his hot palms. "My mother only just told me about it when we heard you were coming to San Diego. I'd also be happy to lend you some of his novels if you'd like."

"Isn't that nice of him, Mary Shelley?" Aunt Eva slipped my hand out of his. "I told him you'd be bored with no school and nothing to read but the dull old dictionary."

"Thank you," I said to Julius. "I'd like to borrow them."

The music stopped. The phonograph's needle traveled to the center of the record with the crackling hiss of static. Julius whipped his head toward the sound. "Gracie, stop gawking at Mary Shelley and attend to the music, please."

"I'm sorry, Julius." Gracie hustled to the phonograph. "I was just so excited to meet her. Stephen always talked about her letters, and I've seen her face so often on your wall there, I almost feel like I'm meeting someone from Hollywood—"

An odd banging erupted from the floor above us.

Gracie's forehead turned as white as her mask. She peered toward the ceiling with an expression of such horror, I half believed something sinister was thumping against the wall upstairs. My heartbeat quickened. I found myself gazing at the ceiling as well, while the painting of the white-cloaked phantom lingered in the corner of my eye.

"Gracie—the phonograph!" said Julius.

Gracie fumbled to replace "Stars and Stripes Forever" with a new record. She turned the crank on the phonograph, and "The Battle Hymn of the Republic" started up at full volume.

"Why are you blasting the room with patriotic music?" I asked Julius over the commotion.

"The spirits of fallen war heroes appreciate it. It makes them feel they didn't die in vain." He steered me by my shoulders, away from my aunt and toward his growing collection of spirit photographs. What must have been a hundred sample photos hung on the longest interior wall, their frames wedged against one another in a fight for space on the walnut panels. The majority of the faceless spirits wore military uniforms and stood behind mortal sitters. Some of the ghosts rested their hands on their loved ones' shoulders.

I heard breathing near the back of my neck and turned my head with a start. Aunt Eva had followed us like a shadow.

"Eva, please have a seat in the chair back there." Julius nodded to a chair in the corner by the door—the pesky relative seat, or so it seemed.

"Do you need me to help with Mary Shelley's hair or—"

"Please have a seat." Julius gave another nod. "The spirits won't want a crowd."

With a wounded look, Aunt Eva retreated, and Julius pressed his fingers around mine again, guiding me across the room. "Let's take off your mask and get you seated."

"I'm not taking off my mask," I said.

"I want to see your whole face in the photograph."

"Are you off your rocker?" I tensed my legs in a solid stance and shook him off me. "I've seen how many people come into this musty, dark room. I'm not risking my life for a photograph."

"All right, all right." He took my hand again and chuckled as though he found my fear entertaining. "Good God, I'd forgotten what a stubborn old mule you are."

"I also have two provisions before I sit for you."

He lifted his eyebrows and laughed again. "And they are?"

I untangled my fingers from his. "First of all, you need to tell Aunt Eva you lied about the way you found Stephen and me the last time I was here."

"Mary Shelley, our host is giving you free photographs," said my aunt from her corner. "Please just sit down for him and stop embarrassing yourself."

"I won't sit down until he tells the truth." I stared at Julius until he could no longer meet my eyes. Over by the phonograph, Gracie scratched at her arm and glanced down at her shoes.

"I may have exaggerated a little." Julius peered straight at me again. "I'm sorry."

"We weren't on the sofa, were we?" I asked.

"No, but you were—" He bit his lip. "My brother said some things to me of a personal, sensitive nature, and—as brothers sometimes fight—I might have added some details about what I saw." He studied my face for a reaction.

I turned toward my aunt. "Did you hear that, Aunt Eva?"

"The entire island of Coronado heard that, Mary Shelley. Please just put this subject to rest and sit down." She rubbed her flushed neck and looked like she wanted to disappear inside the walls.

I returned my attention to Julius. "I'd also like to see Stephen's parcel before I sit."

"Of course. Gracie, pull out the package Stephen prepared for our guest. It's in the top drawer of the desk."

His cousin scuttled over to a small desk topped with three glowing candles, and the flames twitched and danced as she approached. The flickering light made the faces in the nearby photos seem to move.

Gracie squeaked open a drawer and held up a rectangular item wrapped in brown paper. "Is this the one?"

"Yes," said Julius. "Will you assure Miss Black it's Stephen's handwriting on the front?"

"Oh yes, it's his." Gracie beamed at the words on the paper. "His penmanship was always so much better than mine."

That *was* of hers made my blood run cold.

"All right." I gave Julius a nod. "Those were my conditions. As long as you understand I'm only doing this for my aunt's sake and not because I believe in your ghosts, I'll sit for one quick picture."

He gestured toward a high-backed chair with a plum-colored cushion, positioned in front of a black background curtain. "Please have a seat."

I walked over to the chair and lowered myself to the cushion with a shiver. The room felt like a northern basement at the peak of winter, musty odor included. Stephen's words from my last visit entered my mind: *He also runs a fan over ice blocks in between sittings to cool the air in there. He tries to make everyone feel like phantoms are hovering around the studio.*

Julius knelt to position me as he desired and guided my knees to the left in a way that tickled, but I clamped my teeth together to keep from flinching or laughing. He tilted my gauze-covered chin to the right.

"How badly did you injure him that day?" I asked in a voice too quiet for Aunt Eva to hear.

"What are you talking about?"

"You know what I mean. My aunt dragged me out of here so quickly, I never got to ask if those thuds were the sounds of you slamming his head against the wall."

He kept my chin in his hand. "Brothers fight when we upset each other. That's just how we are."

"Is everything all right?" asked Aunt Eva. Uneasiness tinged her voice.

"Everything's fine." Julius got to his feet.

I swallowed. "Has Stephen written? Do you know if—"

An airplane growled overhead and drowned out the music and my question. The thunder of its engine shook the photos on the walls and vibrated in the pit of my stomach.

More thumps and bangs emerged from the floor above. Julius and I both looked at the ceiling.

"What's happening up there?" I asked.

Julius tore his eyes away from the beams overhead. "My studio causes everyone's imaginations to mistake normal house sounds for mischievous ghosts." He strode over to his stepfather's beautiful black camera and ducked his head under a dark cloth behind it. "It's probably just my mother cleaning. She's become a little obsessive. Keeps her from worrying about Stephen."

My eyes drifted back up to the ceiling while he brought me into focus and finished the camera's preparations. I would have felt much better if I could have seen Mrs. Embers myself.

"All right." His head reemerged from beneath the cloth. "Let's get started. Stay still now, and keep looking this way." He leaned his lips toward the camera's outstretched leather bellows and whispered something to the machinery—a ritual I'd seen him perform the last time I posed for him. From the few words I could hear, I gathered he was making some sort of plea to the other side. He then straightened his posture and cried out, "Spirits, we summon you. I bring you Mary Shelley

Black, named after an author of dark tales who believed in the mysterious powers of electrical currents—"

Something dropped to the floor upstairs. Julius flinched and raised his voice: "She's drawn hundreds of mourners to me with her angelic image. Send us another spirit to stand beside her. Bring her a loved one she wants to see." He held up his tray of flash powder. "Mary Shelley Black—summon the dead!"

He opened the cap of a round lens that gaped like the eye of a Cyclops.

The flash exploded with a blinding burst of flames and smoke.

Inside the camera, a chemically treated plate was imprinted with a miniature version of my body.

"There." Julius coughed on a dense white cloud that drifted around his head. "It's done." He screwed the lens cap back into place and inserted the glass plate's protective dark slide inside the rear of the camera.

My eyes watered so much from the scorching air that I had to wipe them with my sleeve. The blast made me remember the Christmas when Stephen's father burned off his eyebrows with a particularly volatile flash explosion.

"Shall I give the package to her now, Julius?" asked Gracie. "Yes."

Another thump from above caused dust from the ceiling's beams to shower upon us. Footsteps pounded throughout the house, far louder than the phonograph's music. I blinked through the smoke and saw Julius's face go as pale as his cousin's.

The pocket doors to the front hall crashed open. Mrs. Embers stumbled into the studio, strands of dark hair falling across her eyes. "I need your help, Julius. I'm hurt." She clutched her stomach.

"Christ!" Julius put down the flashlamp. "Get them out of here, Gracie." He charged across the room and grabbed his mother by the arm to escort her away.

"You need to go immediately." Gracie handed me Stephen's parcel and pushed on my back to get me to move faster.

I looked over my shoulder. "What happened to Mrs. Embers?"

"Please, just go."

"When should we come back for the photograph?" asked Aunt Eva.

"I don't know. Monday morning, maybe." Gracie opened the door and gave me another shove. "A family emergency has arisen," she called to the line of customers, which now spilled over onto the front sidewalk. "The spirits are letting us know they need their rest. Come back another day." She propelled Aunt Eva outside behind me and slammed the door closed on all of us.

Cries of unrest came from the black-clothed grievers.

"What did you do in there, you little hussy?" asked the same heavyset woman who had pushed Aunt Eva off the steps. "Why'd you ruin it for the rest of us?"

"That's Mary Shelley Black," said a young brunette behind her. "You can't talk to her like that."

"I don't care if she's Mary, Queen of Scots. I've been waiting four hours to get a picture taken with my poor Harold, and she just ruined it all."

"I didn't ruin anything—"

Aunt Eva grabbed my hand. "Let's run."

"That'll only make us look guilty," I said.

"Run!"

Two hefty men from the back of the line were now headed our way with murder in their eyes, so I did as she said—I used my Boy Scout boots' double soles of reinforced solid oak leather and bolted across the grass and down the coastal neighborhood's sidewalks, until Ocean Boulevard disappeared behind us.

We didn't stop running until we jumped onto the streetcar, and even then my heart kept racing. I sat beside my aunt on the wooden seat and clutched Stephen's parcel to my chest.

"What was all of that about?" I asked while trying to catch my breath. "What happened to Mrs. Embers upstairs?"

Aunt Eva gasped for air and rubbed a stitch in her side. "I don't know. But I'm sure meeting mourners on a constant basis . . . and worrying about a loved one overseas . . . can destroy one's nerves."

"Poor cousin Gracie seemed as anxious as a frightened mouse."

"Poor cousin Gracie is a flu survivor. Her hair went white

and fell out from the fever. That's why she wears a wig."

"That was a wig?"

My aunt nodded.

I gulped. "It almost seemed to me, with all the spirit activity in that house, the family believes they're being haunted."

Aunt Eva fidgeted in her seat, but she didn't admit the Emberses' house disturbed her. It certainly disturbed me. I could almost understand why Stephen was in such a hurry to get out of there.

I lowered the package to my lap and trailed my fingers over my own name, penned in handwriting I adored—handwriting that mirrored the writer's artistic nature. The *S* in *Shelley* resembled a treble clef. The *B* in *Black* could have been called voluptuous. My odd, dark name always transformed into something lyrical and beautiful through Stephen's pen.

I noticed the string tying the parcel paper together hung loose on one end, as though someone had already slid the string aside to inspect the contents of the package. A small tear also marred the paper. "I think someone's already opened this. Do you suppose Julius—?"

"Mary Shelley." My name passed over my aunt's lips as a tired groan.

I peeled back the tampered end of the paper and slid out a framed photograph. My labored breath caught in my throat. Warmth flushed throughout my face and chest and spread to the tips of my fingers and toes. The strings of my mask tightened with a grin the size of Alaska.

As his last gift to me before leaving for the war, Stephen—fully aware of my love of electricity—had given me a photograph of a jagged lightning bolt striking a sepia nighttime sea.

A TRANSPARENT FIGURE

I HADN'T PLANNED TO HANG ANY DECORATIONS ON THE walls of my bedroom in Aunt Eva's house. Doing so would have been an admission that San Diego was to become my home for a long while.

However, on Sunday, the day after we visited the Emberses, I couldn't help but mount Stephen's lightning bolt on a strip of gilded wallpaper just beyond the foot of my bed. I asked Aunt Eva's permission to pound two nails into her wall and hung both of his photographs side by side, the butterfly and the electricity. I never found any note in his parcel and was certain Julius had taken it. But the picture had finally reached my hands.

I discovered Stephen had crossed out some words in the

lower right-hand corner, perhaps a rejected title, and between gold and white ripples in the ocean, he had written one of his anagrams:

I DO LOSE INK

I squinted and pulled other words out of the letters. *Sink. Die. Nod. Skid. Oiled. Link.* But none of the phrases I deciphered struck me as being the name of a photograph of a powerful storm over the Pacific.

Aunt Eva knocked on my open door and breezed into my room. "I think I'll go pick up Julius's picture of you early tomorrow morning before work. I can catch the first ferry. I'll just wear a skirt over my work trousers."

I stepped away from the images on the wall. "Will the studio be open that early?"

"I assume so. Julius is a hard worker."

"I'll go with you."

"That's not a good idea. You shouldn't be out in public air any more than you have to be."

"I didn't *have* to go to his house yesterday, but you let me. It's mainly clean ocean air we'll be breathing."

"I'll think about it." She spied the mounted photographs. "Are you sure you want those hanging on your wall?"

"Why wouldn't I? They're beautiful."

"Oh, Mary Shelley . . ." She tutted and took my hand. "Come here. Sit down with me for a moment so we can talk about something important." She sat me on my bed and perched beside me on Grandma Ernestine's old blue and white quilt that served as a bedspread. "I know you've never had a mother in your life to teach you the ways of the heart—"

"Don't bring up that morning I kissed Stephen."

"I'm not. I just want to say I know you think you're deeply in love with that boy, but you need to keep in mind you're still so very young. And . . . he might never come home."

"I already know that." I pulled my hand away from her. "Why would you remind me of such a thing?"

"Because every time his name comes up in conversation, your eyes brighten like he's about to walk into the room. And now you're hanging his photos on the wall and further surrounding yourself with him. Did he even ask you to wait for him?"

"He said I didn't have to wait unless I wanted to. He doesn't want me to waste my life worrying about him."

"Oh." She sounded surprised. "Well . . . that was kind of him."

"He's a kind person."

She took my hand again and cradled it in her calloused palm. "If he urged you to be free, then let him go. Don't waste your youth wondering if a boy from your past will ever return to you."

My throat itched with the threat of tears. "I don't think you fully comprehend how much Stephen and I mean to each other."

"Mary—"

"Did I ever tell you how we became friends?"

Her hazel eyes softened behind her glasses. "No, I don't think you did."

"I was eight at the time, and he wasn't yet ten. I'd seen him at school before, but he was always just a nice, quiet boy with an interesting last name, and I mainly played with girls. This one day, though, he brought this little Brownie pocket camera to school." I used my hands to demonstrate the camera's width, about eight inches. "It was just a small one with a beautiful deep-red bellows and an imitation leather covering. I was walking home with my friend Nell and two other girls, and I saw him in the distance, taking pictures of a tabby cat lying on the steps of an old church. Well"—my shoulders tensed at the ensuing memory—"these older boys swaggered up to him and teased him about being Julius's sissy brother. They grabbed his camera and threw it onto the sidewalk. I heard a terrible crack and watched pieces scatter across the cement. And then those boys shoved him in the shoulder and walked away."

Aunt Eva cringed. "I'm sure their father was furious that a camera got broken."

"That's what Stephen shouted after them. He said, 'My father's going to call the cops on all of you,' and then he added some colorful curse words I'd never heard come out of a nice boy's mouth before. I told my friends to go on home, and then I joined him to help find all the lost pieces. Some screws had come loose, and part of the wood casing had split apart beneath the fake leather. Stephen said I wouldn't be able to help him because I was a girl, but I sat right down on the steps of that church and screwed everything back in place with a little spectacle repair kit Dad had given me. I also pulled my ribbon out of my hair and wrapped up the cracked body to avoid any further damage before he could glue the wood back together at home."

"Ah, yes." Aunt Eva nodded. "Wasn't that around the time Uncle Lars decided to buy you a larger tool kit?"

"I think so."

A smile lit her face. "I'd forgotten all about that."

"So there I was," I continued, "piecing Stephen's camera together like a puzzle, fastening the nickel lens board back in place, chatting about the book poking out of his satchel— Jack London's *White Fang*. And all the while Stephen stared at me as if I were something magical. Not the ugly way other people sometimes stare at me, like I'm a circus freak. But with respect and recognition, like he was meeting someone in a foreign country who spoke his language when no one else could. That's how it's been between us ever since. We understand each other, even when we astound each other."

Her eyes dampened. "I just don't want you to get hurt. I hope you'll be able to move on and find other things in life that make you happy."

"Just let me keep hope in my heart for him for now, all right? Let me leave his photographs hanging on my wall to remind me that something beautiful once happened in the middle of all the year's horrors."

She pulled me against her side and sniffed back tears. "All right. But keep your heart guarded. I know what it's like to have love turn agonizing. There's nothing more painful in the world."

NO ONE ANSWERED THE STUDIO DOOR AT DAWN. WE stood outside the Emberses' house in a fog so thick we couldn't see the Pacific across the street.

I tugged my coat around me. "Should we knock on the front door?"

"I don't know." Aunt Eva waddled down the side staircase and peered through the mist toward the main entrance. She wore a blue plaid skirt over her work trousers to disguise her uniform, and the pants beneath produced so much bulk that she looked like a giant handbell—skinny torso, bulbous hips. "I don't want to disturb his mother. She seemed ill the other day."

"You can't be late for work, though."

"I'm not sure what to do." She trekked back up the stairs and knocked again.

The sound of an automobile motor sped our way. We both craned our necks to see the approaching vehicle through the fog: a plain black Model T. The car careened around the corner, clipped the curb with its carriage-sized wheels, and squealed to a jerking stop on the side street next to the house.

A man with uncombed black hair spilled out of the passenger seat.

Aunt Eva rubbed her throat and asked in a whisper, "Is that Julius?"

I squinted through the fog. "I think so."

"You going to be OK, Julius?" asked the driver, a solid-looking, bespectacled fellow who appeared to be closer to my age than Julius's. "You sure you don't want me running the studio instead of closing it for the day?"

Julius ignored the driver and stumbled up to the house, his shirt untucked, his chin dark with whiskers. His face resembled Uncle Wilfred's in the throes of tuberculosis: gray, clammy, sunken. His red-rimmed eyes caught sight of us standing on the steps. "Why are you here?" He didn't sound pleased.

"We came for Mary Shelley's photograph. Are you unwell, Julius?"

He blustered past us, smelling of cologne and something sweet, even though he looked like he could use a bath. "Come in and take it quickly. Then please go. I'm not feeling well."

Aunt Eva jumped out of the way. "It's not the flu, is it?"

"No, it's not the damn flu." He fumbled to open the door and reached around to a switch that lit a quartet of electric wall lamps. "Wait here. I'll get it." He went in.

Behind us, the Model T rumbled away.

I stepped a foot inside the studio and watched Julius disappear through a doorway next to the dark background curtain.

I'd always assumed the door led to a closet, but it appeared to be the entrance to an office in which photographs hung on a string to dry like laundry on a clothesline.

"What's wrong with him?" I asked.

Aunt Eva still massaged her throat. "I have no idea. I've never seen him like this."

"Is it the opium?"

"Mary Shelley!"

Julius walked back into the studio with a brown folder. "Here, take it." He held out the concealed picture in the tips of his fingers.

I approached and took it from him, feeling my stomach dip with nervousness as I did so.

His red eyes watered. "Now go. Please."

"I'd like to see the photograph first."

"Go."

I held my breath and flipped the folder open. There I was, in black and white, seated on the velvet-cushioned chair with my camphor pouch and clock-gear necklace strung around my neck. My pale eyes peered at the camera above my flu mask.

A transparent figure stood behind me—a handsome brown-haired boy in a dress shirt and tie.

Stephen.

Stephen was the ghost in my photograph.

Aunt Eva took the folder from my hand. "Oh no, Julius. Is that your brother?"

The words cut deep. I realized what they implied.

"Is he . . ." Aunt Eva's lips failed to shape the word.

Julius cleared his throat. "We just learned he died in battle. The telegram said it was a ferocious fight at the beginning of October. He went heroically."

All the oxygen left that room. I held my stomach and heard the warning signs of unconsciousness buzz inside my eardrums. My vision dimmed. My legs started to give way.

Aunt Eva took hold of my arm to steady me. "Mary Shelley, are you all right?"

Julius turned his back on me. "Take her outside."

A scream from upstairs jolted me to my senses. We all peered toward the ceiling.

"Stephen!" cried Mrs. Embers, as if someone were tearing her heart to shreds. "Stephen!"

Julius grabbed my arms and turned me around. "I said take her out of here. Both of you, get outside. Go far, far away. My brother's childhood sweetheart is the last person we need to see right now."

My feet tripped from the reckless way he steered me across the floor. Before I could regain my balance, Aunt Eva and I were back outside in the fog. The door slammed behind us. We could still hear Mrs. Embers's screams beyond the walls, even over the thunder of the waves.

"Let's go." My aunt took my hand and guided me down the steps. "We need to let them mourn. What a terrible, terrible thing to lose a loved one clear across the world."

My body felt out of control. I couldn't walk or breathe right. Pain squeezed my lungs so hard that Aunt Eva had to shoulder my weight to help me move.

"I warned you not to long for him." She put her hand around my waist to better support me. "I knew he'd break your heart."

"I want—" I choked and sputtered as if I were crying, but no tears wet my eyes. "I want you to throw that photograph in the bay when we're on the ferry. Stephen . . . he would have hated seeing it."

"I don't think that's a good idea with the way you're acting. I'll keep it for you in case you change your mind."

"No."

"You may want it in the future."

"No."

"Shh. Just concentrate on walking. You'll feel better when you get back home."

"My home's in Portland. I'll never get back there. I'll never feel better."

We continued to hear Mrs. Embers's screams, even as we made our way past the house next door, before the crash of waves swallowed up her cries.

6

THE BUZZ OF ELECTRICITY

WE PARTED AT THE FERRY LANDING ON THE SAN DIEGO side of the harbor. I could tell from Aunt Eva's pinched eyebrows she regretted sending me off alone, but she had to go to work. I staggered away without looking back at her. The photograph floated somewhere halfway across the bay, ripped from its protective folder and thrown in the corrosive salt water.

The quarantine had silenced the heart of downtown. A stray newspaper page scuttled down the sidewalk on the wings of a southerly wind. Overhead a pair of seagulls cried to each other as they soared toward the ocean, eager to escape civilization. I didn't blame them. A handful of men and women departed a yellow electric streetcar near Marston's Department Store at Fifth and C. Like me, they were all dressed in dark clothing and masks, heads bent down with the weight of the world, eyes on the watch for death.

We all looked like bad luck.

The word CLOSED hung from every other shop door, and the stores that did stay open lacked customers. I passed a barbershop in which the barber stooped in front of his mirror and trimmed his own hair, probably out of boredom. The tobacco shop next door displayed a poster with a bloody German handprint. THE HUN—HIS MARK, it said. BLOT IT OUT WITH LIBERTY BONDS.

The Hun—Stephen's Killer, was all I could think.

"No, he's not dead," I murmured. "He's not dead. He's supposed to come home. He's supposed to send me another letter."

A man in a derby hat with a sandwich board slung over his shoulders crossed the street on the other side of the intersection. "Sin is the root of all evil in the world," he yelled to no one in particular. "God is punishing us with pestilence, war, famine, and death." The sign around his neck read THE FOUR HORSEMEN OF THE APOCALYPSE HAVE ARRIVED! YE WHO HAVE SINNED SHALL BE STRICKEN DOWN.

I watched him with horror and realized, *We're all simply waiting to be killed. All that's left is blinding sorrow and a painful death by drowning in our own fluids. What's the point of being alive?*

I couldn't breathe. I turned to face a sandstone wall, removed my mask, and gasped for air. I gulped and gulped until I swallowed as much of the tuna-scented breeze as possible, even though the odor made me sick. Everything made me sick. Why wasn't I the one to get killed by germs or bombs? Why was I standing alone in the middle of a deserted city? Why did a bright and talented boy have to go and do a stupid thing like enlist?

Unable to divine any answers from my empty street corner, I trudged on like a sleepwalker, my feet as thick as sandbags. My erratic breathing mutated into hiccups that stabbed my sides.

In the residential district I spied—and smelled—from across the street an undertaker's clapboard house with a grisly scene in the front yard: stacks of pine caskets, piled two to three high. Even worse, four little boys climbed over the coffins as if they were playing in a wooden fortress. They chanted a rhyme I'd heard at the beginning of the school year, when the flu first raised its monstrous head:

I had a little bird,
Its name was Enza,
I opened the window,
And in-flu-enza.

"Hey, get off there!" I yelled at the children. "You're climbing over dead bodies. Can't you see the flies? You're going to get sick."

The leader of the group—a brown-haired boy in knee pants—balanced his feet on the teetering wood and called out, "It's the Germans, boys. Shoot 'em!"

The other chubby-cheeked kids leaned over the caskets and fired rounds at me from invisible rifles.

"Where are your parents?" I asked.

"Keep firing, men. Show the filthy Boche what you've got."

They continued to attack me with pretend ammunition, with no sign of leaving their disgusting playground. A rumble of thunder in the purpling sky to the west set off a series of delighted *oohs* and *wows* from the boys.

"That's the blast of our cannon, Boche," said the leader. "You're going to die."

"You're going die if you keep playing there, you stupid kids. Get out of there." I marched up the low slope of the yard, into the thick of the stench and the flies, and grabbed the brown-haired boy by the arms. "I said get out of here."

"Let go of me."

"No." I gripped him with viselike strength and dragged his flailing body off the undertaker's property.

"Let me go!"

"Go back home to your mother." I pushed him away down the sidewalk. "I don't want to hear about any more dead boys."

"You're crazy, you know that?" He glared at me over his shoulder and wandered away. His friends fell into place behind him, snickering.

Before I could get to the end of the block, the brown-haired boy shouted from down the street, "For your information, my mother's lying in the hospital with the flu. I *can't* go home to her."

I rubbed away tears with the back of my hand and kept walking.

Three blocks later I arrived at Aunt Eva's yellow house and discovered someone had parked a bicycle next to her roses. A lanky boy no more than twelve, in an official-looking cap and black tie, waited on the front porch with an envelope and a clipboard. He saw me making my way up the path and came toward me at a brisk gait. I braced for more bad news.

"Hello, miss." The boy's voice sounded muffled inside his mask, which looked as if it were tied tight enough to hurt. "Are you Mrs. Wilfred Ottinger or Miss Mary Shelley Black?"

"I'm Miss Black."

"Please sign here."

The words he directed my way on the clipboard blurred together in my tired eyes. All I could make out was WESTERN UNION at the top. Someone had sent us a telegram.

"Oh no." I shoved the clipboard back at him. "I can't take another death today. Don't give it to me. Don't tell me my father's dead."

"I don't read the messages, miss." He pushed the board my way. "Please sign it. I can't leave without delivering the telegram if someone's home."

I wobbled and had to clutch the boy's arm to avoid passing out.

"Please, miss. It'll be all right."

He steadied me, and with shaking fingers I scratched a sloppy version of my signature. I took the tan envelope, tore it open, and read a short message from Uncle Lars in Portland:

```
THEY'RE HOLDING HIM WITHOUT BAIL.
    TRIAL SET FOR DECEMBER.
  POSSIBLE 20-YEAR SENTENCE.
     KEEP M.S. WITH YOU.


              L.
```

Twenty years.

If a jury decided that fate for my father, he'd be sixty-five at his release. I'd be thirty-six. And all because Dad hated war.

The message fluttered out of my fingers to the sidewalk. I marched a dirty footprint across the paper on my way into the house and slammed the door behind me with enough force to rattle windows. Oberon squawked from his cage. That Western Union boy probably jumped out of his skin and pedaled away as fast as his bony legs could take him.

I thumped upstairs to my room and yanked off my mask. Stephen's photographs still hung on the gilded wallpaper, teasing me with memories of a time when he was alive and my father wasn't rotting away in jail. I paced the floor and pulled at my hair until my scalp ached. "Get me out of here. *Get me out of here!*"

A low boom echoed in the distance. My eyes shot to the window. I held my breath. Ten seconds later, the menacing clouds to the west flashed with light, followed by another crash of thunder.

A lightning storm.

I pulled up the window's sash and felt the tiny hairs on my arms bristle with static. Lightning ignited the air, and I wanted its bolts to shock me out of my nightmare world and send me back into my old reality.

I scrounged around my room and found the makings of a kite—the parcel paper from Stephen's package for the body, wire coat hangers for the frame, and a rope of hair ribbons for string. My clock-gear necklace would act as my conductor. I slipped my aviatrix goggles out of my leather doctor's bag, fitted them over my face, and hurried downstairs with my creation.

The claps of thunder now followed the lightning by two seconds. The wind whipped my hair across my face, while fresh-smelling rain streaked my lenses and soaked the string of ribbons, rendering them useless. How stupid to have thought the fabric wouldn't get drenched and heavy. The parcel paper would never soar. My name written in Stephen's handwriting bled into black smudges, gone forever.

Lightning shot across the sky in an erratic streak more blinding than Julius's flashlamp. Thunder reverberated against the soles of my boots a mere second later. The storm gathered overhead. My blood craved the buzz of electricity to replace the poison of the world. I wanted to touch it. I *had* to touch it.

I grabbed the clock gear and held it in the air with my bare fingers.

Another streak of light illuminated the front yard. A roll of thunder clapped overhead, and a slight shock of static zapped the tips of my fingers.

But that was all.

"Come on!" I yelled. "Give me something I can feel."

Someone shrieked from across the street, distracting me enough that I turned my head, but then the world went yellow and crashed against my ears. Electricity burned my hand, threw me backward to the ground.

And killed me.

7

DEATH

THE SCIENTIFIC METHOD HELPED ME COMPREHEND THAT I was no longer alive.

First you formulate a question: *Am I dead?* Then a hypothesis: *If I'm sitting up here in Aunt Eva's eucalyptus tree, looking down at my own body sprawled across the grass in the rain, then I must be dead.* The test: *A redheaded woman in an apron runs across the street, sees my smoking clothing and my lifeless eyes staring through my goggles, and tries to shake my limp body back to life—to no avail. "Oh, dear God, she's dead," she yells to another woman sprinting across the lawn. "The lightning struck this poor girl dead."* The conclusion: *Mary Shelley Black is indeed no longer alive.*

Oh, God, I thought. *What did I just do?*

I looked up: a black cumulonimbus cloud bellowed around the eucalyptus like a seething beast. A siren cried out from somewhere nearby. Neighbors in flu masks gathered below me.

"What did I do?" I called down to the people, although no one seemed to hear. The version of me that sat in the tree looked solid and mortal, in my opinion, but I feared I was little more than a mirage up there. "This doesn't feel right. What am I supposed to do?"

A black police ambulance drove into view. The neighbors waved it down with frantic arms. Men in uniforms jumped out of the vehicle and grabbed a stretcher. I could still see my prone, empty body, with its singed fingers and gray face, and no one, not even the men from the ambulance, could revive me. One of the men pushed my goggles to my forehead and pulled my eyes shut, and my skin looked cold and hostile and ugly. The idea of dropping back into that lifeless flesh sickened me, and I guessed the landing would be excruciating. But sitting in a tree above myself wasn't right, either. This wasn't at all the way death was supposed to be. There were no angels, harps, or pearly gates—just me staring down at my corpse, not knowing what to do.

Go back, I told myself when the officers lifted my body onto the stretcher. *It's clearly not your time. Quick! Before it's too late.*

I pushed myself off the eucalyptus branch, and down I plunged into that unappealing shell of a girl with the torturous sensation of falling into a pool of arctic water. Every square inch of me stung. I gasped for air like a dying fish and heard a pair of doors slam shut near my feet.

My arms and legs sank deep into a canvas bed in the back of a dark compartment. I had entered the too-small skin and bones of a freezing-cold girl made of lead, whose skull throbbed and right fingers burned with a pain more intense than anything I'd ever experienced. Beside me, a person gurgled and wheezed, sounding like he was drowning. The automobile's motor vibrated against my vertebrae.

A few minutes later, we careened around a corner with a squeal of tires, and the wheezing person and I slid to the right, where my knee and elbow hit a metal wall.

A pothole threw me into the air and slammed me down again. The brakes screeched to a stop and I skidded toward the front of the compartment. More metal banged against me. Doors slammed shut. Footsteps scrambled around the vehicle.

A gangly man in an olive-green police uniform opened a set of doors just beyond my feet, blinding my eyes with the glare of the sunlight that must have followed the storm.

"Holy—" The policeman's round eyes widened above his mask. "She's alive!"

"What?" A plumper male face popped up beside him.

"The girl with no pulse. She's alive."

"But—"

"Look at her."

They stared at me as if they were witnessing a foul and bloated corpse rising from the grave.

The gurgling person beside me gasped once more and then fell silent. A whisper of a breeze shivered across my skin, drifted to the top of the ambulance, and passed through the roof, where it disappeared in a flood of yellow warmth.

"The person beside me just died," I found myself saying.

TWO MASKED NURSES IN HATS LIKE GIANT ASPIRIN TAB-lets wheeled me on a gurney through the hallways of a stark white hospital. Cots crowded both sides of the passageways—temporary beds for shivering flu victims who curled on their sides and coughed up blood. I saw cheekbones covered in mahogany spots and entire faces an unnatural reddish purple, which, like black feet, signified the end. The scent of antiseptic cleaning solutions burned my nostrils.

The stockier, white-haired nurse peeked over her mask. "Put your head down. You're lucky to be alive, young lady. Let's keep you that way." Fatigue rolled off her body, exhausting me. "We're in the middle of a plague, sweetheart, and you better heal up quick before this hospital kills you."

They maneuvered me into one of the examination rooms, but a beady-eyed man in a white coat flailed his arms and shouted, "We're out of room. She needs to go in the hall."

"She got hit by lightning," said the stocky nurse. "It's not the flu."

"There's no room. Put her in the hall."

The nurses swiveled me out the door and around the corner, and I gripped the sides of the gurney to make sure I didn't slide and bruise like during my ambulance ride. More flu victims trembled on all sides of me. A rotten flavor lined my mouth. We seemed to travel down those writhing, wheezing, rancid corridors for a good five minutes.

Finally the nurses shoved me in a dark corner. I could see a black foot with a toe tag on a neighboring gurney, but the lack of light kept me from making out the rest of the body.

I grabbed a nurse's cold hand. "Is my aunt here?"

"I don't know, dear."

"Please find her. Her name is Eva Ottinger. She works in the shipyard."

"I'll make sure we contact her. Stay here and rest. The doctor will see you soon."

The nurses pattered away in their soft shoes, leaving me alone with the toe-tagged foot, the darkness, and the macabre chorus of drowning flu victims echoing off the walls.

"WHERE'S MY NIECE? MARY SHELLEY! MARY SHELLEY Black!"

I blinked my eyes open and saw Aunt Eva storming toward me in her greasy work clothes, blond hair flying, glasses shoved up on her nose, flu mask swelling and deflating from violent breaths. Anger radiated from her in pulsating waves, and strangely enough, I could taste her rage—hot, metallic, like a fork that's been heated in an oven.

She gripped the side of my gurney. "My sister didn't die bringing you into the world just so you could take yourself out of it. How dare you spit on your mother's memory?"

"I'm sorry—"

"I've spent day and night worrying about you dying from the flu, and then you go and stick yourself in the middle of a lightning storm."

"Stop shouting."

"I will *not* stop shouting. They told me you died for several minutes. Someone at the front desk just showed me your blackened clock-gear necklace and those stupid goggles—"

"Please. Sick people are trying to sleep." I grabbed her hand with my undamaged one.

The effect my touch had on her was immediate.

The metallic taste faded and transformed into a flavor sweet and light and airy, like whipped cream when it's reached its point of perfection. Her shoulders lowered. She studied my fingers surrounding her flesh. I could see her hazel eyes watching my hand through her spectacles.

"What is it?" I asked. "Why are you looking at my hand that way? That's not the one wrapped in bandages."

"It's nothing. I . . ." Her eyelids closed, and a blissful sigh escaped her lips beneath her mask, as if I'd given her a sedative. "I just don't want you to die."

I chewed my dry and cracking lip and tried to figure out how to tell her what had happened when I *did* briefly die.

"Is the library still open during the quarantine?" I asked.

Her eyes opened. "Why on earth are you asking about books? All you should be thinking about is healing."

"I wonder if there are any books that discuss returning from the dead."

"You shouldn't read horror novels at a time like this."

"No, not a novel, a textbook that discusses what typically happens when people die for a short while like I did. I'm curious if what happened to me is normal."

She lifted her eyebrows. "What do you mean?"

"I need to tell you something, Aunt Eva, but you have to swear you won't bring up Julius's spirits."

She nodded as if she wanted me to continue. "Go on."

"Do you swear you won't mention his name?"

"I swear."

I swallowed, which made my parched throat ache. "I left my body and sat on the branch of your eucalyptus tree for a bit. I saw myself down there, with my clothes smoking and the neighbors gathering around me. It didn't feel right, like I was stuck between life and death, and I wasn't sure where to go."

"You mean . . . you were a spirit?"

"I'm still not saying I believe in all that."

"Was Wilfred there? Or your mother?"

"I didn't see anyone. An ambulance showed up, and I decided to push myself back into my flesh, which hurt like mad."

She squirmed with excitement. "We should tell him."

"Don't say his name. Don't you dare compare what happened to me to those photographs."

"He should know you've been to the other side. Oh, Mary Shelley, can you imagine what he'd photograph now if you posed for him? Do you realize how much serenity your body is emanating? I can feel it in your touch. It's like you're partially still in the spirit realm."

"Don't say that." I snatched my hand away from hers. "I've had a hard enough time fitting into this world without thinking I'm only halfway here."

"That's what it feels like."

"Stop."

"Oh, Mary Shelley." She clutched my arm. "What an opportunity you've been given. You've gone somewhere the rest of us have only dared to imagine, and you've brought a portion of its wonders back with you." She removed her glasses and wiped her watery eyes with the back of her wrist. "This is going to change everything. I just know it."

I studied the hand that had soothed her and tried to figure out if I looked or felt any different than before. My trembling fingers still seemed to be made of flesh and bone. No heavenly glow surrounded my body. Spirits didn't huddle around my bed and try to make their presence known.

But she was right. Something had changed.

THE EXPERT

8

THE HOSPITAL RELEASED ME AS SOON AS I COULD STAND
up on my own. I wasn't gasping for my last breath; therefore,
they didn't have any spare time for me. Nurses were tying toe
tags around flu patients who hadn't died yet, so I made no
complaint about vacating my dark corner.

My head still throbbed, as did my fingers wrapped in
bandages, and my back was sore from being thrown to the
ground by the force of the shock—not to mention the bruises
sustained during that ambulance ride. Aunt Eva hired a taxi
to take us home so I wouldn't have to walk.

I stared at the back of the driver's black cap and balding
head through the window of the enclosed passenger area.

"My father goes on trial in December," I told my aunt. "Uncle Lars sent a telegram."

"He did?"

"I dropped it on your front lawn. I don't know if it's still there."

"It's on my front lawn?" Aunt Eva clutched her handbag to her stomach. "It doesn't mention the word *treason*, does it?"

"No. But Uncle Lars said Dad could be sentenced to twenty years."

"Twenty years?"

I tried to nod, but the movement hurt my head. "He shouldn't even be in jail."

"Do you know what he did up there, Mary Shelley? Do you know his crimes?"

I wrapped my arms around my middle. "I believe he helped men avoid the draft."

"That's right. Uncle Lars said your father was running some sort of group out of the back of his grocery store. Do you know how much trouble the rest of us could be in if anyone learns we're related to a traitor?"

"Don't call him a traitor. He's a good man."

"Then why are you a thousand miles from home, sticking yourself in lightning storms, winding up half-dead in a hospital? If he was so good, why didn't he worry more about keeping his own daughter safe?"

I leaned back against the padded taxi seat and clenched my jaw, unable to come up with an answer.

BACK AT HER HOUSE, AUNT EVA TUCKED ME INTO BED and told me to push aside all the unpleasantness that had coaxed me out into that lightning storm.

"Your job right now is to heal," she said as she pulled the warm sheet up to my chin. "Don't use your brain to do anything else."

So heal I did.

I lay there in bed with my skull splitting in two and my fingers burning and itching inside my bandages, but I refused to take any medicine to kill the pain. I wanted to be able to think without any substances blurring my mind. While Oberon chattered downstairs and Aunt Eva divided her time between the shipyard and me, my body repaired itself. All the tiny cells, nerves, and tissues worked like an efficient machine below the surface of my skin, and I longed to learn more about anatomy and physics and lightning and to listen to music that would challenge the recovering synapses of my brain. But the schools remained closed, and my body continued to stay stuck in a bed with springs that sounded like an accordion, my head and arms surrounded by bags of garlic-scented gum. Aunt Eva insisted the bags would chase away the hospital's flu germs. She also made me wear a goose-grease poultice on my neck and stuffed salt up my nose. I felt like she was preparing me as the main course for a dinner party instead of protecting me from an illness.

Stephen's photographs watched over me from beyond the foot of the bed the entire time, their presence a source of both comfort and anguish. Sometimes, when I let my body relax and my mind go numb, I almost believed I saw him standing there, directly in front of his photos. I almost believed the lightning had indeed brought me in touch with the spirit world.

And sometimes, when I was feeling strong enough to lift my head, I investigated another odd new phenomenon I'd discovered shortly after Aunt Eva first put me into that bed. It involved Uncle Wilfred's brass compass in the wooden case, which I kept on my bedside table.

The needle no longer pointed north.

It pointed to me, even if I moved the compass around. It followed me.

"Holy smoke," I whispered every single time I saw the needle swing my way.

I was now magnetic.

ONE WEEK INTO MY CONVALESCENCE, WHEN I WAS ABLE to sit upright without feeling like someone was whacking my spine with a sledgehammer, Aunt Eva came into my room with a forced smile on her face. "I've sewn a covering for Oberon's cage to keep him quieter during the day while you recover." She carried a long beige cloth as well as a white envelope.

I tilted my head for a better look at the envelope. "What's that?"

She drew in her breath. "It's from your father."

"My father?"

"I forgot to look at yesterday's mail. I just found this below the bills." She gave me the letter. "I'll let you read it in peace, but try not to get agitated by whatever he has to say. Let me know if you need me to come back."

I nodded, and murmured, "Thank you."

She left me alone to stare at the top line of the return address—the name of my father's new home:

PORTLAND CITY JAIL

Those three brutal words churned up all the hurt and rage from the night he left me—the night before I climbed aboard that train crammed with paranoid passengers bound for San Diego.

I remembered the two of us huddled around the kitchen table, finishing a bland meal of rice and beans and dry bread made of cornstarch instead of wheat. Dad ran his fingers through his whitening brown hair and told me, "Mary Shelley, if anything happens to me—"

"You're not going to die from a measly flu germ, Dad," I said.

"I don't necessarily mean dying. If something—"

"What? What's going to happen to you?"

"Shh. Let me speak." He wrapped his sturdy fingers around my hand. "If something happens, I would like you to go straight to Aunt Eva's. The weather's not so cold there. You'd be more likely to survive the flu with open windows and sunshine. And we'd keep the Oregon side of the family out of trouble."

"What type of trouble?"

He avoided my questioning stare.

"Tell me, Dad."

He cleared his throat. "Trouble that comes from doing the right thing, even if it's not safe. That's all I'm going to say about it, because I don't want anyone pressing you for information." He swallowed down a sip of coffee. "Eva's been living all alone in that house ever since Wilfred succumbed to his illness. I'm sure she'd be grateful for the company. Pack your bags after supper, just in case."

I glared at him, my nostrils flaring.

"Mary, please don't ask any questions. I'm not going to give you answers."

He only dropped the second part of my name when he was deadly serious.

I jabbed at my food with my fork until the tongs screeched against the porcelain and made him wince, but I didn't ask anything else. There was no point. If he didn't want to elaborate, he wouldn't. He was as bullheaded as I.

And here I was, more than a thousand miles away, all alone except for a jittery aunt, a chattering magpie, a broken heart, and an envelope with the words PORTLAND CITY JAIL.

I inhaled a calming breath and ripped open the paper.

October 20, 1918

Dear Mary Shelley,

I hope you are safe. I hope you are healthy. I hope you can forgive me for what I have forced you to endure. You may not be able to understand the reasoning behind my sacrifices, but one day when you're older and your anger at me has diminished, perhaps you will see the two of us are alike. We have a great deal of fight inside us, and sometimes our strength of spirit forces us to choose truth and integrity over comfort and security.

I know the world seems terrifying right now and the future seems bleak. Just remember human beings have always managed to find the greatest strength within themselves during the darkest hours. When faced with the worst horrors the world has to offer, a person either cracks and succumbs to the ugliness, or they salvage the inner core of who they are and fight to right wrongs.

Never let hatred, fear, and ignorance get the best of you. Keep bettering yourself so you can make the world around you better, for nothing can ever improve without the brightest, bravest, kindest, and most imaginative individuals rising above the chaos.

I am healthy and, for the most part, doing well. No need to worry about me or the store. I'm letting the bank take possession of

the business so we don't have to trouble your uncles. Take care of
yourself. Please write me soon so I know you are still alive.

Your loving father

I gritted my teeth and breathed through silent tears that
plunked wet stains upon the paper.

"Oh, Dad," I said to his tidy loops of black handwriting.
"Why should I bother making the world better when some of
my favorite parts about it are gone?" I wiped my eyes. "You're
locked away and Stephen's dead, and I don't feel like one of
the brightest, bravest, and kindest individuals without you."

THE FOLLOWING EVENING, AFTER AUNT EVA RETURNED
from work, a familiar baritone voice drifted up to my bedroom from the entryway.

My father's voice.

I swear up and down—I heard my dad.

I hurled myself out of bed in my nightgown and bolted to
the staircase, wondering if the telegram and the letter were
mistakes—or mere dreams. Dad wasn't going to be sentenced
after all. He had come to fetch me.

"Dad!" My bare feet scrambled halfway down the steps and
slipped out from under me. My backside slammed against
wood.

"Don't break your neck, Mary Shelley!" said Aunt Eva
from down in the entryway. "Why are you running?"

I regained my balance and pulled myself upright. "I heard—" My fingers went limp around the banister when I got a good look down below. My aunt stood by the front door with a slender stranger in a brown suit. Not my father.

"Oh." I stooped with disappointment. "I didn't know you had a visitor."

The gentleman's face, aside from his blue-green eyes, was hidden beneath a flu mask. He removed his derby hat and said, "Good evening, Miss Black," and I saw receding hair the glistening golden red of copper wire.

I lifted my chin. "Do I know you?"

"No," said Aunt Eva, "but you've heard of him. This is Mr. Darning."

"Mr. Aloysius Darning?" I took a single step downward. "The photography expert who's been investigating Julius?"

He nodded. "The one and the same. I was just across the bay at Mr. Embers's house, paying my respects for his brother, and he told me the young model from his handbill had experienced a recent taste of death."

"I told you not to tell Julius what happened to me," I snapped at my aunt.

"Don't get huffy in front of our guest, Mary Shelley. I simply telephoned Julius to let him know you'd been badly injured."

"He seemed concerned about you," said Mr. Darning. "And once I learned your name, I realized I knew your aunt."

"Mr. Darning attends my church." Aunt Eva rubbed the

back of her neck in a nervous manner. "While I don't care for the fact that he questions Julius's photography, he is a kind man."

Mr. Darning's eyes smiled above his gauze. "I appreciate that, Mrs. Ottinger. I know supporters of Julius Embers often view me as the villain."

"I want you to know," I said, traveling two more steps, "I had no idea Julius Embers used me in that advertisement until I arrived in San Diego over a week ago."

"Oh . . . really?" He lifted his copper eyebrows. "He didn't obtain your permission?"

"No, and I wouldn't have given it to him, either. Stephen told me all the ways Julius doctors his images. Double exposures, alterations in the developing process—"

"Believe me, I know all about the tricks of the trade, Miss Black. I've investigated all those possibilities with Julius Embers numerous times, but I'm afraid the man is either outsmarting me or genuinely photographing spirits."

"But Stephen was so insistent it's all a hoax," I said.

"I know, I know—I understand Stephen's concerns entirely. An amateur photographer who becomes a false celebrity is just about the worst thing a real photographer can encounter. But I can't find one shred of evidence that Julius is a fake."

I squeezed the handrail. "Isn't there anything else you can do?"

"Mary Shelley." Aunt Eva shook her head at me. "Please don't tire yourself out with subjects that upset you. Go back to bed." She turned to our guest and grabbed the doorknob. "Thank you so much for stopping by to see how she's faring, Mr. Darning."

"If there's anything I can do to help with your investigation," I said before Aunt Eva could shut the door on the man, "please let me know."

"Thank you," said Mr. Darning. "I'll keep that in mind." He took a parchment-colored business card out of the breast pocket of his brown coat. "And when you're feeling better, I invite you and your aunt to come to my studio for a complimentary sitting. I'd love nothing more than to show Julius Embers I can create a superior print of one of his prized subjects—even without a spirit involved." He handed my aunt the card, placed his derby back on his copper hair, and bid us a cordial good-bye in that gentle baritone voice that made me ache for home.

Aunt Eva shut the door and looked my way, her eyebrows raised. "Why were you calling for your father when you came down?"

"His voice sounded like Dad's."

"Oh." She averted her eyes from mine and hugged her arms around herself. "I know how that feels. There's a man at church who sounds like Wilfred."

"May I have Mr. Darning's business card?"

"Why?"

"Just to have it."

"No." She tucked the card into her apron pocket. "I don't

want you trying to get Julius in trouble when he's grieving for his brother."

"I wouldn't. If Mr. Darning is interested in debunking frauds, I'm guessing he enjoys science. I'd like to write to him and ask him some questions—to give me something to do."

"You don't need to be corresponding with a grown man you barely know. I'll put his card in my file in the kitchen, and we can consider the complimentary photograph in the future." She pointed upstairs. "Now go back to bed before I make supper and draw your bath. You're still paler than a ghost."

"Have they buried Stephen yet?"

She lowered her arm. "What?"

"Have they held his funeral while I've been recovering?"

"No. Not yet." She cast her eyes away from me again. "They've been waiting for his body to come home."

A sharp pain pierced my stomach. "Let me know when they do, all right?"

She nodded. "I will."

I retreated back up to my room on unsteady legs.

To chase away images of Stephen's body coming home in a casket, I forced myself to imagine him crawling through the porthole windows of his family's studio to save the photography equipment from the salty air, as he told me he did. He probably had to somehow scale the outside walls just to reach the high openings and risked breaking an ankle to jump down to the studio's floor. My lips turned in a small grin at the thought of Stephen's acrobatic feats of heroism. But I had to wonder what was happening to the camera's precious metal and glass now that he was no longer there to protect it.

I pulled a box of matches from the top drawer of my bedside table, lit the pearl-hued oil lamp, and checked in with Uncle Wilfred's compass before climbing back into bed. My legs found their way under the sheets, and I was about to sink my head into the pillow when my brain registered something my eyes had just seen. I sat upright and looked again at the compass. My mouth fell open. A shivery chill breezed down my spine.

The needle had stopped following me. For twenty-two more seconds, the little metal arrow directed itself with steadfast attention toward two objects across the room—two objects related to the person who had just dominated my thoughts.

The needle pointed to Stephen's photographs.

9

BLUE SMOKE AND WHISPERS

· *October 29, 1918* ·

AUNT EVA WOKE ME UP THE FOLLOWING MORNING BY exhaling a loud sigh next to my bed.

I held my breath and opened one eyelid. "What's the bad news?"

She held her mask in her hand, so I was able to see her pursed, whitened lips. "Julius telephoned me last night. They're burying Stephen this morning. I'll be working an extra shift later so I can take some time off work to go to the funeral. The Emberses were so kind to me when Wilfred died."

"I want to go, too."

"No, you need to heal."

"I want to be there. Please don't make me miss saying good-bye to him."

She sighed again. "All right, but I'm bringing you home the moment you seem too unwell to be there. I'll feed you onion hash this morning to make sure you stay safe, and I'm putting us in another taxi so we don't have to ride on the streetcars."

"OK." I closed my eyes, for they had started to sting.

Aunt Eva patted my arm. "Pick out your nicest dress. We need to leave in an hour."

EVERYTHING I PUT ON MY BODY THAT MORNING—FROM A big blue hair bow to my black silk taffeta dress—felt like iron weights bearing down on my bones. My healing lightning burn itched worse than a poison oak rash beneath my bandages. Even my mouth hurt, probably because Aunt Eva made me eat enough onion hash to disintegrate my taste buds. I felt like a broken, clumsy version of myself as I made my way back into the briny outside air for the first time in more than a week.

The funeral rooms of Barrett & Bloom, Undertakers, were located on a hill east of downtown, inside a white colonial-style house with black shutters and two front doors that seemed three feet taller than a normal entryway. If caskets of flu victims had flooded the premises like at the undertaker's house where I'd seen the children playing, then Mr. Barrett and Mr. Bloom must have kept them well hidden. All I saw on the lawn were trim hedges a vibrant shade of green and magenta bougainvillea that climbed the wall, twisting toward the second-story windows.

We entered a white foyer, and I stiffened at a disturbing sight: a glowing purplish-blue haze that drifted across the floorboards and rose to the ceiling like a restless band of traveling phantoms. The smell of freshly lit matches permeated my mask.

I inched backward. "What is this?"

"They've sprinkled sulfur over hot coals to fight the flu." Aunt Eva nodded toward a metal bucket half hidden by the ghostly plumes. "They tried that same technique at church before the quarantine closed it down. The smoke burns blue."

"That's because it's sulfur dioxide." But knowing the scientific reason for the eerie blue smoke didn't make me feel any better. "I don't like it in here."

"It's to keep us safe." She hooked her arm around mine. "Come on. I'll be by your side."

We followed the sound of voices and organ music through a doorway and found ourselves in a room about thirty feet long, wallpapered in a pale yellow. More buckets of smoking coal bathed the masked mourners in that noxious blue haze and made my eyes smart. If we hadn't been wearing the gauze, none of us would have been able to breathe.

At the far end of the room, a bronze electric chandelier illuminated a closed, flag-draped casket shrouded in smoke, on display in front of amber curtains. My knees went weak, but I forced myself to stay upright, even though the luminous blue clouds billowing around the coffin made it look like the undertakers had placed Stephen in the middle of a giant laboratory experiment. A photograph of Stephen in his army uniform—the same portrait he had mailed to me—sat propped on a white pillar.

Aunt Eva squeezed my arm to give me strength and led me farther inside the sulfuric room.

Two dozen or so masked mourners milled about in the smoke or sat in the spindle-back chairs facing the coffin. A handful of girls my age, perhaps slightly older, dabbed their eyes with handkerchiefs, and I wondered, with a sting of jealousy, if any of them had ever been Stephen's sweetheart. We had never discussed an interest in other people in our letters.

I tore my eyes away from the girls and met Mr. Darning's gaze across the room. He was busy conversing with a few professional-looking men, so he merely gave me a polite nod of recognition. I was tempted to walk over to him just so I could hear that comforting voice of his.

Stephen's cousin Gracie wandered by Aunt Eva and me, looking lost. Her stringy wig slid down the left side of her head, revealing a bald patch above her ear. Her flu mask—poorly tied—hung off her chin like a deflated balloon.

Aunt Eva touched the girl's broad shoulder. "Gracie, how are you?"

Gracie turned our way with pale brown eyes that didn't seem to focus on us. "I don't know. Stephen's mother couldn't come. Nothing's going well at all."

"I'm so sorry." Aunt Eva embraced the girl in a firm hug. "You've been through so much lately, what with Stephen . . . your mother . . . your own fight with the flu." She helped Gracie pull her wig back into place to hide the ravages of the illness.

I tried not to stare. "Where's Stephen's mother?"

"She's away for a while." Gracie lowered her head. "She hasn't been the same since Stephen . . ." She swallowed, and a peculiar emotion rose off her like a vapor—I could taste it over the sulfur, the same way I had tasted Aunt Eva's metallic rage in the hospital. A sour, rotten flavor, like curdled milk.

Julius, wearing a mask for the first time that I'd seen, came our way. At his side strolled the bespectacled young man with the solid build who had driven him home the morning I learned of Stephen's death.

"Go sit down, Gracie—you don't look well." Julius turned our way. "Thank you for coming, Eva. Mary Shelley, I was sorry to hear about your lightning accident. Are you better?"

"Yes. Thank you."

Aunt Eva touched his arm. "How are you doing, Julius?"

"Not well. Um . . . There was something . . ." He rubbed his swollen eyes. "Uh . . . What was I just going to say? Oh— have you met my other cousin? This is Gracie's twin, Grant."

I gave Grant a polite nod. "It's nice to meet you."

"Nice to meet you, too," said Grant. "I've seen your picture enough times, even though I can barely recognize you in that mask. Girls look ludicrous in that gauze."

I opened my mouth to retort that he probably looked better *with* the gauze than without, but I pressed my lips shut out of respect for Stephen.

Aunt Eva kept hold of Julius's arm. "Gracie told us your mother's not well."

"No, she's not," he said. "She's in a terrible condition. Everyone in this miserable family is either dying or cracking to pieces. It's getting hard to take." He slipped his arm away from my aunt's and pulled a handkerchief from his coat pocket. Plump tears leaked from his eyes—a sight I hadn't expected. He seemed too masculine to cry, even at a funeral for his own brother, but I tasted the genuine bitterness of his grief.

Everyone's emotions seemed to come alive upon my tongue.

"So strange," I whispered, to which Julius lifted his red eyes.

"What's strange?" he asked.

"Just the way I'm feeling."

I looked toward Stephen's coffin again and had the urge to walk over and touch the surface. Aunt Eva guided Gracie to a chair. Julius wiped his eyes and mumbled something about spirits, but I excused myself and made my way toward the front of the room. Stephen's dark eyes in the photograph watched me through the incandescent blue fog.

Two boys near his age stood by the casket for about a minute before I could approach, and I heard them saying something about "rotten luck" and "the damned Krauts." They patted the lid like they were giving a reassuring touch to Stephen's shoulder and departed with bowed heads.

I stepped toward the casket, my lungs wheezing and my legs rubbery. It was just the two of us up there: Stephen and me. I laid my nonbandaged hand on the flag covering the wood and tried to envision the way he'd looked when he watched me from his staircase—the interest in his brown eyes, the dimpled grin blooming across his face, the Verne novel lying open in his lap. The funeral room closed around us, becoming as intimate as the Emberses' peacock-green sitting room, where we had dared to inch closer to one another.

"Stephen," I whispered, "I've hung both of your photographs on my bedroom wall. I know we've never believed much in ghosts, but I have to wonder, were you in my room yesterday? Were you visiting your photos? Or me?" I closed my eyes and blocked out the hum of conversations behind me. "Do you know who I am, Stephen?"

Nothing happened that indicated he had heard me.

My lips shook beneath my mask. "It's Shell, Stephen. Mary Shelley. I'm here for you, all right? I've been unwell, but I'd never miss saying—" I gulped down a lump as sharp as a razor blade. "I even wore one of my gigantic hair bows for you because I thought it would entertain you. Like when we were kids. I'd give anything to hear you—"

I stopped, for a heavy weight, thick and poisonous, had settled across my shoulders. My mouth filled with the same hot-metal flavor of rage as when Aunt Eva had yelled at me in the hospital. The fabric below my hand prickled with static, which made my heart pound.

"Stephen?" My voice rose an octave. I ran my fingers along the flag and shut my eyes again. "Are you all right?"

The flavor in my mouth grew more intense, and the flag beneath my hand sparked and crackled. Everything else in the room slipped away.

"Is something wrong, Stephen?" I asked again, feeling in my bones I'd hear an answer.

Three heartbeats passed. A whisper brushed against my ear.

"Very wrong."

My eyes flew open. I peered over my shoulder to see if anyone stood nearby, but there was no one within ten feet of me. I dropped to my knees, pulled down my mask, and bent my bare lips closer to the coffin. "Did you just say *very wrong*? Oh, my God, did you just speak to me?"

"Mary Shelley?" called Aunt Eva from behind me.

"Stephen, talk to me again. What's wrong? Why aren't you all right?"

Another word burned in my ear. *"Blackbirds."*

"What are you doing?" Aunt Eva grabbed my shoulders. "Stand up and put on your mask."

"He's whispering to me. I hear him. He's talking."

"Don't say that."

"Please be quiet—I need to hear him. He's not all right. Something's wrong."

Two pairs of strong male hands pulled me backward.

"Wait." I fought to break free. "He's whispering. He's talking to me."

The soles of my dress shoes skidded across the floorboards. Everything else had gone silent: the organ music, the mourners. Stunned eyes looked at me through the smoke over white patches of gauze. The flag-draped casket disappeared from my view.

"Don't take me away!" I kicked and flailed and arched my back. "I heard him in there. He said something about birds. Don't take me away from him. He's talking to me. He's talking to me!"

My captors steered me toward the lobby, out of view of the horrified mourners. One of the men—Julius—turned me around and clutched my arms so hard it hurt. "What's going on?"

"He was whispering to me. I heard him. He said something's wrong."

"Mary Shelley, stop," said Aunt Eva behind me. "Stop it right now."

The Emberses' cousin Grant stood beside Julius with his hands on his hips and his brow furrowed.

Julius studied me with eyes that so resembled his brother's, and I gripped the cuffs of his black coat sleeves. "Open the casket, Julius. What if he's stuck in there?"

"We can't open it."

"Please—open it. I swear I heard him talk."

"We can't open the casket, Mary Shelley." Julius's eyes went bloodshot again. "His head is too damaged."

His words tore into me with a bite a hundred times more vicious than the pain of the lightning bolt. My lips turned cold and sore with the realization that there would never, *ever* be another kiss. I'd never again feel the pressure of Stephen's hand against the small of my back. I'd never receive another letter from him.

His head is too damaged.

A sob shook my shoulders. I hung my head and bawled like I'd never cried in my life.

Julius hugged me against his chest and allowed my tears to drench his coat's black wool. I wept and choked on the blue sulfur smoke, while Aunt Eva struggled to situate my flu mask back over my mouth and nose.

Julius stroked my hair. "Take her back home, Eva. She shouldn't have come."

"That's a good idea." My aunt took my elbow and pulled me away from Stephen's brother. "Come on, Mary Shelley."

"I know I heard him."

"Don't talk about that right now." She guided me to the door. "I know you're hurting, but you need to let Stephen go."

But I couldn't.

Stephen wasn't completely gone.

10

THE BUTTERFLY AND THE LIGHTNING BOLT

MY AUNT AND I RODE HOME IN THE BACK OF ANOTHER taxi without exchanging a word. All I wanted was to be alone. I was relieved when we returned to the house and she almost immediately flew out the front door, headed for work in the shipyard.

The need to write to Stephen hit me after she left.

During the past four and a half years, whenever something upset me or intrigued me more than I could bear, my first response was to spill my thoughts across a blank sheet of paper for him. I'd slip the letter in a mailbox and imagine it bundled in a brown postal bag, traveling down to Coronado by rail, jostling amid all the other letter writers' stamped parcels for friends and relatives. And I'd picture Stephen reading my words with a smile on his lips and his own pen at the ready.

Fetching two sheets of stationery and a fountain pen from my bedside table might make everything feel normal.

But what's normal anymore, Shell? I pictured Stephen asking as I headed up the staircase. *Normal ended a long time ago.*

"I just need to write," I said out loud to the empty air.

I grabbed the writing utensils and went back downstairs to a weathered wooden table in the backyard. It sat under the sagging branches of sweet-scented orange trees. Breathing in fresh California air without my mask, I penned a message I knew I would never be able to mail.

October 29, 1918

My Dearest Stephen,

Do you want to hear something odd? I attended your funeral today.

Yes, you read that grim sentence correctly. Now I have to ask you something, and I want you to answer me truthfully: Did you speak to me when I was leaning over your casket? Do you see me writing this letter right now? Was your brother right all along about spirits hovering around us, waiting to be captured in photographs, or has something changed in me? My sense of smell has become extraordinarily acute—as if I can smell and taste emotions. Then there's the compass needle, and your voice at the funeral—I'm not who I was before being struck by lightning.

You whispered to me that something is wrong—something about birds. I don't care how many times I've skeptically laughed at the talk of ghosts, I heard you, Stephen. You sounded like you were in trouble.

And if something has happened, does that mean you're unable to rest in peace?

Answer me, please—in any way that you can. Tell me what happened. Let me know if you are suffering. I want to help you, even if it means looking at life and death in strange new ways that make me shudder with fear and awe. If you're stuck and afraid, I'll do my best to help you figure out what's wrong.

If you can still be with me again, then come.

Yours,
Mary Shelley

WHEN DAYLIGHT WANED AND THE AIR COOLED TOO MUCH for me to linger outside, I tucked my letter to Stephen in the dictionary I'd been reading all afternoon and opened a cabinet outside the kitchen door to switch on the main gas valve. Then I dragged myself into the house, grabbed a matchbox, and poked flames in the wall lamps' glass globes to ignite the delicate honeycomb mantles hidden inside. The matches smelled of sulfur dioxide—a scent I knew I'd forever associate with Stephen's casket—and the odor made me want to retch. It took me twice as long as it should have to bring the lamps to their full brightness.

Aunt Eva planned to work late to cover her missed morning shift. Five hours to go before she would come home. Five hours of dwelling by myself after dark.

Supper was the furthest thought from my mind, but I knew Aunt Eva and I would both need to eat. I stirred up a bland pot of canned vegetable soup over her coal-burning, nickel-trimmed cookstove and ate in silence, wishing she could have afforded electricity. Not only did I enjoy the soothing hum of incandescent lightbulbs, but the gaslights emitted an eerie white glow far too similar to the blue haze in the funeral room. My shadow rising and falling across the pea-soup-green wallpaper made me jump and peek over my shoulder every few minutes.

When my bowl was halfway empty, a voice called out from another part of the house, "Hello."

I froze. The hairs on my arms and neck stood on end.

The voice then asked, "Who's there?"—a horrible, squeaky sound that resembled a child speaking on a phonograph record.

I braced myself for more words or movements from the other room and eyed the window as a means of escape. Was it a robber? Stephen? Another side effect of the lightning?

A squawk blasted through the silence.

Oberon.

"Oh . . . of course." I sighed. It was just that silly bird talking, not Stephen or an intruder. Just a trained magpie saying what he always asked when someone entered the room.

I returned to my soup, swallowing down limp beans and

carrots that tasted like rocks, when a thought struck me: Why did Oberon ask the question he always asked when someone entered the room *if no one had entered the room?*

I leapt out of my chair and charged into the living room, convinced I'd find Stephen standing by the bronze cage.

Oberon was alone, but he fluffed up his black-and-white feathers, lowered his raven-dark head, and screamed bloody murder at the empty lavender room.

"What's wrong, Oberon?" I approached the bird with cautious footsteps. "Did something scare you?"

"Who's there?" he screeched again.

I spun around and scanned the living room, not liking the atmosphere. I swore I heard one of Aunt Eva's picture frames tapping against the wall.

"Everything's OK, Oberon," I said in a voice meant to soothe the both of us. "Everything's fine."

"Who's there?"

"Please stop saying that."

"Who's there?"

"I said stop!" I tossed the beige cover over his cage.

"Who's there?" Oberon rustled his wings beneath the cloth. "Who's there? Hello. Hello. Who's there? Who's—"

"Stop!"

"Who's there?"

"Shut up, you stupid bird. No one's there. Absolutely no one's there."

I kicked the sofa instead of succumbing to an urge to

knock over his cage, and limped back to the kitchen, where I huddled in my chair with my hands clamped over my ears until the bird stopped yelling.

AUNT EVA TRUDGED THROUGH THE FRONT DOOR SOME-time after her whistling cuckoo announced ten o'clock. She slouched at the kitchen table as though her back ached, and her eyelids drooped, so I served her leftover soup and sat with her for five minutes, never mentioning the bird or the uneasy feeling that had settled over her living room.

"Are you all right, Mary Shelley?" she asked in a voice beaten down by fatigue.

"As right as I can be."

"Go up to bed. Put today behind you."

I nodded and pushed myself up from the chair.

Pots clattered in the sink from her cleaning up in the kitchen while I wandered down the hall and up the groaning staircase.

I stepped across the threshold into my bedroom. The air didn't feel right at all.

The first objects that drew my attention were Stephen's photographs, and I remembered something I had once read: according to everything from Christian lore to Slavic legend, butterflies symbolized the flight of the soul from the body. I felt I was looking at pictures representing him and me—the butterfly and the lightning bolt. The lost soul and the girl who toyed with electricity.

A movement in the corner of my eye distracted me.

Uncle Wilfred's compass.

I crept closer to my bedside table and lit the oil lamp's wick with a match. The compass's needle spun in every direction.

"I'm going to turn off the gas after I change into my night-clothes," said Aunt Eva, giving me a start as she padded across the hall behind me to her bedroom. "Good night."

I blew out the match. "Good night."

I stared at the compass for ten more minutes. It never settled down.

Close to eleven o'clock, I changed into my nightgown and crawled under my blankets, keeping the oil lamp lit beside me. The pine dresser and wardrobe looked calm and homey, but still the strange energy hummed around me. The flames of my lamp grew restless, casting shifting shadows that leapt across the wall. I held my breath in anticipation and fear, re-minding myself to breathe when I felt dizzy, and it must have been well past midnight before I finally fell asleep.

I awoke, curled on my side and facing the wall, as the downstairs cuckoo announced three o'clock. The muted glow of the oil lamp still illuminated my golden wallpaper, but the blackness of night crowded around me as if it were a living creature. The scent of burning fireworks scorched my nostrils. A coppery taste lined my tongue and caused the fillings in my teeth to ache, while my heartbeat echoed inside the mattress, pounding like a second heart.

Someone was with me.

I'd experienced that sensation before, in the dark, fresh out of a nightmare—the belief that something was staring at me from across the room in the shadows of my furniture. In the past, the stranger always ended up being a doll or a chair reflecting moonlight. But this time I was positive someone would be there if I checked.

Just turn around and look, I told myself. My breaths came out as shallow flutters of air against my pillowcase, and I could have sworn I heard that needle spinning around in the compass.

Just look.

I inhaled as quietly as possible, not wanting to disturb the room. I squeezed my eyes shut and counted silently to three.

One.

Two.

Three.

I flipped myself over. Opened my eyes. And found Stephen next to my bed.

11

PHANTOM

BEFORE I HAD TIME TO FIGURE OUT HOW I SHOULD RE-
spond to his presence, he was gone. He jerked back, as if
someone had yanked him by the collar of the white undershirt
he wore, and disappeared.

The buzzing energy in the room died down. The compass
began following my movements again. Stephen's photographs
remained on the wall—motionless, untouched.

I trembled under my sheets, overwhelmed by a barrage
of emotions—terror, shock, amazement, concern, elation,
love—and unsure what I should do next. My lips tried to form
Stephen's name, but they shook too much to function. My
arms and legs couldn't move. Black and gold spots buzzed in
front of my eyes. I panted until I must have passed out, for I

didn't remember a single other thing about the night besides a dream.

A nightmare about a bloodstained sky.

A MASKED FACE SHONE IN THE LIGHT OF A CANDLE IN MY doorway.

I gasped and sat upright.

"What's wrong?" Aunt Eva, not a spirit, came toward me. "What is it?"

"Nothing's wrong."

"Are you sick?"

"No." I looked around the room for signs of Stephen in the weak light.

"What is it, Mary Shelley?" She brought the candle closer to my face. "You're so pale. You look like you've seen a—"

We locked eyes. Her face blanched. The word she didn't speak seemed to hover in the air between us: *ghost*.

"I . . ." I searched my brain for a new subject, unwilling to let the conversation veer anywhere near Julius's conception of spirits when I was grappling to understand my own. "Is it morning now? Are you heading to work?"

She drew the candle away from my face. "Yes, and I want you to stay inside all day. You've been out of this house too many times since you've been here. Don't open the windows."

"Are you sure you don't have any books left in the house besides the dictionary? I really need to read."

"That's all I have besides cookbooks. I had to get rid of all the Swiss and German texts I used in my translation work. Even Wilfred's family Bible was in German."

"*How* did you get rid of them?"

"I gave them away."

I scowled. "Did you burn them?"

"It doesn't matter how I got rid of them. Neighbors had seen them on my shelves. They would have questioned my loyalty to the country if I had left them there."

"What type of world are we living in if we're destroying books? Isn't it the Kaiser's job to annihilate German intellectualism?"

"Shh! Don't talk like that." She waved at me to be quiet and glanced at the window, as if the neighbors had climbed the walls and were eavesdropping from behind the lowered panes. "You sound like your father. You've got to keep opinions like that to yourself."

I flopped back down to my pillow with a huff and pulled my blanket over my shoulders.

"I'm sorry you're stuck like this, Mary Shelley. I know you have no one to keep you company."

Ah, but I do. If that wasn't just a dream.

"You'll find a deck of cards in the living room. Why don't you play some solitaire?" Her footsteps retreated across the floorboards, out of my bedroom. She closed the door, leaving me behind in the near darkness.

Her feet pitter-pattered down the stairs. The front door shut. I sat up, relit my bedside lamp, and drew a deep breath.

The compass's arrow pointed at me.

I looked toward the butterfly and lightning photographs on my wall and remembered the burning air from the night before, the distressed movements of the compass, the restlessness, the fear.

"Stephen? Are you here? Are you safe?"

A mourning dove cooed its five-note song outside my window, but nothing else stirred.

"Stephen?"

The compass remained fixed on me. I slouched back down on my bed and felt as alone as Aunt Eva had thought I was.

THE BELLS ON MY AUNT'S WOODEN TELEPHONE RANG ON the kitchen wall as I scrounged around for breakfast in the icebox. I slid the horn-shaped receiver off the side latch and held the cold metal to my ear.

"Hello. Ottinger residence," I said into the gaping black mouthpiece that always reminded me of the lips of a person shouting "Oh!"

Crackling static met my ears. My heart leapt.

Stephen is somehow on the other end of the line.

"Is this Mary Shelley?" asked a male voice that could have been his.

"Yes."

"This is Julius."

"Julius? Oh." I settled back down on my heels, not even realizing I had risen to my toes.

"I'm in between sittings right now," he said, "and I have a line of customers spilling out to the street again, but I wanted to talk to you a moment."

"About what?"

"How are you?"

"I'm all right."

Static buzzed through the silence again before he asked, "Did you really hear him whisper?"

I swallowed. "Yes."

"Do you believe in spirits now?"

I leaned my forehead against the telephone's glossy oak and debated my answer.

"Mary Shelley?"

Another swallow, one that scraped against my throat. "I don't know about other spirits, but I think . . . I might believe . . . I can communicate with Stephen."

"Do you want to come to a séance with me?"

"Why would I want to do that?"

"I know a spirit medium. She holds séances in an apartment over her grandparents' hardware store downtown. Her circles are legitimate—there's no hanky-panky, no flimflamming, no reason to be afraid. She's an upstanding girl who attends the local Spiritualist church."

"I don't want to contact Stephen through a medium."

"You don't have to contact him. Just come as a learning experience and witness the way other people summon spirit phenomena. You're a smart girl, right? Come see what Spiritualism is all about. You'll fit in with everyone else there. You're like them, Mary Shelley."

I bit my lip, troubled by how much I wanted to go, to find people like my strange new self.

"Are you home alone right now?" he asked.

"Why?"

"That's an awful way to live, sequestered like that, hiding from the flu until you die." His voice sounded louder, as if he had moved his lips closer to the mouthpiece to speak more directly into my ear. "Come with me tonight. These people are all well educated and inquisitive. Everyone's young and eager to learn more about the connection between the living world and the afterlife."

"Aunt Eva would have to come, too."

He paused. "Yes, of course."

"What time?"

"The circle doesn't start until nine o'clock. I'll pick you up at eight thirty."

"I'll try it once, but if I find the experience upsetting, I don't want you to ever talk to me about spirits again."

"You have a deal, Mary Shelley. I'll see you this evening. Dress nicely. No goggles."

He hung up.

AFTER BREAKFAST, I STARED AT STEPHEN'S PHOTOGRAPHS in my bedroom and dared myself to contact him as if I were a Spiritualist medium. Maybe a trance was what I needed to understand these teasing glimpses of his life after death. A spiritual state of mind. Full belief in the other side.

I knelt in front of his photos with my eyes closed and my mind open. I even laid my hands against the picture frames and called his name.

"Stephen. Stephen. Are you there? Stephen Elias Embers."

No. Not quite right. I felt like one of those questionable people who advertised public séances in the newspaper.

TODAY ONLY!
MISS MARY SHELLEY BLACK
A REMARKABLE DEMONSTRATION OF SPIRIT COMMUNICATION
HEAR SHAKESPEARE HIMSELF RECITE *MACBETH*!

I opened my eyes. "You're not like that." I got off the floor and plopped onto my bed. "You've got to approach this more like . . . an experiment. Like . . . Phantom."

That's right: Phantom.

When I was ten, Dad and I had a devil of a time finding a mouse that was chewing through the cardboard cookie boxes in Dad's grocery store. I nicknamed the little pest Phantom, for he came and went in the night like a supernatural entity. None of the traps in the usual places worked. We couldn't find his means of entrance and escape anywhere. All we saw were the mysterious visitor's nibble marks and half-eaten cookies.

After a week of fruitless searching, Dad and I became detectives. We lined the perimeter of the store and the backroom with talcum powder and tracked the tiny footsteps we discovered the next morning. Phantom seemed to be creeping out from somewhere behind the barrel of soap chips. We then used steel bars, springs, and peanut butter bait to build the finest mousetrap a father and daughter had ever invented—much safer than the store-bought ones Dad wouldn't allow me to set. Once we had put our equipment in place, we captured that mouse the very next night.

Stephen was certainly no mouse, and I didn't intend to trap him. But he was something to be coaxed out of hiding.

A mystery to explore.

A scientific mind like yours should want to explore the communication between spirits and mortals, Aunt Eva had said the day I arrived at her house. *It's no different than the mystery behind telephone wires and electrical currents.*

She was right. If I could figure out why I was still able to see Stephen, it would be no different than Thomas Edison discovering how to create electric light out of carbon filaments and dreams. Or the Wright brothers proving humans could fly.

The impossible often turned possible.

Scientific detectives and Spiritualists could be one and the same.

12

COME TALK TO THE SPIRITS

AUNT EVA CAME HOME TO FIND ME DISEMBOWELING HER telephone.

"What on earth are you doing inside my telephone box?" She plunked a crate of onions on the wobbly worktable at the center of the kitchen and put her hands on her hips.

I blew a stray strand of hair out of my eye. "I'm dissecting it."

"What?"

"My brain desperately needs exercise. I decided to see how the wires work."

"Don't play with any wires—not after shocking yourself to kingdom come." She slammed the telephone box closed, just missing the tips of my fingers. "Bolt that up and stay out of there."

I held up the silver bells. "I need to put it back together first."

"Mary Shelley—"

"It'll just take a minute. The phonograph took longer."

"Leave the phonograph alone. It's having trouble as it is."

"Not anymore."

She sighed, pulled down her grease-streaked flu mask, and grabbed two onions from the crate. "While you're cleaning up your mess, I'm going to make supper."

I screwed the bells back into place. "We've been invited to go somewhere tonight."

"We have?"

"Julius wants to take us to a séance."

She let an onion drop to the floor and turned toward me. "A séance?"

"He called about it this morning." I watched her eyes water with disbelief and excitement behind the round frames of her glasses. "I guess you're interested?"

Her cheeks flushed scarlet. "I am not interested in Julius Embers."

"I meant the séance. I already know you're interested in Julius."

"He's four years younger than I am. I'm a recent widow. Don't be ridiculous." She pulled a knife out of a drawer and went to work dicing the onions. The back of her neck glowed a radioactive shade of red. "He knows so many worldly people in downtown San Diego. And it's the night before Halloween.

I bet the séance will be quite the social event. What would I even wear?"

"I have no idea."

"Wait a minute . . ." She turned my way with the knife in her hand. "Why do *you* want to go to a séance with Julius Embers?"

Instead of answering, I shut the telephone box and screwed the front cover into place.

"Oh, Mary Shelley." Her shoulders sagged. "We can't have another episode like the one at the funeral."

"You said it felt like I brought part of the afterlife back with me. What if I have? What if I'm not all the way back from the dead?"

"You look alive enough to me."

"But Stephen—what if he hasn't made it to the other side? What if there's a reason he's not resting in peace?"

"I don't want you causing another scene. It's not healthy to refuse to let someone go."

"Then why have séances? Why have spirit photography? If you think what I'm doing is wrong, why do you support Julius Embers?"

Aunt Eva pursed her lips until she looked far older than her twenty-six years. She resembled photographs of her own late mother, who always puckered her face at cameras like she was sucking on lemons. "It's just . . . different. Julius is a professional." She went back to the onions—*chop, chop, chop, chop, chop.*

I grumbled and put the screwdriver back inside Uncle Wilfred's toolbox, which sat near my feet.

"What time are we supposed to be there?" asked Aunt Eva.

"He's picking us up at eight thirty."

She lifted her head. "In his car?"

"I guess so."

"It's a Cadillac. I've seen it in the garage behind the house." *Chop, chop, chop, chop, chop.* "A Cadillac ride and a downtown séance." She whistled and shook her head. "And here I thought onion soup was going to be the highlight of my night." She rubbed her damp forehead with the back of her hand. "You need to go pick out something nice to wear. I don't know about Spiritualism in Oregon, but séances are formal events here in San Diego. Or so I hear."

"Why don't you let me make the soup, and you go get ready. You're the one who's worked in the shipyard all day." It was my roundabout way of telling her she stank too much to attend a formal social event, but she agreed without offense and hurried off to bathe.

AFTER SUPPER, WHEN THE SUN HAD LONG SINCE SET AND our gas lamps illuminated the house, I sifted through my wardrobe, pushing aside the nicest dress I owned—the black silk taffeta one I'd worn to Stephen's funeral. My second best, a navy-and-white plaid wool dress with a lace-trimmed collar, ended up being the garment I wiggled over my shoulders and buttoned into place. A belt made of the same fabric cinched my waist, and the hem fell mid-calf. I'd have to wear my black Mary Janes instead of my dingy Boy Scout boots. A pair of kid gloves would hide the scaly lightning-burn remnants on my fingertips. I dug around in my doctor's bag for a little beaded coin purse that had belonged to my mother and stocked it with a portion of the money my father had made me pack before I fled Portland.

In the kitchen, where we could heat the curling rod on the stove, my aunt fluffed, knotted, and swirled my long locks into an elaborate style she called a turban coiffure. To be specific, she made me look like I was wearing a fuzzy turban made out of my own chestnut-brown hair. My reflection in her hand mirror didn't even look like me.

"I really regret chopping off all my curls." She nitpicked over the last few pins at the back of my head, jabbing my scalp until I winced. "I feel so ugly these days with my short hair and my red, calloused hands."

"You're not ugly. Your hair is modern and chic, and your job in the shipyard is admirable, both for the country and the women's movement."

Someone rapped on the front door with the metal knocker.

"It's him!" She grabbed her mask and flew down the hall, contradicting everything I'd just said about her being an admirable symbol of the women's movement.

Julius stood on our front porch in a chalk-stripe suit and a charcoal-gray fedora—and again no flu mask, which I found to be arrogant. His face looked pale, and the skin beneath his eyes bulged with bruise-colored bags, as if he hadn't slept the night before. Taking advantage of one of my new peculiarities, I inhaled a deep breath through my mask and tried to detect the emotions rolling off him.

My tongue went numb.

"Good evening, ladies." He took off his hat and revealed slicked-down black hair, stiff and shiny with pomade that smelled like a barbershop. "Are you ready?"

"Yes, we are indeed." Aunt Eva grabbed her handbag and led us out the door. "Thank you so much for inviting us, Julius. How is your mother?"

"Not well. Let's not talk about that."

He placed his hat on his head, and we followed him down the front path to a blue two-door Cadillac roadster convertible with a hood that stretched for miles and a wooden steering wheel as large as a ship's helm. He had parked the car underneath the electric streetlamp in front of the house, and the light shining down through the bulbous globes made the vehicle's paint glisten as bright as sapphires.

"What type of engine does it have?" I asked.

He opened the passenger-side door for us. "Why don't you just try looking pretty for a change?"

I was just about to give him a tart reply when a screaming black police department ambulance sailed around the corner and came to an abrupt stop in front of a house across the street.

Aunt Eva froze. "Oh, dear God. The flu has reached our

block." Her feet skidded on the sidewalk like she was trying to run away on ice, and then she took running leaps back to the porch. "The flu has reached our block!"

"Eva, stop!" called Julius in a voice deep and authoritative enough to keep her from escaping inside the house. "The flu is everywhere. It's not some big, bad monster coming down the street, knocking at each door. It's random, and you and your niece smell enough of onions and camphor mothballs to fight off any germ that gets within ten feet of the two of you."

I watched policemen in high-buttoned green uniforms hustle to the neighbors' front door while maneuvering a beige stretcher. Their clothing reminded me of army tunics. Soldiers engaging in battle against an enemy they couldn't even see.

"Come back down here, Eva." Julius opened the passenger door wider, revealing a plush black seat more luxurious than any sofa my family had ever owned. "We don't want to keep our hostess waiting."

"They're dying right across the street, Julius."

"Eva—come talk to the spirits. They'll tell you there's nothing to fear."

His words acted as an elixir upon my aunt's nerves.

Her shoulders lowered. Her chest rose and fell with a soothing breath. "Oh. I hadn't thought of the séance that way. I suppose you're right." She ventured back to the Cadillac and climbed into the middle section of the seat.

I stepped in next to her with my coin purse dangling off my wrist. Julius helped me push the hem of my skirt into the car so it wouldn't catch in the door when he closed it, and then he strode over to the driver's side.

The officers across the street hauled out a body concealed by a sheet. Long red hair swung off the end of the stretcher.

Aunt Eva turned her face away with pain in her eyes. "That was Mrs. Tennell, the woman who found you dead during the lightning storm, Mary Shelley. The poor thing. She has five children."

I dug my nails into the beads of my handbag. "I should have thanked her for helping me. I should have visited her. I'm too late."

"There's nothing you can do." Julius climbed into the driver's seat and slammed the door shut. "Stop thinking about it." He brought the engine to life with a roar and steered the roadster southward, to the heart of downtown San Diego.

We traveled past houses and storefronts and more black ambulances. On the sidewalk in front of a home as pristine white as a wedding cake lay three bodies a huckleberry shade of blue, dressed in nightclothes. The corpses rested beneath a streetlamp, as if the living had kicked out the dead like garbage. I bent forward and held my forehead in my hands to stave off nausea.

"I heard the Germans snuck the flu into the United States through aspirin," said Julius.

I swallowed down bile. "That's just more anti-German propaganda."

Aunt Eva kicked my ankle. "Don't talk like that."

"I'm not trying to sound un-American," I said, "but the aspirin rumor is stupid. Influenza is an airborne illness. The only way the Germans could have used the flu as a weapon was if they shipped boatloads of sick German people over here and let everyone cough on us. But the flu kills so quickly and randomly that everyone on the boat might have been dead by the time it arrived in an American harbor, like Dracula's victims on the *Demeter*."

"Does she always argue like that?" asked Julius.

Aunt Eva nodded. "Yes, I'm afraid so."

"She sounds like my brother."

A small smile managed to spread across my lips beneath my mask.

Another siren screamed by. That old bully Death breathed down my neck and nipped at my skin, warning, *Don't waste one spare second of time. If there are things you want to accomplish while you're still alive, you'd better do them soon. I'm coming.*

13

UGLY THINGS

JULIUS PARKED THE CADILLAC IN FRONT OF A FIFTH Avenue hardware store. The shop was wedged between a toy store and a restaurant that smelled of juicy grilled hamburgers. The sign in front of the eatery claimed the place specialized in "Liberty Steaks," but that was simply paranoid speak for *We don't want to call anything a name that sounds remotely German, like "hamburger." We're pro-American. We swear!*

A glass door led us to a dark interior staircase that clattered with the echoes of our dress shoes as we climbed the steps. Another door, plain and chipped and brown, waited at the top. Julius knocked.

Someone opened the door a crack and stuck out her head: an unmasked girl, a year or two older than me at most, with long golden ringlets crowned by a sparkling jeweled band. Her eyes were lined in black kohl, her lips rouged a deep red.

"Hello, Julius." She opened the door farther, enough for us to see her wine-colored dress and gargantuan breasts that seemed at odds with the innocent Goldilocks look of her hair. "I didn't know you were bringing two guests."

Julius took off his hat. "Does that throw off your numbers?"

"Sadly, no. Not at all. Francie died over the weekend. We're not sure if Archie and Helen are still alive. Roy saw an ambulance at their house on Monday."

Julius wrinkled his brow. "That's disturbing."

We entered a dim, bare hallway, and the girl shut the door behind us.

"Welcome." She offered her hand to Aunt Eva. "I'm Lena Abberley."

"I'm Eva Ottinger. And this is my niece, Mary Shelley Black."

"Ahh." Lena shook my hand and grinned at Julius. "You've brought your muse, Julius. 'Beauty resides within the sacred studio of Mr. Julius Embers, Spiritualist Photographer.'"

I reddened and let go of her hand, tasting a flavor that stung sharp and hot. "I didn't know he was going to put me on that handbill."

She winked at me. "Don't be modest about the great Julius Embers's interest in a pretty young thing like you. He and I refer clients to one another. You'll find a stack of those hand-bills next to my donation jar in the parlor. Come along." Lena beckoned with her index finger. "Roy is already here." She swished through a doorway to the right of the entry hall with her curls bouncing and her hips swinging beneath her dress.

We followed her into a small living room decorated in fringed electric lamps and paintings of mustard-yellow flowers that weren't particularly pretty. A blond young man with cloudy eyes puffed on a cigarette at a round wooden table in the center of the space. Julius closed the room's door.

"This is my fiancé, Roy." Lena nodded toward the young man at the table. "Roy, this is Julius's muse and her aunt."

"I'm not his muse," I told Roy, who looked straight through me like he didn't care one way or another.

"I have a homemade anti-influenza remedy for you to snack on." Lena picked up a bowl of sugar cubes from the table. "You're going to need to take off your masks for the séance. The gauze scares away the spirits who died before the flu attacked. They worry surgeons are sitting around the table, waiting to operate on them."

Julius snickered. "You just don't want to wear your own mask, Lena. You hate how it looks on you, so you blame the helpless spirits."

"I don't see you spoiling your handsome face with the gauze, either, Mr. Embers."

"If Death is coming for me," said Julius, lifting his chin, "I want him to see my entire face. He's not going to find me cowering behind anything."

Aunt Eva massaged her masked cheek. "Are you sure we

need to take off our gauze? The flu just arrived on my block tonight."

"The flu is *everywhere*," said Roy, sucking on his cigarette.

"That's what I told her." Julius scooted chairs out for each of us. "Sit down, ladies. Take off your masks and eat Miss Abberley's snack so we can begin."

Aunt Eva took the seat next to Julius, so I positioned myself in the chair between her and Roy and dropped my coin purse next to my aunt's bag. I pulled down my mask until it dangled around my throat like a necklace and watched Aunt Eva do the same. Lena presented us with the bowl of sugar cubes, which smelled like my father's hands after he'd fill cans of kerosene in the back storeroom of Black's Groceries.

I sniffed at the cubes again. "Sugar cubes soaked in kerosene? Is that your flu remedy?"

"Precisely." Lena scooted an extra chair between Roy and Julius for herself. "That's how you get rid of germs. You burn them away."

"I'll burn my throat away."

"That's the point." She sat down. "Eat it or leave."

I picked up a glistening cube and studied it.

Aunt Eva placed a piece of sugar on her tongue, grimaced, and swallowed it whole. Her face turned red. Her eyes watered, and I half expected her to breathe fire. "May I have a drink of water, please?"

"Roy, be a gentleman." Lena knocked Roy's arm with her elbow. "Get Mrs. Ottinger a glass of water."

I raised my cube to my mouth but transferred it inside my fist at the last second and pretended to swallow. When Roy hustled back in with the sloshing glass for Aunt Eva, I flicked the cube to the floor beneath the table.

"So, tell me, ladies." Lena leaned forward on her elbows. "Who do you want me to bring to you tonight?"

My jaw dropped. "We can't tell you that information. How will we know whether or not you're a cheat?"

Lena raised an eyebrow. "A cheat?"

"Mary Shelley!" rasped my aunt. "Be polite. We're guests here."

"If I tell you whom I want to see," I said, folding my hands on the table, "and drop clues about what I want him or her to say, we'll have no proof whether or not you genuinely contact the dead."

"Are you insinuating I can't contact the dead?"

"I'm saying, if you can, you don't need to ask whom we want to see."

"Good Lord." Julius rubbed his swollen eyes. "Listen to all those proper *whoms*. No wonder Stephen couldn't keep his hands off her."

Lena's eyes pounced on me. "Stephen? Is that who you want to find?"

I glared at Julius. "I didn't want you saying anything to her about your brother and me. I don't want her summoning him."

"Then why did you agree to come here?" asked Aunt Eva,

her voice struggling back to life after the kerosene. "I thought you wanted to find Stephen."

"I'm here because I'm curious. If you're going to summon a spirit for me, Miss Abberley, I want you to pick someone obscure—someone no one here would have ever mentioned to you. If I see you're genuinely gifted, I'll pay you to show me how you channel your gifts. But I'm not parting with one precious cent if you're going to sit there and ask me to feed you information."

Lena tugged on one of her coiled curls. "Are you setting rules for me?"

"Yes. If I'm to pay you for tutelage, I'd be an employer of sorts."

Roy chuckled and actually spoke more than four words. "You're being challenged, Lena. It's about time, after all that spoiling you get from your doting followers."

"Shut up, Roy. Put out your cigarette." Lena rose from her chair and pressed her hands against the table. "I've got rules for you, too, Miss Black."

"What are they?"

"No getting out of your chair after I turn off the lights. No talking. No breaking the sacred circle. No touching the ectoplasm."

"What's ectoplasm?" I asked.

"Aha! So, you *don't* know everything." She beamed with a show of shiny white teeth. "Ectoplasm is spiritual energy, fully materialized. Imagine an umbilical cord connecting the other side to the mortal world. My body produces ectoplasm that reaches out and moves tables and objects with the strength of human hands. Keep your fingers off it, and while you're at it, keep your fingers off Roy, aside from holding his hand while we create the chain of energy. Are you quite clear on my rules, Miss Black?"

"Yes."

"Good. Then let's begin." Lena plunked the bowl of sugar cubes on a side table that also held a donation jar and Julius's handbills. She *clip-clopped* in her thick heels to a switch by the door and pressed the button that turned off the lights, submerging the room in blackness. Agonizing chills spread down my back and arms. The temperature seemed to drop twenty degrees. I smelled Roy's extinguished cigarette. And mold.

Lena traveled back to her chair in the dark with the same *clip-clop* rhythm as before, which reassured me she hadn't traded places with anyone else. A chair scraped against the floorboards, sounding like she had taken her seat.

"Join hands," she said.

We did as she asked. Roy took my gloved hand tenderly, and Aunt Eva clamped down on my healing fingers until I fidgeted enough for her to loosen her hold.

Lena drew air through her nose and released it through her lips with a slight whistle. "I'm going to fall into my trance now." She breathed in and out again. "Open your mind. Leave your doubts at the door. Turn your thoughts to loved ones who've left this world for the Summerland." She continued her long, audible breaths, each exhalation punctuated by a soft moan that caused Roy's fingers to twitch against mine. I tried to see the outlines of my companions' heads, but the darkness penetrated the room completely. Lena must have sealed off the windows to keep even the slightest hint of moonlight from peeking through the shades.

I didn't turn my thoughts to any loved ones.

The perfume and cigarettes and mold in the air gave the séance a dirty feel. We were not attending a formal social event, as Aunt Eva had said we would. I'd been tricked into another theatrical show, courtesy of Mr. Julius Embers, whose impenetrable emotions reminded me again of Stephen's warnings about opium. Hazy Roy, who sounded like he was starting to snore next to me in the dark, was probably an addict, too.

"Spirits, are you with us?" Lena's new, deep trance voice rumbled up from her belly. "Knock once for yes, twice for no."

Aunt Eva's hand flinched in anticipation.

"Are you with us?" asked Lena again.

SLAM.

A solid knock walloped the table and made me jump.

"How many spirits have joined us tonight?"

SLAM SLAM SLAM SLAM SLAM.

"Five spirits. Marvelous. Do you see your loved ones sitting at this table, spirits? Once for yes, twice for no."

SLAM.

"Do you want to show your beloveds you're here?"

SLAM.

"Then play for us, spirits. Play."

The table vibrated under our hands, as if an electrical current buzzed beneath the wood.

"Join us, spirits. Play. Show us you're here."

The vibrations strengthened, rattling up my arms, jolting my neck, and trembling down my spinal column. The table creaked and shook and tilted back and forth, gaining momentum. Wood crashed against my rib cage, tipped away, and banged against me again. I couldn't breathe. Pain and fear crippled me.

No, no, no, screamed the rational voice inside my head. *This is not what Stephen's spirit feels like.*

The table hit me so hard it knocked the wind out of me. I regained my breath, kicked off my right shoe, stretched out my stocking-covered toe, and felt around in the dark for signs of fraud. After another blow to my ribs, my toes met with something soft and curvy and covered in smooth fabric: a pair of female legs, wrapped around the center post, shaking the table with all their might.

One of the feet gave me a swift kick in the fleshy part of my calf.

"Ow!" I cried.

"Shh," hissed Aunt Eva.

The shaking stopped and Lena called out, "Don't touch the ectoplasm. Keep all hands and legs to yourselves. Behave like proper ladies and gentlemen or you'll do irrevocable harm to the one you want to see." She exhaled five more of her drawn-out breaths, probably to calm herself after my investigative toes. "Close your eyes. Turn all thoughts to the dear souls you miss so much. Don't allow anything else inside your head. No doubts. No fears. *Nothing.*"

I closed my eyes and played along, even though my expectations had soured as much as when Stephen had told me about Julius's photography tricks. I turned my thoughts to Mae Tate, the first student at my high school to die of the Spanish flu. No one in the séance room would have known about her. Mae had worn her dark brown hair in loose braids that hung a full foot below her backside, and she always sat at the front of the classroom because her father couldn't afford to buy her eyeglasses. She collapsed on the floor during the first week of English literature, while we were studying William Collins's "The Passions" in our McGuffey Readers. Mrs. Martin rushed us out of the room, as if the girl had caught fire, and we all stared with open mouths at the way Mae convulsed on the hard wooden floor like the victim of a witch's curse.

That's all I could remember about Mae Tate at that moment. My mind clouded over. Other memories—stronger, richer ones; memories that wanted me to see and feel and taste them—invaded my brain.

A room wallpapered in peacock green.

Stephen's mouth on mine.

Mr. Muse.

Lightning striking a sepia sea.

Four words penned in an artistic hand: I DO LOSE INK.

Blue smoke.

A flag-draped coffin.

A whisper: *Blackbirds . . .*

"I see—the letter *W*," said Lena across the table.

W? I shook my head and reoriented myself. *Oh, Christ. She's going to tell Aunt Eva Uncle Wilfred came through.*

I opened my mouth to stop any fake uncles from emerging in the dark, but my voice got stuck in my throat. The air burned with the same stifling firework smoke I had smelled before Stephen showed up next to my bed. My eyes watered from the uncomfortable change in the atmosphere. The weight of suffering pressed down on my body.

"They're killing me," said a voice behind me.

I turned my head but saw only darkness.

"They're killing me," it said again.

"Stephen?" I struggled to break free of the circle, but Roy and my aunt tugged me toward them. "Stephen, I'm here." I sprang loose from their grip with a force that tipped my chair backward. The wood and my elbow banged against the floor.

Aunt Eva shrieked, and Julius cried out, "What was that?"

"It's all right." I untangled myself from the chair and crouched in the dark. "Stephen, where are you?"

"Help me." Stephen's voice came from a few feet away. "I swear to God they're murdering me."

"You're already dead. I went to your funeral. You died in the war."

"They're coming. Oh, God, they're coming!"

"Stephen?" I reached out but grabbed only air. "What happened to you? Who do you see killing you?"

"Ugly things."

"What types of things?"

"Monstrous birds." He gasped, which made my shoulders jerk. "Don't you hear them?"

"Birds are killing you?"

"Blackbirds. They've tied me down. They're torturing me."

My God, I thought. *Is he halfway in hell?*

"Do you know who I am?" I sat up. "Can you see me?"

A pause followed, long enough to swell with questions from the other sitters. *What is she doing? What's happening? What the hell is going on?*

"Shell." Stephen's voice brushed against my ear and shivered through me in the sweetest way. Static sparked across my hair. "My Mary Shelley."

I lowered my eyelids and smiled. "Yes, it's me. You showed up in my bedroom last night, scaring me half to death."

"You've been pulling me toward you like a magnet. Keep me with you. Don't push me back to France and home again. They've got me trapped there."

"You died in battle. No one's going to hurt you anymore."

"No. You've got it all wrong. They haven't finished with me yet. They're never going to finish with me."

A chair scooted away from the table.

"Keep me with you," he said against my neck.

"Keep coming back to me," I whispered. "I'll help you figure out what's wrong, I promise."

Heavy footsteps clomped across the room.

I opened my eyes. "Someone's going to turn on the lights. Be careful, Stephen—"

The electric lamps buzzed back to life and blazed against my corneas. The smell of fire in the air softened to the lingering wisps of Roy's snuffed-out cigarette. My mouth cooled to a normal temperature.

Stephen was gone.

Lena plodded my way, brow pinched, ringlets jostling. She raised her hand, and before I could duck, she slapped my cheek. "How dare you take over my séance? How *dare* you? Who do you think you are, coming in here, questioning me, insulting me, making a scene in the middle of my sacred trance?"

Julius got to his feet. "All right, all right. Calm down, Lena."

She turned on him and smacked him, too. "Why did you bring her here? Are you trying to make fun of my spiritual skills?"

"No—"

"Get her out of here." Lena ran to the door and swung it open with a crash of wood against wall. "Get her out right now. I don't want to see any one of you on my doorstep ever again, and that includes you, Julius. I hope you never find your brother."

I shot to my feet and tried to lunge at Lena, but Aunt Eva

and Julius took hold of me and escorted me out to the entry hall, where Lena pelted the backs of our heads with balled-up handfuls of Julius's flyers.

AUNT EVA CLIMBED INSIDE THE CADILLAC WITH BOTH OF our beaded handbags quaking in her arms. I put my left foot on the running board to step in beside her, but Julius clasped my elbow and steered me down the sidewalk with enough speed to make me trip.

"Where are you taking me?" I asked in a panic.

He stopped below an electric streetlamp near the hamburger restaurant and yanked me close. "You're not just pretending to see him, are you?"

"No. I hate frauds."

He pushed his fingers into my flesh. His pupils looked as small as pinpricks. "Swear upon his grave you're not lying."

"I swear upon his grave. I still believe your photos are fakes, but I've seen him and heard him, and I just felt him whisper against my skin. He thinks something's still killing him."

Julius's face paled. "What did he say?"

"He told me monstrous blackbirds are tying him down and torturing him. The air burns whenever he comes, and he's terrified, like he's reliving his death over and over."

Julius swayed. He dropped my arm and leaned against the lamppost to steady himself, his skin chalky white.

"I'm sorry, Julius. Did they tell you anything about the way he was killed over there?"

"No."

"Did they mention birds? Or capture by the Germans?"

"No."

"If he comes to me again, I'll ask him more. He begged me to keep him with me, but I don't know how to hold on to him. I was hoping your friend would help, but—"

"Just make him leave. Make him go wherever it is he's supposed to go."

"I will if I can. I feel so sorry for him. He's suffering."

Julius pushed himself off the streetlamp and lurched back to his car, where Aunt Eva waited, clinging to the passenger-side door with blanched fingers. I followed, and we all sat in the Cadillac without a word.

Halfway back to the house, Aunt Eva turned to Julius. "Do you think she's going out of her mind with grief?"

He sniffed and wiped at his nose. "She's sitting right there. She can hear you."

"The lightning seemed to change her. She even feels different when I touch her. Is she really seeing him?"

Julius didn't answer. He held the wooden steering wheel with his right hand and rubbed the bottom half of his face with his left, and I could tell from his rigid jaw and troubled eyes that the fraudulent spirit photographer believed in his brother's ghost.

14

STAY SAFE

I COULDN'T SLEEP.

I thumbed through Stephen's envelopes and reread several of his letters to hear his living voice inside my head. Most of his messages were written on stationery as blue as the sea—his favorite color—with his initials, *SEE*, monogrammed at the top.

One letter, from April 1917, stood out because of his discussion of the war and our friendship.

Dear Mary Shelley,

Happy birthday! How old are you now? Fifteen? Are you still as short as you used to be? Were you really short, or am I just remembering you that way because you're two years younger?

You probably already know this, but people teased me for being friends with a brainy girl. If I ever acted cold toward you when the taunting got bad, I apologize for my idiocy. None of those people ever write to me these days, so it seems stupid to have worried what they thought. They disappeared into my past without a trace, but the friend I considered abandoning because of them still makes me laugh with her brutally witty letters and bold honesty. I have never met a single soul like you, Shell.

So this is war. The declaration changed Coronado and San Diego overnight. The men are all enlisting and everyone is hurrying to make sure we all look like real Americans. One of our neighbors held a bonfire in his backyard and invited everyone over to burn their foreign books. I stood at the back of the crowd and watched people destroy the fairy tales of Ludwig Tieck and the brothers Grimm and the poetry of Goethe, Eichendorff, Rilke, and Hesse. They burned sheet music carrying the melodies of Bach, Strauss, Beethoven, and Wagner. Even Brahms's "Lullaby."

I kept wondering what you would have done if you had caught people dropping books into a hissing fire. I imagined you running over, reaching into the flames, and asking, "Have you all gone insane? Do you realize you're killing art and imagination, not the Kaiser's army?" But I stood there like a coward and kept quiet. I was afraid.

I know this letter has turned much darker than what a birthday letter ought to be, but I find it hard to talk to people around here. Everyone wants to categorize the world as good or bad, right or wrong. There is nothing "in between" in their eyes.

Be careful, Shell. It's a dangerous time to have unusual ideas. Make sure you truly know people before you offer them your trust. There are monsters lurking everywhere, it seems, and they sometimes disguise themselves as friends, neighbors, and patriots. God, I hope no one ever finds this letter and accuses me of being a traitor. That's not how I feel at all. I love our country. I just feel we've all gotten a little lost.

Stay safe. Happy birthday.

Your friend,
Stephen

I had forgotten that particular letter. Perhaps I had pushed it aside in my mind because the contents made me uneasy, but I now realized every sentence—from his shame over his thoughts of abandoning me to his curiosity about my reaction to book burning—was a testimony to how much I meant to him.

I tucked the blue stationery back into the envelope and closed my eyes with my fingers folded around the crisp edges.

THE THREE O'CLOCK CALL OF THE CUCKOO DOWNSTAIRS drew me out of sleep again.

My room appeared to be empty and still. The air didn't burn. I rolled onto my back and settled my head deep into the pillow, half drifting back to sleep.

A minute or so later, something sank down beside my

right hip on the bed. The mattress let out one of its accordion moans. A pair of legs settled beside mine.

I opened my eyes.

My breath caught in my throat.

Stephen sat next to me trembling, sweating.

I could see him.

He slouched against the wall in a sleeveless undershirt and trousers a burlap shade of brown. His hair hung in his face, disheveled and grown since I saw him in April, and he held his head in his fists. "Oh, God, Shell. Please make them stop."

My voice escaped me. I wanted to lift my hand to see if I could touch him, but I worried I'd scare him away. I managed to say one word: "Stephen?"

He wouldn't move at first—he just held his head and shuddered. Then something gave him a start. His shoulders flinched like he had heard a gunshot, and he dove down next to me, pressed his cheek against mine, and squirmed closer.

I stroked his hair above his left ear. "Why can I feel you?" A smooth lock slid between my fingers with the crackle of static. His face was covered in clammy sweat that dampened my skin. "I can feel you. Are we both half-dead?"

"They're killing me."

"It's all right. Nobody's here." I wrapped my arms around him and clutched the soft folds of his cotton shirt. His breath warmed my neck, and his heart drummed against me as if he were still alive. My own heart galloped like a quarter horse. "Nobody's here, Ste—"

He gasped and peered over his shoulder.

"What's wrong?"

"Oh, God." He pushed himself to his elbows. "They're coming."

"Who?" My eyes flew to the wall, and I imagined for a moment I caught the shadow of a large bird soaring across the golden paper.

"Oh, Christ." Stephen crawled all the way on top of me, knocking his knees against mine. "Keep me with you."

"How?"

"Let me be a part of you."

"How?"

"Let me inside."

My shoulders tensed. "What do you mean?"

"Close your eyes."

Another shadow flitted across the wall behind him. My eyelids refused to budge.

"Close your eyes." He cupped my cheek with his trembling hand and breathed the scent of burning candles against my face. "Please. Close your eyes and open your mind to me. Help me stay with you."

"Will it hurt?"

"I don't know."

"I'm scared."

"You're safe. I'm not. Help me."

At those words, I shut my eyes. He pressed his mouth against mine and kissed me in that urgent way of his, guiding my lips apart with his own, tasting of smoke and fire. My head went dizzy and buzzed with a violent hum that grew more deafening with every second. I couldn't move beneath him. I couldn't breathe. The oil lamp's flame blew out beside me, which made the dizziness worse, like someone was spinning me around and around on a swing in a pitch-black room. Stephen no longer felt like Stephen but a massive weight I couldn't lift. Lights flashed in front of my face—blinding, fiery explosions that singed the air and clogged my throat. Hungry eyes watched me from the corners of the room, ready to come closer. My wrists and ankles burned with the bite of heavy rope. I was going to die. Oh, my God, I was going to die.

"Get me out of here!" I freed my mouth and tried to get up. "I don't want to be here. Get me out of here." I kicked and fought and struggled, but the bindings dug farther into my skin. Everything burned—my wrists, my lungs, my nose, my stomach. All I could do was shriek and writhe in the black, black world.

A pair of hands reached around my shoulders.

"No! Don't shoot me. Get me out of here. Don't kill me."

Someone scooped me upward, as if pulling me out of water.

I broke through the surface and gasped for air, a light shining bright against my eyes. My room came back into view. My oil lamp glowed beside me again.

Aunt Eva's face hovered in front of mine, as pale as moonstone. She gripped my shoulders and stared at me as though she didn't recognize me. "Mary Shelley? What were you screaming about? Are you all right?"

I fought to catch my breath and looked around the room—the last thing I wanted to see was any creature with wings and a snapping beak—but there was nothing with us. My skin dripped with sweat, and my bones turned as heavy as when I had returned to my flesh after the lightning strike. My eyelids weighed a hundred pounds.

"Mary Shelley?" Aunt Eva pressed her icy hand against my forehead. "Do you have a fever? Is it the flu?"

"No." I fell out of her hands and collapsed against my bed. "No. It was something else. It's as bad as what he said. It's worse. What were those eyes?"

A thermometer jabbed me in the mouth. I tried to fight it at first, but my aunt held me down and wedged the glass beneath my tongue.

"You're talking like you're feverish." She stared at me. "Either that or that séance went to your head. We should have never left the house tonight. We should have never gone inside that trashy room with that cheap-looking girl."

My aunt's spectacles blurred until the two lenses expanded into four wavering bottle caps. My eyelids closed. I fell asleep before she could even take the thermometer out of my mouth. My brain simply slipped away, and I was gone—completely gone without a single dream—for the rest of the night.

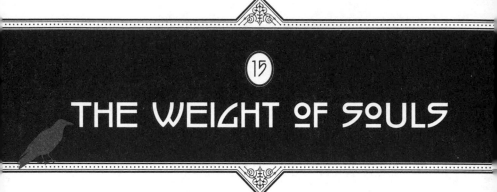

15
THE WEIGHT OF SOULS

A MASKED FACE STARTLED ME IN THE DARK.

"Don't hurt me!"

"Stop saying things like that." Aunt Eva brought her candle closer to her face and walked to the side of my bed. "It's just me. I'm getting ready to leave for work. Are you feeling all right? Can I leave you alone?"

My bleary eyes wandered around the rest of the room and caught sight of the outlines of Stephen's photographs on the wall, my flu mask dangling off a dresser knob, my sturdy Boy Scout boots sitting upright on the floor.

"I said, are you all right?" She leaned over me.

"Yes." I breathed a sigh that rustled her hair. "I'm fine."

"Have you been having nightmares?"

"No. Not since you woke me up last night."

She stroked my cheek with her chilly hand. "Take my phonograph apart again today or do whatever you want inside this house, but don't dwell on that séance."

"I won't," I said. It was a lie.

Her eyes studied my face one more time before she disappeared from my room and down the stairs. Oberon spoke his name to her in his gravelly bird voice, and then I heard the front door shut.

A half hour later, I got dressed and emptied my black doctor's bag of everything but sheets of blank writing paper and some cash. Down in the kitchen I ate an apple and pulled Mr. Darning's business card out of a little silver box my aunt kept next to her cookbooks. I then plunked myself on the living room sofa to yank my boots over my stockinged feet.

"Who's there?" asked Oberon from his cage.

I glared at the bird.

"Who's there?" he asked again.

"I told you to stop saying that. It's not amusing anymore." I laced up my boots, grabbed my mask and bag, and clomped out the door.

A crow cawed from the roof next door and gave me a sideways stare I didn't care for in the slightest. I tied my mask strings around my head, hurried my pace, and glanced over my shoulder, making sure the black bird didn't follow me. The crow flapped away with a whoosh of large wings and disappeared among the browning leaves of an oak tree.

Three blocks to the south I passed the undertaker's wretched-smelling house across the street. Four men in coveralls hustled to assemble more makeshift caskets on the front lawn, and I felt the vibrations of their saws inside my bones.

"Have those boys stopped playing on the caskets?" I called to the workers.

A graying man with a thin, masked face looked up from his sawing. "What's that you said?"

"I saw a group of boys playing on the caskets the last time I walked past here."

"You mean those little scamps we've been chasing away this past week?"

"Yes."

The man nodded toward a pile of smaller coffins beside him. "They're in there now."

His words socked me in the stomach. I turned my eyes toward the ground and pretended I hadn't heard the response.

The reinforced soles of my Boy Scout boots clopped down the sidewalk.

Death snapped at my heels—*I'm coming. Are you watching out for me?*

Five blocks farther south, I dug Mr. Darning's business card out of the black bag, for the addresses were getting close. I scanned the shop windows for the photography studio, passing a hat shop, the Dream Theatre, a grocery store, and hotels. Eventually I found it—Darning Studio—a modest storefront on the northeast corner of Fifth.

Two display windows showcased Mr. Darning's work: a collection of twenty photographs, ten per window, not a single one of them tainted by spirits, flu masks, or even the war. I saw babies in long white christening gowns and plump-cheeked children in sailor outfits. Brides in airy veils posed in front of clean-shaven men in three-piece suits. The members of a high school football team, clad in black jerseys and knee pants, folded their arms and gazed at the camera with stern expressions. A pretty young woman with dark curls piled on her head peered at me with eyes like pools of ink. On a white card below her frame someone had written, *San Diego's beautiful chanteuse Vivienne Boudreaux.*

The photos brought a smile to my face beneath my mask. They were all lovely.

I opened Mr. Darning's glass door, next to a black sign engraved with golden letters:

MR. ALOYSIUS P. DARNING
PHOTOGRAPHER AND RENOWNED DEBUNKER
OF SPIRITUALIST FRAUDS

A jingling brass bell announced my entrance, and I stepped into a small waiting area with three oak chairs.

"I'm with a customer," called Mr. Darning from around a partition. "I'll be with you in a moment."

"Sit still, Billy," said a woman's voice. "Daddy wants to see how big his boy is getting."

More picture frames hung in the lobby, lined in a neat row along gold- and burgundy-striped wallpaper. I perused the contents of the frames while I waited, reading letters thanking Mr. Darning for catching fraudulent photographers. I looked at newspaper photos of well-dressed gentlemen clapped in handcuffs, their arms clutched by unsmiling policemen. A handwritten letter from the mayor of Los Angeles offered Mr. Darning grateful phrases such as "Your display of integrity amid a turbulent era is to be commended, sir." And "It is never easy to stand up for what is right when so many people want to prove you wrong. I thank you from the bottom of my heart for saving countless Los Angeles families from becoming victims of fraud during this current craze for Spiritualism."

The mayor's words gave me chills. They echoed those of my father in his letter: *Sometimes our strength of spirit forces us to choose truth and integrity over comfort and security.*

A burst of light exploded around the corner, and a child screamed.

I peeked around the partition.

Deep in the middle of a dense haze of smoke, a woman and a boy of about two or three posed on a wicker chair in front of a canvas backdrop painted to look like a lush springtime garden. Both mother and child wore flu masks, and the boy choked on tears and flashlamp smoke as he fought to pull off his gauze.

"I think that should do it, Mrs. Irvine," said Mr. Darning, waving the thick white cloud away with a piece of heavy paper. "You're all done, Billy. You were such a good boy, I'm going to give you a stick of candy."

I seated myself in one of the lobby chairs and kicked my black bag under my skirt so no one would ask why I was lugging a doctor's bag around town in the middle of a flu pandemic. For the first time it struck me as being a strange thing to do, and I didn't want Mr. Darning thinking me strange.

The little boy waddled out of the studio first, wiping his red, runny eyes and shoving a purple candy stick under his flu mask. He smelled like a sticky grape mess. The copper-haired photographer, dressed in a black coat and tie and, of course, a gauze mask, escorted the mother out on his arm. Her blue cotton dress hung off her thin body like an empty sack of flour.

"Thank you, Mr. Darning," she said, taking her little boy's hand. "I hope my William appreciates the photograph. His letters have turned so somber since he fought at Belleau Wood."

"I'm sure he'll adore the photograph. And I'm sure he's fine over there. I wish I could be there myself, but I'm prone to asthma."

"I know I look a fright after the flu, so I'm not sure I'll be much comfort to him."

"Nonsense—you're enchanting. Your husband will love seeing the two of you alive and well." Mr. Darning opened the door for the pair. "I'll have the photograph ready in two days, and then you can put a wonderful little package in the mail to raise his spirits."

"Thank you."

They said their good-byes, and Mr. Darning closed the door and swiveled toward me. "Miss Black. How are you?"

I pushed myself out of the chair. "I'm all right."

His blue eyes warmed with compassion. "Are you sure?"

"Yes, I—" I remembered that the last time Mr. Darning had seen me, Julius and Grant were dragging me away from Stephen's casket while I kicked and screamed about Stephen's whispers. "Um . . . you offered me a free photograph when you visited my aunt's house, and I would like to take you up on that opportunity."

"Certainly. But didn't your aunt want to come along, too?"

"She's at work, so I'm here on my own. If you don't mind, I also have some questions I'd like to ask you about spirit photography."

"Ah, I see. Well, I'd be happy to answer them." He waved for me to join him in the studio. "Come on back and you can ask me whatever you'd like while we set up your portrait."

I followed him around the corner, and the familiar atmosphere in that main room knocked me off balance. I had to hold on to the back of a nearby armchair to recover from a painful wave of nostalgia for Stephen's father's old studio up in Portland. The assortment of props piled next to the staging area—fake boulders, parasols, teddy bears, Parisian fans with long white feathers—summoned memories of rainy Oregon weekends spent inside Mr. Embers's workplace. Stephen and I would wear grown-up-size costume hats and read books or play games while lounging on the studio's velvet-upholstered chairs and settees. I remembered the scents of darkroom chemicals and smoke and the lingering sweetness of customers' perfumes, as well as the sacred silence of Stephen's father developing his photographs.

"Are you sure you're all right, Miss Black?" asked Mr. Darning.

I nodded. "I'm fine."

He slid a rectangular wooden holder containing the used photographic plate out of the back of his boxy camera. "Let me go put this glass plate in my darkroom. I'll be right with you." He strolled through a doorway to the left, but he was back in less than a minute, rubbing his hands, ready to jump into work. "Now," he began as he scooted the wicker chair he had been using for the previous portrait to an empty spot at the side of the studio, "what did you want to know about spirit photography?"

"Well . . ." I picked at a navy string dangling off my right cuff and tried to figure out where to start. "My aunt said you've been exposing fake spirit photographers across the country."

"That's right." He rolled up the backdrop with the painted garden. "I traveled during the summer mostly, before the flu started shutting down cities. Far too many photographers have added spirit images to their repertoire, I'm afraid. The wave of grief sweeping across the land has resulted in desperation and gullibility."

"'Like rummies chasing bottles.'"

He peeked over his shoulder. "What was that?"

"That's how Stephen Embers described the desperation when he talked about his brother's customers. He said he'd hear them crying downstairs and it broke his heart. It's sickening to think of people preying upon grief."

"It is sickening, but the crooked photographers all use the same tricks, so they're easy to catch. They believe they're skilled enough to fool me." He pulled down a plain gray canvas. "The only one who's proven to be a challenge is our own Julius Embers."

"I'm guessing you'll catch him one day, though."

"Perhaps."

I stopped picking at my sleeve. "You don't think he's telling the truth, do you?"

"Part of me wants to believe."

"Really?"

Mr. Darning didn't respond at first. Instead, he dragged a large silver urn holding a silk cherry tree into the center of his staging area. I noticed his eyes glistened with tears. The bitter bite of grief scoured my tongue—it had a flavor similar to vinegar and was equally painful.

I cocked my head at him. "Are you OK, Mr. Darning?"

He stopped tugging on the urn and put his hands on his hips, exhaling a muffled sigh into his mask. "A close female friend of mine was one of the first San Diegans to die from the flu. A beautiful young singer, only twenty-four years old."

"Oh. I'm so sorry." I stepped forward two feet. "Is she the

dark-haired woman in the photograph in the window?"

He nodded and drew a handkerchief out of his breast pocket. "I started off so skeptical about spirits when I first hunted down frauds." He wiped his left eye. "But now I'm compelled to find tangible proof that we all go somewhere when we die. It hurts more than anything to think of a sweet soul like Viv's"—he pressed his handkerchief over his right eye and squeezed the other one closed; a stifled sob escaped his lips as a pained moan—"as being gone forever. I'm so sorry. I don't mean to break down like this. It's highly unprofessional."

My throat stung from the grief and embarrassment saturating that room, and it took me several seconds before I could respond without a hoarse voice.

"It's—it's all right." I rubbed my swollen throat. "I understand completely."

"I'm sure you do." He sniffed back his emotions and struggled to tuck his handkerchief back inside his pocket.

"Have you found any other possible true spirits?"

"I've read about scientists investigating the spirit world." He cleared his throat and fussed with the arrangement of silk flowers. "A physician named MacDougall conducted experiments involving the measurement of weight loss at the moment of death. He theorized he was demonstrating the loss of the soul, which, according to his studies, weighs about three-fourths of an ounce."

My eyes widened. "How in the world did he get volunteers to die on a scale?"

"At a home for incurable tuberculosis patients. He would push a cot holding a dying man onto an industrial-sized silk-weighing scale, and he kept his eyes on the numbers while his assistants watched for the final breath."

"Holy smoke." I shook my head in disbelief. "My uncle died in a home like that, but he certainly didn't have people hovering over him, waiting with bated breath for him to go."

"He received their written consent beforehand. It's not as cold and unfeeling as it sounds. Other men have conducted similar research on mice. Some are using X-rays and cylindrical tubes to study the physical manifestation of the soul."

"Maybe I should show them my compass."

"I beg your pardon?"

"Nothing." I looked down at the toes of my brown boots. "Just a thought I had about turning myself over to a laboratory."

"Are you referring to anything related to your experience with Stephen Embers?"

I played with the exposed pink skin of my lightning-burned fingers.

"I'm not scrutinizing you as if you were a trickster photographer, Miss Black. I'd honestly like to know what happened at his funeral. I was there, remember? I heard you insist he was talking to you."

"I know." I covered my eyes with my hands. "You probably think I'm either crazy or a liar."

"No. You seem an honest girl." He walked closer to me

with footsteps that scarcely made a sound. "Do you believe you're communicating with Stephen?"

I dropped my arms to my sides and decided to be truthful. "Yes. I'm positive I am."

Hope burned in his eyes. "Really?"

"That's partly why I want you to photograph me today. I don't want to go to Julius, because I'm afraid he'll tamper with the image. But I'm so curious to see if a camera can capture any sign that Stephen is here with me."

Mr. Darning glanced around the room. "Do you think he's here with you right now?"

"No. I don't know." I shrugged and shook my head. "Oh, this all sounds so crazy when I talk about it out loud. I know how hard it is to listen to someone who sounds like she's full of bunk, but everything changed after I died—after I was struck by lightning. I experience the world in an entirely different manner."

"What other types of things do you experience?"

"I taste emotions. Your grief just now when you were discussing your loss felt as though I were swallowing a bottle of vinegar."

"Really?"

"And I affect a compass. The needle follows me around the room, like I'm a ghost. Unless Stephen is there. Then it follows him."

He stared at me without saying a word.

I pulled at the edges of my gauze mask, which rubbed

against my chin. "It sounds insane, I know. I never believed in spirits before this happened, and I'd love to find a scientific explanation. I'm planning to go to the library today."

"Would you show me the compass phenomenon?"

"Yes." I sighed in relief. "Yes, definitely—that would be really nice, actually. I'd love to get a professional's opinion."

"May I come over this weekend?"

"Hmm . . ." I rubbed my forehead and tried to remember what day of the week it was. "Oh, today's Halloween, isn't it? A strange day to be discussing spirits. That means tomorrow's Friday. Aunt Eva will be home by five thirty. I suppose you could come over any time after six. You could stay for supper, if you'd like—although Aunt Eva mainly prepares onion dishes that incinerate taste buds and stomach linings."

He laughed. "No, no, I don't want to impose. I'd just take a look at you and the compass and be on my way."

"That would be fine."

"Well, this is indeed intriguing." He rested his hand on the top of his camera. "Shall we take your photograph, then? See what happens?"

I nodded. "I'm ready."

He showed me the entire process as we went along, demonstrating the prepackaged glass plates he purchased directly from Kodak, which he tucked into a protective wooden holder in the darkroom before sliding the holder into the slot behind the bellows. "This is the stage where the phonies typically cheat," he said. "A trickster's plate will contain a previously photographed image, and that image will look like a transparent ghost when the picture is developed."

"A double exposure."

He nodded. "That's correct. Now, I don't guarantee anything will come of this photograph. I make no claims to possess mediumistic skills."

"I know. But let's just try it and see what happens. For the sake of science."

The skin around his eyes crinkled in a way that told me he was smiling behind his mask. "For the sake of science."

He positioned me in front of the gray backdrop with my arms folded behind my back. I gave a weak smile while he prepared the shot with his head ducked beneath a black cloth, and he took my photograph with nothing but the kindest display of professionalism.

Yet, in the aftermath of the violent flash, an empty feeling pestered me.

Stephen doesn't want to use his energy to show up for a casual picture, you idiot, I realized as stinging tendrils of smoke crept over my hair and skin. *Why would he pose for a photograph when he's suffering? You're wasting your time trying to satisfy your own curiosity.*

Stop playing.

Go help him figure out what's wrong.

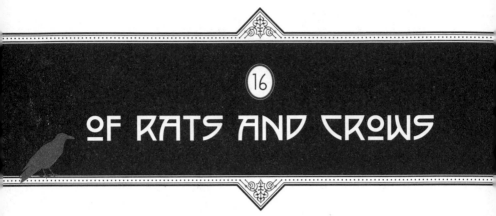

16
OF RATS AND CROWS

ON THE CORNER OF EIGHTH AND E STOOD A GORGEOUS white mansion with Grecian pillars flanking the entrance. A trim green lawn lined with rustling, feathery palms led to castle-sized wooden doors that promised knowledge, adventure, and hope. This was San Diego's library.

Inside, the same surreal sulfur smoke as at Stephen's funeral emerged from burning buckets of coal and blurred the view of the central desk and the pale green walls. Sunshine tried to stream through long windows, but the blue clouds blocked the light and cast drifting shadows across the solid oak furniture. I choked on a sulfuric stench that reminded me of rotten eggs, even with the gauze covering my face.

A masked brunette with a soft splay of wrinkles at the

edges of her eyes walked toward me through the burning haze. "May I help you?" she asked in that eager way of speaking all librarians possess.

"I need to look up quite a few subjects."

She noticed my black bag. "You're not a physician, are you?"

"No, I just brought this to hold my notes. It used to be my mother's bag."

"Ah, I thought you looked a little too young to be saving lives. You made me feel better for a moment, thinking you'd be able to help if anyone falls ill. Quite frankly"—she peered over her shoulder and lowered her voice to a conspiratorial tone—"I'm surprised the city hasn't shut us down entirely. Only the reading rooms are closed."

"Oh . . . they're closed?" My posture wilted. "I was really hoping to do some studying here this morning. I need to read through too many books to carry home."

"What subjects did you need to find?"

I ran through my mental list of categories. "Well, I'd like to find books on modern war poetry, trench warfare, German military practices, prisoners of war, blackbirds, birds in mythology . . ." I stopped for a moment to take stock of everything else. "Lightning injuries, electricity, magnetic fields, spirit photography, Spiritualism, and true experiences of life after death."

Her eyes stopped blinking. She looked like a mouse that had been cornered by a cat. "Are you familiar with card catalogs and the Dewey decimal system?"

I nodded. "Yes."

"We allow our patrons to find their own books from the stacks. You seem an ambitious girl. Why don't you try looking up these subjects on your own? I'll even sneak you into the women's reading room to make up for your troubles."

"You will?"

"Yes."

I exhaled an appreciative breath. "Thank you so much. Where is the card catalog?"

She pointed to the wooden files beyond the wall of smoke behind me. "Right over there."

"I don't have a library card yet. I'm new to the city."

"I'll leave an application for you in the reading room."

I thanked her again and headed over to the drawers of cards that indexed books by subject matter.

By the time I reached the empty women's reading room, I carried a stack of ten books in my arms, my muscles quivering from the weight of all those cloth- and leather-bound volumes. The handles of my black bag dangled from my right hand beneath the pile and cut off circulation to my fingertips. I parked myself at an oak table, all alone save for those blue sulfur-dioxide phantoms.

The librarian had left me both the library card application and a copy of the day's newspaper. A story below the latest flu death tolls caught my eye: the opening of a Red Cross House for healing war veterans, whom the paper described as "Uncle Sam's convalescent nephews." In the accompanying photograph, two local women in tailored black dresses served tea to a young man who looked like he'd just been dragged off the battlefield. His hair was as wild as mine after the lightning blasted through me, and his eyes seemed to be saying, *What I don't need after a war is two crazy society bats pushing cups of tea my way.*

An urge to visit those healing soldiers and sailors welled up inside me. I wanted to learn how the war that snatched away Stephen had affected other boys—and to find some sort of clue that would explain why he claimed to be tortured by birds. Plus that soldier's distressed face saddened me. I felt compelled to help people like him, to lend a sympathetic ear and offer comfort that extended beyond cups of tea.

At the top of my first sheet of writing paper, I scribbled, *Visit the Red Cross House and talk to returning men.*

Next, I opened *A Treasury of War Poetry*, published just the year before, and read firsthand accounts of the trauma of the trenches, told through bold and brutal poems such as "The Death of Peace," "I Have a Rendezvous with Death," and "The Hell-Gate of Soissons."

"Into Battle," by Julian Grenfell, mentioned a blackbird:

The blackbird sings to him, "Brother, brother,
If this be the last song you shall sing,
Sing well, for you may not sing another;
Brother, sing."

A chilling reference to crows appeared in Frederic Manning's "The Trenches":

Dead are the lips where love laughed or sang,
The hands of youth eager to lay hold of life,
Eyes that have laughed to eyes,
And these were begotten,
O Love, and lived lightly, and burnt
With the lust of a man's first strength: ere they were rent,
Almost at unawares, savagely; and strewn
In bloody fragments, to be the carrion
Of rats and crows.

With shaking fingers I transcribed *to be the carrion of rats and crows*, and gagged on both the mental image of birds feasting on dismembered dead soldiers and the rotten-egg fumes stealing through my mask. I put the poems aside and continued through the rest of the books, reading about lightning strikes, magnets, prisoners of war, and modern battle strategies. I studied trench combat, gas warfare, and a condition called shell shock that affected soldiers' minds. I investigated Spiritualism and found stories of desperate, educated men like the novelist Sir Arthur Conan Doyle and the physician Duncan MacDougall, he of the soul-weighing experiment, who were risking their reputations to find proof of the afterlife.

Desperate, I wrote on my paper. *They're always desperate.*

I read about ectoplasm that was proved to be cheesecloth, unexplained spirit voices, spirit lovers, spirit writings, spirit photographs, spirit manifestations, and even two girls in Cottingley, England, who claimed to be photographing fairies. My brain raced, and my sheets of paper filled with notes and diagrams and formulas and poetry.

But I still had no idea why Stephen thought monstrous birds were tying him down and killing him.

"DO YOU KNOW HOW I CAN GET TO THE NEW RED CROSS House in Balboa Park?" I asked the same brunette librarian who had helped me before.

She slid my stack of five checked-out books across the polished countertop. "Take the Fifth Avenue streetcar up to Laurel. You'll find a bridge crossing the canyon to Balboa Park."

"Is the park small? Will it be hard to find?"

She raised her eyebrows. "You've never been there?"

I shook my head.

She laughed. "Well, I guarantee you won't miss it when you get to the bridge. It's the former site of the Panama-California Exposition. The military owns the area now, but somebody could probably direct you to the Red Cross House. Do you know someone recuperating there?"

"No, but I'd like to volunteer."

She leaned her gauze-swathed chin against her fist and studied me. "How old are you?"

"Sixteen."

"Does anyone know you're wandering around in the quarantined city by yourself?"

"I said I'm sixteen, not six."

"That doesn't answer my question."

Instead of responding, I opened the wide mouth of my mother's black bag and crammed it full of books.

The librarian ducked below the counter. "Here." She stood up straight again and slid a red pack of garlic-flavored gum across to me. "Take a stick or two. I can't stand the thought of sending a kid across town without some flu protection."

"You sound like my aunt. If she had her way, I'd be bathing in onion soup every night."

"Just take it, please. Take the whole pack. I can buy another." She folded her slender hands on the counter. "It would be a shame to waste all that curiosity to the flu."

I took the pack, and to make her feel better, I even slipped my mask down for a moment and popped one of the foul sticks of gum in my mouth. Instant tears careened down my cheeks. "Ugh." I spit the gum out in my hand. "This is awful."

"Just chew it, OK? Stay safe out there." She nodded toward the exit. "Now go on. I'm getting tired of crying over kids who don't have anyone to watch over them anymore." She turned away from me and stooped down to a collection of books on a low shelf behind her.

I hesitated, soothed by the taste of concern trailing off her, almost tempted to stay. She looked back to see if I had gone, her eyes shining with tears, so I thanked her and slipped away.

17

KEEP YOUR NIGHTMARES TO YOURSELF

I GAGGED ON THE TASTE OF THE GARLIC GUM WHILE A bright yellow streetcar carried me along the rails to the hills above San Diego. Three businessmen in smart felt hats rode with me, probably on their lunch break. They buried their gauze-covered noses in the *San Diego Union*, and one of them read the October influenza death tolls out loud.

"Philadelphia: over eleven thousand dead and counting—just this month. Holy Moses! Boston: four thousand dead."

The use of cold statistics to describe the loss of precious lives made me ill. I crossed my fingers and hoped that Portland wasn't a big enough city to mention. Hearing the death toll up there—worrying about my father in that crowded jail—would have probably killed me.

"New York City: eight hundred and fifty-one in just one day—*eight hundred and fifty-one*! Can you believe that?"

"Laurel Street," called the conductor from his post by the center doors.

I pressed a fancy little nickel-plate button inlaid in mother-of-pearl, relieved for the chance to escape. The car came to a gentle stop on a flat part of the street.

"Where's the bridge to Balboa Park?" I asked the conductor before heading down the steps.

"Straight to the east." He pointed with a long arm, and like the librarian, he added, "You can't miss it."

He was right. A nearsighted person without glasses could have spotted it from more than a block away: an elaborate arched concrete bridge spanned a pond and a canyon, and on the other side of the hundred-foot drop rose a city of Spanish colonial palaces, straight from the pages of a fairy tale.

I walked briskly across the bridge, eager to reach the Red Cross House and urged on by a feeling in my gut that someone there would be able to help me with Stephen. I ran below curved balconies, wrought-iron railings, and plaster pillars sculpted with intricate flowers, grapes, and rambling vines. It would have been amazing to simply stand there and gape at the architecture, but not when I had a mission.

The building I sought stood out like a beacon, for a large red cross marked its roof. I slowed my pace as I approached the daunting entrance, my heart thumping as if I were about to come face-to-face with Stephen himself.

Inside, the main room must have stretched two hundred feet across, and bandaged, wounded men were everywhere. They read and slept on sofas and padded leather chairs, or hobbled about on crutches. Others were confined to wicker wheelchairs. A few groups who didn't look as battered as the rest huddled around tables and played cards. Canaries sang from wire cages. Two open fireplaces warmed the air. No one, save those warbling canaries, made much noise.

Along with the garlic fumes heating my tongue, the rancid taste of suffering drenched my mouth, as if someone were pouring week-old soup prepared with spoiled meat and stagnant water down my throat. I yanked off my gauze and threw the wad of gum into a wastebasket.

A woman with eyes as amber and narrow as a cat's came my way in a white Red Cross hat and clip-clopping heels. She straightened her flu mask over a nose that appeared rather large, smoothed out the crisp apron covering her pressed gray uniform, and took a long look at my doctor's bag.

"I'm not a doctor," I said. "I'm just carrying some library books in the bag." I tugged my gauze back over my mouth and nose. "It belonged to my mother."

"Oh." She blinked like she didn't know how to respond to such an introduction.

"My name is Mary Black," I tried again, omitting the "Shelley" to avoid associations with *Frankenstein* and Germany in an American Red Cross building. "I'd like to volunteer to help the men."

She surveyed my appearance, from the childish white ribbon tying back my hair at my neck to the worn-out Boy Scout boots that were coming unlaced. "How old are you?"

"Sixteen. And a half."

"That's a little young to be witnessing the state of some of these men. Most of our volunteers are married women who've seen a bit of life already. They've experienced childbirth. They've lost husbands."

"I just buried a boy who meant the world to me, ma'am. I've seen corpses as blue as ripe huckleberries lying in front yards out there. There's no need to protect me from anything." I shifted my sagging bag to my other hand. "I'm tired of sitting around doing nothing."

She swallowed. "Very well. Are you up to serving the men refreshments and making sure they're comfortable? Helping them write letters and whatnot?"

"Yes."

She stepped closer and softened her voice. "Several of the men are amputees, and some of their faces are quite damaged beneath their bandages. You may see signs of deformed cheeks and chins and missing facial bones. Are you sure you can do this?"

"I'm positive."

"All right, then. Please avert your eyes if you need to, but try not to express disgust. Our goal is to help them recover in the most soothing environment we can offer."

"I understand." I peeked at the quiet gathering of broken

boys beyond us. "Why are so many of their faces disfigured, if you don't mind me asking? Is it the explosive shells they're using over there?"

"I'm told it's the machine guns. Curious soldiers will often lift their heads out of the trenches, thinking they can dodge bullets in time, but there's no way they can possibly avoid the hail of machine-gun fire." She glanced over her shoulder. "We tend to also see several missing left arms because of the way they position themselves for shooting in the trenches. Their bones shatter into tiny fragments and their wristwatches become embedded in their wounds. There's no way to save the limbs."

I didn't cringe, for I felt she was testing me, and I was determined to prove I could handle the horrors. "What can I do first?"

Her heels clicked over to a woven tan basket sitting on one of the front tables. "Well, I was just about to pass around these oatmeal cookies. Why don't you give that a try?" She carried the basket my way. "Heaven knows, these boys would probably love to be offered baked goods by a pretty young girl. Just be careful none of them gets too fresh with you."

I looped the basket handle over my arm and soaked up the scents of baked oatmeal and roasted nuts—a divine combination that curbed the rancidness inside my mouth.

"Is there a particular part of the room where I should start?" I asked.

"It doesn't matter. They're all in need of cheering. If

the men are too much for you to take, come into the back kitchen. We can always have you help bake something or roll bandages."

"I'll be fine. Thank you." I dropped my black bag by the front door, and then I journeyed into the main room, trying to convey confidence in my stride.

Where to start, where to start? I wondered, unsure if I would be more helpful in one direction versus another. At random, I picked the right.

The first two young men I approached were sitting in fat leather armchairs reading outdated copies of the *Saturday Evening Post*. I remembered the picture of the clown on the rightmost cover from way back in May or June. The black-haired boy reading that particular issue was missing both his legs, his trousers sewn to hide the two stumps. The other young man, a handsome devil with golden-brown hair and smoky-gray eyes, wore bandages over his left wrist where his hand ought to have been. An unlit cigarette dangled from the scarred fingers of his surviving hand.

"Would you like a cookie?" I asked the black-haired one.

He looked to be of Mexican descent, with olive skin and dark irises that brightened when he found me standing over him. "Yes, please," he said.

I handed him one of the lumpy oatmeal cookies and kept my attention from straying to his two stumps. "Here you are."

"Thank you." He untied the top strings of his flu mask and revealed a boyish round face with a healing pink gash across his chin. "You're much younger than the ladies who usually help around here," he said. "*Qué bonita.* Very pretty."

"Thank you."

"No, thank you, *querida.*"

"Please excuse Carlos," said the other boy with a cockeyed smirk I could see through a round opening cut in the center of his mask. "They dope him up with morphine so he doesn't feel the . . ." He pointed with his cigarette to Carlos's missing legs. "He's under the delusion he's still a Latin lover."

"I'm twice the man you are, Jones."

"Said the man with no legs," chuckled the blondish boy.

"Not funny, friend. You're just jealous the ladies fuss over you less." Carlos leaned back in his chair and beamed up at me. "Do us lovesick fellows a favor, *querida.* Take down your flu mask. Let us see your entire beautiful face."

"You don't need to see my whole face."

"But I do," said Carlos.

"You'll be sorely disappointed." I lifted another cookie out of the basket. "I have huge warts and buckteeth hiding under my mask."

"Don't tease us." Carlos gave me a pleading look with his big brown eyes. "We're starving for female attention, *querida.* Just one quick peek."

"I'm afraid not." I offered the cookie I was holding to his friend Jones. "Would you like one of these?"

"No." The blondish boy slid his cigarette between his lips through his mask hole. "But I'd love a light." He raised his narrow hips and yanked a matchbook out of his back pocket with a grimace. His other arm, the one with the missing hand, lay across his left leg as if it were something dead.

"They're bad for your breathing, you know," I said, nodding to his cigarette. "And if these masks do help fight the flu, that gaping hole in the front of yours isn't going to do you a lick of good, either."

"Who are you, my aunt Gertie?" He jerked his chin at me and bit down on the cigarette. "I bet you're also part of the noble crusade to outlaw booze."

"I just know some of the easier ways to avoid an early grave." I set his rejected cookie back into the basket. "You should take care of yourself so you can heal. You're still young. What are you, about nineteen? Twenty? Twenty-one at most?"

He stared me down. "Just light my match, sweetheart." The cigarette fluttered in his lips as he spoke. "This little cigarette is the only thing keeping me from putting a bullet in my head."

The chill in his gray eyes made me want to recoil, but I kept my face stoic. I lowered the basket to the ground and lit his cigarette for him with trembling fingers, as if he were an explosive I was afraid of detonating.

He exhaled a stream of smoke out of the side of his mask instead of directly into my face, and his eyes softened. "Thanks. You're a doll."

"You're welcome." I looked at his good hand. "Are those scars from the war?"

He exhaled another white cloud. "Barbed wire. We rolled entanglements between us and the enemy's trenches, and it was sharp as hell. I came back from war a real cutup."

I reached down for the basket, ignoring his dark pun, and felt his gaze burn against the top of my head.

"I'd give you a hand, doll," he said, "but the Krauts already got it."

"Stop it, Jones." Carlos lowered his half-eaten cookie. "Don't pay any attention to him, *querida*. He's got a strange sense of humor."

I picked up the basket. Jones was staring straight at me while he took a long drag on his glowing cigarette. I turned away and left the two of them behind. My back slouched more than before. Confidence left my stride. The harsh scent of bitterness surrounding that boy hurt worse than the smell of kerosene.

The other masked soldiers turned my way, their expressions expectant, as if I could truly do them good with a simple basketful of cookies. They welcomed me with misshapen, bandaged faces, empty sleeves where arms should have been, healing burns, gashes with red, crusted skin, crutches, absent legs, joints throbbing with rheumatism, and the taste of an indescribable weariness that made my own muscles ache.

Unlike Jones, most of the men were polite and sweet, offering quiet words of thanks.

I came upon a boy who was missing his left arm and leg. Between the bandages and his flu mask, his head was a jigsaw puzzle of intermingled gauze that swallowed up more than seventy-five percent of his face. He slept in one of the leather chairs, head tilted to the right, his chest rising and falling with easeful slumber.

"That one's in the arms of Madame Morphine," said the man sitting in the chair across from him—a graying fellow with an eye patch. "I'll take his cookie for him."

"I'll save it for when he wakes up," I said.

"He might not wake up for a couple hours."

"If you were sleeping as peacefully as he is"—I handed the man his own fair share—"wouldn't you be upset if someone else took your cookie?"

The man wrestled down his mask to show a wistful grin. "I would give far more than a cookie to be able to sleep as peacefully as that, little miss."

"You don't sleep well?"

"Not anymore I don't. Not after they dropped me down in the trenches with the rats."

I fetched another cookie out of the basket and nudged it into his hand.

He patted my elbow. "Thank you, miss. I won't tell a soul."

"Get some good sleep," I said. "You're not in the trenches anymore."

My next stop was a table of three young men playing poker, their wounds less visible than the others', although a pair of crutches leaned against the back of the shortest one's chair. They sat with more ease than the rest of the convalescing fellows, and they enjoyed touching my fingers when I handed them their treats.

"Thank you, blue eyes."

"Much obliged, girlie."

"Aren't you a sweet thing?"

The tallest of the group, a scarecrow of a man with a bulging Adam's apple, sang "Pretty Baby" to me, and I blushed and thanked him and wished he would stop. In an armchair next to them, a curly-haired redhead with a leg wrapped in bandages leaned his forehead against the palm of his hand and wept silent tears.

"Would you like a cookie?" I asked him while Mr. Scarecrow kept on singing behind me.

The man didn't answer. He didn't even look my way. Another long tear rolled down his masked cheek and soaked into the gauze.

Mr. Scarecrow cut off his serenade mid-chorus. "That's Mulroney. He cries all the time, which is pretty dang embarrassing to watch. You may as well keep walking so you don't have to look at him."

I bent down closer to the weeping soldier and put my hand on his arm. "I know how you feel. The world's been getting the best of me, too."

The soldier's eyes met mine.

"Would you like to escape from your troubles for a while?" I asked. "I'd be happy to go find a book I can read to you. Maybe we can both take a short vacation from the real world."

He nodded.

"Something funny, maybe?"

He nodded again, with more vigor.

"I'll be right back."

I left a cookie on his lap and sought out the Red Cross woman who had greeted me.

Society ladies were entering the building to start their afternoon shift of administering aid—a glistening, perfumed whirlwind of starched white blouses, feathered hats, waved hair, and jewels.

"Do you know if there are any books to read to the men?" I asked them.

A tall, spindly woman around Aunt Eva's age beckoned with a manicured fingernail. "Over here, dear. How nice to see a young girl giving her time." She led me to a battered crate shoved beneath a table and scooted the box out for me to see. "These were donated just yesterday."

I knelt and thumbed through a dusty pile of clothbound books. Chaucer. Milton. Tolstoy. Melville. Hawthorne. Bunyan. None of them were right for men in need of cheering.

Down at the bottom, a lighter choice caught my eye: *The Adventures of Tom Sawyer.*

"Aha! That's more like it." I maneuvered Twain's novel out from under the stack. It had a red cover and looked to be in fairly new condition.

"A children's tale?" asked the society woman in a tone that told me she was wrinkling her nose beneath her mask.

"I don't feel like reading anything somber." I stood back up. "And I doubt any of them want to hear grim stories of tortured men and tragic women. Let's give them Tom and Huck."

I tucked *Tom Sawyer* under my arm, borrowed a spare chair from the poker players' table, and returned to the side of the weeping curly-haired soldier.

"'Chapter One,'" I read after I gave a comfortable sigh, "'Tom Plays, Fights, and Hides' . . ."

A collective silence hushed the poker table beside me. Knees turned my way. Heads lifted. Every single man nearby perked up his ears and listened to the "children's tale."

While the ladies glided around the room and poured tea into fine bone china without a single spilled drop, the soldiers and sailors leaned on the arms of their chairs and laughed at Tom Sawyer's shenanigans. Their chuckles rumbled around me, growing richer with each chapter, and I thought, *Maybe I am doing some good. Maybe Stephen would be pleased to know I'm helping people like him. Maybe Dad would be proud.*

"'Chapter Four: Showing Off in Sunday School' . . . 'Chapter Six: Tom Meets Becky' . . ."

I read and read until my throat turned dry, and then I took a drink of water and read some more. The canaries and society women and that foul taste of suffering fell away, replaced by Tom's aunt Polly's house with the whitewashed fence, and the island where Tom and Huck pretended to be pirates.

"'Chapter Ten: Dire Prophesy of the Howling Dog' . . ."

Despite the good I seemed to be doing, however, the section of the room where the boy called Jones smoked in his armchair still weighed me down. He was like a dark stain on a delicate fabric, and I couldn't stop my eyes from occasionally drifting his way.

It wasn't until I had read nearly one hundred pages that I finally figured out why he bothered me so.

Jones seemed bright. The way he cracked an instant joke—as dark as the jokes may have been—demonstrated a quick wit. It indicated he could've been someone I'd enjoy as a friend if that brutal bite of bitterness wasn't getting the best of him. Perhaps he had once even been gentle enough to have loved a girl. Maybe he held that girl close the day before he left for training and promised in a voice not fully sure of itself, *I'll be fine.*

He bothered me because if Stephen were sitting in that chair instead of Jones, Stephen might have also stabbed my soul with the chilling stare of a person who now knew things he should have never learned.

AT FOUR THIRTY, I SAID GOOD-BYE TO MY AUDIENCE AND went to the door to fetch my bag.

My pace slowed as I drew nearer the exit. The same feeling of dissatisfaction that had pestered me at Mr. Darning's studio turned my legs sluggish. I hadn't accomplished one single thing for Stephen. I had worried too much about upsetting the men to ask them the questions baffling my brain.

My feet came to a halt.

I turned toward the person in the room who had spoken to me with the most honesty and marched in his direction.

"Ah, Aunt Gertie returns." Jones twirled an unlit cigarette around with his fingers like a baton.

"You seem unafraid of honesty." I stopped in front of him. "I need to ask you a question about the war."

I could see his mouth harden through the hole in his mask. Clenching my fists, I fought off my fear. "What would you think if a soldier told you he was being tortured by birds over in France?" I shifted my weight from one foot to the other. "What would that mean to someone who's been over there?"

Again he studied me with those watchful, penetrating eyes that didn't seem to blink. "I'd say, 'Keep your nightmares to yourself, pal. Those aren't the things we're supposed to be discussing with other people.'"

"You'd think they're just nightmares?"

"If I mentioned out loud half the things that torture me in my dreams, I'd be put in a straitjacket faster than you can say *crackpot*. And I guarantee you every man sitting in this building feels the same way."

I looked out at all the other men and experienced a depth of concern so overwhelming it made me tremble. I took a breath to steady myself and turned back to Jones. "There was nothing over there resembling murderous birds, then? Nothing that could have pinned a soldier down?"

"I don't know." He crossed his right leg over his left knee

and bit the cigarette between his teeth. "Reality and night-mares have a funny way of blurring together when a man's fighting down in the bowels of mother earth." He twitched his foot and kept his gaze on my face. "Why do you want to know this stuff? Who's telling you he's getting pinned down by birds?"

I bit my lower lip and debated whether I should answer.

He gave a short laugh that was more of a shrug. "You're as bad as the doctors, aren't you? Wanting to know what's going on inside our heads but scared sick of the answers. Maybe you shouldn't go asking about things your naive female brain can't handle. Go back to your quilting bees and tea parties or whatever the hell you all concern yourselves with."

This time I was the one who responded with an unflinch-ing glare. "A dead boy is the one telling me," I said. "A dead soldier."

His eyes lost a hint of their chill. "What are you talking about?"

"Even us naive women find ourselves haunted by the war, you see. And some of us have even tried killing ourselves, like you claim you're tempted to do. I can tell you firsthand it's not worth the heartache and pain. So don't do it."

I turned and left the building.

THE PIRATE KING

A ROW OF ELECTRIC LIGHTBULBS BURNED ACROSS THE ceiling of the southbound streetcar, illuminating a green-tinged poster that hung on one of the closed windows.

REMEMBER BELGIUM! BUY BONDS FOURTH LIBERTY LOAN

Below the boldfaced words, a silhouetted soldier in a spiked German helmet dragged a little girl away from her Belgian village.

I shifted in my seat and stared at the poster while the streetcar rocked back and forth. Conflicting thoughts about the war stabbed behind my eyes like a headache.

In saving U.S. boys from heading overseas, I realized, Dad may have been allowing Germans to kill Belgians.

The U.S. government saved Belgians . . . by allowing Germans to kill and maim our boys.

Lives were being traded for other lives. The line between right and wrong blurred into a haze. Dad and Stephen could be called heroes, murderers, or victims, depending on how you looked at the situation, and the Germans, too, for that matter. Nothing about the war made sense. None of it seemed right. The kaisers, kings, and presidents should have just had a good arm wrestle over their differences instead of bringing regular people into their mess.

The stabbing behind my eyes worsened.

"God, don't let it be the flu," I murmured loud enough for a woman in a maid's uniform to turn my way with fear in her eyes.

I BLEW THROUGH AUNT EVA'S FRONT DOOR JUST AS DARKness was settling over the house, and I was immediately assaulted with another "Who's there?" from Oberon. His feathers rustled in his cage, and I could have sworn a pair of wings brushed against my hair. I swiped at the back of my neck, grabbed a candlestick, and ran upstairs to drop off my black bag and sweat-soaked flu mask. My goggles—my steadfast companions during my last moments with Stephen and my lightning death—lay on my bed amid the other treasures I had taken out to make room for books and notes. I fitted the lenses over my eyes and adjusted the leather straps around my head for old time's sake.

After making the rounds to light the downstairs lamps, I soothed my parched throat with a cup of cool water in the kitchen. My headache began to ease its firm grip on my skull. I filled the glass again and browsed Aunt Eva's collection of phonograph records out in the living room, hunting for the musical equivalent of *The Adventures of Tom Sawyer*. She owned several songs from the opera *The Pirates of Penzance*, which would do nicely.

I wound the phonograph's hand crank and put the needle in place. The record crackled to life. An actor with a dramatic stage voice announced he would live and die a pirate king, and a bouncy harpsichord introduction began. I leaned back in the rickety white rocking chair and listened to the pirate and his harmonious crew fence and sing about how glorious it was to be a pirate king.

Oberon's big bronze cage was starting to smell like it needed to be cleaned. The magpie swallowed seeds from a metal bowl, but I tried to ignore the movements of his crow-like head by gazing out at the empty street through my snug goggles. The world was still for the moment, unless the sirens of ambulances had become so ingrained in my ears that I no longer heard them. A glowing jack-o'-lantern smiled at me from the porch rail of a bungalow across the way, and I remembered it was Halloween. No one else seemed to be celebrating a holiday a little too closely associated with death. And nightmares.

I sighed and held the glass to my chest. "Those poor men and their war dreams," I said to the empty room before taking another sip.

During the song's second verse, I spied a roadster with shining round headlights cruising into view in front of the house. The Pirate King continued to belt out his piratical joy, while the car's driver steered his vehicle in a one-hundred-eighty-degree turn and bumped the front tire into the curb. He backed up two feet, shifted again, and pulled alongside the pavement. The roadster was a Cadillac. Its sapphire-blue paint glimmered beneath the streetlight.

Julius's Cadillac.

I sat up straight and stiff.

Aunt Eva was in the passenger seat—I could see the silhouettes of her work cap and flu mask. I tore off my goggles and ran to the front door.

The two of them climbed out of the vehicle and shut the doors. Julius wore the same gray fedora as the night before, and he lugged a crate of oranges under his arm. Aunt Eva laughed and chatted with so much giddy enthusiasm that she didn't even notice me standing guard in the doorway until they reached the porch steps.

"Mary Shelley!" She grabbed her chest. "You scared me, just standing there. What are you doing without your mask?"

Julius thumped up the porch steps behind her. "Would you look at that? It does have a mouth and a nose." He gave my chin a flick, but I jerked away.

"What are you doing here?" I asked.

"Julius surprised me at the factory and offered to drive me home." Aunt Eva gestured for us to hurry inside. "Come in, both of you. Shut the door, Mary Shelley. Julius, please have a seat in the living room."

Julius sauntered in with his crate.

"Who's there?" asked Oberon.

I grabbed my aunt by her wrist before she could take two steps up the stairs. "Why is he here?"

"He's lonely and grieving, so he picked me up from the shipyard. I invited him to supper. Go in and sit with him."

"Where are you going to be?" I asked.

"Upstairs."

"Why?"

She yanked me toward her and spoke through gritted teeth: "Because I wasn't expecting him, and I need to change out of these awful, smelly work clothes. I'm embarrassed beyond words right now. Please be a kind hostess while I make myself presentable." She pushed me toward the living room and announced in a cheerier voice, "If you'll both excuse me for a moment . . ."

She hurried up the rest of the stairs. A smell of grease and perspiration so thick I could almost see it lingered in her wake.

I headed into the living room and plopped myself in the

rocking chair across from Julius. "Why are you here?"

"Why do you sound upset?"

"I just want to know what you want."

He tossed his hat on a cushion beside him and sank back into Aunt Eva's flowery ivory sofa—a tiny piece of Victorian doll's furniture compared to his long body. As usual, he wore no mask, and a pale and worn appearance soured his entire face. His eyes were bloodshot and his pupils pinprick small, as they were the night before.

"You should be nice to me," he said. "I brought you something."

I turned my attention to the fruit crate sitting at his feet. "Oranges?"

"No." He hoisted the crate with a grunt, carted it over to me, and dropped down on one knee by my side. A chalky flavor numbed my tongue—a feeling emanating from Julius that I couldn't identify.

"I brought you Stephen's books," he said.

I opened my mouth to react, but no words found their way to my lips—only a shaky flutter of air.

He placed a leather-bound volume on my lap: Jules Verne's *Around the World in Eighty Days*. The cover's rich mahogany scent filled my nose, bringing me back to rain-soaked Oregon afternoons spent with Stephen.

A second book followed: *The Mysterious Island*, the novel Stephen had been reading the day we last saw each other. I touched the embossed title and remembered how the book had rested on his knee when he sat at the bottom of the staircase. I smelled briny sea air and heard the low thunder of waves crashing against the beach across from his house, as well as the ticking of the grandfather clock with the pockmarked moon face and the swinging brass pendulum.

A tear burned down my cheek. Julius pulled a handkerchief out of his coat pocket and offered it to me.

"Thank you." I wiped my eyes.

He rose from the floor and sat on the little round end table next to me. "I know how close the two of you were since you were children." His chilly hand settled around my shoulder. "And I've been thinking quite a bit about what you said after last night's séance. I don't think you're crazy."

I kept my eyes on Stephen's books.

"Mary Shelley," said Julius as he moved his fingers to the back of my hand, "will you please help me remove his spirit from my house?"

Those words got me to look straight at him. "Do you see him, too?"

"No, but I hear him. In his room. Sometimes, even in the middle of the day, the floorboards groan, and I know it's him."

"Is that what those noises were when I last posed for you—when you and Gracie kept looking up at the ceiling in horror and your mother got hurt?"

"I—yes, I think it was." His hand trembled against mine. "I can't even sleep in that house anymore. I want to move, but I need money."

"Are you planning to sell the house?"

"I can't. My stepfather left the property to Stephen and my mother."

"What about all the money from the spirit photographs?"

He snorted. "I'm not a fellow who saves up his nickels and dimes. I have an expensive image to maintain. Customers to impress. Hobbies . . ."

"Then don't complain about being stuck there. Maybe if you hadn't tossed out Stephen's photographs or hurt him—"

"I told you before, brothers fight. That's just how it is."

"You've destroyed his work. He called you violent and a fraud."

"I called him meddlesome and spoiled. It's all a matter of perspective."

"I'm going to see if Aunt Eva needs anything—"

He clasped my elbow before I could step past his big feet. "Don't go. I'm sorry. I just want you to help him. Please, Mary Shelley. Put him to rest."

"Why do you even care?" I asked. "You were never nice to him."

"That doesn't mean I want him to suffer. He was just a kid, for Christ's sake. He . . ." Julius's voice cracked, and grief's sharp sting overpowered the ice-cold numbness on my tongue. "He did a stupid thing by running off to war when he could barely even put up a fight here at home." He closed his eyes and clenched his jaw, and I could feel his battle against tears in his squeeze of my arm. "Jesus, look at me." He shook his head and let out a pained laugh. "Who knew that little pip-squeak of a brother would ever make me cry?"

I removed his hand from my elbow with a delicate motion. "I am trying to help him. If you have even the smallest inkling why he thinks birds were killing him overseas . . ."

"Germans shot him. There were no birds."

"But something terrified and hurt him before he died. And I bet he won't ever leave this earth until he understands what happened to him."

"He died in combat. What more does he need to know?" Julius pulled his handkerchief out of my hand and wiped his eyes.

"Maybe he's like Hamlet's father's ghost, needing justice for his murder." I rubbed my arms to fight off an outbreak of gooseflesh. "I still think he may have been a prisoner of war. He seems mistreated—tortured."

The taste of Julius's grief dissolved in my mouth, replaced by numbness again, as if he were retreating from pain.

"What else could possibly help him feel at peace, Julius?" I asked. "You lived with him all his life. What do *you* think I could do to convince him to move on?"

Julius lifted his lashes and regarded me with his deep brown eyes. A strange look of serenity washed over his face, and his breathing softened. "I just heard him."

"What?" I cocked my head and listened for whispers, but I heard only Aunt Eva's footsteps bustling around upstairs. "Are you sure you didn't just—"

"Mary Shelley . . ." Julius took me by the elbow and guided me down to the rocking chair. His voice dropped to a conspiratorial whisper. "He said . . . he knows you threw that photograph into the bay."

I froze.

Julius leaned close, his forehead a few short inches from mine. "He said he wants another picture of the two of you together. Before he goes. That's what he needs."

"How . . . ?" I swallowed. "How do you know I threw that photo in the bay? Did Aunt Eva—"

"He just told me. You shouldn't have done that. It upset him. He thinks you don't want to remember him."

"No . . . he doesn't think that. It's those birds—"

"He wants a photograph."

I searched Julius's face for signs of trickery, but he kept his eyes on mine. His stoic expression showed me nothing.

He gathered both my hands in his freezing palms. "I'll capture you together one last time. I'll give you a copy of it to keep somewhere special. And then you can tell him good-bye."

"But . . ."

"Mary Shelley." He smiled in a pitying sort of way. "What did Stephen want more than anything else in the world? What made his heart beat fastest?"

My face flushed. I turned my eyes toward the floorboards. "To be as skilled a photographer as his father."

"No. You know that's not the right answer." Julius nudged his knee against mine. "He wanted you."

I shut my eyes to stave off more tears.

Julius bent close again, his breath brushing against my cheek. "He doesn't want you to ever forget him."

"I wouldn't."

"Help him. With a photograph. Invite his spirit into another picture with you. Prove you'll always remember him."

"But . . . he hated spirit photography."

"Please, Mary Shelley." Julius strengthened his hold on my hands. "I just need one . . . last . . . picture."

I looked him in the eye again, and this time I saw something wild and unstable staring back. "Wait . . ." I squirmed. "What's all this about, Julius? Why are you really here?"

"It's about you helping Stephen and me get out of that godforsaken place."

"How could one photograph get *you* out of that house?"

"I'm going to send it to a contest. A scientific publication is looking for proof of the existence of spirits." His eyes gleamed like a child's on Christmas morning. "And they're offering a prize of two thousand dollars for solid evidence."

"No." I pulled my hands out of his. "I'm not helping you get any money."

"I'd give you a fair percentage of the prize money if you brought him to me." He clasped my shoulder. "I bet we could produce solid evidence—a photograph of Stephen that would make the judges' scientific eyes pop with fear and awe and respect."

"No!" I shot to my feet. "Absolutely not. Cripes, Julius, I

thought you were here because you truly cared about your brother."

"I do care. If you turn down this opportunity, you're the one abandoning him, not me. Why would you do that to him? Why would you let him suffer?"

I drew in my breath to give myself confidence. "I'm sure one of the reasons he's unsettled inside your house is because he hates what you did to his father's studio."

Julius shrank back, so I summoned the courage to go further. "Stephen said your drug abuse and fraudulence probably led to his father's heart failure. Maybe he wants you to stop lying and to stop doctoring those photographs."

He absorbed my words for another silent moment. His eyes watered and reddened, and he seemed on the verge of either bawling or erupting with rage. He stood up and towered above me at his full, intimidating height. "I am not a fraud. I do not doctor photographs. I did not drive my stepfather to an early grave."

"But you're a drug addict."

"You don't know what you're talking about."

"I can tell just by being next to you." I breathed in again, the chalky scent coating my throat like novocaine. "You're numb. Maybe if you sobered up, you wouldn't feel the need to prey upon innocent people."

He grabbed both of my arms and lifted me to my toes. "You try living with your brother's ghost and sending your mother away half out of her mind. You try growing up with a stepfather who loved your brother more than you and tell me you wouldn't touch one speck of a substance that takes away the pain."

"You're hurting me."

"Don't ever accuse me of being an addict and a fraud again."

"Let go of me."

"I came to you for help." He shook me. "I came to you as the brother of a boy who loved you."

"Let go of her!" Aunt Eva ran up behind Julius and pulled on his shoulders.

"Leave me alone, Eva."

"What are you doing to her?"

"Leave me alone you stupid, clingy woman!" He let go of me and shoved my aunt to the floor.

The room fell silent, aside from my rapid breathing and the clicking of Oberon's talons as he paced his perch.

Aunt Eva slowly propped herself up on her elbows. She was wearing a brown silk dress, and she smelled powdered and perfumed. Little tortoiseshell combs dangled from stray blond strands. Her glasses hung cockeyed on her nose. She wasn't wearing her flu mask.

"Get out of my house." She pushed herself up to a standing position and straightened her spectacles. "I don't ever want you near my niece again."

"No—I can't. I need her to help me!"

"I said get out." She charged at her wall of photographs,

yanked down the picture with the white-draped figure and me, and pitched the frame at Julius's head. He deflected it with his arm, and the frame crashed to the wooden floor in a shower of glass.

He backed away. "You're crazy."

She grabbed the framed article with his soldier spirit photos and threw that at him as well. He jumped away and let the glass shatter at his feet.

"I'm calling the police if you don't get out of here this minute!" She pulled down another photo—the one with Uncle Wilfred's spirit. "I'm sure Mary Shelley has marks on her arms from your fingers."

The third frame whacked him in the temple. She then pelted him with his hat.

He grabbed the fedora, yelled obscenities I'd never even heard before, and bounded down the hall. He must have swung the front door closed with all his might, for the house shook and the rest of the photos on Aunt Eva's living room wall were knocked crooked.

Aunt Eva exhaled in a way that sounded like a sob. She put her hands on her hips and hung her head, taking deep breaths that wheezed from the depths of her lungs.

I hesitated between comforting her and cleaning up the glass.

"Are you hurt, Mary Shelley?" Her voice turned choppy. "Do you need a doctor?"

"No. You got to him before he could hurt me too badly."

"I can't believe—I don't understand." She tromped out of the room and into the kitchen.

I followed after her.

With her back to me, she opened the surface of her tan cookstove, lit a match, and stirred up the smoldering coals like she was jabbing the poker into Julius's heart.

"I can cook, if you'd like," I said.

She kept digging at the coals.

I rubbed my arms, still feeling Julius's finger marks throbbing beneath my sleeves. "I'm sorry about what he did to you."

"I wasted nearly a year of my life wanting that man. I spent Wilfred's last months hoping Julius would be my chance to have someone who wouldn't waste away and die on me. I had no idea he thought so little of me that he could come over and bully us like we were nothing. Why was he hurting you?"

"We were arguing about Stephen."

She shook her head and slammed the stovetop closed. "It's my fault for always pushing you at him. It's my fault for allowing you to see your childhood friend again. I could have saved us both so much heartbreak if I hadn't been swept away by—" She wiped her wet cheeks with a dishcloth. "And here I am, twenty-six years old, with no husband or children of my own."

"I'm surprised you'd still want children after dealing with me."

She sputtered a small laugh. "But I do. And I—I lost my husband just as I was starting to age. I'm not pretty like you and your mother. I'll never find someone to love me again."

"You are pretty, Aunt Eva, even though you never seem to think so. And you're not old. My mother didn't give birth to me until she was thirty."

"But she died when she gave birth to you."

"Because of severe bleeding that had nothing to do with her age. There's still time for children. Isn't it amazing that right now you have the opportunity to head downtown in trousers and short hair to build ships—to join in some of the same adventures as men?"

She blew her nose into the dishcloth. "A job doesn't hold you when you're lonely. It doesn't comfort you when a killer flu comes barreling into town."

I walked over and placed my hand on her smooth, silk-covered shoulder. "I'm here for you, though. We'll take care of each other."

At the hospital my touch had soothed her, and again she relaxed under my palm. She faced me with eyes swollen with tears. "Are you really communicating with Stephen? Did you honestly hear him and feel him in that séance room?"

I pursed my lips and nodded. "Yes."

"Are you sure you're not just imagining him? I know you're desperately lonely, too. You have no friends here. You have no father and no school, which I'm sure can cause—"

"It's truly him, I swear. He seems to need my help in under-standing his death. Otherwise, I doubt he'll ever rest."

Her mouth quivered. "Do you believe he's been with you anywhere else besides that séance room and his funeral?"

I lowered my eyes.

"Mary Shelley, where do you think you've encountered him?" She gulped. "In this house?"

I nodded and met her gaze. "He comes to me at night. I've seen him. I've felt him. I think someone did something terrible to him."

A deep groove of concern formed above the bridge of her nose.

"Don't be afraid of him," I said. "He doesn't seem to want to do any harm. He's just scared. I think between the war and the flu, no one's going to escape getting haunted. We live in a world so horrifying, it frightens even the dead."

She left my side and grabbed an onion and her knife from the worktable. "Go clean up the broken glass while I fix supper. Let's put the subjects of death and the Embers brothers to rest for the evening. I've had enough for one day."

I did as she asked, for the kitchen was drenched with the taste of heartbreak, and I could barely breathe.

19
A BLOODSTAINED SKY

I BROUGHT *THE MYSTERIOUS ISLAND* TO BED WITH ME THAT night. My room sweltered with a heat unthinkable for an Oregon girl in fall, so I wore my sleeveless summer nightgown made of batiste and embroidered lace and stretched out on my bed beneath the oil lamp's light.

Part One, I read silently to myself, *Dropped from the Clouds*. Jules Verne and his brilliant writing transported me into a hot-air balloon that careened toward a South Pacific island on the winds of a catastrophic storm. The lingering pain of finger marks on my bare arms faded the further I dove into the story, and the ache of missing Stephen and my father softened to a point I could almost tolerate. Warmth spread like candle wax through my blood. I fell asleep ten chapters in, with Stephen's book squished between my cheek and the pillow.

An awful dream visited me. A crow as large as a bald eagle sat on my chest. I pushed at its lung-crushing body to get it off me, but it cawed and flapped its black wings and sliced my skin with its snapping beak.

"Don't!" I yelled with enough force to pull myself out of sleep.

My eyes opened.

I gasped.

Stephen was on me—not a bird.

I regained my wits, pushed him off, and crawled backward to the corner of my bed. "Stay back. Don't come any closer."

He lunged toward me, so I stood upright on the mattress and shoved my spine against the wall. "Get back, Stephen!"

"Don't push me away." He clutched my hips and tugged me down.

"Let go of me! You can't get close to me the way you did last night."

"I need you, Shell." He pulled me to my knees. "Come closer."

"No." I shoved him with enough fear-fueled strength to send him falling backward on his elbows. "You're pulling me into your darkness when you get too close." I stood again. "You have to stay back if you want me to help you."

He remained on his back and watched me with eyes black and fearful. He wore that white undershirt again, and I could see an unhealthy thinness in his arms and stomach.

His cheekbones had become more prominent since April.

"I see red marks on your arms," he said. "They're killing you, too."

"I'm all right, Stephen. Just scoot back a few feet so I can think clearly."

He kept staring at Julius's marks on my skin.

"Scoot back if you want to stay with me," I repeated. "You need to listen to what I say so we can keep each other safe. Do you understand?"

He edged backward a foot.

"Do you promise not to come any closer? Look me in the eye."

He did as I asked, and a small spark of the old Stephen inhabited his brown irises again. I could still see the handsome boy I loved inside that changed, haunted person.

"Will you stay right there?" I asked.

He nodded.

"You promise?"

He nodded again.

"Talk to me, Stephen, so we can make sense of the ugly things and send them away." I swallowed. "Tell me about France."

He dropped his gaze, and his photographs behind him shook with an unnerving *tap, tap, tap, tap, tap* against the wall.

"Last night at the séance you asked me to stop you from going either there or to your house," I said. "What parts of the war do you experience?"

"I'm not talking about France."

I lowered myself to a kneeling position. "I need you to tell me what happened so I can help you get some rest. What do you see?"

The picture frames trembled harder.

"Tell me, Stephen."

"Trenches flooded with rainwater. Mud. Filth. Gas masks." He sat upright and pulled his knees to his chest. "Blood-soaked bodies hanging on barbed wire. Artillery shells whistling and screaming overhead. Rats the size of cats crawling over me. Flashes of light that bring out the huge, dark birds."

My flesh went cold. "Tell me more about the birds."

"I don't know where they come from." He buried his face against his knees. "But they're like no creature I've ever seen. I can't tell how many there are. They show up, and I expect them to peck out my eyes, but they just keep watching me and killing me, and they never go away."

"How are they killing you?"

His body shook as if something cold had surrounded him. "It's dark and shadowy. I'm struggling too much to see them through the smoke and flashing lights. My wrists are tied to something. They stick the tube of a copper funnel down my throat and gag me."

"Were you tortured over there? Did the Germans capture you?"

"I don't know."

I inhaled a gust of fiery air. "The air burns whenever you're with me. What do you smell when you're with these birds?"

"Fire, yes. And those goddamned flashes of light explode over and over and over and over."

His lightning photograph whacked against the floor, saved from shattering by the braided rug.

I heard a movement in Aunt Eva's bedroom down the hall—a squeak of her mattress. I held my breath, counted to twenty, and turned my attention back to Stephen. My voice dropped to scarcely above a whisper. "What do you see when you're in your bedroom?"

He lifted his face, his eyes dim and weary. "A bloodstained sky."

"In your bedroom?"

"Yes. And the closed door and windows that won't let me out."

"You feel trapped in your bedroom, then?"

"Yes."

"Is your brother ever there?"

"No, just the birdmen, when it's dark."

"Birdmen? They're part man?"

"I don't know. It's dark. They've got hands and beaks."

"You see them in your room? Not just on the battlefield?"

"I don't know if it's my room or not. It's hot from all that light . . ." He brought his hand to his left temple.

"Are you all right, Stephen?"

He winced. "It hurts my head."

"What does?"

Mr. Muse's frame banged hard enough to make a dent in the wall.

"Oh, God." He opened his eyes. "I want to shoot them."

"Please stop that knocking sound. Aunt Eva will hear you."

"You've got to keep them from getting at your eyes."

"There aren't any birds here, Stephen. Listen—your brother gave me some of your books, and I can feel the warmth you experienced when you read them. I wonder if going inside your house and touching anything left over from your time in France—"

"No! Stay away from that house."

"I can't go to France, but I can get into your bedroom."

"No. Don't go anywhere near there. If they're there, they'll take your beautiful eyes."

"How am I supposed to help you, then?" I raised my voice. "Tell me. What am I supposed to do?"

I heard Aunt Eva running across the floor of her room. I turned toward my door and heard the second frame clatter to the ground. By the time I leapt over to the pictures to hang them back on the wall, Stephen was gone.

Aunt Eva walked in just as I placed the lightning bolt image back on its nail. I saw the expression on her face when she caught my fingers wrapped around his photograph—the slump of her shoulders, the sudden downturn of her mouth. The previous glow of awe in her eyes when I'd mentioned communicating with the spirit world had now dimmed to deep concern.

She didn't say a word about Stephen. She told me to go back to bed and left my room.

The compass's needle followed me again. The smoke and frustration in the air lifted. I tucked myself beneath my blankets, but I couldn't sleep until the early hours of the morning, when the crickets stopped chirping and the first strains of light glowed through the lace of my curtains. I could only lie there and think of a white, bloodstained sky and Stephen's insistence that he was being watched and murdered by those hideous dark birds.

20

PAUL SPITZ

WITH MY MASK TIED TIGHT AND MY BOOTS LACED FIRMLY
in double knots, I returned to the Red Cross House in the
morning, an hour after Aunt Eva left for work.

I grabbed *The Adventures of Tom Sawyer* from the donated
book pile and headed back into the throng of bandaged men
and twittering canaries, the latter of which set my nerves on
edge with their erratic, fussy, twitchy bird movements.

"Are you all right?" asked a woman's voice.

I pulled my eyes away from a cage of yellow birds and
found the Red Cross nurse with the amber cat eyes standing
next to me. "Yes. Why?"

"You've been staring at that cage for at least two minutes.
One of the men who's been eagerly awaiting the end of *Tom*

Sawyer called me over and asked what you were doing."

"Oh." I blinked away a foggy haze muddling my head. "I'm sorry. I didn't sleep well last night. I'm sure I'll be fine once I sit down and start reading again."

"If this is too much for you—"

"I'll be fine. I'm happy to be here again. I want to help."

Her eyes seemed to ask, *Are you sure about that?* I gave her a confident nod and watched her walk away.

Then my attention wandered to the part of the room where Jones and Carlos had rested the day before, and I half expected to hear myself called Aunt Gertie again.

Carlos sat in his same leather chair, reading another old issue of the *Saturday Evening Post.*

The seat beside him was empty.

Fear twisted inside my gut. Had Jones killed himself?

I strode over to Carlos, whose dark eyes shimmered above his mask when he saw me. "Good morning, *querida.* You've come back to us."

"Of course I came back." I nodded to the empty chair. "Where's Jones?"

"Jones?" He knitted his eyebrows like he didn't understand. "Oh, the joker there. That wasn't his real name. I just called him that because so many of you gringos are named Jones."

"Oh." I glanced around the room. "Well, where is he? Is he sitting somewhere else today?"

"He's in the influenza ward. They found him burning up with a fever in the middle of the night."

"What?"

"A nurse told me this morning."

I hugged *Tom Sawyer* to my chest and clawed the cloth cover. Tears pricked at my eyes.

"Don't cry for him, *querida*. He was kind of a bastard."

"I'm not crying for him specifically." I wiped my eyes with my fingers. "I don't know. Maybe I am."

"He might not die. Not everyone does."

"I know."

An awful silence passed between us, which made Jones's chair seem all the emptier.

"I heard you say something about a dead soldier yesterday." Carlos reached his hand toward me across the armrest. "Did you lose a sweetheart?"

I nodded. "His funeral was only three days ago." I sniffed and wrapped my fingers around Carlos's. "Oh, this is silly. I'm supposed to be the one comforting all of you. That Red Cross nurse is going to give me the boot at any second."

"Shh. It's all right." He gave my hand a squeeze. "I lost my sweetheart, too. She did not die, but she took one look at my missing legs and ran away. I have not seen her since I got back to San Diego in early October."

"I'm sorry." I sniffed again. "Maybe she'll get braver with time."

"Maybe." He shrugged. "I don't really think so, though." He gave my fingers another squeeze—a gentle gesture that reminded me I wasn't standing there all alone in the world.

"Where was your boy from, *querida*? Around here?"

"Coronado. He was supposed to finish his studies at Coronado High School last spring, but he enlisted instead."

"Oh, I wonder if he knew that Coronado fellow who's convalescing here."

"What? Did you—" My lips couldn't function for a moment. "There—there's a person from Coronado here?"

"You may have seen him—the poor *hombre* missing the left side of his body. I remember Jones making another one of his terrible jokes about the boy. 'That Coronado bugger is *all right*,' he'd say whenever anyone wheeled him by."

I remembered the boy—the sleeping one from the day before whose head was a mess of gauze. *That one's in the arms of Madame Morphine,* the man with the eye patch had said before asking for his cookie.

"Do . . . do you think . . ." My tongue struggled to keep up with my thoughts. "Do you think he might have known my friend Stephen?"

"I don't know." Carlos let go of my hand. "Go ask him yourself."

"Are you sure you don't mind me going over there right now?"

"I'm not going to chase after you." He snickered and gestured with his chin toward his missing legs.

"Thank you so much for telling me about him." I pulled down my mask and kissed the top of Carlos's head through his thick black hair. "Thank you, thank you."

"You're welcome, *querida*. Thank you for not having huge warts and buckteeth."

I slid my mask back up and took off across the room, slowing my pace when I realized how jarring it would be for the Coronado boy to wake up to the crashing of boots against tile.

I found him in the same chair as the day before—a mangled young man who could have been Stephen's age. His head seemed to have caved in on one side and now hid beneath all those crisscrossing bandages, including his left eye, which may or may not have still resided in its socket. The left sleeve of his button-down shirt lay empty and deflated, as did the left leg of his tan trousers. All I could see of his actual body was a hand, a pale eyebrow, and an open right eye the color of green tea.

He drew in his breath beneath his flu mask. "Oh, sweet Jesus." He sounded like he could only talk out of the right side of his mouth; each *s* that he spoke whistled through his teeth. "I thought I was a goner."

"I'm sorry I scared you."

"You looked like an angel." He took a few shallow breaths. "I don't mean that in a flirtatious way. You honestly looked like a golden beam of light. I thought you were going to take me away."

I shook my head. "No, I'm just a person." The chair where the man with the eye patch had been the day before was empty, so I pulled it closer to the boy and lowered myself into its cushion with a squeak of leather. "Are you in much pain?"

"They keep me on morphine. I'm too far gone to care about the pain when I'm doped up like this." He chuckled a little. "It's nighttime that's the worse. That's when everything aches and the nightmares come breathing down my neck."

"I'm sorry to hear that. I've heard the others talk about the nightmares, too. I'm sure it's not easy." I found my hands shaking. "Umm . . . look . . . someone told me you were from Coronado."

"Yes." He pushed himself up a little straighter. "That's where I've lived all my life. Except for my time in the army, of course."

"Did you go to the high school there?"

"Yes. Good old Coronado High."

"Did you know Stephen Embers?"

"Stephen?" He nodded. "Yes, definitely. We've been friends since he first moved to the island."

My heart beat faster. "D-d-did you see him in France?"

"Yeah, a group of us from school joined up at the same time." He cocked his head at me and raised his visible eyebrow, as if he suddenly recognized me, even with my mask covering most of my face. "Say . . . what's your name?"

My entire name counted too much to hide any part of it. "Mary Shelley Black."

"Ohhh . . ." The soldier's eye brightened. "No wonder you look so familiar. Stephen pulled out that photograph of you all the time."

"He did?"

"I was there when he first got it in the mail, and boy, you would have thought you had sent him a pile of gold from the way he reacted." He held his chest and took a longer break to catch up with his breathing.

"Are you all right?" I asked.

"Sorry. It's sometimes hard . . . to get the words out." His labored speech sounded like it was tiring him, and every *s* whistled worse than before, but he kept going. "I was just going to add that Stephen wedged your photo inside his helmet when we were down in the trenches. He mooned over it—when he was feeling well. He told the rest of us boys you were the prettiest and smartest girl in the world."

"He said that?"

"I was even"—the exposed section of the boy's forehead turned pink—"a little jealous of him."

I blushed as well, and smiled so much the strings of my mask tautened enough to hurt. My eyes smarted with tears, but I snitfed and held myself together for the sake of Stephen's friend.

"How's he doing?" asked the boy.

My blood drained to my toes. "What do you mean?"

"Have you seen him yet? Or did they put him in a hospital on the East Coast first? They said that might happen."

My eyes narrowed in confusion. "Weren't you there when it happened? Stephen died in battle in the beginning of October."

"October?" He shook his head. "No, that's not possible. He wasn't even overseas in October."

I clutched the armrest. "Pardon?"

"They had to send him home."

"Alive?"

"Yes."

"When? Why?"

He answered in a tone so hushed I had to balance myself on the last two inches of the chair to understand him. "It was pretty bad. I hate to be the one to tell you."

"Please, just tell me."

The boy swallowed. "Stephen sort of . . . well . . . he lost his mind over there in the trenches. Got to the point where he couldn't even move anymore. He'd just huddle in the mud, shaking. They tried to help him in one of the field hospitals once—examined him to see if he was faking. But then they sent him straight back into battle . . . and he got worse than ever."

I folded my hands to conceal how much they jittered. "What did they do to him then?"

"They discharged him and shipped him home. He wasn't the only one like that. Hell—excuse my language—but hell, most of us went a little off our rockers over there. You couldn't help it. Some of the fellows' bodies and brains just stopped working right. Scary as heck." The soldier rubbed the right side of his bandaged forehead and wheezed a little. "Stephen was so bad off I didn't think anything could fix him. It was like something inside him broke." He turned his eye back to me and looked like a lost pup. "You don't know where they took him once he got back to the States, then?"

I shook my head. "I don't know anything. His brother said he died a hero's death over in France. He never said anything about him coming home."

"I wonder if he died during transport. Maybe it was the flu. The family could be misinformed. The army gets antsy about the men whose minds leave them."

"He died somewhere, somehow. I went to his funeral."

Stephen's friend got quiet. I snapped out of my shock enough to realize I'd just informed a drastically injured boy his close friend was dead.

"I'm so sorry I had to tell you that news," I said.

"He was a good fellow." Tears blurred his visible eye. "A really good fellow."

"Yes." I nodded. "He is. Was."

"Some of the other soldiers gave me trouble because my father was born in Germany and my last name's Spitz. They called me slurs like Kraut and Boche. But Stephen . . ." The boy's eye brightened a moment. "He would tell them all to shut their damned mouths. Oh . . . sorry . . ." He lowered his head. "There goes my language again."

"It's all right. I've heard words far worse than *damned*—sometimes from Stephen."

The soldier wiped away a tear and sniffed. "Oh, Christ, what a waste." He shook his head and squeezed his eye closed. "Such a waste. I hope he went quickly and didn't have to keep suffering." He leaned his elbow on the chair's arm and rested his head against his fist. Another tear spilled from his eye and glistened against his mask.

"What's your name?" I placed my hand around his upper arm, feeling the soft satin of his sleeve and the lack of nourished flesh beneath.

His meager muscle relaxed beneath my fingers. "Paul."

"I hope you heal soon, Paul. I hope the nightmares stop bothering you and your pain leaves your wounds."

I moved to take my hand off him, but he tensed again and said, "Can you keep touching me a little longer? Again, I don't mean that in a flirtatious way, especially now that I know you're Stephen's girl. But . . . you remind me of something I experienced after that shell went off next to me."

"I do?"

He nodded. "I thought I'd died for a while and went somewhere peaceful. I'd forgotten what that felt like until you touched me."

I held his arm again and watched his eyelid fall.

"Can I ask you one last question, Paul?"

"Yes."

"Did Stephen ever seem to be afraid of birds when he was over there?"

Paul didn't answer, and for a minute I thought he'd fallen asleep. I gave up waiting for a response and shifted my legs to get more comfortable, when he drew in his breath and replied, "None of us liked the crows. They ate us when we died. They hovered on the edges of the trenches and stared down at us, watching us, waiting for us to get shot or bombed. Sometimes we even had to fight them off the boys who weren't all the way dead."

My stomach tightened. "Oh. God. I'm so sorry."

"Why do you ask?"

"Just a strange dream I've been having. I'm sorry I brought up such an unpleasant subject. Please rest now, and heal."

"Thank you. I'm sorry to be so blunt. I think . . . I've forgotten . . . how to speak in polite—" His tongue sounded like it had grown too heavy to finish his sentence. His chin sank forward on his chest, and he dozed off.

We sat like that for at least a quarter hour, amid the restless chirps of the flitting canaries, the tinkle of teacups on society women's trays, and the soft swish of cards flipping at the poker game several feet away. Paul's body relaxed until his gentle breathing indicated he was in a deep sleep. Quiet snores snuck out from beneath his mask.

I remained next to him, touching him, holding on to a tangible piece of Stephen's life, haunted by his words. And even when I moved along to the other men and finished reading *Tom Sawyer*, all I could think about—it consumed my entire being—was the image of Stephen shivering in the shadows of hungry dark birds while his mind crumbled.

21

THE COMPASS PHENOMENON

SOMETHING MOVED ON AUNT EVA'S PORCH.

I snuck up the front path with noiseless footfalls and craned my neck to see beyond the post that blocked my view. I could make out the shape of a crouching person.

"Who is that?" I asked.

The person shot up with a cry of surprise, and I spotted a pair of large round spectacles balanced above a sagging flu mask. Brown hair grew from the top of the stranger's head like a thicket of grass.

"Is that Grant?" I shielded my eyes from the setting sunlight. "Stephen's cousin?"

"That's right." Grant slunk down the porch steps.

"What are you doing here?"

"Julius wanted me to bring you something." He nodded backward to the porch.

"Why didn't he bring it himself?"

"He's busy at his studio." Grant stuck his hands in his pockets and slithered away from the house. "Plus I think he's afraid of you."

"Julius isn't afraid of anyone." I grabbed Grant's arm before he could dart away. "Hey, wait. I need to ask you something."

"What?"

"I just heard something about Stephen's last days in France."

Nervous air pulsated off him. "Why don't you chat with Stephen about it instead?" He tried pulling away from me. "You're the one who's supposed to be summoning him."

I tugged him closer. "Does the family know Stephen was sent home alive?"

His breathing quickened.

"Did he make it home, Grant? Tell me. Do you know what happened to him?"

"Look, Shell—"

"Don't call me Shell. Only Stephen could call me that."

"Look, Frankenstein . . ." He spoke so close to my face he would have spit on me if we weren't wearing masks. "My mother choked to death from the flu right in front of my eyes five weeks ago. My father's drifting around somewhere in the middle of enemy waters with the U.S. Navy. And my sister lost her hair from a fever so high I can't believe she's not buried like our ma." He yanked himself free of me. "Gracie and I are just trying to survive on our own right now. We don't need anyone pestering us about us working in Julius's studio."

"I'm not pestering you about Julius's studio. I'm just asking about Stephen—"

"Stephen's a dead war hero, all right? Leave it at that. I don't know who's telling you otherwise, but they've got their story wrong."

He turned and walked away.

"A friend who was with him overseas told me otherwise," I called after him when he reached the front sidewalk. "Stephen didn't die in battle."

Grant stopped with his shoulders hiked as high as his chin.

"How did he die, Grant? If you know, please tell me."

He stayed stone-still with his back curved into a lazy C and his eyes directed at the sidewalk in front of him. "You ever heard of shell shock?"

I flinched at the question. I had read about that condition at the library. It could have described what Paul told me about Stephen.

"That's what they're calling the psychological trauma from the war, isn't it?" I asked.

"It's a cowardly way to behave. I've heard the British execute their soldiers who get it, because of the shame."

I wrapped my arms around myself and strove to keep my

voice from breaking. "Is our army doing that to our men, too? Is that what happened to Stephen?"

Grant shook his head, still speaking to the ground. "I'm thinking his friend is the one who's shell-shocked. The friend who's lying to you. Stephen died in battle." He squinted up at me through the sun-bright lenses of his glasses. "If you really are seeing his ghost, spooky Frankenstein girl, ask him yourself. I bet he'll swear he's still over in France, picking off Germans."

Before I could even think to respond, Grant hustled down the sidewalk to his black Model T and leapt into the driver's seat. The engine popped and rattled as it sputtered to life, and he sped away in an oily cloud of exhaust.

I watched him careen around the bend with a squeal of tires before I climbed up to the porch to see what he had left.

A gold Nabisco Sugar Wafers tin sat by the front door, an envelope bearing my name resting on its lid. I ripped open the paper and tugged out a note written on letterhead from Julius's studio.

Dear Mary Shelley,

I apologize for my behavior last night. Grief for my brother and concern for my mother are bringing out the worst in me. You're right, I bury my pain in ways I shouldn't, but I swear to you I'm an honest businessman who is doing nothing to tarnish the good name of my stepfather's studio.

I am giving you something of Stephen's I found in his room. You seem the best person to have it. Perhaps it will make a complete set.

Please come to Coronado for another photograph as soon as you can. You know in your heart it would help us all. It is the right thing to do.

Yours with sincerest apologies,
Julius

I knelt and removed the box's lid.

In the golden tin lay Stephen's name and address, scrawled in black ink across a pile of pastel envelopes in my own handwriting. All the letters I'd ever written to Stephen since his move to San Diego—the companions to his own letters from the summer of 1914 to early 1918—were tucked inside the cookie tin. I sifted through the envelopes and postcards and heard the sound of our shared lives in the crisp rustle of paper.

"It's just a bribe for a spirit photograph," I whispered to myself. "Just a bribe. Don't you dare go running over there, Shell. Don't do it."

I snapped the lid closed, rose to my feet, and braced myself to be greeted by the black-and-white bird that dwelled within Aunt Eva's walls.

"OBERON. HELLO. WHO'S THERE? OBERON."

The bird would not shut up. I slammed my bedroom door

against the nonstop whistling and squawking and set to work
mapping out what I knew.

June 29
Stephen's last letter, written from France.

Sometime between June 29 and October 1
Stephen sent home.
Taken to East Coast hospital?

Sometime between summer and October 19
Stephen loses his life.
*(Grant just mentioned executions of soldiers suffering psycho-
logical trauma. Did that happen to Stephen?)*

Saturday, October 19
Restless sounds heard above Julius's studio during my sitting.
Julius says that may have been Stephen's ghost.

Monday, October 21
*We pick up my photograph in Coronado; the picture includes
Stephen's "spirit."*
Julius tells us Stephen died a hero's death.
My lightning accident.

Tuesday, October 29
Stephen's funeral.

Seeing all the dates and pertinent information laid out on paper helped my brain feel a little more organized. Yet so many questions jumped out from the gaping holes in the diagram. The unexplained pieces remained just as unexplained as before.

A siren howled outside, blaring loud and close enough for me to abandon my notes and look out a front window in Aunt Eva's bedroom. A black ambulance stopped in front of the house next door, and the neighbors' yard exploded into a scramble of stretchers, officers, and hysterical family members who rushed about in the fading daylight.

Out of the chaos charged my running and screaming aunt.

"The flu is next door!" came her muffled yell from behind the closed pane. "Oh, dear Lord, the flu is next door. Mary Shelley!"

I hurried to meet her downstairs.

"The flu is next door!"

"I know."

"What are we going to do?" She pushed the door closed and locked it tight, as if she were able to barricade us against germs with a dead bolt.

"Don't panic, Aunt Eva."

"It's next door!"

"I'll start boiling onions for supper. Why don't you change out of your uniform and get comfortable?"

"We'll wash ourselves in the onion water." Her eyes bulged. "I want to smell the onion fumes in my hair."

"That sounds fine." I patted her shoulder. "Go get changed."

She clambered upstairs and climbed out of her grubby work clothes while I lit the gaslights and cookstove with more matches that smelled like Stephen's funeral.

When my aunt tromped back downstairs, she wore an apron and carried a sponge, and she insisted we scrub the insides of all the windows with hot water. I stuffed salt up my nose at her urging and wiped down the kitchen windowpanes while the scent of boiling onions overpowered the air. My stomach cramped and groaned.

Someone knocked on the front door, and only then did I remember my invitation to Mr. Darning to come over and view the compass phenomenon. I thundered down the main hall to get to him before my aunt, but she was already opening the door.

"Who's there?" asked Oberon. "Hello. Hello."

"Oh. Mr. Darning." Aunt Eva wiped her hands on her apron. "This is a surprise. Please, come in—quickly." She grabbed the photographer's arm and yanked him across the threshold. "The flu just hit next door. I don't want to leave the house open." She slammed the door closed and locked it tight again. "Oh, good heavens, I just washed my mask and won't be able to wear it."

"Is this a bad time?" he asked.

"Hello. Who's there?" said the blasted magpie.

I sidled up next to Aunt Eva. "I'm sorry, Mr. Darning. I forgot to tell her I invited you over."

"You invited him over?" asked my aunt.

Mr. Darning removed his hat. "She was going to show me the compass phenomenon."

Aunt Eva raised her brows. "The compass phenomenon?"

"I haven't yet mentioned my compass experiences to Aunt Eva." I backed up the stairs. "Again, I'm sorry—I've been preoccupied. I'll go get it and bring it to the living room." My feet sounded like an elephant stampede as I scrambled up to fetch Uncle Wilfred's mahogany case with the weighted brass compass mounted inside.

"Did she call you on the telephone to invite you over?" I heard Aunt Eva ask when I returned to the top steps.

"No," said Mr. Darning.

I came to a halt.

"She invited me when she came to my studio for her portrait yesterday."

Oh no.

"What?" squawked my aunt, as loud as Oberon. "She left this house?"

"Was she not supposed to?"

"No. I thought she was at home all day. Mary Shelley Black! Get down here this instant."

"I'm coming, Aunt Eva." I squeezed the compass to my chest.

She and the photographer stood together in the living room, and the glare she shot my way could have frozen the Sahara. "What were you thinking? Why don't you just go to the hospital and let flu patients cough in your mouth, get it over with? Is that what you want?"

"I'll go crazy if I just bury myself in onions at home all day. I have to get out."

"I'm going to write your father."

"Fine—write him. He'd be proud of me. I've been helping convalescing veterans at the Red Cross House."

"What?"

"Should I go?" asked Mr. Darning.

"No, please, not yet." I lugged the case over to the game table in front of the windows. "I want you to see the compass, and I want Aunt Eva to witness it, too."

With hesitation, Mr. Darning rested his brown derby hat on the sofa and approached the compass. Aunt Eva crept our way with her mouth pinched tight and her hands on her hips. Oberon whistled and squeaked.

The photographer leaned over the device and rubbed his gauze-covered chin, and I noticed he smelled like the fine leather seats of an automobile. Out the window, I could see a shiny red touring car with a foldable top parked beneath our streetlamp.

He drew a sharp breath. "Ahhh, yes. I see what you mean."

The needle pointed squarely at me.

"Ahhh, yes! This is absolutely fascinating, Miss Black. Absolutely fascinating."

"The needle even stays on me when I move." I stepped around to the right side of the table, holding out my arms as if I were walking a tightrope. Mr. Darning backed out of the way for me, and I crossed over to the left. The needle followed my movement like a devoted duckling.

Aunt Eva watched and gasped. "I had no idea that was happening. When did you discover this?"

"When I came home from the hospital."

"Hmm, I wonder . . ." Mr. Darning returned to the compass and pressed his hands against the case. "Did the lightning change your magnetic field? Or did your experience of momentarily dying—of becoming a temporary spirit, as it were—do this to you? Is your soul having trouble settling back inside your body?"

I shook my head. "I don't know. I haven't yet found any information about the otherworldly effects of getting struck by lightning."

"You say the needle also follows Stephen when you think he's around?" he asked.

Aunt Eva gasped again. "What?"

"It does." I nodded. "Once, the needle moved everywhere, like he was upset or confused. Another time it pointed to his photographs hanging on my wall."

Mr. Darning shook his head in amazement. "This is remarkable. Like MacDougall's scale experiments on the dying. I'm so impressed with all of this." He rubbed his arms and tittered like a schoolboy. "You've given me gooseflesh."

"You don't think I'm going out of my head with grief, then?" I asked.

"This needle seems to be telling us otherwise, doesn't it?" His eyes beamed at me. "Would you bring the compass to my studio Monday and let me photograph the way you affect it? Better yet, I'll bring my own compass so I know nothing's being rigged."

"But you dislike supernatural photography," said Aunt Eva.

"I dislike fakes. As with everyone else, I'd love to find proof of the survival of the spirit beyond death. Maybe Mary Shelley's body is demonstrating that the soul exists as a magnetic field." He leaned his elbows against the table and bent even closer to the apparatus. "Come to my studio Monday, say around ten o'clock in the morning, and I'll record what you're experiencing. Bring Stephen's photographs as well, and we'll see if we can attract signs of him."

"All right." I peeked at my aunt's bloodless face. "As long as Aunt Eva doesn't mind me leaving the house again."

"Let's see what the flu does to our block first. We might not even be here Monday." She massaged her forehead with her hands balled into fists. "I hate to be rude, Mr. Darning, but I'm overwhelmed by everything that's been happening and really need to feed Mary Shelley her onions."

"Please, don't let me keep you." Mr. Darning tore his eyes off the needle and fetched his hat from the sofa. "I'm sorry to interrupt your evening, but this has been remarkable. Thank you for allowing me to be a witness."

"You're welcome, Mr. Darning." I followed Aunt Eva and him to the door. "Did my other photograph reveal anything?"

"No—oh, I forgot to bring that with me. I'll give that to you on Monday as well."

"Nothing peculiar showed up, then?"

"I'm afraid not. But let's not give up. I think we're on to something here. Perhaps we'll open an unchecked door in the world of psychical research."

I smiled. "Thank you so much for coming. I feel better now that I've shown the compass to someone with your background."

We said our good-byes, and Aunt Eva allowed him to slip out a small crack in the door before she locked us up again.

She grabbed me by the sleeve and pulled me close. "You should have told me he was coming."

"I'm sorry. I've been distracted and forgot."

"That's the second day in a row a man has shown up while I look a mess."

"You look fine."

"I have salt hanging out my nose." She brushed at her nostril.

"I'm sure he understands."

"That doesn't make it any less embarrassing." She pushed me away. "I'm so furious at you for leaving this house, Mary Shelley. What is wrong with you?"

"Stephen didn't die in battle in October."

She gawked at me like I was speaking in tongues. *"What?"*

"I met one of his friends at the Red Cross House today, a boy named Paul from Coronado. He said Stephen lost his mind over in France and the army sent him home before October. Julius lied—Stephen didn't die heroically."

She closed her gaping mouth. "Well . . . perhaps the family was embarrassed about the actual cause of death. The push to have a war hero might make people say things that aren't true."

"Why was he tortured, then?"

"You don't know that he was. Maybe he caught the flu on the way home."

"He probably came home before the flu even spread. He might not have lived long enough to know about the pandemic. And that doesn't explain the birds and the burning air."

"What birds?"

"He's haunted by birds. They troubled the men in the trenches because they ate the dead."

My aunt stepped back with terror in her eyes. "You need to let this morbid fascination go, Mary Shelley."

"I told you, he's coming to me—I'm not making it up. He needs my help."

"Even if he does, how on earth is a sixteen-year-old girl supposed to help a dead young man who lost his mind in France? There's nothing you can do for him."

"That's not good enough." I stormed back into the living room to fetch the compass and accidentally knocked an elbow into Oberon's cage, which sent the bird flapping and screeching. "Oh, be quiet, you awful bird."

"Don't take out your anger on Oberon." Aunt Eva placed

protective arms over the magpie's cage. "Maybe you should speak to the minister at church. You're starting to scare me."

I hoisted the compass. "A minister would think I'm either crazy or possessed by the devil. I'm tempted to speak to Julius."

"No." She blocked my path to the stairs. "Don't you dare speak to Julius after what he did to us yesterday."

"I want him to tell me how Stephen died."

"I told you, the family might be embarrassed and too upset to discuss it. Maybe that's why Mrs. Embers lost her nerves. Sometimes the truth is too terrible to discuss. Do you truly believe I tell the girls at work the real reason why you came to live with me?"

The compass slipped in my sweaty hands, but I caught it before it fell.

"I tell my friends your father went to war," she said, "just like Stephen's family is saying he's a hero. The world is an ugly place right now, and some things need to be hidden. Don't go poking around in other people's business."

I sighed in disgust.

She squeezed my arms. "Will you promise me you won't contact Julius?"

I gritted my teeth and nodded.

"Good." She jutted out her chin. "Now let's go eat our onions. Put Wilfred's compass away and then come right back downstairs—but be careful with that. It's been in his family for years."

"I will."

Oberon jabbered and screeched as I took the compass upstairs, and my mind replayed Paul's conversation about the birds.

They ate us when we died. They hovered on the edges of the trenches and stared down at us, watching us, waiting for us to get shot or bombed.

You've got to keep them from getting at your eyes, Stephen had told me when he spoke from the shadows of my bed. *They'll take your beautiful eyes.*

At the top of the stairs, I murmured under my breath, "'And strewn in bloody fragments, to be the carrion of rats and crows.' No wonder they haunt you so much, Stephen. But did they really kill you?"

I set the compass on the end table next to my bed, and the needle jerked away.

"What . . . ?" My blood sped through my veins. "Are you . . . ?" I turned and searched the room for signs of Stephen, but saw only furniture and his crate of books.

"Are you here?" I asked. "Are you with me right now?"

The arrow swayed and shifted in every direction. Pressure mounted in the air like a kettle about to boil. Smoke engulfed my nose.

I clutched the compass's case. "I'm sorry if I scared you with that poem. Please don't be upset. Please come back and talk to me."

Something whacked against the floor.

I jumped and turned again.

At first I didn't see anything out of place. Nothing moved. Nothing rustled in the quieting, rapidly cooling atmosphere.

I poked around the room and discovered the source of the sound—Stephen's lightning bolt photograph lay facedown on the braided rug, stiff and motionless, like the dark blue bodies on the sidewalk when Julius drove us to the séance. I held my unsettled stomach and picked up the frame. The fall had cracked the wood, but the glass remained intact, as did the photograph beneath. I hung the picture back on its nail, and the anagram Stephen had written between the golden waves caught my attention:

I DO LOSE INK

"Link," I whispered, picking out the verbs. "Soil. Lend. Nod. Sink. Don. Die—"

A headache flared between my eyes. I rubbed my forehead above my nose.

"Mary Shelley," called Aunt Eva from downstairs. "Are you all right? Did something fall up there?"

"Everything's fine. I'm coming." I straightened the lightning bolt's frame and whispered, "I'll figure it out, Stephen. I'll figure everything out. I just need to think. I'm sure the answers will come."

22
LIVING AND BREATHING

DRESSED IN MY WHITE NIGHTGOWN, MY HAIR FREED FROM
its ribbon, I gathered the strength to write my father a letter
by the oil lamp's light.

November 1, 1918

My Dearest Father,

*I received your letter, and I am relieved to hear you are well. Are
they giving you enough food? I would feel better knowing that you
are eating properly. If I sound like a little mother, perhaps that's
because Aunt Eva fusses over me night and day and shows me how
to be an expert worrier. She's caring for me well, but you can probably guess which one of us is the braver member of the household.*

Is there any chance they'll drop the charges before your trial? Do you have a lawyer? If there's any possibility you won't stay in jail, please tell me as soon as you can. I really miss you. I was just remembering the other day about the time we built that mousetrap together and hunted all over the store for that little pest Phantom. And remember when you taught me how to fix our phonograph? I figured out how to make the same repairs on Aunt Eva's machine just two days ago. You would have been proud.

Now for the hardest part of this letter: my sad news.

Stephen died. Can you believe that, Dad? Stephen Embers died. I am doing better than expected, so please do not worry. His funeral was lovely. Everyone treated him like a proper war hero.

I have been reading quite a bit to keep my brain active—and to help me understand the war better. I have a question for you: when you were in the Spanish-American War, did you see soldiers whose bodies and brains had stopped working right? They're calling it shell shock now, but I'm sure it happened before they invented shells. I'm curious about that subject and would like more information. Perhaps when I am older, I will try to learn how to repair broken minds in addition to exploring the inner workings of machines and electrical devices. These damaged men need help, and figuring out how to heal them seems a worthy challenge.

I am healthy and safe, Dad. Please keep yourself the same way.

Your loving daughter,
Mary Shelley

My hand cramped from the tension coursing through my fingers. I had kept the tone of the letter somewhat optimistic for Dad's sake, but I longed to say so much more. Penning the words *Portland City Jail* on the envelope made the muscles burn even worse.

I set Dad's letter aside and fetched the stack of Stephen's envelopes—the ones he had addressed to me—so I could read words written by the boy whose mind was still intact. What could his voice from the past tell me?

At the bottom of the stack lay the very first letter Stephen had written after he moved to California. I opened the blue envelope and pored over his message.

June 21, 1914

Dear Mary Shelley,

We finally unpacked enough for me to find my writing paper and pen. The house is just as I remembered from when I visited my grandparents: large and drafty, with the wind whipping through the boards at night, making the walls creak.

The house faces southwest, with a view of the wide-open Pacific. L. Frank Baum wrote the last books of his Oz series when he wintered down here, just a few blocks away from where I'm sitting right now. If I ever see him walking down the street, I'll tell him I know a crazy girl up in Oregon who's read all his books at least five times apiece.

Glenn Curtiss, the aviation genius, owns a naval flight school on North Coronado Island, and his airplanes buzz over our house and rattle the china cabinet several times a day. My mother worries that all the plates and cups will shatter from the ruckus. It scares her something awful. I've seen Curtiss's flying boats, which are normal biplanes with pontoons attached to the bottom. They take off from the Spanish Bight, the strip of water that separates the two Coronados, and the pilots circle them over the Pacific outside my bedroom windows (yes, windows, plural—you should see this place, Shell!). Imagine what it would be like to feel that free, flying through the air, gazing down at the earth like a seagull. Maybe one day I'll join the navy and learn how to fly. I bet you would, too, if they allowed women. Better yet, Curtiss would hire you to work for him, and you could lecture him about all the ways he could improve his engines.

Are you lonely up there without me, Shell? I already miss our chats. I genuinely doubt I'll find any girl around here who spends her spare time fiddling with clocks and poring over electrician's manuals. Have you read any good novels I should know about? Is it still raining in Portland, or did summer weather finally arrive? Summer lasts year-round here. While you shiver up there this winter, I'll be swimming in the ocean and basking in the sunshine on the beach. I'll send you a sand crab.

Write soon.

Your friend,
Stephen

I sputtered up a laugh and remarked aloud, "I remember telling you *exactly* what you could do with your sand crab."

I laid the letter next to the lamp and sighed into my hands, my elbows digging into the table. "Are you in the room with me right now, Stephen? Can you hear me?" A quick check with the compass told me I was the only magnetic force gripping the atmosphere at the moment. "Why can't you come when I call you? Why do I have to be half-drunk with sleep for you to completely show up? In fact . . ." I stood. "I'm going to bring a chair upstairs so I can sleep sitting up."

After the long day at the Red Cross House and all the bickering with Aunt Eva, my arms shook with exhaustion as I lugged a dining room chair up to my bedroom. Aunt Eva's door was shut, the space beneath it dark, so she didn't have to witness my preventive measures against waking up with a boy or a bird on my chest.

I sat on the scratchy needlepoint cushion and attempted to get comfortable. "All right." I nestled my head against my arms on the table. "Come if you can, but don't scare me." I closed my eyes.

At first only the soft whisper of the oil lamp's flame met my ears—a soothing nothingness. Minutes later an entire brigade of sirens tore through the streets like an invasion of wailing banshees. Their cries made the hairs on the back of my neck bristle. I must have drifted off counting how many ambulances there were—at least four of them—while the oil lamp turned the backs of my eyelids orange.

A dream ran through my head: I lay on my back some-where outside and watched the blackness of the nighttime sky dissolve into a milky shade of white. A gunshot hurt my ears. Streaks of red splattered across the heavens.

I awoke with a gasp, fear blazing across my tongue and static snapping in my hair. I heard another gasp, and Stephen thrust his arms around my waist and buried his cheek against my stomach as if I were a life preserver, his face pale and damp in the lamplight. He shivered against me.

I wrapped my arms around his head. "Are you all right, Stephen?"

He didn't answer. He could barely breathe.

"It's OK. I'm here. You're safe. It was just a dream." I lowered my right hand to his shoulder and found the wide cotton strap of the sleeveless undershirt he was always wear-ing. To soothe him, I ran my fingers down the curve of his bare arm, meeting with cold flesh and scars that reminded me of the barbed-wire wounds on Jones's hand. I puzzled over Stephen's lack of a proper shirt. "Where were you when you put on these clothes?"

I bit my lip in anticipation of his answer. The question seemed like a stroke of genius for the five or six seconds after I asked it.

He didn't respond—he just quaked and panted—so I elab-orated. "You're wearing a sleeveless undershirt, a brown pair of pants that look like civilian trousers, and gray socks without any shoes. Do you remember where you were when you put on this clothing? Do you remember why you're not wearing a regular shirt?"

He slowed his breathing enough to answer. "No."

"Are you sure? Please think hard, Stephen. Think back to the moments before the birds arrived. Where were you?"

"I don't know." He closed his eyes and tightened his grip around my waist. "I just remember it being hot. There was too much sunlight. Too many windows. I didn't like wearing sleeves."

"Were you in a hospital?"

"Maybe. I just . . ." His eyes opened wide. "Oh . . ." He exhaled a sigh heavy with remembrance.

My heart raced. "Oh what?"

"I just remembered something."

"What?"

"I think I hurt her."

"Her?" I swallowed down my jealousy. "A girl was there?"

"The Huns flew over us. Their planes were practically right on me. The bombs were about to drop. I don't know why she was there."

"Who was there?"

"My mother."

"Your mother?"

"She was reaching over me, and I kicked her so hard she stumbled several feet backward and landed on the ground. I heard her cry out in pain."

"Your mother was in a hospital with you? Is that what you

mean? Or was there a nurse who looked like her?"

"It was her. She said my name."

"But—that can't be." I shook my head.

"She was there. I was panicking about the plane, but she was there, and I hurt her."

"Wait a second . . . wait . . ." The little clock gears inside my head clicked into place. "Oh, God." My diagram of the events leading up to his death repositioned itself in a brand-new order in my mind. A sentence from Stephen's letter sitting right there next to me on the bedside table leapt off the page: *airplanes buzz over our house and rattle the china cabinet several times a day . . .*

"Oh, my God."

I remembered back to the day I posed for that second spirit photograph in the Emberses' house—the biplane soaring over the roof, footsteps scrambling across the room above our heads, dust shaking loose from the beams, Mrs. Embers tearing into the studio, saying, *I need your help, Julius. I'm hurt.* She had grabbed her stomach as if she had just been kicked, and Julius shouted, *Christ! Get them out of here, Gracie.*

It wasn't a ghost that made everyone stare up at the ceiling with whitened faces. A spirit didn't somehow hurt Mrs. Embers.

It was an eighteen-year-old boy, deep in shock from the war, reacting to a sound that reminded him of battle.

"You were still alive that day." I grabbed the sides of Stephen's face. "When Julius took my photograph and Gracie gave me the package, you were living and breathing in the bedroom directly above my head."

He scowled and shook his head. "I'm still alive, Shell. Stop saying I'm not."

"You came home, Stephen. You're not still in the trenches."

"But the minute you let me go, I'll be back in the mud and the dark and the shit and the blood. I hear them whispering right now." He peered over his shoulder. "Don't you hear them?"

"What are they saying?"

"All sorts of things. One of them wants to know how long it's going to take."

I pulled his head against my stomach and buried my face in his brown hair. "Tell them to go away. Tell them you haven't been on the battlefield for a long while. Tell them you came home."

His fear seeped inside me, pounding in my pulse and drumming against my ears. Our breaths blended into a staccato beat. All I could think about was Julius standing next to his camera while patriotic music blared from the phonograph to cover the bangs and thumps from the room above the studio.

"What happened to you?" I asked. "Did someone do something to you in your own house?"

"They're killing me."

"I know." I kissed the top of his head through his smoke-laced hair. "I know."

He breathed into the folds of my nightgown. "Keep me with you."

"I'll try."

"Keep me close." His lips kissed my stomach through the airy fabric—a flutter of pleasure that penetrated the pain. "I want you so much, Shell."

"I want you, too. More than anything else."

The room trembled with frustration and longing until even the curtains swayed, and my mouth filled with the rich flavor of a feast I could only taste but never, ever consume.

"I wonder what would happen if you pushed the darkness out of your thoughts." I drew in a deep, quivering breath. "If you remembered the parts of your life that had nothing to do with death. I wonder what it would feel like if you moved closer to me without those suffocating memories weighing us down."

He looked up at me, his eyes dark and curious.

"I wonder . . ." I pushed myself off the chair and grabbed his hand to help him to his feet, even though my own legs shook. "Can you stand up with me?"

He rose up above me, and we stood face-to-face for the first time since the morning we held *Mr. Muse* between us in his house. I cupped his cool cheek and guided him toward me by his waist. His hands ran across my back and seemed to grow warmer against my fabric. For a moment, the fear throbbing through him faded to a mere whisper of trepidation, barely there, like a weak heartbeat.

His attention switched to the ceiling. He tensed against me and held his breath.

"No, come back." I grabbed both sides of his face again. "Come back to me. Think of something good. Think about kissing me in your house. Do you remember that?"

His eyes wouldn't leave the dark air above us, and I, too, heard the flapping of restless wings.

"Think about how it felt when we kissed with your photograph tucked between us. Do you remember that?" I lowered his face until his forehead bumped against mine. "Did your heart beat as much as mine did, Stephen? Do you remember your lips on my mouth and neck? Do you remember the way you made me breathe?"

He closed his eyes with a sigh that shuddered straight through me.

"You remember, don't you?" I whispered.

"Of course I remember."

"I'm here now." I brushed his lips with a kiss that tasted far less like smoke than the other night. "Stay with me. Don't think of anything else. Not a single thing. Let's see if I can keep you with me."

He caressed the back of my neck, and we kissed again. The sensation was stirring and sweet. The closer we got, the more the feeling bloomed into a rush of pleasure far more delicious than even the bliss of flesh against flesh. My head clouded over with a dizzying sense of exhilaration. My legs lost their ability to stand.

"I need to sit down." I pulled away from him but grabbed his arm so he wouldn't disappear. "Come with me." I guided him back toward my bed with careful footsteps. "Are you still with me?"

"Yes."

We sat on the edge of the bed, and our mouths returned to each other. His fingers explored the curves of my body from my neck to my chest, and down to my waist. Lovely breezes shivered across my skin. He slid my nightgown up past my knees and kissed the small of my throat.

"Is this all right?" he asked. "Can I pull your skirt up farther?"

I nodded, and he kissed my neck again with a touch that melted straight through me. His hands edged my nightgown up to my hips.

I lay back against the cool quilt and allowed him to climb on top of me.

His lips warmed my chest through the nightgown's fabric. "For some reason, Shell, I can't ever take off these clothes. I don't know why."

"It's all right. Just be close to me."

"I want to be as close as I can."

"We'll make the best of it."

I held on to his back and felt him push against me with a sigh that traveled deep inside my own lungs. I still wore my cotton drawers, and he kept his trousers buttoned, but an electrifying current pulsed between us.

"See," I murmured, "we're even closer than we could have been before."

Energy coursed through my blood and brought a smile to my face, and I could tell by the way Stephen breathed and lowered his eyelids that he was experiencing the same rapture. We toyed with the provocative sensation, his trousers brushing against my legs in a hushed rhythm, until he broke the silence with another whisper.

"This is the way Julius told them he found us."

"No—don't bring up anything upsetting right now." I gripped his arm to keep him from slipping back into the darkness.

"I was just going to say I sometimes wish he had actually found us this way." He eased himself all the way on top of me and breathed into my hair. "Even though it would have been wrong and it could have led to trouble, it would have been nice to have felt that with you, even just once."

I closed my eyes and pulled him closer still, until he surrounded me completely. Until I felt him inside my soul.

23

THE CAGE

A NOISE INTERRUPTED US.

A squawk.

Somehow we heard it, beyond the walls and the floor, and the noise sent blood streaming back into my brain. I opened my eyes.

"What was that?" Stephen lifted his head and stared at me as if I had just stabbed him in the gut. His pupils swelled as wide as saucers.

I gulped. "I think it was a bird."

His lips twitched. "A bird?"

I nodded. "There's a pet bird downstairs."

He looked over his shoulder, and the flame of the oil lamp rose and danced, streaking topsy-turvy shadows across the wall. The needle of Uncle Wilfred's compass quivered beneath the glass.

Stephen's eyes returned to mine. "We've got to kill it."

Like the lamp and the needle, I trembled with his terror.

The bird squawked again, and we both jumped.

"It hears us," he said. "Kill it before it finds us."

"It's a pet."

"Have you ever seen what their beaks can do to a person, Shell? Do you know what they'll do to your eyes?"

I winced.

"It's either you or him," he said. "Get a gun."

"I don't have a gun."

"Then get a knife. Or even a pair of scissors." His hot breath against my face fanned a fire inside me. All I could think of was a crow as large as a bald eagle bearing down on my chest. The stringy taste of feathers filled my mouth.

"Kill it," he said in a voice that vibrated inside my brain, as if the thought were coming from my own mind instead of his lips. "Hurry."

I rose from the bed.

Part of me knew what I was doing was wrong—so very wrong—but that other part, the part getting louder and more anxious, powered my feet across the bedroom rug. I peeked over my shoulder and no longer saw Stephen on the bed, but his fear continued to burn in my lungs. He was still with me.

I twisted the doorknob and left the room, tense with anticipation of another sound emerging from the thing downstairs.

The pitch-black stairs groaned under my weight, but I kept going, oblivious to anything but that squawking, violent, sharp-beaked creature.

When my feet reached the bottom of the stairs, the house itself seemed to rumble with apprehension. The *click click click* of talons scuttled somewhere unseen.

"Who's there?" asked a voice in the dark.

I froze against the banister behind me.

"Who's there?"

The bird was talking to me. I gagged and clutched my stomach, smelling death and mud and poisonous fumes.

Kill it, Shell.

"There's a pair of scissors in the sewing box in the living room," I whispered. "But I have to go past the cage."

Run past. They're coming. Hurry!

I leapt into the living room but took a bad step, which sent me crashing against the floorboards on my hands and knees. The thing beneath the covered cage beat its wings and screeched, "Who's there? Hello. Hello."

They're coming. Oh, God, they're coming.

I scrambled across the room to the shadow of a wooden sewing box next to the rocking chair and dug out a pair of scissors that glinted in the moonlight.

"Who's there?"

Bile rose in my throat as I tiptoed toward the cage.

"Who's there? Who's there? Hello."

Just do it, Shell! Kill it!

I held my breath and reached out to the beige cloth covering the bronze wires.

"Who's there?"

Do it!

I pulled. The cloth tumbled down.

An ear-shattering screech pierced the night, and I stumbled backward and fell to the ground in horror. A huge black crow-faced bird with a luminous white beak and hands like a man's gripped the bronze bars. It raised its back feathers and bit at the cage with its furious mouth, and the air from its wings beat down on me, sending a wall of stinging smoke burning down to my stomach.

"What's happening?" asked a female voice.

I saw a candle out of the corner of my eye, but all I could do was lean back on my elbows with tremors convulsing my body.

"Mary Shelley?"

"Kill it!" I managed to shout, the scissors feeling sturdier in my hands. "Kill it before it kills me. Shoot it!"

"What's wrong with you?"

"Give me a gun." I sprang to my feet.

"No." A woman with short blond hair pulled the cage away from me and swung open a door to a world screaming with ambulance sirens.

My legs gave way and I fell to the ground again. My mouth tasted dirt and blood from a cracked lip. The sound of machine-gun fire reverberated around my head, as well as shouts and commands and the whistle of a shell about to hit. The earth rocked below me. A woman cried and yelled something about telephoning a minister. Nothing made sense. It was far too much to bear—far too much to keep living through, so I shut myself off to the world and curled into a ball until nothing but stark silence echoed in my ears.

24

DISCOVERIES

SOMEONE WAS KNOCKING ON A DOOR.

I opened my eyes and stared up at the crisscrossing white beams of Aunt Eva's living room ceiling. The batiste fabric of my nightgown clung to my legs and stomach like a film. My sweat smelled of onions. My head, thick with sleep, felt disoriented by the morning sunlight as well as the fact that I was lying on the floor in the middle of a room.

The flu, I thought. *Did I just have a flu fever?*

I sprang up to my elbows and checked for blue-black feet.

The toes wiggling beyond the hem of my nightclothes were still their normal shade of pasty Oregon white. Plus I sweated instead of shivered, and people with the flu always shivered like they were freezing from the inside out.

Not the flu. It wasn't a fever dream that lay with me in my bed the night before and urged me to go downstairs to kill a bird. Not at all.

Another five-beat knock came from the back of the house, sounding like someone was at the kitchen door. I wobbled up to my feet and lurched past the empty space where Oberon's cage used to sit.

Through the kitchen window I could see a masked girl with red braids. She stood beside a wooden pull wagon full of food crates and looked harmless enough, so I opened the door.

She leapt back when she saw me. "Oh no! Do you have the flu?"

"No." I wiped damp hair off my cheek. "What I have isn't contagious."

"Oh." With a worried brow, the girl pulled a crate stuffed with golden onions off her wagon. "Mrs. Ottinger orders her groceries to be delivered every Saturday morning. You need to tell her we could only give her one dozen onions instead of two because there's a shortage."

"All right." I glanced over my shoulder for signs of my missing aunt, but I neither heard nor saw any trace of her.

The girl set the box of onions at my feet, then pulled out a larger crate packed with carrots, potatoes, string beans, apples, and eggs.

"Do you need me to pay you now?" I asked.

"Mrs. Ottinger usually pays on credit. But with everyone getting sick . . ."

"All right. I'll get you some cash." I remembered seeing Aunt Eva fetch taxi money from a Gibson's Cough Lozenge tin kept on top of the icebox, so I paid the girl her two dollars and sixty-three cents and brought the crates inside.

The girl went on her way to the tune of squeaky wagon axles that needed a good oiling. I would have helped her out by liquefying some soap and slicking up the metal if I didn't need to hunt down my aunt. It was Saturday, so Aunt Eva wouldn't have been at work. Normally she was up long before I was—and I doubted she would've left me lying on the living room floor.

"Aunt Eva?"

My voice bounced off the ceiling of the empty house. No one responded.

I sprinted upstairs.

"Aunt Eva?" I crashed open her door, and she screamed from her bed, clutching a two-foot-tall crucifix that looked like some medieval relic. Garlic and onions rolled off her pillow and bounced across the floor.

"Stay away from me!" she cried.

"I'm sorry, Aunt Eva."

"Sorry's not good enough. What type of person crouches in the dark in the middle of the night, scissors in hand, yelling about killing a poor, innocent bird?"

"Where is Oberon?" I entered her room.

"Don't come near me!" She scooted against her headboard with wild eyes.

"It's just me now. Everything's fine."

"Everything is *not* fine."

"Where's Oberon?"

"I set him free before you could hurt him." Two loud coughs shook her chest, then transformed into a fit of hysterical tears. "The poor thing's wings were clipped, so I don't know how far he made it. Hopefully, far enough that he'll never come back here again."

"I'm so sorry—"

"Your voice sounded like yours, but those words coming out of your mouth . . ." She sniffed and sobbed. "I hid all the scissors and knives in the house, and then I tried calling my minister, but his whole family is sick. His wife referred me to another minister, but he was sick, too. The doctors wouldn't come, because they're too busy, and even that Mr. Darning wasn't answering his telephone." She hugged her crucifix against her cheek and wept thick tears across the tarnished gold. "We're all alone. It's just you and me and that lunatic boy."

"Don't say that about him."

"What do you expect me to say? If he truly returned to this earth as a spirit, why are you letting him near you? Why aren't you sending him away?"

"I can't."

"Try."

"Even if I tell him to leave me alone," I said, wringing my hands and venturing closer to her, "I know in my heart he'll keep reliving his death until he understands who or what hurt him. It's terrifying him and infuriating him."

"There's no possible way you can learn that information."

"Yes, there is. He was still alive when Julius took my last picture, Aunt Eva. Those noises coming from upstairs—that force that hurt Mrs. Embers—that was *him*. I bet they were hiding him up in his room."

"You don't know that."

"Wait right here. I want to show you something."

I raced off to my bedroom, where I pulled my diagram of Stephen's last months out of the drawer beneath Uncle Wilfred's compass. With careful strokes to avoid messing up my work with inkblots, I crossed off information that no longer seemed accurate and added new discoveries.

June 29
Stephen's last letter, written from France.

Sometime between June 29 and October 1
Stephen sent home.
Taken to East Coast hospital?

~~**Sometime between summer and October 19**~~
~~*Stephen loses his life.*~~
~~*(Grant just mentioned executions of soldiers suffering psychological trauma. Did that happen to Stephen?)*~~

Saturday, October 19

Restless sounds heard above Julius's studio during my sitting.

~~*Julius says that may have been Stephen's ghost.*~~

MRS. EMBERS COMES DOWNSTAIRS, LOOKING LIKE SOMEONE HAS JUST HURT HER.

STEPHEN IN CORONADO AND STILL ALIVE AS OF MY 10:00 A.M. PHOTOGRAPHY APPOINTMENT!

Monday, October 21

We pick up my photograph in Coronado; the picture includes Stephen's "spirit."

Julius tells us Stephen died a hero's death.

MRS. EMBERS SCREAMS STEPHEN'S NAME UPSTAIRS. (DID SHE JUST FIND HIM DEAD??)

I returned to my aunt with my notes. "See? I think he died somewhere between October nineteenth and twenty-first—somewhere between my Saturday morning sitting and the Monday morning we picked up the photograph."

Her eyes scanned the paper forced into her lap, and her lips whitened. She shook her head. "What are you implying?"

"Remember the state Julius was in when we picked up my photograph early that morning? He seemed dazed and upset, and I asked you if he was on opium. Then their mother screamed Stephen's name upstairs, and she hasn't been seen again."

"Julius . . . he's not a murderer. He can't be. He wouldn't

kill his brother *or* his mother." She shoved the paper off her lap. "He even cried at Stephen's funeral—remember?"

"Were they tears of sorrow or guilt?"

"Why would he risk finding his brother's spirit at a séance if there was a chance Stephen would call him a murderer?"

"But Stephen doesn't know who killed him." I picked up my diagram from the floor. "The war and reality seem to have blurred together into a jumbled mess in his head. All he talks about are bird creatures attacking him."

"Don't talk to me about birds, Mary Shelley," she warned with a stony glare.

"I need to go to his house."

"No!" She grabbed my arm. "Even if I get the flu and drop dead, promise me you won't ever go over to Julius's. Promise you won't let him pour his honey into your ears."

"You're not going to drop dead from the flu, Aunt Eva."

"Promise me."

I squished my lips together. "I don't think I can promise that. Julius is probably one of the only people who knows what really happened to Stephen."

Lines of concern wrinkled her forehead, making her look older. "But while you're helping Stephen, who's going to help you? Why don't you ever think about saving yourself?"

"My mother saved other people. I thought you wanted me to be like her."

"Your mother was a trained physician. You're a sixteen-year-old girl." She pointed to the window. "Listen to the world out there. Do you hear all the sirens? It's not safe to go any-where. You stay inside this house."

"Then Stephen will be staying inside with me. I've got to find out how he died."

"No, you don't." She erupted into another mess of soggy tears. "You don't need to do anything but listen to me for once in your life. Take all his belongings out of your room, throw them into the backyard—"

"No!"

"I feel like the only adult left in this world right now, and I don't know what else to do. Please just stay in this house and rid yourself of anything that has to do with that boy." She began to sob so hard that her face turned a disconcerting shade of purple.

I rubbed my face and steadied my breath. "All right. I'll stay inside for now to make you happy. Please stop crying so much. You're going to make yourself sick." I dropped my arms to my sides and watched her wipe her eyes and leaking nose with a handkerchief pulled from beneath her covers. "If we're not going anywhere, can I please make us a breakfast that doesn't involve onions?"

She hiccupped. "Take a bath first. You look and smell aw-ful. Unless you think that boy will show up in the tub with you—"

"He's not going to show up in the tub, for pity's sake." My skin sizzled with a blush. "You stay here and calm down, and I'll go get washed up. Everything will be fine."

．．．．．

AUNT EVA'S FEAR OF STEPHEN SHOWING UP IN MY BATH
got me thinking.

If I tipped the back of my head against the porcelain-enameled rim of the tub and let my body go limp in the sudsy water, would my mind grow drowsy enough to see him? Would he get too close again and fill the house with his terror? Or could I lure him for just a breath of a moment?

He had come to me in the daylight before—when his whispers burned at my ear at his funeral and when his photograph dropped to my floor just the previous afternoon. If I pushed away the commotion of the sirens outside and let myself sink downward, downward, downward . . .

My arms relaxed over the tub's curved lip.

My chin tilted upward. My head lightened. The center of the earth dragged me toward it, as if I were riding in an unlit elevator on a rushed descent.

Down.

Down.

Down.

The world above me faded to white. Pain seized my head. Something exploded across the clouds, and the sky turned a deep red. I rose toward the bloodstained surface. Voices cried out in panic below.

"Mary Shelley."

I jolted upright with a frantic splash of water. Fresh air rushed into my lungs, and my slippery fingers clutched the sides of the tub to regain my bearings.

"Gracie is here, Mary Shelley," called my aunt through the door. "Can you be out and dressed in a few minutes?"

"Gracie?" I slicked back my wet hair. "Stephen's cousin Gracie?"

"Yes."

"Did she say why she came?"

"I told her she can't have what she came for, but she wanted to talk to you just the same."

"What did she come for?"

My aunt didn't respond.

"I said, what did she come for, Aunt Eva?"

"A séance. To find Stephen."

I leapt out of the tub with a loud cascade of water and grabbed my towel. "Let me just get dressed. I'll be right there."

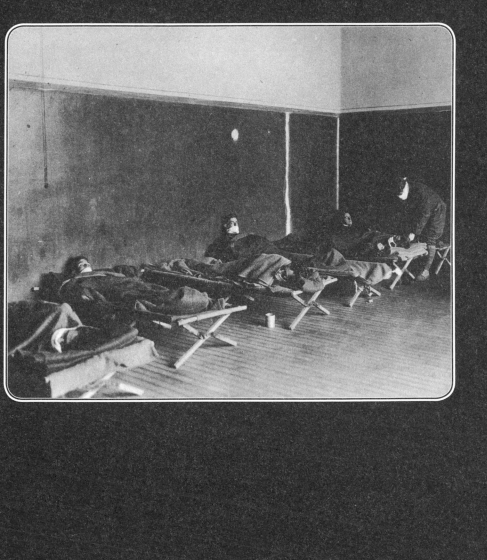

25

COUSIN GRACIE

I PADDED OUT TO THE LIVING ROOM ON BARE FEET AND twisted my hair into a braid to avoid dripping all over my navy-blue dress with the sailor-style collar. I had worn the same garment the first time I met Gracie, I realized, when she had bustled about Julius's studio, changing phonograph records to smother the sounds of Stephen upstairs.

Gracie watched me approach with round, inquisitive eyes—the look of a captured owl. She sat, shoulders stiff, in the middle of Aunt Eva's sofa, her flu mask lowered to her throat, hands clasped in her lap as if they had been locked together with a key.

My aunt looked equally rigid and uncomfortable in the rocking chair across from her.

"Hello, Gracie." I parked myself beside our guest, which made the girl stiffen even further. "It's good to see you again."

"It's good to see you, too." Gracie dropped her gaze. "I've wanted to come over here ever since I heard about what happened at that séance the other night. Grant heard about what happened from Julius, actually, and then Grant told me. I haven't been working in the studio lately."

"Why not?" I asked.

That nasty, curdled taste of spoiled milk I remembered from the funeral spread across my tongue.

"I haven't . . ." Gracie sniffed. "I haven't wanted to go back to that house since Stephen . . ."

I sat up straight with the realization that she may have just confirmed my suspicion that Stephen died in that house. "But Grant still works there?" I asked.

"He says he has to. When our mother died, he quit his job at a restaurant downtown. He said we both needed to work at Julius's studio to be with family and to earn decent money. Our father is off in the navy, you see, so it's just the two of us right now."

Aunt Eva rocked in her chair with soft creaks of wood. "Don't you live on Coronado as well?"

Gracie shook her head and grinned, embarrassed. "We're the poor relations. Our father used to be the swim instructor at the Hotel del Coronado—that's how he met our mother. She used to go swimming in the hotel's pool when the Emberses wintered in that big house over there. Mama didn't get to inherit the house, because she was the female heir. Stephen's dad got it, so we've always lived right here in San Diego."

I squirmed at the idea of Stephen being part of the rich side of the family. "I don't think Stephen ever felt comfortable living on the island," I said. "He told me he was heading to war to avoid becoming corrupted by his surroundings. He probably would have preferred switching houses with you."

"Many people would give their right arm to live in such a beautiful community," said Aunt Eva.

"I've seen men with missing arms," I muttered. "I'm sure they'd choose intact bodies over ocean views any day."

My aunt frowned and changed the subject. "Would you like some breakfast, Gracie? Mary Shelley and I haven't yet had ours."

Gracie shrugged. "I guess breakfast would be nice. But what I really want is a séance."

Aunt Eva stopped rocking.

Gracie looked at me from the corners of her eyes. "Like I said, I've wanted to visit you ever since I learned you spoke with Stephen at that séance." She fidgeted with her interlocked fingers. "That's not true, actually. I've wanted to come ever since Grant and Julius dragged you away from Stephen's casket."

"Oh?" I squirmed again. "Why didn't you come sooner?"

"I've been nervous. I didn't want to bother you."

"You're not bothering me." I pressed my fingers over the back of her clammy hand. "I'm glad you came."

She turned her face away from me. "Last night I dreamed you died of the flu."

"Oh," Aunt Eva and I said in unison.

"I'm sorry if that's a terrible thing to dream, but I realized I should come before it's too late. I know you and Stephen were close—he told me stories about you ever since he used to come down to visit as a child. I . . . need to speak to him."

My heart beat faster. "What did you want to say to him?"

"I want to tell him . . ." Her eyes brimmed with tears. "I just want to say . . . I'm sorry."

"Sorry?"

"I—I want to tell him I miss him."

I looked to Aunt Eva, who scowled and shook her head.

"My aunt is uncomfortable with the idea of me summoning him." I stroked Gracie's wrist. "Maybe you should join us in the kitchen for some breakfast, like she said, and we could chat for a while. I'll tell you the types of things Stephen has been saying to me, and you can help me figure out what's troubling him."

Gracie lifted her head. "He's troubled?"

I scraped my teeth against my bottom lip. "Yes. Very much so."

"Contact him for me, please!" She squeezed my hand. "Please let me speak to him. What if you do get this flu? How am I going to communicate with him then?"

Aunt Eva rose from her chair. "Let's go have some breakfast—"

"No—look at me." Gracie pulled off her wig and revealed a startling bald head with a downy covering of new white hair. "Look what the flu did to me. I'm one of the survivors, and look what it did. Grant thought I was dead one night, and he even laid a sheet over me and called an undertaker. I'm one of the lucky ones, and look what I'm like. When this flu gets you, I might never get a chance to talk to my poor cousin."

"Come into the kitchen." I stood and pulled Gracie to her feet. "We'll contact him out there."

Aunt Eva blanched. "No!"

"Keep all the knives and scissors hidden." I brushed past her. "Open the windows so the neighbors can hear you scream if something goes wrong, but let me help him."

"I don't want him in this house."

"Then let us put him to rest, Aunt Eva, so he can leave. You can talk to him yourself if you'd like, or go hide in your room, but this needs to be done."

Gracie tugged her wig back over her head, and I led our guest back to the pea-soup-green kitchen, where the little circular table would make a fine spot for a séance.

"Do we need candles?" asked Gracie.

"That doesn't seem to matter." I pulled out a chair for Stephen's cousin and lowered myself into a seat that faced away from the windows. I didn't want to see any crows or blackbirds perched on the orange trees out there . . . or even banished Oberon, trying to find his way back in.

To my utter shock, Aunt Eva rushed into the room and

slipped into one of the two remaining chairs. "Do it quickly. I swear, if anyone gets hurt—"

"He doesn't want to hurt any people. Everyone will be safe."

"Should we hold hands?" asked Gracie.

"Not yet." I placed my palms on the table. "I'd actually like to start by asking you some questions, Gracie."

"Me?" Gracie recoiled. "What types of questions?"

"Be kind, Mary Shelley," warned Aunt Eva. "Remember what I said about prying into other people's business."

"I know. But I need answers." I peered straight into Gracie's pale brown eyes. "Tell me the truth—does Julius seem like an honest person to you?"

Gracie flinched, and an avalanche of curdled milk sloshed down my throat. I gagged on the stomach-souring awfulness and braced my hands against the table to keep from retching.

Aunt Eva reached out to me. "What's wrong?"

I gulped down the guilt-soaked flavor with a grimace. "I'm fine. Just a moment . . ."

"Are you going to get sick?" asked Aunt Eva.

"I'm fine." I cleared my throat with a deep, uncomfortable sound. "Um . . . all right . . . let me be more specific, Gracie. When you helped Julius at his studio, did you ever see him cheat?"

Gracie shook her head, and the sour taste softened. "I didn't ever go into Julius's darkroom with him, but I was there when Mr. Darning came to investigate him one time."

"What did Mr. Darning do?" I asked.

"He marked his initials on blank photographic plates to make sure Julius wasn't switching them with used ones. And Julius passed all his tests, which seemed to puzzle Mr. Darning. There were reporters there and everything. Oh, and look." She popped open a silver locket dangling around her neck below her flu mask. "Here's a photo Julius took of me and my mother's spirit."

I leaned in close, but I saw only a fuzzy streak of light behind a somber image of Gracie, who was seated in front of Julius's black background curtain. "I just see a blur."

"That's probably her."

"Oh." I sank back in my chair and furrowed my brow. "So. He seems an honest man to you, then?"

Gracie snapped the locket shut. "I don't know about that." She bowed her head. "He wasn't always nice to Stephen."

"What did you see him do to Stephen?"

"I know . . . ," said Gracie, scratching the back of her neck. "He sometimes stole Stephen's photographs off the wall and burned them."

Aunt Eva's jaw dropped. "He burned his brother's photographs?"

Gracie nodded. "Stephen was worried that all of his work would be gone by the time he returned from the war, so he packed up most of his pictures and negatives and hid them about a week before he left."

I leaned forward. "Do you know where he put them?"

She shook her head. "He wouldn't even tell his mother what he was doing with them. He was probably afraid she'd slip and mention their whereabouts to Julius. She thought he might have purchased a safe-deposit box in a bank or a post office and stored them there."

"Why did Julius destroy Stephen's photographs?" asked Aunt Eva.

Gracie's eyes moistened again. "My cousins always fought like a pack of wild dogs, and their fights turned vicious after Stephen's father passed away. Aunt Eleanor considered asking Julius to move out, but she always favored him a little, even if she never said so out loud. She and Julius escaped her terrible drunk of a first husband together. She always felt sorry for him starting life with a bully for a father."

I traced my fingernail along a scratch in the tabletop and pondered the missing photos. "Stephen gave me two of his pictures before he left for training . . . but the rest must have already been stored away. He never mentioned anything about hiding the others, but we didn't have all that much time together . . . I don't think that's why he's troubled. I don't know . . ." I looked to Gracie. "I met one of his friends from his battalion at the Red Cross House yesterday."

Gracie hunched her back the same way her brother had when I questioned him about Stephen's condition.

"What that friend told me about Stephen's last days in France was upsetting and confusing to hear," I continued. "May I mention what I heard?"

She gave a nod that was more a quiver of her round chin.

"He said Stephen didn't die in battle." I hesitated a moment, for the air was thickening. "He said he lost his mind over there in the trenches. The army tried to help him in a field hospital, but he just got worse. They had to send him home." A searing pain clogged my lungs, but I breathed through it and forced myself to keep talking. "Did you know about his discharge?"

Gracie's lips shook. Her eyes watered until a flood of tears ran down her cheeks. "We were supposed to keep it a secret."

"Why?" I asked.

"All the Emberses' friends boasted about their boys receiving medals, or they could at least say their sons died in combat, fighting for liberty." She sniffed. "None of their young men were sent home in shame. Aunt Eleanor . . . she worried Stephen would be viewed as a coward . . . and a traitor. She even blamed herself for the way she raised him. Stephen was always so quiet and artistic. I can't even imagine a gun"— Gracie squeezed her face into a pained expression as the flow of tears streamed harder—"in that boy's hands."

I held on to her wrist. "He made it back to Coronado, didn't he?"

She sniffled and attempted to steady her voice. "His mother had to fetch him from a hospital on the East Coast. A nurse went with her. They found him sitting in a bed, not speaking, shaking, just staring with eyes that looked like he was watching Death breathe in his face."

I winced.

"They brought him home sedated," she continued, "and hid him up in his room. Aunt Eleanor investigated the nearest asylums, but she said they all used barbaric water treatments. Patients were chained to beds. The doctors wanted to sterilize them all so they couldn't transfer their madness to future generations." She stopped and wiped her eyes with a handkerchief tucked inside the black sash of her dress. "Aunt Eleanor insisted on keeping him at home, waiting until he came out of his shock enough to go to some of the places offering to help recuperating servicemen."

I lifted my face. "How did Julius feel about that decision?"

"Well . . ." Gracie sniffed. "He said he didn't like it, but Stephen didn't make any noise during the first week. None of Julius's customers knew he was up there. Julius told us to keep saying Stephen was still overseas. This was all around the time Mother died from the flu, and I didn't know what to do. Julius said if Stephen got bad enough we should just tell people he'd gotten shot in combat and put him away."

A profound sadness settled in my bones. I wanted to lower my head and cry for everything I'd ever lost in my life, but I pushed my arms against the table, elbows locked, to keep myself upright. "What happened after the first week? Did he start making noise?"

"Yes." Gracie sniffed again. "He started to wake out of his fog a little. He wasn't yet talking, but he started yelling whenever he heard certain noises—the buzz of the doorbell, the telephone ringing, the flashlamp, the Naval Air Station planes. Anything loud and sudden panicked him. He even kicked his mother in the stomach once when one of the planes flew over the house. Julius had to take her to the hospital to make sure she didn't have any internal damage."

"That was the day we were there for my most recent photograph," I said.

"Yes."

"Did you see Stephen when he was up in his room?"

"No, I stayed away from him. I didn't want to see him that way."

I rubbed my eyes, which throbbed and burned with phantom smoke. "Stephen says he often sees creatures watching over him while he's strapped down. No one tied him to his bed, did they? Either in that East Coast hospital or at home?"

"Oh, heavens. I don't know. He may have been chained to that hospital bed. I didn't ask Aunt Eleanor how they were keeping him calm after he kicked her." Gracie tugged my hand away from my eye with a firm grip. "Is he here? Does he know what I'm saying?"

"I think he's trying to come, but I don't want him to get any closer until you answer the most important question—the one that may help him rest in peace." My throat and mouth ached from the smoke and the fight to hold back tears. I realized the cause of his death, spoken aloud, might make him disappear from my life, so selfishly I let a few more seconds tick by before I asked my question: "How did he die, Gracie?"

Gracie's face contorted again. She tried to hold on to my hand, but her tears ran down to the bodice of her black dress at such a rate, she had to let go to wipe them. My aunt just sat there, stunned and mute.

"What happened?" I asked. "Please tell him. He needs to know."

"Stephen . . ." Gracie lowered her eyes. "My poor cousin . . . You shot yourself."

My head slammed against the table. My neck simply refused to hold up my skull any longer, and I found myself lying there with my cheek pressed against the wood. A terrific headache erupted in my left temple.

"Are you all right, Mary Shelley?" Aunt Eva grabbed at my shoulders. "I told you not to do this. Sit up. Sit up, and tell me you're all right."

"How did he get a gun?" I somehow found the strength to ask.

"Julius kept one to protect the house from intruders," said Gracie.

"Where was Julius?"

"He slept at our house that night. He rode over from Coronado on the last ferry and showed up at our door after getting a drink in the city. He said he needed a break from taking care of Stephen."

"What time was that?"

"I don't know—maybe eleven o'clock. He's always coming over to stay the night so he can be in the city."

"And he was there all night?"

"Well . . . he was in San Diego all night, I know that for sure. I went to bed shortly after he arrived, and I found him lying on our living room floor early the next morning. He was . . . he and Grant . . . they sometimes . . ."

My eyes widened. "They sometimes what?"

"They sometimes go to—please don't tell Grant I'm telling you this . . ."

"Where do they go?" asked Aunt Eva for me. "Please just tell her so she'll sit up and act like a normal person again."

"I'll wake up in the morning," said Gracie, "and find them passed out in various parts of the house, and their eyes don't look right. They're like pale sleepwalkers who can barely move. Grant says he's only been smoking pipes in that den with Julius since our mother died—he says it helps him with his grief. Please don't call the police on him. I know it's opium, but he'll stop using it soon. I swear he will."

I tried to piece the timeline together in my head. "So . . . after you found Julius on the floor that morning, Grant must have driven him home to Coronado. Aunt Eva and I saw Grant drop him off when we were waiting to pick up my picture."

"Yes." Gracie nodded. "Then Grant drove straight back to our place. Julius didn't feel like opening the studio that day."

"Why not?"

"More and more people were hearing Stephen upstairs. Customers got frightened. Some of them left before sitting for their photos." Gracie pressed her handkerchief over her eyes and exhaled a long sigh. "Julius telephoned—later that Monday morning. He was in tears. He said their mother had found Stephen, dead, with the gun in his hand, and there was blood everywhere. The police had to come. My aunt hasn't been the same ever since."

I massaged my temple and kept going. "Where is Mrs. Embers now, Gracie?"

"In a local sanitarium . . . one of those health resorts with fresh springwater and relaxation treatments. She probably needs more care, but we couldn't imagine putting her in an asylum. Not after she fought so hard to keep Stephen out of one."

"Is she any better?" asked Aunt Eva, now clinging to my shoulders as if her safety depended on it.

Gracie shook her head. "I've gone to visit her every day. She grabs my hand and mutters something about poison and a gunshot and her strong sleeping pills. Other times she's quiet and looks like a lost little girl. I wish I could help her. I don't know what I can possibly do to make her come back to us."

I knitted my brow. "Why is she talking about poison?"

"I don't know." Gracie mopped her face with her cloth. "Maybe Stephen tried poisoning himself first."

"You're sure no one else was in the house when Stephen died?" I asked.

"I'm positive. Grant and Julius were in San Diego."

"They couldn't have gone to Coronado after you went to bed?"

"No. The ferries were closed for the night, and the drive around the bay is too long and risky in the dark. The peninsula leading to Coronado is just a thin strip of land." She wiped her tears again and knocked her wig off center. "The police confirmed it was a suicide, but Julius paid them to keep quiet so he could keep insisting Stephen had been in France the whole time. The undertakers were so overwhelmed by the number of funerals for flu victims that we delayed his burial by more than a week. That allowed Julius time to tell people we were waiting for Stephen's body to come home. It was all so horrifying." Gracie balled her cloth between her hands. "To lose a loved one at such a young age is unthinkable, but then to have to lie about the circumstances and watch his mother go out of her mind with grief . . . I don't know what to do, Mary Shelley. Is Stephen here yet? Will he speak to me and forgive me for going along with the war hero charade?"

I closed my eyes and drew in a deep breath of the smoke working its way into my lungs and under my skin. An exhausting weight curled around my back and pressed against my spine.

"Stephen," I whispered to him, feeling my aunt's fingers pull away from my shoulders. "I know this all must be disturbing for you, but now you know what really happened. Is there anything else you need us to do to help you rest? Is there anything you want me to tell your cousin before—"

Rage singed my tongue. Without warning, violent tremors seized my torso and legs, and the window behind me rattled in response to my movements. Every object hanging on the walls—from the cuckoo clock to the spice rack—soon clanked and shuddered and sounded like a living creature struggling to break free from its nails, and there was nothing I could do to stop the shaking.

Gracie whimpered. "Stephen?"

"I don't believe it," he growled, so close to me—so very, very close. "And I know exactly why my mother's talking about poison." His anger churned in my veins, and his voice took on a raspy tone that didn't even sound like him. "The blackbirds pour it down my throat."

"Stop it, Mary Shelley," begged Aunt Eva.

"Stephen?" asked Gracie. "Stephen, I'm so sorry we couldn't help you. I'm so sorry."

"Tell her, Shell," said Stephen over the cacophony of rumbling glass and gas pipes groaning at their seams. "Tell her I didn't kill myself. Tell her someone pours poison down my throat. They're killing me. They won't stop killing me."

The window cracked, shocking me out of my convulsions.

The shaking stopped.

The room fell silent.

Aunt Eva thumped against the floor. Gracie's skin turned a seasick green, and she swayed like she'd also faint at any minute. She gripped the table's edge and lowered her forehead to the surface to keep from toppling over.

I didn't blame either of them. I nearly fell unconscious myself.

For Stephen's voice hadn't burned against my ear or emerged from the air a few feet away from my head. His shouts weren't something for me alone to hear in the private confines of my brain.

His voice—his actual deep voice—came directly from my mouth.

26

SOLDIER'S HEART

I WAITED ON THE COLD FLOOR OUTSIDE AUNT EVA'S ROOM
with my face pressed into my sweating palms. Gracie had
helped revive my aunt and steer her to bed, but after that she
simply shut down, as if someone had closed up shop inside of
her. She wandered from our house with an empty stare.

Waves of dizziness threatened to knock me over, but I kept
my wits about me and tried to fit Gracie's account of suicide
into Stephen's blackbirds story. Did he shoot himself because
he was convinced birds from the battlefields had followed him
home to haunt him? If that was the case, why did both Stephen and Mrs. Embers insist poison played a role?

"What if his mother killed him to put him out of his misery?" I asked myself aloud.

The echo of my theory banged around my brain until a vein in my forehead pulsated. I fidgeted with guilt for even considering the possibility. But, still . . . what if Mrs. Embers didn't want her son to suffer? Perhaps that's why she had to be taken away after his death. Maybe Stephen's mind transformed his mother into a monstrous creature to protect him from the truth.

A HAND NUDGED THE BACK OF MY ARM. "WHO ARE YOU right now?"

I blinked away my drowsiness and found my aunt standing over me with her crucifix in her hands like a baseball bat. The lengthening shadows of late afternoon stretched outside her bedroom door behind her.

"You're not going to hit me with that, are you?" I asked.

"Are you Mary Shelley?"

"Yes, it's me. Please put that down."

Her arms relaxed around the cross, but her face remained tense. "I don't want you out here."

"Do you feel better?"

"Go to your room and lie down. I'm fetching a glass of water for myself. I'll bring one to you in a moment."

"All right. Thank you."

I made my way to my room and flopped facedown on the mattress.

Aunt Eva went downstairs and made a commotion in the kitchen, slamming cupboard doors and yelling about the crack in the window. She thumped back up and plunked herself down on my bed with enough force to rock me back and forth. "Don't ever talk like him again." She set a glass of sloshing water on the table beside me.

I buried my face in my goose-down pillow. "Grant looks strong enough to be of use to someone trying to get rid of an embarrassing family member."

"Stephen took his own life. You heard what Gracie said— his mother found him holding the gun. I'm sure it's hard to fathom the boy you knew doing something like that to himself, but it sounds like he wasn't even remotely the same person by the time he got home."

"I don't believe he committed suicide. I think they killed him."

"People don't commit murder because of embarrassment."

"They didn't know what else to do with him." I turned my head to the side to look at her and her cross. "Do you think a mother could be capable of killing her own son to put him out of his misery?"

"No!" Her eyes got huge. "That's a horrible thought. I'm sure Mrs. Embers held hope in her heart for Stephen's recovery. Please, Mary Shelley, I don't want him to keep coming to you. Tell him to stay away. Tell him if he has any decency left, he'll leave you alone."

"I can't let him go until I find out why he's still partway here."

"It was as if the devil himself possessed you."

"That wasn't the devil."

"He was no angel."

I exhaled a long breath through my nose. "Do you know what my father told me about monsters and devils?"

She shook her head. "I almost hate to think what your father's opinion on that subject would be."

"He said the only real monsters in this world are human beings." I licked my parched lips. "It was a frightening thing to learn, but it makes so much sense. We can be terrible to one another." I dug my cheek deeper into the pillow. "And do you know the oddest thing about murder and war and violence?"

"Oh, Mary Shelley, please stop talking about those types of things."

"The oddest thing is that they all go against the lessons that grown-ups teach children. *Don't hurt anyone. Solve your problems with language instead of fists. Share your things. Don't take something that belongs to someone else without asking. Use your manners. Do unto others as you would have them do unto you.* Why do mothers and fathers bother spending so much time teaching children these lessons when grown-ups don't pay any attention to the words themselves?"

Aunt Eva nuzzled her chin against the crucifix. "Not every grown-up forgets those teachings."

"But enough of them do. If someone killed Stephen, they didn't treat him as they'd want to be treated. And those men who arrested my father punched him in the gut before they hauled him away. The Espionage Act already allowed them to take him away from me, but they also hurt him to teach him a lesson. He sank to his knees and couldn't breathe after they were done with him."

"Wartime isn't like normal times."

"But that's the point. We wouldn't even have wars if adults followed the rules they learned as children. A four-year-old would be able to see how foolish grown men are behaving if you explained the war in a child's terms. A boy named Germany started causing problems all over the playground that included beating up a girl named Belgium on his way to hurt a kid named France. Then England tried to beat up Germany to help France and Belgium, and when that didn't work, they called over a kid named America, and people started pounding on him, too."

My aunt lowered her cross to her lap. "It's not that simple. Africa and Russia are involved, Germany and England were competing to build bigger navies, the Serbs assassinated Archduke Ferdinand—you can't break down the causes in a child's terms. And you better not say those things in public. That's exactly why your father went to jail." She leaned forward. "You have to realize, he was once like Stephen. That's where his anger comes from."

My arms and legs went cold. "What are you talking about? How was he like Stephen?"

"They called the condition names like soldier's heart during the Spanish-American War, this thing they're saying is shell shock nowadays. The unexplained effects of war upon a person's mind. Your father still had it when he met your mother."

I lifted my shoulders and head. "Are you sure? He's never shown any signs . . ."

"I remember him coming over to visit your mother when I was about seven. We'd all be talking about something that didn't even have anything to do with the war, and he'd sort of drift away. He'd look off into the air in front of him and not say a word for at least five minutes. Your mother would take his wrist, check his pulse, and call his name, and eventually he'd shake out of it and ask what we were just talking about." Aunt Eva sat up straight and put the cross aside. "My parents worried about my sister's relationship with him. They thought she was confusing concern for a sick man with love, and they feared she considered him the ultimate test of her skills as a physician."

"But they did love each other, didn't they?"

"I'm sure they loved each other. Your father gradually got better, and they seemed happy enough. His own father worked him hard in that store to make sure he kept up a routine in his life. The marriage lifted his spirits, certainly. But I didn't stop seeing those fading-away episodes until after you were born. Maybe he realized you were too important to lose."

I sighed in disbelief and sank my head back down on the pillow. "Then if Stephen's family had just given him a chance and found him help, he might have eventually recovered, too."

"His family didn't kill him."

"But—"

"No." She pressed her hand against my back. "He's dead because he wanted to be dead. There's nothing you can do for him. I know it sounds cruel, but he chose to leave. And he should stay gone."

I NAPPED FITFULLY AFTER AUNT EVA STOPPED RUBBING my back and left me alone in the room. I kept dreaming about that bloodstained sky. A gunshot would ring through my head, and the world above me would be splattered in the darkest red. I'd awaken with the sensation of a bird pressing down on my lungs, yet nothing was there but the taste of smoke and copper and Stephen's photographs staring at me from the wall beyond the foot of my bed.

Those photographs. *Mr. Muse* and the mysterious *I Do Lose Ink*.

"I Idle Nooks," I murmured, trying to decipher the lightning bolt's anagram to keep my mind from drifting back to blood. "In Kilo Dose. Oilskin Ode . . . No, that doesn't sound like a title at all. None of it makes sense. Nothing makes sense. I've got to work on my diagram again . . ."

I'd fall back to sleep, and the nightmare would haunt me again, like a motion picture running on an endless loop.

When darkness swallowed up daylight and I couldn't stand the thought of any more dreams, I pushed myself upright, lit the oil lamp, and shook the sleep out of my head.

"Think, Shell, think," I told myself in my own clear voice. "Put together a new set of notes. You can do this."

I grabbed a fresh sheet of paper from the drawer and went to work.

Saturday, October 19
1. Stephen panicked about an airplane and kicked his mother during my 10:00 a.m. photography appointment.
2. Julius was so worried about Mrs. Embers's injury that he risked taking her to a hospital during this plague. (I wonder, did he want Stephen to leave the house more than ever after Stephen harmed their mother?)

Sunday, October 20
1. Julius showed up at Grant and Gracie's house, around 11:00 p.m., saying he had first stopped for a drink after taking the last ferry.
2. Between approximately 11:00 p.m. and the following morning, Julius and Grant presumably visited an opium den.
3. Meanwhile, Mrs. Embers was in her bed in Coronado, having taken a sleeping pill.

Monday, October 21
1. Gracie found Julius lying on her living room floor in the morning.
2. Grant drove Julius home.
3. Julius handed me the "spirit photo" and told us Stephen died a hero's death.
4. Mrs. Embers screamed Stephen's name upstairs.

Key Observations/Questions:

1. Did Julius prepare the photo before Stephen's death, knowing Stephen would either be killed or taken to an asylum after their mother's injury? Gracie said Julius wanted to start telling people his brother was dead if Stephen got bad enough.

2. Why were Mrs. Embers's pills so strong that night? Did someone give her an increased dose?

3. What did Mrs. Embers hear or know about a gun and poison? Was she on her pills in her room, or was she there with Stephen?

And at the bottom of the page I wrote the one question I'd been asking all along but still couldn't completely answer, which frustrated me to no end:

HOW DID STEPHEN EMBERS DIE?

THE DARKEST HOURS

AFTER A SILENT SUPPER OF ONION SOUP WITH AUNT EVA,
I returned to my bed and read Stephen's Verne novels until
my eyes no longer stayed open.

I dreamed of the little boys who played on top of the coffins in front of the undertaker's house. Flies buzzed around
their brown caps as they climbed over the foul-smelling caskets and pretended to hunt Germans. This time they sang the
nursery rhyme "Sing a Song of Sixpence."

> *The king was in the counting house, counting out his money,*
> *The queen was in the parlor, eating bread and honey,*
> *The maid was in the garden, hanging out the clothes,*
> *When down came a blackbird and pecked off her nose.*

I jerked awake, paranoid once again that a bird was on my chest, watching me while I slept.

I turned to my side, blinked through the dim glow of my oil lamp's light and saw nothing but my bedroom, quiet and still. My lungs breathed without the burden of anything squashing the life out of them. Stephen's photographs hung on the wall across the way, undisturbed.

Yet the air burned with his presence.

I heard a sound—something wet, splashing against my bedsheet behind my back. I clenched my eyelids shut and dreaded flipping over, for I didn't hear any rain outside my window, and so the ceiling couldn't have been leaking.

I counted five more drips before Stephen's beaten-down voice emerged from behind me in the bed. "Please keep me with you. I can't stand it anymore."

I kept my eyes closed. "We'll figure this out soon so you can have some peace. We're so close now."

"I didn't kill myself."

"I know."

"They're killing me."

"I know." I shut my eyes tighter. A warm liquid seeped across the sheets and soaked my nightgown, but I swallowed down my fear and kept talking to him. "Stephen, does one of the blackbirds look like your mother?"

Three more drips. "What?"

"Is your mother ever there when you're suffering from the poison?"

"No."

"Are you sure?"

"She isn't there."

"What about your brother and cousin?"

"They're blackbirds. Enormous, vicious creatures. I see their beaks—huge, luminous scissors that could tear you to shreds."

"You keep saying that, but I don't understand. I need to touch the place where you—"

"No—they'll rip you to pieces. Don't you dare go anywhere near that bed, Shell. You'll see them."

"I want to see them. I want to know who did this to you."

"Please, no." He flinched enough to jerk the mattress. "Don't go to my room. Swear to me you won't."

"Then tell me what I'm supposed to do. I can't keep you with me. It's—scary. It's dangerous. I can't do it, Stephen." My eyes welled with tears. "I've got to let you go." I covered my face with quivering fingers and cried.

Stephen wept as well—I could hear him shaking and sniffing behind me, which made me sputter sobs into my pillow all the more.

"Don't . . ." He choked on tears. "Please don't cry, Shell—"

"I should have stopped you from leaving for the war that day. I should have done something."

"There was nothing else you could have done. I had already signed the papers to go."

"We should have had the chance to be together again. You shouldn't be dead. I've lost my entire life." The pillow beneath

my cheek absorbed my tears until the fabric felt drenched—
and all the while the dripping liquid oozed its damp and sticky
heat across the left side of my body. I coughed and struggled
to find my voice. "Are you bleeding, Stephen?"

He sniffed again. "My head really hurts."

I wiped my eyes with a corner of the quilt. "I'm going to get
off the bed now. I'll move slowly."

"Don't let me go yet. I'm not ready."

"I'm just standing up so I can see what you look like." My
blood turned sluggish in my veins. I had to fight against the
weight of his sadness to rise to a standing position. But I
made it. I stood upright.

With the softest of steps, I turned around and faced him.

"Oh, Stephen." I slapped my palm over my mouth and
burst into tears again.

Blood, thick and dark and blackish red, caked his face and
shirt. I couldn't even see his eyes and mouth—only the in-
nards of his head. He huddled against the wall and held his
hand against his left temple, but a stream of crimson seeped
through his fingers and fell to a puddle on my sheets.

My legs buckled. My knees slammed to the floor. I lowered
my head to the rug and fought against black spots buzzing in
front of my eyes.

"It's too late," he said while my brain swayed on a swelling
sea of dizziness. "They're here."

Unconsciousness stole me away before I could see who
"they" were.

DOWNSTAIRS, THE CUCKOO ANNOUNCED HALF PAST FIVE in the morning.

I opened my eyes, and after several more minutes spent on the floor regaining my strength, I pushed myself to a standing position with the wobbling legs of a newborn deer.

Stephen was gone. My empty sheets looked clean and white, without one speck of blood staining them.

But I remembered what he looked like.

I staggered out to the dark hallway with nothing but the feel of the wall under my hand guiding me to my aunt's half-open door. "Aunt Eva? Can I sleep with you until you have to get up?"

She didn't answer, so I entered her unlit room.

"Aunt Eva?"

Strange little breathing noises rasped from her bed, as if she were crying but trying to stifle her sobs.

"Did you hear him?" I asked her. The soles of my feet found their way across her unseen floorboards. "Is that why you're crying? I'm sorry. I'm trying to let him go. I know I need to."

She kept breathing in that odd way. My stomach sank. The sounds didn't resemble sobs anymore.

She was shivering.

"Oh no." I lunged toward her bedside table and lit a match. "Oh, Christ."

She was curled in a ball beneath her covers and trembled as if all the blankets in the world couldn't warm her. Her face had turned tomato red, and her sweaty hair clung to her cheeks and lips. Her eyes stared at nothing.

I covered my mouth and nostrils with my hand to protect myself, even though the germs were just as likely to be waiting on my skin as traveling through the air. The match burned down to my fingers, searing my flesh, so I blew it out, struck another one, and lifted the glass chimney of her oil lamp to ignite the wick.

"The flu got inside the house," she wheezed. "Leave before it finds you."

Every square inch of my skin went cold at the way she described the flu like one of Stephen's blackbirds. "I've got to help you, Aunt Eva."

"Go."

I laid my palm against her forehead. "You're hotter than that match that just burned me."

"Don't touch me." She tried to swipe her hand at my arm. "Pack your things and leave before it gets you, too."

"I don't have anywhere else to go."

"Go. Leave. Get out of the house." She shut her eyes against a violent bout of shivering that gripped her the same way Mae Tate had convulsed on the floor of our high school English classroom.

"I'm going to make you some tea and onion soup—"

"Go!"

I jumped backward at the force of her words. "Who's going to take care of you?"

"It doesn't matter. I can't face your mother and tell her I let you die. She'd never forgive me. She'd want you to live." She grimaced through the pain of her chills. "Go. Go!"

I backed out of the room, unsure what to do. At any second I might drop to the floor with the same convulsions. My life could end in a matter of hours. Stephen would never be free.

But I couldn't leave my aunt. I couldn't—not when I could possibly save her.

The day before my father's arrest, I read an article about a Portland woman who cured her four-year-old daughter of the flu by burying her in raw onions for three days. The mother had fed the child onion syrup and smothered her in pungent bulbs from head to toe. Dad had remarked, "It's like the Gypsies hanging garlic above their doors to ward off evil," and I shook my head in dismay at the woman's desperation.

But that Portland girl survived. She lived. Her mother saved her.

I could save Aunt Eva.

I ran downstairs, switched on the main gas valve outside the back door, and poked matches inside the globes of the kitchen wall lamps to set them glowing. Light burned through the darkness in that cold, still room.

The pile of onions delivered the day before sat in a crate on the kitchen floor. Eleven of the dozen remained. I plunked three of them on the kitchen worktable.

"The knives!" I smacked my forehead. "She hid all the kitchen knives."

I charged back upstairs to Aunt Eva's room. "Where are the kitchen knives?"

"Go away."

"I need to chop onions. Where are they?"

"Wilfred's violin case."

"I don't see a violin case." I pulled at my hair. "Where is it?"

"Under the bed." She groaned through her spasms. "It's so cold in here. Why is it so cold in San Diego? The weather was supposed to cure Wilfred."

"I'll get more blankets. I'll be right back." I dashed away and tugged my blankets and Grandma Ernestine's quilt off my own bed, dragged them down the hall, and laid them over Aunt Eva's twitching body. "Here you go. Nice and warm."

"*Kalt.*"

"What?" I asked.

"*Kalt.*"

"I don't know what you're saying, Aunt Eva."

"*Eiskalt.*"

"Are you speaking German?"

"Don't speak German, Mary Shelley." She whimpered through her chills. "They'll arrest you. *Gefängnis.*"

"I've got to find the knives. Where's his blasted violin case?" I dug through shoes and boxes stuffed beneath the bed. "Here it is. Cripes, you really wanted to hide it, didn't you?" I popped open the latch of a curved leather case.

The knives and scissors were tucked around Uncle Wilfred's cherrywood violin. I snatched a knife with an accidental strum of the E string and returned downstairs, so fueled by fear I didn't yet feel tired from being up so early.

My fingers chopped those golden bulbs as fast as they could without severing a thumb. I stuck an onion wedge in my mouth and sucked on its potent fumes to keep my own body from breaking down. Water blurred my eyes.

"Wait—why am I chopping them?" I spit the onion out of my mouth. "She needs to be buried in them. This is crazy. What do I need to do?" I paced the kitchen floor and yanked my hair again until my scalp hurt. "All right . . . let's make the chopped ones into soup and syrup and cut the other ones in half to stir up the odors. We'll put the halved ones in her bed. Her feet—oh, damn, I forgot to check her feet!"

Another frenzied dash upstairs. I flapped the ends of her blankets off her legs and fell to my knees in thanks at the sight of shivering white feet.

"Oh, thank God. They're not black."

But some of the victims die within a matter of hours, I remembered the newspapers warning. *Some last for days before a deadly pneumonia sets in, and there's nothing you can do to free their lungs from that suffocating blood-tinged fluid.*

Aunt Eva coughed a wicked cough that rattled inside her chest. Her nose bled into her pillowcase.

"Why is there blood?" I mopped her up with a handkerchief, but the flow kept coming. "Hold this against your nostrils with as much strength as you can give. I have to get the onions. We've got to get you covered."

I took off again, and I heard my father's words of advice from his letter in the rhythm of my footsteps pounding through the halls.

Human beings have always managed to find the greatest strength within themselves during the darkest hours.

The phrase spurred me onward to the kitchen.

Human beings have always managed to find . . .

It sliced through the onions with eight swift beats.

. . . The. Great. Est. Strength. With. In. Them. Selves . . .

It rustled in the papery onion skins shuffling in a pouch made of my nightgown's skirt.

. . . during the darkest hours. Human beings have always managed to find the greatest strength within themselves during the darkest hours.

I lifted the blankets off my aunt.

"No," she screamed. "It's too cold. *Kalt! Kalt!*"

"I'm smothering you in onions. You'd do the same for me, and you know it."

I scattered the onion halves over her upper body while she pulled her knees to her stomach and hacked and shivered. More blood gushed out of her nose, this time in a stronger flow. I wiped her up again and changed her pillowcase, but she stained the new case within five seconds. I attempted to give her an aspirin for the fever, but she threw it up.

"I should call a doctor."

Human beings have always managed to find the greatest strength within themselves during the darkest hours.

Back in the kitchen I picked up the telephone's black, horn-shaped earpiece and turned the crank on its boxy oak body. It took a hundred years for the operator to answer.

"Number, please," said a female voice at the other end.

"I need a doctor."

"A specific doctor?"

"Any doctor. My aunt's sick with the flu, and her nose won't stop bleeding."

"Is it a dangerous level of blood loss?"

"I don't . . ." I massaged my eyes. "Yes—it seems dangerous. She's burning up with a fever and throwing up, too. I can't give her an aspirin."

"I'm afraid most doctors are too busy to answer their phones right now. I'll try connecting you to an ambulance dispatcher. One moment, please."

A series of clicks traveled down the line, and all I could think about was how swiftly time was passing. The cuckoo clock would be striking six in the morning in three minutes.

A man from the San Diego Police Department picked up, but he told me I'd have to wait at least twelve hours before an ambulance would be available.

"I hear sirens outside my house," I shouted into the mouthpiece. "Why can't one of those ambulances just stop by and get my aunt?"

"Because they're already being used to transport other patients. We'll put her name and address on a list and get a car there as soon as possible."

"What if she dies before then?"

"Then cover her with a sheet and put her outside. A separate ambulance is making the rounds to pick up bodies."

I hung up on the man and pressed my forehead against the telephone's sharp wooden edge. "This can't be happening. It's too much." I whacked the green wall with my fist. The sensation felt exquisite, so I whacked it again until the cuckoo clock bounced off its nail and splintered on the floor. The second hand still ticked, so I stomped on the clock's face with my bare foot and kicked the contraption across the kitchen, where it cracked against the icebox with a terrific *crash*.

The ticking stopped.

I had killed a clock.

I should have been saving my aunt and my dead first love, but instead I had murdered a beautiful Swiss timepiece, handmade in the nineteenth century by one of my great-grandfathers up in the Alps. My fist throbbed. Little clock handprints bruised the sole of my foot.

Death gave a good chuckle. *I'm beating you, little girl. You see? You can't fight me. Why even try?*

I grabbed clean cloths and returned upstairs to Aunt Eva.

THE REST OF THE DAY UNFOLDED MUCH THE SAME: NON-stop running up and down the stairs with soup and tea and cold compresses. Fruitless telephone calls to find doctors and ambulances. Bloody noses. Rasping coughs that sounded like the last gasps of a drowning person. Skin color checks. Onions. Vomit. Curse words that would have made my father cringe. Clothing changes when I couldn't stand the mess of fluids on my own skirts.

I opened a cookbook and learned how to make onion syrup by filling a jar with alternating layers of onions, brown sugar, and honey, but the concoction would need to sit overnight to be ready to consume. When my stomach growled, I stopped to eat an apple and drink a glass of water, but my breaks couldn't have lasted more than two minutes apiece. There was no time to slow down.

Somehow, night returned before it seemed due. Aunt Eva had made it onto a list for an ambulance, but every time I called for an update, the dispatcher added another twelve hours to the wait.

"I'll pay you money," I told the man near midnight. "I'll pay you to pick her up sooner. I bet you're fetching rich people faster than the poor souls who slave away in the shipyard. That poor woman worked her fingers to the bone to keep the navy safe, and you're just letting her die up there."

"Miss, her name is on our list. We'll get her as soon as we can."

"You're not a true patriot. You're not one hundred percent American."

"Miss—"

"I'm sorry, that was a terrible thing to say. I hate when people say that. I'm sure you're a fine person."

"Miss, you sound tired. Are you ill as well?"

"I'm fit as a fiddle. I've never been better. It's lovely weather we're having, too, isn't it? A grand day for a cup of tea with my beautiful dead boy and my dying aunt."

"Miss, get some sleep. We'll send an ambulance."

"He was just eighteen."

"Get some sleep."

"She's twenty-six."

"Miss . . ."

"All right." I rested the earpiece on its hook and tottered on my feet. "All right."

I STRUGGLED TO STAY AWAKE, TO KEEP HELPING AUNT Eva, but my arms and legs refused to move at a normal rate. A snail of a girl was what I'd become. An old woman shuffling about in the stooped body of a sixteen-year-old.

Candlelight illuminated a little porcelain clock on Aunt Eva's bedside table. The morning ticked its way toward five o'clock. Almost twenty-four hours had passed since I'd first found her with the flu. The oil for her lamp had run out, so I hunkered down on her floor in the shadows with my arms wrapped around my bent legs.

"I wonder how that Jones boy is doing, or whatever his name was," I said to my aunt's wheezing, weakening body. "The one who unsettled me at the convalescent home. Is his flu as bad as yours? And I wonder about Carlos and Mr. Darning, and Stephen's friend Paul. Are they still alive? Is my dad alive? Will today be the end of the world? Because it sure feels like it." I sank my head against my knees and smelled onions and blood on my black skirt. "It wasn't all that frightening to die, come to think of it. Returning was the hard part, landing back inside this broken body and waking up to the war and the flu and people who do cruel things to other people." I bit my lip and tasted dry skin. "Why did I even return? What a nasty joke to send a girl back inside her body, only to show her there's nothing she can do for anyone in the world."

Aunt Eva muttered something in German and gibberish.

"Hmm . . . maybe the onion syrup is ready. I should give that a try." I grabbed the side of her bed with one hand and hoisted myself off her floor. "Let's give that a try, shall we?"

A cry of shock escaped my lips.

My aunt's face was brown. Those mahogany spots—the purplish, brownish signs of a body losing oxygen—were overrunning her cheeks and ears. She gurgled and sputtered, and blood again leaked from her nose.

"No, that's not fair!" I dug my fingers into her mattress. "I'm trying my hardest to save you, so you can't turn purple. Don't you dare let this beat you, Aunt Eva. Don't you dare—"

An ambulance wailed through the neighborhood outside.

What would happen if I jumped in front of the vehicle to make it come to a stop? What would happen?

"Let's find out." I left my aunt's side and galloped down the stairs in the dark, somehow arriving at the bottom without breaking my neck. Outside a salty breeze blew through my hair and skirt, and the moon was a thumbnail sliver in the still-black sky. A cluster of voices murmured down the street, and I turned and smiled for the first time that day.

There would be no need to jump in front of an ambulance, for there an ambulance sat—one block down.

"Thank you!" I took off running to make sure I reached the driver before he could drive away or fade from sight. "Don't be a hallucination. Please don't be a hallucination."

Two uniformed policemen hauled a young woman out of an adobe-style bungalow with a red-tiled roof. Her unshaven husband ran his hand through his tousled brown hair while holding a toddler in his other arm. A grandmotherly woman beside him rocked a crying infant.

"Please take my aunt, too!" I ran at the officers at the speed of hurricane winds. "Take my aunt; she's in my house."

"There's no room," said one of them—an ugly man with squinty eyes and enormous ears.

"She's not very big. You can make room." I was aware of my arms waving around me as if they had a mind of their own, but I couldn't control them. "Please! Stop telling me to wait twelve more hours. This woman here isn't nearly as sick as my aunt. Her face isn't even close to turning purple."

"We don't have another stretcher."

"Then I'll carry her myself, you lazy, useless—"

"I can help." The flu victim's husband put down the toddler and came my way. "I'll help you carry her."

I stepped back, caught off guard by his kindness. "What?"

"Stay right here," he told the officers. "Where is she?"

"This way. Thank you. Thank you." With tears turning the road ahead of me into a blurry, bobbing streak, I led the man to our house, and we tore up the dark stairs together. "Thank you. She's in here. She's turning that brownish-purple color."

The man scooped my shivering aunt into his arms by the light of the candle.

"*Kalt*," she muttered. "So *kalt*. *Grippe*. Wilfredededed . . . *mein Liebchen*."

"Don't speak German, Aunt Eva. She's not even German, she's Swiss." I followed the man and my aunt out of her room, back into the blackness of the upper hallway. "She was born in America, and I killed her Swiss cuckoo clock. I kicked it clear across the kitchen as though it were causing our problems. Just like Oberon and those scissors that nearly got him."

"Do you have the flu, too?" asked the man on our way down the stairs. "You sound feverish."

"No, I'm fine. I just haven't slept in twenty-four hours, and no one would come get her, and Stephen's waiting for me."

He maneuvered Aunt Eva out the front door. "Where is someone waiting for you?"

"He's probably shivering down in the shadow of blackbirds again . . . um . . . Coronado, I mean. Did I just tell a stranger about the blackbirds?"

Something rustled in the white branches of the eucalyptus when we passed beneath its long, fragrant leaves, and I wondered if Oberon was perched up there, waiting for the door to open again so he could fly inside.

"Where are your parents?" asked the man. We were half-way back to his house.

"Gone. Dad said the flu wouldn't be so bad in San Diego with all the warm, fresh air, but that's not the first time he made a mistake. Why are you helping my aunt when you must be sick with worry about your wife?"

"It's better than thinking I allowed someone to die."

"That's good of you." Goodness—there was still goodness in the world. "I started thinking I was the only one left alive."

The ugly officer waved at us to move faster. "Hurry up—we need to get going."

The man nestled Aunt Eva in the back of the ambulance, squeezing her between his shaking wife and a white-haired woman with a face too young for her hair. They all wore dainty ivory nightgowns. Three sleeping angels. The last thing I saw before the officers shut the door was three pairs of bare feet, lined up in a row. Aunt Eva's looked darker than the others.

"Wait!" I lunged for the door. "Her feet looked black."

The ugly officer grabbed my arms and pushed me away. "We can't wait any longer."

"Her feet looked black."

"It's too dark to tell."

"They looked black. Let me see."

"We've got to go!" He forced me down to a seated position on the street. "Stay right there, and don't you dare get up. You're not helping anyone right now." He took off toward the driver's seat.

"Let them go." The man who had carried my aunt seized my elbow before I could shoot back toward the ambulance. "Your aunt is in good hands."

"Her feet looked black."

"It may have just been the lack of light."

"I didn't even say good-bye."

"She'll be all right . . . It's all right." The man put his arm around my shoulders and led me over to his crying children and the grandmotherly woman, while the sirens blared. "Do you want to come inside with us? None of us are feeling well, but at least we can be sick together. You seem to be alone."

I shook my head. "Stephen told me in that letter about the war to be careful offering my trust to people. He's waiting for me. If I'm going to drop dead from the flu, I need to go to his house while I'm still able. I'm so tired."

"Why don't you get some sleep before you find this person? You really look like you're getting the flu."

"I'm not sick. I'm just tired." I pulled myself out from under the man's comforting arm and backed away. "Thank you. I've got to go. I've got to help someone before I die. My mother didn't lose her life just so she could send a useless girl into the world. There's got to be something more."

28

STEPHEN'S ROOM

BACK IN MY BEDROOM, I STUFFED MY MOTHER'S LEATHER doctor's bag full of my treasures—Stephen's photographs, his letters, my goggles, *The Mysterious Island*, my mother's coin purse, Dad's note. I crammed everything inside the cloth-lined compartments with the same urgency as when I had packed for San Diego the night my father warned me people might be coming for him. The brass gear necklace with the lightning burn went over my head and shimmered on the bodice of my best dress—the black silk taffeta one I'd worn to Stephen's funeral. The garment still smelled of sulfur and sorrow, but my plans for the morning required my finest clothing.

Downstairs, I put on my coat and tucked an onion in my pocket. And a potato. Our next-door neighbor in Portland,

Miss Deily, insisted a potato in the pocket would scare away the flu, and I was willing to do absolutely anything to buy a few more minutes. I tied my flu mask in place and lifted my leather bag by its handles.

Outside, the sky to the east blushed pink, a color that would have looked brilliant in a chemist's glass flask. I pulled my coat around me and headed south to the center of the city, feeling like the earth's sole survivor. Smoke hung across the sky in a cloud that sprinkled ashes on the silent streets and sidewalks. I didn't know if I was smelling chimneys battling the November chill or crematoriums disposing of the dead, but the city looked and felt like the Germans had just bombed us. The stacks of coffins in the undertaker's front yard spilled out to the sidewalk, and the stench was overwhelming. I held my breath and kept walking.

Death bit at the backs of my ears. *I told you I was coming. Get ready. I'm here.*

"You're not here yet," I said. "I'm still upright and walking, aren't I?"

I clutched my mother's bag and walked five more blocks to Mr. Darning's photography studio, not far from the site of the Liberty Loan drive where Aunt Eva had purchased my goggles in another life. The red automobile that had been parked outside our house during the photographer's visit sat next to the curb.

I hurried to the studio's door and banged on the glass. "Mr. Darning? Are you in there?"

I held my breath. A figure moved inside.

"Mr. Darning?" I banged again. "Please open up. It's Mary Shelley Black. I need your help."

The photographer appeared behind the glass with rumpled hair and blinking eyes. With his mask in his hand, he opened the door, and for the first time I saw his entire face, including a trim mustache that matched his copper-wire hair.

"Miss Black. You caught me off guard. I slept here last night because my neighbors all have the flu."

"It got Aunt Eva, too. I'm scared it's going to take me at any minute."

"Oh, Jesus." He pulled away from me.

"I've been breathing the same air she has. I'm dead—I know it. Please take me to Stephen Embers's house before it knocks me down."

"What?"

"Take me over there, and convince Julius to allow me inside Stephen's bedroom. Julius wants to take a picture of me for a contest. We can tell him the best place for a spirit photograph is up in Stephen's room."

"But—"

"I swear to you I'll show you evidence of a soul who's departed his body. I swear you'll feel better about that girl of yours who died."

He tied his mask around his face. "I don't know if I should allow you in my car—"

"That's her picture right there, isn't it?" I pressed my hand against the window that separated me from the photograph of the beautiful dark-haired woman.

"Yes, that's Viv."

"If you had only a few hours left to live," I said, my fingers running pale streaks down the glass, "and you knew you could spend those last precious moments freeing her soul so she could rest in peace, wouldn't you do anything you could to help her?"

His eyes shone with tears. "Of course I would."

"Then help me free a soul I love." The vinegary sting of grief nipped at my taste buds. "Keep me safe from Julius while I call Stephen to me one last time."

He craned his neck toward me. "You're—you're going to let his spirit go?"

I nodded. "It's time. They all need to move on, Mr. Darning."

He blinked, and a tear escaped his left eye.

I took my hand away from the glass. "But I promise you, what you'll witness in Stephen's room will be better than Mac-Dougall's scale experiments, better than my compass, and far better than Julius Embers's usual photographs. You'll have proof your Viv lives on in some other place."

He turned his gaze from me to the picture of the brunette woman, which told me his answer.

He would be coming.

I would be safe to explore Stephen's last memories in the very room where he died.

I SPENT MY FINAL CROSSING OF SAN DIEGO BAY IN THE
automobile section of the Coronado ferry, seated on the passenger side of Mr. Darning's ruby-red vehicle, my black bag
tucked beneath my legs. Once the *Ramona* docked, Mr. Darning slammed his foot on the gas pedal and we sped across
the island that wasn't an island, past the streetcar tracks that
had carried Aunt Eva and me to the Emberses' house, and
alongside the restless Pacific until we reached the two-story
cottage with brown shingles.

He pulled the car next to the curb and shut off the motor.

Three crows were perched on the Emberses' roof. Their
sinister caws laughed over the ocean's roar, and I swore they
stared me in the eye.

"Oh no." A headache erupted across my skull. "You were
right." I slunk down in my seat.

Mr. Darning popped open his door. "I was right about
what?"

"I can't get out of the car until those birds go away."

"Why not?"

"I see their beaks."

"Pardon?"

"They're like scissors. They could tear me to shreds. I don't
like how they're looking at me."

Mr. Darning didn't move.

"Kill them," I shouted in a husky tone that startled the
both of us.

He stepped out of the car and smacked his hands together. "Shoo. Go away, birds. Get out of here."

The calculating birds didn't budge.

"Throw something at them." I slid farther down against the leather. "Hurry, before they smell the gore on my clothing."

"What gore? Why are you talking like that? Your voice sounds different."

"Just kill them."

"I can't go throwing rocks at somebody's roof. Let me fetch my box of photographic plates from the backseat so we can go inside. Ignore the birds."

"I can't ignore them. Look at their eyes. They're watching me."

He backed away from the car. "You're starting to scare me. Please . . . let me fetch my plates from the backseat."

The dark thugs on the roof flapped their wings and took flight. I ducked and gasped and covered my head with my arms while their feathers beat against my neck.

Mr. Darning touched my back and made me jump. "The birds are headed east. They're nowhere in sight. You don't need to be afraid of them. All right?"

I lifted my head and made sure the birds were truly gone. "All right." My voice resembled my own again. "I'm sorry. They bother me these days."

He opened my door for me. "Calm yourself and stop shaking so much. There's nothing to fear." Despite his bold words, his own hands trembled.

A disorienting bout of light-headedness threatened to stop me from making my way up to the front porch, but I gulped deep breaths and persevered, still keeping an eye out for crows. And the flu. My dizziness and confusion could have been the first signs of fever.

Mr. Darning's raps against the front door sounded as loud to my ears as cannon blasts. We waited almost a minute, with no results, and then he knocked again.

I reached out to the wall below the porch light for support. "What if Julius isn't home?"

"Shh. Let's listen for his footsteps and make sure he's not avoiding us."

We tipped our ears toward the door and stood stock-still, but I only heard waves breaking on the shore across the street.

Mr. Darning swallowed and looked my way. "He might be dead."

"Oh no." I jiggled the brass doorknob. *Locked.* "No!" I pushed against the door as if I were truly strong enough to break it down. "This can't be happening. His cousin came to our house just yesterday. Julius was alive as of her visit."

Mr. Darning shook his head. "Being alive yesterday doesn't mean a thing with this flu."

"Don't remind me. My aunt . . ."

"I'm sorry."

I glanced behind me at the empty lawn where the lines of photography customers had waited. I thought of the studio . . . and the porthole-style windows.

"Oh . . . wait . . . Stephen's entrance." I tore down the front steps.

"Where are you going?"

"Stephen used to climb through the studio's windows," I said, my feet squishing across the dew-soaked front lawn, "to save the equipment at night when Julius left them open."

Mr. Darning trailed after me with his brown case of glass plates in hand.

Around the corner, beyond the studio's entrance, I saw three round windows—all open to allow the chill from the night to settle inside the house. Or else left open by a man unavailable to shut them.

Stephen's grandparents had built the openings six feet off the ground, so the portholes were more a useless nautical decoration than a means of view or escape. A larger window faced the ocean at the front of the house, but I had always seen its shutters closed and locked, perhaps so Julius could further provide a dim and ghostly atmosphere inside the studio.

Two options existed: a coral tree with thick branches that reached out to the windows and a sturdy white trellis that was attached to the wall next to the leftmost porthole. I didn't feel like shinnying up a tree trunk in my taffeta dress, so I grabbed hold of the trellis's latticed wood and started to climb.

"You can't go into that house alone," said Mr. Darning. "Not when Julius might be in there."

My head still felt dizzy, so I didn't dare look down at him.

My hands brushed past a flowering vine that tickled the backs of my fingers. "I'll run"—I grunted and kept going upward—"straight to the side door . . . and let you in right away. I just hope Stephen isn't furious at me for coming."

"Why would *Stephen* be furious?"

I wrapped my right hand around the bottom edge of the left window. "He believes there are creatures inside the house that want to hurt me. Nightmare creatures." I peeked inside the studio.

"Do—do you see anything in there?"

I shook my head. "It's empty. The lights are off. I'm going in." I clutched the trellis again and went a few inches higher. "Please turn away, Mr. Darning. This won't be ladylike."

"Be careful."

"I'll try." I reached out to a nearby tree branch, gripped it with both hands, and swung my feet to the bottom edge of the round window. I then slid my legs carefully through the opening so I wouldn't take the six-foot drop in one loud go. With my fingers still locked around the branch, I held my breath and listened for Julius's footsteps. Or Stephen's voice.

"Are you all right?" Mr. Darning called from down below.

"I'm fine. I'm going to push the top half of my body through and see if I can twist around and hang on to the ledge before dropping."

Somehow, I did exactly that. With a swish of black taffeta and the thuds of tumbling feet and elbows, I landed on the studio floor—bruised but intact.

The house inside tasted of smoke and poison and blazing-hot metal. It felt wrong to be there, and I would have bolted out the door if I hadn't felt in my gut that Stephen's room hid the missing piece in the puzzle of his death.

"What are you doing in here?" asked someone behind me.

I leapt to my feet.

Julius came toward me through the open pocket doors, but he staggered rather than walked. His pace was slow and his footsteps unsteady, like the movements of a drunk. His pale face had grown thin compared with his appearance just four days earlier, and his wild black hair needed a good brushing.

I ran over to the side door and opened it for Mr. Darning.

Julius stopped in his tracks when he saw the other photographer entering the studio. "Why are you both here?" he asked.

"We thought you were dead from the flu." I grabbed hold of Mr. Darning's arm for support. "You weren't answering the door. We got worried."

Julius took four more labored steps and spoke as if we were idiots. "Why. Are. You. Here?"

I steadied my breathing. "I'm here to put your brother to rest. I'll sit for that photograph you want."

Julius's eyes—so bloodshot they must have burned—blinked as if I'd just woken him from a long sleep. He stood up straight and made his voice deeper. "Why are *you* with her, Darning?"

"I'm curious about her abilities. I agreed to accompany her to ensure you'll be sending a legitimate photograph of your brother's spirit to that contest." Mr. Darning lifted his brown case. "As usual, I've brought my own plates, marked with my initials, to prevent you from switching to your own doctored versions."

Julius scrutinized Mr. Darning through uneasy eyes. "You sure you're not plotting to get me arrested?"

Mr. Darning lowered his case. "I swear I'm only here for the sake of psychical research. I believe this girl is genuinely capable of luring your brother into a photograph. If we can get him to come, there would be no need for you to be arrested, would there?"

I lifted my chin and tried not to let my fear get the best of me. "Please let me help your brother, Julius. I know he'll come to me. *You* know he'll come to me."

Julius leaned his hand against the wall for support, right next to the picture of the white-draped phantom and me. He sniffed and rubbed his nose. "You look terrible, Mary Shelley. Are you sick or something?"

"No—just tired and anxious to contact your brother. Will you let me?"

He shifted his weight from one foot to the other and hesitated some more. My eyes and throat stung as if a cloud of cyanide hovered overhead, and Julius looked equally sickened by the toxic atmosphere.

To speed things along, I spoke to his way of thinking. "Are

we ready to win this prize, Julius? Should we help both you and Stephen get out of this house for good?"

"How much is the prize?" asked Mr. Darning.

I kept my eyes on Julius. "Two thousand dollars for solid proof of the existence of spirits. Isn't that right, Julius?"

Julius stirred back to life once again. He pushed himself off the wall. "Bring Stephen quickly . . . and then send him far away from here. I don't want him anywhere near me, so don't—"

I hurried out to the house's main entryway.

"Hey! Where are you going, Mary Shelley?"

Julius and Mr. Darning followed me out to the hall, their footsteps amplified in the deep, hollow space, which still reminded me of the belly of a ship with its dangling brass lantern and knotty wood walls.

"Why are you out here?" asked Julius. "The studio's back—"

"Shh." I lifted my finger, for I thought I had heard a whisper down the way.

The grandfather clock continued to preside over the far end of the hall, but the second hand ticked louder than I remembered. A shadow hiding the round white moon face seemed to lengthen across the wall to the clock's left and stretch toward the staircase. I remembered what the stairs looked like—the shine of the dark wood, the green runner trailing up the steps behind Stephen. An electrical hum rose in their direction, drowning out the ticking of the clock.

I kept an eye on that back portion of the house. "We have

to photograph him in his bedroom to catch him with your camera."

Julius shook his head. "No! Absolutely not. You are not going into his room."

"Isn't that where you hear him?" I asked.

"I don't want you in there."

"Then there's no point in trying. That's where he is. I bet if I called to him right now, he'd make a sound up there . . ."

"No." Julius ran over and grabbed my shoulder to stop me from going to the staircase. "Don't call him."

"I'd listen to her, Embers," said Mr. Darning. "She seems to know how to find him. He was already coming to her in my car outside your house."

Julius turned even paler. "He was?"

Mr. Darning nodded. "I heard him. This is going to be a spectacular photograph. I can feel it."

Julius gulped like he might throw up. Then he said, "All right. I'll take the photograph upstairs. But I have conditions, too."

I tensed. "What are they?"

"You have to take off that mask. No more photographs of you in goggles or gauze or other bizarre accessories. This has to be a professional sitting. You're here only to pose for the picture and to send him away. No dramatics. No snooping."

I looked to Mr. Darning, who gave me a comforting nod and said in that gentle tone of his, "You know it's probably already too late for gauze masks. The judges would appreciate seeing your face. You don't want to look like you're hiding anything."

I nodded. "I'll take the mask off, then. May I use your washroom to cool my face before the sitting?"

"I—all right." Julius rubbed his eyes and swayed for a moment. "Go make yourself presentable. I'll fetch my equipment and start setting up." He pointed at Mr. Darning. "You wait right here, Darning. I don't want you sniffing around his room before I'm up there." He stumbled back inside his studio, and I half wondered if he'd collapse and pass out.

Mr. Darning set his brown case of photographic plates on a small marble table in the hall and popped open the lid. "Go get yourself comfortable, Miss Black. You're doing well. I've never seen a braver girl."

"Thank you," I said, although I didn't feel brave in the slightest. The vile tastes of poison and blood flowed across my tongue and warned of imminent pain.

I wandered down to the grandfather clock on unsteady legs and stopped for a moment to watch the brass pendulum swing in its hypnotizing rhythm. The second hand journeyed to the bottom of the white moon face, and the gears—those thin cuts of circular metal moving in perfect synchronicity— spun and clicked deep inside the heart of the contraption.

I glanced back at the staircase and longed to hear Stephen ask me again what I saw through my goggles' lenses. I wanted to tell him a new answer: *I see the future, and I know it can all be changed if you stop yourself from heading off to the army when you're still in school. Don't run away from your home life just yet. The battles will rob you of your mind, and someone will destroy your body. Your photographs will be lost. You'll never get to grow up.*

I clenched my fists and continued through the house, past the humming staircase.

The washroom consisted of a pull-chain toilet, a white shell sink, and more cedar wall panels that smelled of wood and toxic fumes. Only a sliver of natural light came through a small window near the ceiling, so the room felt dark and crowded and uncomfortable. I removed my mask and splashed cool water over my sweating cheeks and nose. The peaked face staring back at me in the mirror above the sink belonged to a petrified kid, not a confident spirit medium. My skin lacked all color, and my hair seemed darker than usual. I already looked like a black-and-white photograph.

I dried my face on a limp yellow towel that reeked of darkroom chemicals. The noxious air inside the house kept me from inhaling deep enough to calm my racing heart. With my throat dry, I twisted the doorknob and walked across the hallway in my double-reinforced Boy Scout boots that could still help me run at a moment's notice.

I approached the bottom of the staircase, my pulse beating in the side of my neck. I could feel Stephen there, sitting the same way as when I saw him back in April. My left foot slipped on a polished floorboard, but I righted myself, regained my balance, and inched farther. The bottom step of the staircase came into view, along with a foot in a gray sock. The buzzing of electricity grew so loud my eardrums felt they would burst.

I stepped around the corner and saw him.

Black-red blood still covered his entire face and shirt, so close and clear and grotesque in the daylight. I shut my eyes and gagged.

"Don't go up there," he told me. "Get out."

"You don't look right." I braced myself against the wall and tried so hard not to ruin everything by vomiting all over the floor.

"Are you ready?" asked Julius in a voice that buzzed as much as the stairs.

I peeled one eye open and couldn't see Stephen anymore.

Julius thumped down the staircase in his huge brown shoes. "Mr. Darning just observed me placing his own plates in the camera upstairs. The equipment and lighting are ready."

"I'm ready, too," I said in a voice that sounded as if my vocal cords had turned to sandpaper. My head pulsated with pain to the beat of the blood churning through my veins. My body wouldn't last much longer—if the flu didn't overtake me, my nerves would. The need to reach Stephen's bedroom fueled my strength to endure the walk up that staircase.

I'd read about pilots describing a change in air pressure when their planes ascended into the sky. That's how it felt climbing up to the Emberses' second story. My stomach rose into my chest the way it did on a Ferris wheel, and the blood vessels in my temples seemed poised to pop. My throat burned hotter. I gripped the rail for support, as my legs melted beneath me.

At the top of the staircase, Julius turned right, toward a bedroom. The broiling air gusting out the opened doorway blew against my face like heat from an oven. The sound of a thousand lightbulbs, restless with electricity, droned within.

"Do you hear the buzzing?" I asked Julius.

"What buzzing?"

I eyed a wooden bed across from the door, below one of three windows that washed the room in an eerie sunlight I'd seen in photographs of empty barns and graveyards.

Mr. Darning waited for us just inside the door, offering me another nod of encouragement. "It's all right, Miss Black. I'm here."

Julius entered ahead of me, and I noticed the unsteadiness of his legs, the hesitancy with which he approached his camera. The leather bellows stretched toward the mattress, which was covered in nothing more than a dusty brown blanket. A chill spread from the nape of my neck to the small of my back. That ratty old cloth was probably hiding Stephen's blood. There was no longer a pillow.

"Well?" Julius steadied himself by holding on to the black box of his camera's body. "Aren't you coming in?" His voice squeaked an octave higher than usual. He kept his neck stiff and his eyes alert, searching for something over his shoulder.

I stepped across the threshold of Stephen's bedroom, which smelled rancid and stale. My legs might as well have been wading through a pool of molasses. The air pushed me backward as if it were alive, forcing me away from that buzzing and angry bed, breathing hot fumes against my face.

I staggered forward and reached my hand out to the brown blanket, the same way I'd try to grab a log if I were drowning in a river. Static stung my palm. I knew touching that mattress would give me a shock as potent as the lightning bolt's, but I bent forward, pushed through the molasses air, and climbed onto that bed.

A jolt of electricity whacked me in the back. I fell and shut my eyes through spine-rattling pain that shuddered through my teeth and made me bite my tongue. The room went black.

When I opened my eyes, I found the world dark and my wrists bound to a bed by coarse ropes that burned through the layers of my skin. I was on my back, and there was whispering near the door.

"Wait until I put on the mask. I don't want him recognizing me."

"Who cares if he recognizes you?"

"I don't want anything in his eyes slowing me down, all right? I didn't smoke enough dope tonight. I'm losing my nerve."

"I told you, too much dope might slow us down. What a waste it would be to forget to photograph him."

"Are you sure something's going to show up?"

"We've got to try, right?"

I struggled against my ropes. Dark figures shuffled around

me, guided by the dull light of a single candle. They wore black clothing and kept the flame far enough from their faces for me to see anything but pure-white surgical masks and the glint of their watchful eyes. One of them positioned a camera near the bed. I heard the turning of the tripod's handle and smelled the firework scent of magnesium powder poured across a flashlamp's tray. Scuttling noises emanated from everywhere, as if rats were scurrying around the room. Every sound was magnified.

One of the figures turned toward me, and his mask mutated into an enormous white beak. I sucked in my breath and blinked my eyes, but he wouldn't change—the creature looked like an ungodly bird with the body of a man.

A light flashed, and I was deep in the belly of a trench in France, cradling my rifle, waiting for the sound of artillery fire alongside other panting men. The mixed stink of rotting flesh, cigarettes, sweat, rum, urine, and stagnant mud turned my stomach into mush. I huddled on the ground at the far end of the line, and not more than six feet down from me lay the body of a soldier with reddish-brown hair, his flesh soft and pale, the blood on his face still drying.

A group of cawing carrion crows descended over the poor soul and pecked at his glassy brown eyes with their scissor-sharp beaks jabbing, jabbing, jabbing—fattening themselves on the ruins of war, gorging on a dead nineteen-year-old boy. One of the birds raised its head and stared at me with its beak smeared red and hunger brightening its ravenous eyes. I'd woken with one of its kind pressed against my rib cage before, digging at my uniform, smelling the blood in the fibers until I fought it off me to prove I was still alive.

I aimed my rifle at the crows on the boy and shot the largest bird dead, which sent a flurry of black wings flying past my face and a spray of machine-gun fire raining down upon us.

Then I was back on the bed in the unlit room, and one of the birdmen propped up my head on a pillow and forced the narrow tube of a copper funnel between my teeth. I gagged and struggled to free my wrists and ankles from the ropes. There was so little light; all I saw were those luminous beaks. I heard a bottle uncork and smelled the sting of darkroom chemicals in the air. Panic charged through me. I tried pushing the funnel out of my mouth with my tongue, but the figure shoved the tube farther inside, making me gag all the more.

"I'll try to keep his head up," said one of the birdmen in a strained whisper. "Unless . . . do we want to drown him with the acid? Maybe he'll look more like a flu victim in the photograph if he's choking."

"I don't know. I just want to get it over with."

The creature tilted a bottle, and then he poured.

Liquid fire careened down my throat and scorched my insides, burning all the way down to my stomach. I choked and coughed and spit out a substance that seared my face with the pain of a thousand pinpricks.

A light exploded, white and fiery like a bomb. I was back in the trench in France, running through the mud with a rifle in my hands, bullets whizzing overhead, a gas mask covering my head and magnifying my wheezing breaths. The man in front of me went down, collapsing in a spray of blood and muck that splattered across my mask. A green mist settled over me, as poisonous as that liquid the dark birds poured inside me.

I was back on the bed again, and the creatures were arguing over whether a picture had just been taken.

"Was I in that picture?"

"No."

"Are you sure about that?"

They shoved the copper funnel back in my mouth, and the volcanic river again sloshed down my throat. I turned my head and coughed out the poison into my pillow, burning my own flesh a second time. I cried out in horror.

The figure jumped out of the way. Another flash of light and smoke erupted five feet away, momentarily illuminating the dark human halves of the birds, who watched me from by the camera.

They were photographing me.

"Why are you poisoning me?" I tried to yell, but my larynx had been so burned by chemicals it made my voice coarse and weak. "Don't peck out my eyes."

"How long is it going to take?" asked one of the creatures in a deep and whispery voice.

"I have no idea. Have patience. Take some more pictures. He really does look like he's dying from the flu. I think the choking helps."

"What about the ropes? Dying flu patients aren't tied to beds."

"Damn it. I didn't think of that. Get those off him."

The creatures surrounded me again, studying me as I writhed and hacked out the stinging poison.

"He looks like he'll still fight. He's strong when he's delirious."

"I thought you were sticking him with morphine."

"Why the hell did I let you talk me into this?"

"Think of the huge impact on the world of psychical research if we capture his soul as it's leaving!"

"You only think that because you're more of a doper than I am, and he's not your brother."

"He's hardly a human being anymore. He's as good as dead, right?"

"Why did he say we were going to peck out his eyes?"

"Because he's a lunatic."

"I'm getting my gun."

"No! His spirit will leave too quickly. We won't have time to photograph it."

"I can't stand this. He's looking at me. I'm getting my gun and putting him out of his misery."

"No!" I cried in a voice that didn't sound human anymore. "Don't shoot me. Get me out of here. Don't kill me."

A flurry of action surrounded me—the rush of feathers, the scuttling of feet, voices arguing whether or not they should speed up the process. One of the creatures released my wrists from the ropes, but the deep-voiced one wrestled him to the ground and cussed him out. The room spun as if I were on a carnival ride. My throat and belly raged with fire. I turned on my side to curl up in pain and saw the silver metal of a gun shining on the bedside table.

My salvation.

I reached out, desperate to kill the squabbling birds with the bullets before they could finish with me. My clumsy fingers grasped the weapon. A brutal force knocked me in the head. The world slowed to a crawl, and a gunshot echoed in the black and heavy atmosphere. A white, bloodstained sky beckoned from overhead, tugging my soul toward it, while someone shouted from below, "Quick! Take a picture. We're going to miss it! We're going to miss it!"

And the scene started over again. I opened my eyes and found the world dark and my wrists bound to a bed by coarse ropes that burned through the layers of my skin. I was on my back, and there was whispering near the door.

This time someone grabbed my arms and shook me. I heard the name "Mary Shelley" and got confused. *Mary Shelley? Why is she here?*

"Leave us alone," I shouted. "Don't poison me. You're killing me."

A hand smacked me across the face. "Stop saying that. Why are you saying that?"

"Don't kill me. Please don't poison me."

"Stop it. I'm not poisoning you. Why are you talking like

you're him?" My attacker shook me until a bare, sunlit room came into view. Julius's face—not a bird's—stared down at me. I didn't see a single bird anywhere.

Beyond Julius's head, dark stains marred the ceiling's white plaster—the shadows of blood. Stephen's own blood was the red and white sky that haunted him.

"Oh, God. Oh, my God." I regained my bearings and tried to sit up, surprised to find my wrists weren't tied with ropes. "Stephen? Can you hear me? Those weren't monsters poisoning you."

"Don't you dare say I was the one poisoning him." Julius shook my shoulders. "Do you hear me? It wasn't me."

"What do you think you saw, Miss Black?"

I jumped at the sound of the other male voice as if I'd heard another gunshot. Mr. Darning stood by the camera and calmly sprinkled a box of powder across the flashlamp's tray as if preparing for a normal studio portrait. "You looked like you were in a trance," he continued. "I took a photograph of your intriguing state and can't wait to see if we've captured a record of your communication with the other side."

My stomach lurched.

Our conversations about spirits and science ran through my mind: *A physician named MacDougall conducted experiments involving the measurement of weight loss at the moment of death . . . at a home for incurable tuberculosis patients . . . He would push a cot holding a dying man onto an industrial-sized silk-weighing scale, and he kept his eyes on the numbers while his assistants watched for the final breath . . . I'm compelled to find tangible proof that we all go somewhere when we die. It hurts more than anything to think of a sweet soul like Viv's as being gone forever.*

"What did you see?" asked Mr. Darning again, his voice eager, his eyebrows raised. He positioned the loaded flashlamp into a holding stand next to the camera. "His spirit?"

"No." I steadied my breathing, even though the truth was falling into place with sickening clarity. "I witnessed two blackbirds experimenting on a delirious war veteran in the confusion of the dark."

Julius squeezed my arms. "Why are you talking about blackbirds, too? There were never any birds in this house."

"His attackers looked like birdmen with their dark clothing and beak-like flu masks. He wanted to shoot them, but he grabbed the gun wrong and must have pulled the trigger. It wasn't a suicide—he was disoriented and fighting for his life. He died struggling to live. He wasn't as good as dead."

"He wanted to shoot them?" asked Mr. Darning.

"Did you hear what she just said, Darning? 'As good as dead.' That's what you kept calling him that night."

"Perhaps you should stop damaging your brain with illegal substances, Julius." Mr. Darning ducked his head under the black cloth behind the camera. "I certainly wasn't anywhere near your brother when he was in the throes of his neuroses."

"Get me off this bed before it happens again." I squirmed

to escape Julius's grip. "I can taste the poison and the smoke from the flash. Don't make me repeat that."

"Let's take another photograph before she gets up," said Mr. Darning. "I've got this new plate ready to go."

"Would you stop taking photographs?" shouted Julius. "Get out from under that cloth and stop treating my house like a laboratory. I'm sick of your morbid psychical research haunting me each night. I'm sick of listening to my brother's bed shaking up here because of you."

Mr. Darning's face reemerged. "Keep your mouth shut, Julius."

"I sometimes hated Stephen, but he was my brother. I never would have done anything so twisted if I'd been in my right mind. You became obsessed with death after your girl-friend died."

"Stop putting ideas into Miss Black's head."

"She already has the ideas in her head. She knows who was in his room, Darning. Didn't you hear her? She felt you poisoning him."

Mr. Darning left the camera and grabbed my shoulder. "Tell me exactly what you think you saw, Mary Shelley. No one's going to hurt you if you tell me the truth. Who did those blackbirds look like?"

"Stephen!" I cried out. "Stephen Embers, where are you?"

"Don't bring him here right now." Julius covered my mouth with his hand, but I sunk my teeth into his flesh and freed my lips.

"It wasn't otherworldly creatures who tortured you." I twisted and tried to get away. "It was two desperate men trying to win a contest. It's in my notes from the library—*they're always desperate.*"

"Quiet!" Mr. Darning shoved me by my shoulders down to the scratchy brown blanket. "Just settle down. No one did anything wrong."

"Why did you have to treat him like he was nothing? He was a person—not an experiment."

"Boys in Stephen's condition are better off dead, Miss Black."

"That's not for you to decide."

Mr. Darning pinched my nostrils shut and forced my jaw closed with his free hand. My eyes bulged. My lungs fought to find oxygen. I scraped my nails into his hands, but he only clamped down harder. I kicked my legs and pounded on his knuckles.

"Are you killing her?" asked Julius in a panic.

"She'll tell someone. Why did you have to blabber about everything? She's a nice girl."

"I don't want another kid dying in here."

"Well, I don't want to go to jail. I don't deserve to waste away behind bars for your goddamned lunatic of a brother who ruined our experiment."

The flashlamp exploded.

An eruption of smoke and light attacked the room with the violence of shells blasting in Stephen's war zone.

Mr. Darning jumped off me and gaped at the Cyclops lens staring us down through the dissipating cloud of white. The flashlamp's fiery aftermath—the same burning air Stephen carried with him to his death—invaded my nostrils and lungs.

Julius stumbled toward the camera. "How did that go off by itself?" He covered the lens, as if he could hide everything they'd done by screwing the round cap into place. "What just happened, Mary Shelley?"

I struggled to find my voice through gasps of air. "You wanted me to bring Stephen for a photograph"—I pushed myself to my elbows—"and he came."

The air boiled with rage, and the panes of all three windows shuddered in their frames with a fury that took away my breath. Mr. Darning froze. Julius peered at the restless glass with eyes large and black. I scanned the bedroom to see if Stephen stood anywhere against the wood panels, but I saw only faded rectangles where his pictures used to hang. His anger heightened all around us. The room felt ready to implode.

Somebody pulled me off the mattress and dragged me under the bed, where I buried my face in my arms just moments before the windows shattered with a crash that rang in my ears. Shards of glass skidded across the floor and nipped my hands, and the men cried out in pain. They dropped to the floor with an impact that jolted my elbows.

Then silence.

I lay there beneath the bed, terror-stricken, shaking, my ears still ringing, but the air around me lightened a hundredfold. The bedroom's toxic taste dissolved with the gentleness of cool milk tempering the bitterness of a cup of tea. I realized someone was holding me under the bed, keeping his arm around me, imparting warmth and a feeling of safety to my trembling body. "Grab the photographic plate that shows him trying to kill you," whispered Stephen near my ear. "Tuck it inside that satchel lying next to you and run."

I lifted my head and found, to my right, the silhouette of Stephen's old leather camera satchel caked in dust. I managed to get the tan strap over my shoulder in the cramped space beneath the bed and crawled out, careful not to cut myself on the battlefield of broken glass.

I grabbed for the camera but lost my footing for a moment when I saw Julius and Mr. Darning lying on the floor, streaked in blood. Glass had sliced their faces and clothing and hands, each tiny wound bleeding a stream of bright scarlet. Julius stared at his bleeding palms like he didn't understand what was happening.

I had witnessed enough photography in my life to know to push down the dark slide sticking out of the top of the camera to protect the glass plate inside. I then pulled out the wooden plate holder that carried the fragile piece of evidence.

"Mary Shelley," groaned Julius. "I'm in agony. Get me my painkillers from my bedroom."

I stuck the plate holder in Stephen's empty satchel. "I'll call an ambulance when I'm a few houses down."

"No! Don't call anyone."

"I'm calling the police." I moved to leave, but someone gave me a shove from behind that sent me toppling toward the glass on the ground. All I remembered after hitting the floor was peering over my shoulder and catching the fleeting image of Mr. Darning's face and the camera coming toward my head. Pain walloped my skull.

My spirit slammed up to the far corner of the ceiling.

My body remained below.

DEATH, AGAIN

DOWN ON THE GROUND, MY FORMER SHELL LAY IN A twisted heap—an empty body with Stephen's satchel still strapped over my shoulder. A welt on my forehead bled and swelled like rising dough. Mr. Darning collapsed with the camera in his hands, crumpled over my feet, and seemed to lose consciousness. Julius curled into a ball four feet away and sobbed.

"I told you to stay away from my house," said a nearby voice.

I looked beside me. Stephen was also crouching up there in the upper corner of the room with his back against the ceiling and his feet pressed against the wall. He looked less wounded and bloodied, although I could see where the bullet had entered his head. Burn marks marred the skin around his mouth.

I edged closer to him. "He hit me with the camera. What if I stay dead? What if no one finds me or understands what happened?" My frustration rumbled down to the room and rocked Stephen's bed against the wall.

Julius sobbed harder. "Stop haunting me, Stephen. Leave me alone. Go away."

"Is everyone all right in there?" asked a woman outside the window, down below on the front lawn.

"Who's that?" I asked Stephen.

"She sounds like our neighbor."

"I heard the glass break," called the woman. "Are you up there, Julius? Is anyone hurt?"

Julius struggled to lift his head. "Get me help! I'm bleeding to death here."

"I don't know if I'll be able to find an ambulance. I'll fetch my husband and bandages."

"I need my painkillers! I'm in agony."

Mr. Darning groaned as if he were coming to but remained limp across my feet.

I turned my attention to the windows with their demolished panes and strained to hear the neighbor's feet running to her house. I thought I detected the squish of heels hurrying across grass.

Stephen wrapped his arms around his legs. "Those weren't birds, then?"

"No." I slid all the way next to him and leaned against his side. "They were people."

"Did they really try to kill me to win a contest?"

"Yes, they did. I'm so sorry." I laced my fingers through his. "Mr. Darning loved a young woman who died. He was desperate for proof of the afterlife, and your brother was desperate for money. I guess they were both out of their minds on drugs. Maybe they became friends because of their addictions, or maybe—" A thought struck me. I remembered the peculiar puzzle of Mr. Darning catching every other flimflamming photographer except for Julius. "No, wait—did they already know each other before Mr. Darning started saying he was a fraud catcher?"

Stephen cocked his head. "You mean Aloysius Darning?"

"Yes. Did you know him?"

"That was the name of a two-bit photographer whose business was about to shut down before I left for the war. I died because of *him*?"

"One played the mysterious photographer. The other played the expert. And both profited. No wonder Mr. Darning always denied finding proof that Julius was a fake. He probably also posed as the spirit soldiers." I looked down at the man who I once thought shared my father's voice. "He was scamming me the entire time. I was just as desperate as everyone else, wasn't I?"

A door opened somewhere downstairs.

Stephen braced himself against the ceiling. "If they find the glass plate inside the satchel, they'll have documented proof of him attacking you while Julius stood by. People will ask questions. They might discover photographs from the night of my death."

"But what if they don't see the plate? What if nobody searches inside the satchel?"

"Go back down there and show them the plate yourself."

I shrank back against the ceiling's plaster, terrified of dropping into that damaged flesh below. Down there, my body grew grayer and colder by the minute.

"Go on," said Stephen. "I can't ever leave, knowing you died because of me. Push yourself back into your body. Stop the world from mucking up everything so badly."

A gray-haired couple blew into the bedroom with rolls of white bandages tucked in the crooks of their arms. They contemplated the blood and the glass and struggled to make sense of the scene. The man knelt beside my body and searched for my pulse.

"Go back, Shell." Stephen stroked my hair with soothing fingers. "You'll be all right."

"What if the world never gets any better?"

"It'll have a far better chance if you're in it. Go on. The only way I can rest is if you survive."

I met his brown eyes. The same sense of urgency that had gripped us in his family's sitting room overcame me.

"Send me off as a happy young woman," I said.

"What?"

"I want to go off to my battles the same way you went to yours. Send me off as a happy woman."

Gravity gave me a sharp tug that threatened to pull me away from him. We clasped hands before I could slide too far.

He leaned down and kissed me, and his touch no longer summoned images of bloodstained skies, battlefields, and murderous blackbirds. Instead of smoke and fire, his mouth tasted of the divine sweetness of icing on a cake when the sugar isn't overdone. The taste of love before any pain gets in the way.

Our lips stayed together until gravity proved too strong.

He held tight to my hand. "Go live a full and amazing life, Shell. Come back when you're an old woman and tell me what you did with the world."

I nodded and clung to his fingers. "Swear to me you'll rest."

"I swear."

My body down below appeared closer than before. At any second I'd plunge into an excruciating pool of ice. Our arms stretched farther apart, and our hands shook against each other. Every precious second we had spent together during our shared lives—from the day he brought his little Brownie camera to school to the morning I spied him through my goggles at the bottom of his Coronado staircase—warmed my soul and killed the darkness. I was ready.

A silent count to three.

A plea that the end wouldn't hurt—for either of us.

I closed my eyes and let him go.

I DO LOSE INK

IN THE MINUTES FOLLOWING MY DROP INTO THAT FRO-
zen, leaden body, I somehow found the strength to reach
inside Stephen's satchel and hand the wooden plate holder to
the Emberses' neighbor, who was shouting to his wife that I
wasn't dead.

"Here." I forced the smooth wood into the man's hand. "Here's
evidence that the people you found me with are monsters."

Before my eyelids drooped closed again, a flood of yellow
warmth brightened the far corner of the ceiling—and disappeared.

MY MEMORIES OF THE MOMENTS AFTER MY BRIEF DEATH
in Stephen's bedroom were a muddled assortment. Chills

that penetrated down to my bones. Pain boring into my skull. Salty broth forced between my lips. Muscle aches. Wheezing. Flooded lungs. Gasps for air. Delirium. Drowning.

Somewhere toward the end of my suffering, I dreamed about the anagram Stephen had written at the bottom of his lightning bolt photograph.

I DO LOSE INK

In the dream, the words stared at me from behind the glass of his battered and splintered picture frame that had fallen to my floor too many times. I tried with all my might to unscramble his hidden meaning, but the letters slid around in the sepia waves and repositioned themselves into dozens of nonsensical phrases.

Oiled oinks. Kid loonies. Doe oilskin. Die ski loon. Ski on oldie.

My brain hurt. I massaged my exhausted eyes and tried to make the real title come into focus.

Sink. Die. Soil. Ink. Look. Slide. Side.

Before the dream ended, I saw it, sharp and clear:

LOOK INSIDE

I AWOKE IN AN UNLIT CORNER OF THE HOSPITAL WITH sweat-soaked bandages wrapped around my head and something stringy tied to my right foot's big toe. Perspiration drenched the hospital gown sticking to my body. My mouth tasted pickled. I strained to lift my head to get a look at the end of my cot and found a toe tag tied around my flesh, awaiting my death.

"Lord, have mercy! She's still fighting to live." The stocky nurse I remembered from my lightning injury waddled toward me with cobalt-blue eyes shining above her mask. "You've been struck down by lightning, given a concussion that knocked you dead, and spent a week getting clobbered by the flu—but here you are, blinking at me like a confused newborn. I wish all my patients possessed your mighty will to live."

I stared at the woman with my lips hanging open. "I had the flu?"

"Yes, you most certainly did." She set her clipboard beside me on the cot and placed her cold hand against my forehead. "Your temperature was one hundred and five degrees when they hauled you in here with that head injury, and you developed a bad case of pneumonia. Some detectives have been asking to speak with you, but I told them they'd need to find a spirit medium if they intended to chat with you anytime soon."

I wiggled my itchy foot. "Is that a toe tag on me?"

"It is. I half wondered if tying it there would make you mad enough to prove me wrong about dying again." She went to the foot of the bed and untied the string. "I guess it worked."

"How long have I been here?"

"Well, it's Sunday, November tenth . . ." She flipped through her clipboard. "You came in November fourth, just about a week ago. Kaiser Wilhelm abdicated the throne and escaped to Holland since then."

"He did? Is the war over?"

"Not yet, but soon, we hope. Very soon." She pulled a thermometer out of her white pocket and gave it a good shake.

"Did anyone bring a doctor's bag that belonged to me?" I asked. "I left it inside a red automobile in front of a house on Coronado."

"It's sitting right below your cot."

"I need to look at a photograph tucked inside."

"I need to take your temperature first."

"Please let me have my—"

She shoved the little glass tube inside my mouth before I could say another word. The thermometer made the insides of my cheeks itch, and I was tempted to pop it out with my tongue, but I needed her help.

She kept track of the time using a wristwatch, and after a grueling wait that seemed to ramble along for an hour, she fetched the stick from my mouth. "Ninety-eight point six." Her eyes glistened. "Congratulations, my little fighter. You're beating the infamous Spanish influenza."

I tried to sit up. "May I have my bag now?"

"Lie down, lie down—you're not completely healed yet." She lowered me back to the cot by my shoulders. "I'll pull out whatever it is you need, but then we need to get you resting and eating and drinking so we can send you on your way. Why do you own a doctor's bag, anyway?"

"My mother was a doctor."

"A lady physician for a mother?" She whistled. "No wonder you're a bold one, missy."

I heard her click open the black bag's clasp beneath me, and I swallowed with anticipation.

"I see a pretty photograph of a butterfly—"

"It's the other one. The lightning bolt."

"Here it is." She set Stephen's picture on my stomach. "My, my, my. That's a beauty. Must have been taken by quite the photographer."

"Yes. It was." I ran my fingers down the chipped frame to his words written at the bottom. The letters—written below an older, scratched-off title—were just as I remembered:

I DO LOSE INK

LOOK INSIDE. Not a title at all.

A request.

The nurse patted my knee. "All right. I'm going to check on some of the other patients, and then I'll bring you clear broth and get a doctor to examine your lungs and head. Don't go anywhere." She chuckled and shuffled away on the soft soles of her shoes.

I pried open the frame's back cover and saw the shine of a gold key—and a note, written on the photo's cardboard backing in Stephen's gorgeous handwriting.

April 20, 1918

My Dearest Mary Shelley,

*My mind keeps replaying the events of yesterday and giving our
time together a new ending, one that doesn't involve Julius ruining
everything for us. That morning feels like an unfinished work of art,
interrupted and spoiled. If I could have had just five more minutes
with you, I would have kissed you until our lips ached, and I would
have told you I've loved you from the moment you fixed my camera
on those church steps when we were little kids.*

*Even when the world seems like it's spinning out of control,
you're always there for me, Shell, whether in person or through your
letters. During my darkest moments, you have always reminded
me that life is interesting as hell (pardon my French, but there's no
other way to put it). If nothing else, I will fight in this war to ensure people like you remain free to dream your dreams and become
whatever you desire.*

*This photograph is for you—a small compensation for putting
up with my brother's spirit games and for sending me off to battle
with a contented soul. I photographed the lightning storm from my
bedroom window last winter. I'm guessing you would have loved seeing the bolts pierce the Pacific. I wish you had been here beside me.*

*You'll also find a key to a safe-deposit box at the main San Di-
ego post office (I've written the box number, as well as my military
address, below). I don't have time to put this parcel in the mail
myself, unfortunately. The idea of giving this key to you just struck
me as I was getting dressed to leave this morning. Hopefully, my*

mother will send it before Julius snoops and you'll be as skilled at this anagram as you were with Mr. Muse. A regular letter would likely disappear in Julius's hands.

Please take the contents of the box and do with them what you like. I don't want to risk writing them into a will or leaving them in my house. Julius would get to them somehow. My mother has copies of her favorites, but the negatives are in the box. You may keep the photographs or sell them if you can. Never send any profits to my brother.

If I lose my life in France, perhaps show my work to a few people as proof that I was once in this world. It's hard to imagine disappearing without a shred of evidence that I existed. I would be eternally grateful.

Thank you for coming back into my life before my departure to the unknown. I will never forget you, Mary Shelley Black.

Yours with all my love,
Stephen

P.S. Don't ever worry what the boys who don't appreciate originality think of you. They're fools.

MARY SHELLEY BLACK

A DOCTOR SIGNED MY HOSPITAL RELEASE PAPERS THE same day the war ended: November 11, 1918.

Fireworks whistled and exploded somewhere out in the city, and when I flinched from the commotion, the nurses told me a German delegation had signed the armistice to end the fighting. Faraway battles would stop snatching the minds and lives of our boys and men in the dark bellies of the trenches. The carrion crows would have to fly to other hunting grounds.

During the twenty-four hours before my release, I'd been subjected to oversalted soup, cold fingers and stethoscopes prodding at my skull and chest, eye exams, mental exams, and stiff detectives in dark suits questioning me about Julius and Mr. Darning. The detectives told me Grant and Gracie were being cooperative about their knowledge of Julius's whereabouts during the night of Stephen's death. Yet the men warned there'd be trials and potential ugliness.

"We discovered some grisly photographs in our searches through the two men's studios," said the older detective with the least compassionate voice. "The road ahead may be rather upsetting for a sixteen-year-old girl. I'm afraid your delicate female eyes and ears will experience some ugliness."

"Oh, you silly, naive men." I shook my weary head and genuinely pitied their ignorance. "You've clearly never been a sixteen-year-old girl in the fall of 1918."

WITH MY HEAD SHROUDED IN BANDAGES AND MY LEGS shaking from lack of use, I wandered with my black bag through the shivering, rasping bodies toward the hospital's exit. The tangy sweet smell of the doctors' celebratory champagne drifted above the fetid stench of fever surrounding me on the cots, and my heart ached to see people still suffering when one half of the nightmare was ending.

"Get better," I told them on my way through the white corridors. "Please get better. The war is over. It's done. Don't miss this. Keep fighting."

I reached the last hallway and came to a stop. I recognized the face of a patient sitting on one of the cots on the right-hand side of the corridor.

She was eating a bowl of soup, her legs nestled beneath a patched-up green blanket, and I would have missed her if she had been facing the opposite direction. Her blond hair had turned pure white.

"Aunt Eva?" I ventured closer to make sure the hazel eyes and bottle-cap lenses were truly hers. "Oh, my goodness. Aunt Eva. It is you!" I threw my arms around her bony shoulders and squeezed her as hard as I could without hurting her. "You didn't die. Your feet weren't black after all. I could have sworn they were black."

"Mary Shelley . . ." She breathed a relieved sigh into my hair and clutched my head against hers. "They told me you were in here, fighting the flu and recovering from a concussion. I've been so worried about you."

"A doctor just released me. Oh, I'm so glad you're not dead."

We held each other close for a good minute or more, sniffing back tears, ensuring neither of us was about to disappear.

"I buried you in onions and nearly went crazy with worry." I dropped to my knees beside her cot. "And I was so certain it had been for nothing. Your face was brown, and some man from down the street helped me get you into an ambulance. He carried you like a hero."

"Which man?"

"Well . . . he's already married."

"Mary Shelley!" A weak blush rose to her cheeks. "I wasn't asking to hunt down a husband. I want to know whom to thank."

"Oh. I'll show you where he lives when we're both home."

I grabbed her cold hand. "You are going to be able to come home, aren't you?"

"Yes." She steadied her soup on her lap. "The fever's gone. I just need to regain some strength. I feel like a train ran me over and left me on the tracks to die."

"I completely understand. I think I must have lost at least ten pounds. Just look at my blouse." I tugged on the loose fabric gapping above my waistline. "I look like a scarecrow."

"But your beautiful hair is still brown." She ran her fingers through my mess of tangled tresses. "Mine's white . . . isn't it?"

I sank my teeth into my bottom lip. "It might be temporary. It's a striking color, actually."

"It might fall out, like Gracie's. I've seen some clumps."

"It might not."

"And to think I was so worried about my chin-length hair before." She clamped her hand over her mouth, and her shoulders shook as if she were either laughing or crying—or both.

"Shh." I helped her stabilize her sloshing bowl. "It doesn't matter. You're beautiful because you're breathing. And you're not purple—I can't believe you're not purple."

Aunt Eva wiped her eyes behind her glasses. "When I heard you had a head injury, I worried you'd gone to save your ghost. I kept dreaming about Julius shaking you in my living room."

"I did save Stephen. And he saved me. He's at peace now." I swallowed. "We let each other go."

"Oh." She gave a small nod. "I'm glad." She directed her

eyes toward her soup with a weighty sigh. "Oh, Mary Shelley. I hope I can be strong enough to take care of you."

"You will be." I rubbed the remnants of her mighty shipyard biceps. "Soon enough you'll be back at home, putting up with me dissecting your telephone and arguing my way through everything again. You're stronger than you think you are, Aunt Eva. You're my battleship-building aunt, after all."

The corners of her mouth lifted in a smile. "Thank you." She wiped another tear. "Despite everything, I'm glad I've had you by my side these past weeks. You may have driven me to the edge at times, but you excel at fighting to save the people you love."

"So do you."

She nearly argued that point, but she closed her mouth and seemed to accept my words.

"Keep eating and resting for now, OK?" I grabbed the handles of my black bag. "Keep getting better and stronger. I need to go fetch something at the post office, and then I'll put my things away at home and come straight back to be with you again."

"Don't tire yourself out."

"I won't. I promise to take good care of myself."

"Ah . . ." She nodded. "Now *that* sounds like your mother."

"My mother took good care of herself?"

"She did. She really did."

"Then maybe I'll start giving that a try." I kissed her forehead. "I love you, Aunt Eva. Thank you for living." I squeezed her hand, scooped up my bag, and left the hospital to rejoin the world outside.

MY FINGERS SHOOK AS I SLID THE GOLD KEY INSIDE A lock on the austere brass door of Stephen's safe-deposit box. Inside, I found a black leather case engraved with silver letters that spelled out *SEE*—Stephen Elias Embers's initials. A fitting companion to *LOOK INSIDE*. I slid the case out of the receptacle with care, and right there on the cold post office tiles, I snapped open the latch and met Stephen's treasures.

In sepia-hued and color-tinted images, his view of the world unfolded for me across glossy photographic paper. Golden clouds rolled in from the ocean's horizon at the brink of sunset. Sandpipers waded in foamy seawater that looked as frothy as the top of a lemon meringue pie. California missions stood against a backdrop of clear skies, their adobe walls cracked and crumbling and faded with time. Fields of wild poppies brought beauty and life to the dry desert floor. Biplanes glided over the Pacific, casting wrinkled shadows across blue-tinged waves.

I also found his older photographs from Oregon, which didn't possess the same clarity and skill as his more recent work, but they were beautiful just the same. Mighty Mount Hood with its snow capped triangle of a peak. Portland's Steel Bridge spanning the Willamette River in the heart of the city. My eleven-year-old head, smothered beneath one of my giant white bows, while I perched on the picket fence at the edge of my front yard. Stephen had written one simple word on the back of my photograph—*Shell*—as if I didn't need further explanation. I liked that. It made me feel I wasn't as confusing and complicated as I thought.

He even included a self-portrait in his collection, taken December 1917, before his dad had died. Stephen sat on the boulders of the seawall across the street from his house and held up a sign that read A PORTRAIT OF THE ARTIST AS A YOUNG MAN. Strands of his short brown hair blew across his forehead, and I could practically taste the salt on the breeze rustling around him. He smiled in that way of his that revealed the dimple I enjoyed, and his eyes looked peaceful and free.

Glass negatives also awaited inside the case, nestled in protective sleeves, as fragile as if they were his children. I imagined taking his treasures to his mother, laying them in her lap, and coaxing her back to the world through his work.

"You're not disappearing without a trace," I said to his face in the photograph. "Not if I can help it. Not a chance." I ran my finger down the picture's smooth edge. "I promise to try to stop this world from mucking up everything so badly. And you know I'm good to my word."

I repacked his case and clicked the lid shut.

With one hand clutching the handles of my mother's bag and the other gripping Stephen's treasures, I left the post office and walked home through the swelling celebrations of the war's end. Model Ts puttered down the streets, their squeaky horns honking like ecstatic ducks. Americans of all ages and sizes and colors crept out of their bolted-up houses and remembered what it was like to smile and laugh and throw their arms around one another for a kiss. Firecrackers popped and shimmered on the sidewalks. "The Star-Spangled Banner" soared out of windows. Drivers tied cans to the backs of cars and wagons, and the air filled with the joyous music of tin clattering against asphalt.

The festivities rose out of the crematorium smoke and the rambling piles of coffins and the black crepes scarring neighborhood doors, which made the bliss of victory all the sweeter. We were all survivors—every last one of us who limped our way out to the sidewalks that afternoon and spit in Death's cold face.

I tightened my hold on Stephen's case of photographs and my own treasures and kept plodding forward to my new home on the edge of a city that had sheltered me during the worst of the storm. The weight of the world lifted from my shoulders enough for me to raise my chin and hold my head higher. A warm breeze whispered through my hair. My own restless soul settled farther inside my bones.

I was ready to live.

Ready to come back fighting.

I BECAME INTERESTED IN THE BIZARRE AND DEVASTATING year 1918 around the age of twelve, when I saw an episode of a television show called *Ripley's Believe It or Not!* I learned about two girls in England in 1917—sixteen-year-old Elsie Wright and her ten-year-old cousin, Frances Griffiths—who claimed to have photographed fairies. Several investigators, including the novelist Sir Arthur Conan Doyle (Sherlock Holmes's creator) and the photography expert Harold Snelling, deemed the girls' fairy pictures genuine, and the two cousins became famous. The narrator of *Ripley's* explained that people believed in the photographs because World War I was so horrifying. I wondered exactly how atrocious the era had been if grown, educated people were convinced fairies could be caught frolicking in the English countryside.

As an adult, I read "The Man Who Believed in Fairies," by Tom Huntington, an article that appeared in *Smithsonian* magazine, and I again learned about Elsie and Frances and Sir Arthur Conan Doyle and grew further intrigued by their story. The article described the Victorian era's Spiritualism craze, which had spread like wildfire across America and

Europe starting in the 1840s. Spiritualism had gained new popularity during the desperate years of the First World War.

Why was the World War I period so horrifying? For starters, innovations in war technology, such as machine guns, high-explosive shells, and mustard gas, provided new means of terror, injury, and death on the battlefields. Furthermore, the influenza pandemic of 1918 (this particular strain was known as the "Spanish flu" and the "Spanish Lady") killed at least twenty million people worldwide. Some estimates run as high as more than one hundred million people killed. Add to that the fifteen million people who were killed as a result of World War I and you can see why the average life expectancy dropped to thirty-nine years in 1918—and why people craved séances and spirit photography.

The flu hit hard and fast in the fall of 1918, targeting the young and the healthy, including men in the training camps and trenches. The baffling illness then waned shortly after the war's end, on November 11, leaving as mysteriously as it had arrived.

Flu vaccines were crude and scarce, so people resorted to folk remedies to save themselves from the illness. Every preventive flu measure and cure described in this book came from historical accounts of the pandemic.

The contest that Julius Embers tries to win is based upon *Scientific American*'s 1923–24 offer of twenty-five hundred dollars to the first person to produce authentic paranormal phenomena in front of a committee of five. Renowned escape artist and magician Harry Houdini loathed phony mediums and their use of magic tricks in the dark, so he helped judge the entries. No one ended up going home with the prize.

Dr. Duncan MacDougall truly did weigh dying tuberculosis patients on an industrial-sized scale in 1901 to explore the loss of the soul at the moment of death. Most scientists consider his work to possess very little merit due to the many weaknesses in his studies.

For more odd and fascinating forays into psychical research and Spiritualism, explore the wealth of information found in such books as *Spook: Science Tackles the Afterlife*, by Mary Roach (W. W. Norton & Co., 2005); *A Magician Among the Spirits*, by Harry Houdini (Arno Press, 1972; original printing 1924); and *Photography and Spirit*, by John Harvey (Reaktion Books, 2007).

For more information about World War I's devastating effects on the lives of the people who fought and on Americans back home, I recommend *The Last Days of Innocence: America at War, 1917–18*, by Meirion and Susie Harries (Vintage Books, 1998); *Shell Shock*, by Wendy Holden (Channel 4 Books, 2001); and *Bonds of Loyalty: German Americans and World War I*, by Frederick C. Luebke (Northern Illinois University Press, 1974). Be sure to also explore poems and books by such writers as Wilfred Owen, Siegfried Sassoon, Ernest Hemingway, and Katherine Anne Porter: gifted artists who were actually there.

ACKNOWLEDGMENTS

TO MY PATIENT, OPTIMISTIC, HARDWORKING AGENT, Barbara Poelle, who swore we'd get this book published even if it meant she'd have to bruise her knuckles banging down doors: Thank you from the bottom of my heart. We did it!

To my editor, Maggie Lehrman: Thank you for your amazing, insightful, and inspiring notes and for sharing (and improving upon) my vision of this novel. I'm so incredibly grateful you took a chance on my historical tale. To everyone at Abrams who's helped me share this book with the world (Maria T. Middleton, Laura Mihalick, and the rest of the crew): I'm honored to have your talents behind this book.

To my early readers, Carrie Raleigh, Ara Burklund, Kim Murphy, and Francesca Miller: Thank you for your time, feedback, and unwavering encouragement.

To Bill Becker of PhotographyMuseum.com, Sophia Brothers and Sophie Richardson at the Science & Society Picture Library, Holly Reed at the National Archives and Records Administration, David Silver of the International Photographic Historical Organization, and Stephen Greenberg, Crystal Smith, and Douglas Atkins at the U.S. National

Library of Medicine: Thank you for fielding all my historical image questions.

To Mrs. Betsy Martin and Ms. Kathie Deily, formerly of Crown Valley Elementary School: Thank you for making my writing feel special when I was a kid.

To my grandpa, Ward Proeschel, born in 1915: Thanks so much for sharing your memories of the early twentieth century with me.

To my parents, Richard and Jennifer Proeschel: Thank you for my life, and thank you for giving me the gift of the love of reading.

To my sister, Carrie Raleigh: You've been my first reader ever since we were children, and your love, companionship, and enthusiasm mean the world to me. I love you, Bear!

Last, but most certainly not least, thanks to my husband, Adam, and our two kids, for their steadfast patience, love, and support. This one's for you, my loves.

ABOUT THE AUTHOR

CAT WINTERS WAS BORN AND RAISED IN SOUTHERN CALI-
fornia, near Disneyland, which may explain her love of
haunted mansions, bygone eras, and fantasylands. This is
her first novel. She lives in Portland, Oregon, with her family.
Visit her online at her main haunt, catwinters.com.

This book was designed by Maria T. Middleton. The text is set in 10.5-point Minister, a typeface designed by Carl Albert Fahrenwaldt for the Schriftguss foundry in 1929. The display fonts are P22 Arts and Crafts Tall and Regular.

This book was printed and bound by RR Donnelley in Crawfordsville, Indiana. Its production was overseen by Alison Gervais and Kathy Lovisolo.

Stories for Children

ISAAC
BASHEVIS
SINGER

STORIES
FOR
CHILDREN

Farrar/Straus/Giroux

NEW YORK

Contents

Author's Note

I never believed that I could write for children. I always had the false impression that those who write for children are not real writers, and those who illustrate books are not real painters. It is true that as a child I read the Brothers Grimm in German and also translations of Hans Christian Andersen's stories and I loved them. I will never forget the great joy I felt reading a Yiddish edition of Sherlock Holmes stories by Conan Doyle. Just the same, the idea of writing for children never entered my mind. But editors often know more about writers than the writers themselves. This particular editor, Miss Elizabeth Shub, was convinced that I could write for children, and nothing I could say to her changed her conviction. She was after me for a long time, and I finally wrote the stories which are now to be found in the collection *Zlateh the Goat and Other Stories* and in a dozen other books for youngsters. Many of them were translated into English by Miss Shub and myself.

This particular collection of my children's stories is especially important to me. Although I love illustrations to stories for children and in many cases they are a very propitious addition to the story, I still think that the power of the word is the best medium to inform and entertain the minds of our youngsters. Most of the stories I read as a young boy were not illustrated. Needless to say, the stories in the Bible, which I read and reread, had no illustrations. In this volume I'm happy to speak to my young readers just in words. I still believe that in the beginning was the Logos, the power of the word.

I.B.S.

New York, 1984

Stories for Children

The Elders of Chelm
& Genendel's Key

It was known that the village of Chelm was ruled by the head of the community council and the elders, all fools. The name of the head was Gronam Ox. The elders were Dopey Lekisch, Zeinvel Ninny, Treitel Fool, Sender Donkey, Shmendrick Numskull, and Feivel Thickwit. Gronam Ox was the oldest. He had a curly white beard and a high, bulging forehead.

Since Gronam had a large house, the elders usually met there. Every now and then Gronam's first wife, Genendel, brought them refreshments—tea, cakes, and jam.

Gronam would have been a happy man except for the fact that each time the elders left, Genendel would reproach him for speaking nonsense. In her opinion her highly respected husband was a simpleton.

Once, after such a quarrel, Gronam said to his wife, "What is the sense in nagging me after the elders have gone? In the future, whenever you hear me saying something silly, come into the room and let me know. I will immediately change the subject."

"But how can I tell you you're talking nonsense in front of the elders? If they learn you're a fool, you'll lose your job as head of the council."

"If you're so clever, find a way," Gronam replied.

Genendel thought a moment and suddenly exclaimed, "I have it."

"Well?"

"When you say something silly, I will come in and hand you the key to our strongbox. Then you'll know you've been talking like a fool."

Gronam was so delighted with his wife's idea that he clapped his hands. "Near me, you too become clever."

A few days later the elders met in Gronam's house. The subject under discussion was the coming Pentecost, a holiday when a lot of sour cream is needed to eat with blintzes. That year there was a scarcity of sour cream. It had been a dry spring and the cows gave little milk.

The elders pulled at their beards and rubbed their foreheads, signs that their brains were hard at work. But none of them could figure out how to get enough sour cream for the holiday.

Suddenly Gronam pounded on the table with his fist and called out, "I have it!"

"What is it?"

"Let us make a law that water is to be called sour cream and sour cream is to be called water. Since there is plenty of water in the wells of Chelm, each housewife will have a full barrel of sour cream."

"What a wonderful idea," cried Sender Donkey.

"A stroke of genius," shrieked Zeinvel Ninny.

"Only Gronam Ox could think of something so brilliant," Dopey Lekisch proclaimed.

Treitel Fool, Shmendrick Numskull, and Feivel Thickwit all agreed. Feivel Thickwit, the community scribe, took out pen and parchment and set down the new law. From that day on, water was to be called sour cream and sour cream, water.

As usual, when they had finished with community business, the elders turned to more general subjects. Gronam said, "Last night I couldn't sleep a wink for thinking about why it is hot in the summertime. Finally the answer came to me."

"What is it?" the elders chorused.

"Because all winter long the stoves are heated and this heat stays in Chelm and makes the summer hot."

All the elders nodded their heads, excepting Dopey Lekisch, who asked, "Then why is it cold in the winter?"

"It's clear why," replied Gronam. "The stoves are not heated in the summer, so there is no heat left over for the winter."

The elders were enthusiastic about Gronam's great knowledge. After such mental effort, they began to look toward the kitchen, expecting Genendel to appear with the tea, cakes, and jam.

Genendel did come in, but instead of a tray she carried a key, which she gave to her husband, saying, "Gronam, here is the key to the strongbox."

Today of all days Gronam was confident that his

mouth had uttered only clever words. But there stood Genendel with the key in her hand, a sure sign that he had spoken like a fool. He grew so angry that he turned to the elders and said, "Tell me, what foolishness have I spoken that my wife brings me the key to our strong-box?"

The elders were perplexed at this question, and Gronam explained his agreement with Genendel, that she should give him the key when he talked like an idiot. "But today, didn't I speak words of high wisdom? You be the judges."

The elders were furious with Genendel. Feivel Thick-wit spoke out: "We are the elders of Chelm, and we understand everything. No woman can tell us what is wise and what is silly."

They then discussed the matter and made a new law: Whenever Genendel believed that her husband was talk-ing like a fool, she was to come in and give the key to the elders. If they agreed, they would tell Gronam Ox to change the subject. If they did not agree, she was to bring out a double portion of tea, cakes, and jam, and three blintzes for every sage.

Feivel Thickwit immediately recorded the new law on parchment and stamped it with the seal of Chelm, which was an ox with six horns.

From that day on, Gronam could talk freely at the meetings, since Genendel was very stingy. She did not want the elders of Chelm to gorge themselves with her beloved blintzes.

That Pentecost there was no lack of "sour cream" in Chelm, but some housewives complained that there was a lack of "water." But this was an entirely new problem, to be solved after the holiday.

Gronam Ox became famous all over the world as the sage who—by passing a law—gave Chelm a whole river and many wells full of sour cream.

Translated by the author and Elizabeth Shub

A Tale of Three Wishes

Frampol. This was the name of the town. It had all the things that a town should have: a synagogue, a studyhouse, a poorhouse, a rabbi, and a few hundred inhabitants. Each Thursday was market day in Frampol, when the peasants came from the hamlets to sell grain, potatoes, chickens, calves, honey, and to buy salt, kerosene, shoes, boots, and whatever else a peasant may need.

There were in Frampol three children who often played together: Shlomah, or Solomon, seven years old; his sister, Esther, six years old; and their friend Moshe, who was about Shlomah's age.

Shlomah and Moshe went to the same cheder and someone there told them that on Hoshanah Rabbah, which is the last day of the Feast of Tabernacles, the sky opens late at night. Those who see it happen have a minute's time to make a wish, and whatever they wish will come true.

Shlomah, Moshe, and Esther spoke of this often. Shlomah said that he would wish to be as wise and rich as King Solomon, his namesake. Moshe's wish was to be as learned in religion as was the famous Rabbi Moshe Maimonides. Esther desired to be as beautiful as Queen Esther. After long discussions, the three children decided to wait until Hoshanah Rabbah, to stay awake the whole night together and, when the sky opened, to utter their wishes.

Children must go to bed early, but the three stayed awake until their parents fell asleep. Then they sneaked out of the house and met in the synagogue yard to wait for the miraculous event.

It was quite an adventure. The night was moonless and cool. The children had heard that demons lurk outside, ready to attack those who dare to go out on a dark night. There was also talk of corpses who after midnight pray in the synagogue and read from the Holy Scroll. If someone passed by the synagogue at such a late hour, he might be called up to the reading table, a most frightening event. But Shlomah and Moshe had put on fringed garments, and Esther had dressed in two aprons, one in the front and one in the back, all meant to ward off the evil powers. Just the same, the children were afraid. An owl was hooting. Esther had been told that bats flew around at night and that if one of them got entangled in a girl's hair she would die within the year. Esther had covered her hair tightly with a kerchief.

An hour passed, two hours, three, and still the sky did not open. The children became tired and even hungry. Suddenly there was lightning and the sky opened. The children saw angels, seraphim, cherubim, fiery chariots, as well as the ladder which Jacob saw in his dream, with winged angels going up and down, just as it is written in the Bible. It all happened so quickly that the children forgot their wishes.

Esther spoke up first. "I'm hungry. I wish I had a blintz."

At once, a blintz appeared before the children's eyes.

When Shlomah saw that his sister had wasted her wish on such a petty thing as a blintz, he became enraged and cried out, "You silly girl, I wish you were a blintz yourself."

In an instant, Esther became a blintz. Only her face looked out from the dough, pale and frightened.

Moshe had loved Esther for as long as he could remember. When he saw that his beloved Esther had turned into a blintz, he fell into terrible despair. There was no time to lose. The minute was almost over, and he exclaimed, "I wish her to be as she was."

And so it happened.

Immediately the sky closed again.

When the children realized how foolishly they had squandered their wishes, they began to cry. The night had become pitch black and they could not find their way back home. They seemed to be lost in some strange place. There were no mountains in Frampol; still, the children were climbing up a mountain. They tried to walk down again, but their feet kept climbing by themselves. Then there appeared an old man with a white beard. In one hand he held a stick, in the other a lantern with a candle inside. His robe was girded with a white sash. A strong wind was blowing, but the candle did not flicker.

The old man asked, "Where are you going? And why are you crying?"

Shlomah told him the truth, how they stayed awake all night and how they wasted their wishes.

The old man shook his head. "No good wish is ever wasted."

"Perhaps the demons confused us and made us forget our wishes," Moshe suggested.

"No demons have any power in the holy night of Hoshanah Rabbah," the old man said.

"So why did the sky play such a trick on us?" Esther asked.

"Heaven does not play tricks," the old man answered. "You were the ones who tried to play tricks on heaven. No one can become wise without experience, no one can become a scholar without studying. As for you, little girl, you are pretty already, but beauty of the body must be paired with beauty of the soul. No young child can possess the love and the devotion of a queen who was ready to sacrifice her life for her people. Because you three wished too much, you received nothing."

"What shall we do now?" the children asked.

"Go home and try to deserve by effort what you wanted to get too easily."

"Who are you?" the children asked, and the old man replied, "On high, they call me the Watcher in the Night."

As soon as he said these words, the children found themselves back in the synagogue yard. They were so weary that the moment they came home and put their heads on their pillows, they fell asleep. They never told anybody what had happened to them. It remained their secret.

Years passed. Shlomah had become more and more eager for knowledge. He showed so much talent and studied so many books of history, trade, and finance that he became the adviser of the King of Poland. They called him the King without a Crown, and King Solomon of Poland. He married the daughter of an important man and became famous for his wisdom and charity.

Moshe had always been deeply interested in religion. He knew the Bible and the Talmud almost by heart. He wrote many religious books and he became known as the Maimonides of Our Time.

Esther grew up to be not only beautiful but a learned and highly virtuous young lady. Many young men from rich houses sent matchmakers to her parents to ask for her hand in marriage, but Esther loved only Moshe, as he loved only her.

When the old rabbi of Frampol died, Moshe was made rabbi of the town. A rabbi must have a wife, and Rabbi Moshe married his Esther.

All the people of Frampol attended the wedding. The bride's brother, Shlomah, came to his sister's wedding in a carriage drawn by six horses, with grooms riding in front and on the back of the carriage. There was music and dancing, and the young couple received many gifts. Late at night, the bridegroom was called to dance with the bride, and so were all the guests, the bride holding one edge of the handkerchief and her partner the other, according to custom. When someone asked if everyone had danced with the bride, the wedding jester said, "Yes, except for the night watchman." As he uttered these words, an old man emerged from nowhere with a stick in one hand, a lantern in the other hand, his loins girded with a white sash. The bride, her brother, and the bridegroom recognized the old man, but they kept silent. He approached the bride, placed the lantern and the stick on a bench nearby, and began to dance with her, all the people staring in amazement and awe. No one had ever seen this old man before. The band stopped playing. It became so quiet that one could hear the sputtering of the candles and the chirping of the grasshoppers outside. Then the old man lifted up his lantern and gave it to Rabbi Moshe, saying, "Let this light show you the way in the Torah." He offered the stick to Shlomah with the words: "Let this stick protect you from all your enemies." To Esther, who was holding the white sash, he said, "Let this sash bind you to your people and their needs forever."

After saying these words, the old man vanished.

In the years following, it happened quite often that the Jews came to ask Esther to intercede for them before the rulers of the land. She would fasten the white sash around her waist, and she never failed to help her people. Everyone called her Queen Esther.

Whenever Rabbi Moshe had difficulties in understanding some fine point of the law, he opened the ark where the lantern stood with its eternal light, and things became clear to him. When Shlomah was in trouble, he would take hold of the stick and his foes became powerless.

All three lived to a ripe old age. Only before his death

did Rabbi Moshe reveal to the people of Frampol what had happened that night of Hoshanah Rabbah. The rabbi said, "For those who are willing to make an effort, great miracles and wonderful treasures are in store. For them the gates of heaven are always open."

The Extinguished Lights

It was the custom to light the Hanukkah candles at home, rather than in a synagogue or studyhouse, but this particular studyhouse in Bilgoray was an exception. Old Reb Berish practically lived there. He prayed, studied the Mishnah, ate, and sometimes even slept on the bench near the stove. He was the oldest man in town. He admitted to being over ninety, but some maintained that he was already past one hundred. He remembered the war between Russia and Hungary. On holidays he used to visit Rabbi Chazkele from Kuzmir and other ancient rabbis.

That winter it snowed in Bilgoray almost every day. At night the houses on Bridge Street were snowed under and the people had to dig themselves out in the morning. Reb Berish had his own copper Hanukkah lamp, which the beadle kept in the reading table with other holy objects—a ram's horn, the Book of Esther written on a scroll, a braided Havdalah candle, a prayer shawl and phylacteries, as well as a wine goblet and an incense holder.

There is no moon on the first nights of Hanukkah, but that night the light from the stars made the snow sparkle as if it were full of diamonds. Reb Berish placed his Hanukkah lamp at the window according to the law, poured oil into the container, put a wick into it, and made the customary benedictions. Then he sat by the open clay stove. Even though most of the children stayed at home on Hanukkah evenings, a few boys came to the studyhouse especially to listen to Reb Berish's stories. He was known as a storyteller. While he told stories he roasted potatoes on the glowing coals. He was saying, "Nowadays when snow falls and there is a frost, people call it winter. In comparison to the winters of my times the winters of today are nothing. It used to be so cold that oak trees burst in the forests. The snow was up to the rooftops. Bevies of hungry wolves came into the village at night, and people shuddered in bed from their howling. The horses neighed in their stables and tried to break the doors open from fear. The dogs barked like mad. Bilgoray was still a tiny place then. There was a pasture where Bagno Street is today.

"The winter I'm going to tell you about was the worst of them all. The days were almost as dark as night. The clouds were black as lead. A woman would come out of her kitchen with the slop pail and the water turned to ice before she could empty it.

"Now hear something. That year the men blessed the Hanukkah lights on the first night as they did every year,

[16]

but suddenly a wind came from nowhere and extinguished them. It happened in every house at the same time. The lights were kindled a second time, but again they were extinguished. In those times there was an abundance of wood to help keep the houses warm. To keep the wind out, cracks in the windows were plugged up with cotton or straw. So how could the wind get in? And why should it happen in every house at the same moment? Everybody was astonished. People went to the rabbi to ask his advice and the rabbi's decision was to continue rekindling the lights. Some pious men kept lighting the candles until the rooster crowed. This happened on the first night of Hanukkah, as well as on the second night and on the nights after. There were nonbelievers who contended that the whole thing was a natural occurrence. But most of the people believed that there was some mysterious power behind it all. But what was it—a demon, a mocker, an imp? And why just on Hanukkah?

"A fear came over the town. Old women said that it was an omen of war or an epidemic. Fathers and grandfathers were so disturbed that they forgot to give Hanukkah money to the children, who couldn't play games with the dreidel. The women did not fry pancakes as they had in former years.

"It went on like this until the seventh night. Then, after everyone was asleep and the rabbi was sitting in his chamber studying the Talmud, someone knocked on his door. It was the rabbi's custom to go to sleep early in the evening and to get up after midnight to study. Usually his wife served him tea, but in the middle of the night the rabbi poured water into the samovar himself, lit the coals, and prepared the tea. He would drink and study until daybreak.

"When the rabbi heard the knocking on the door, he got up and opened it. An old woman stood outside and the rabbi invited her to come into his house.

"She sat down and told the rabbi that last year before Hanukkah her little granddaughter Altele, an orphan, died. She had first gotten sick in the summer and no doctor could help her. After the High Holidays, when Altele realized that her end was near, she said, 'Grandmother, I know that I'm going to die, but I only wish to live until Hanukkah, when Grandpa gives me Hanukkah money and I can play dreidel with the girls.' Everybody in Bilgoray prayed for the girl's recovery, but it so happened that she died just a day before Hanukkah. For a whole year after her death her grandparents never saw her in their dreams. But this night the grandmother had seen Altele in her dreams three times in a row. Altele came to her and said that because the people of the town had not prayed ardently enough for her to see the first Hanukkah candle, she had died angry and it was she who extinguished the Hanukkah lights in every house. The old woman said that after the first dream she awakened her husband and told him, but he said that because she brooded so much about her grandchild, she had had this dream. The second time when Altele came to her in her dream, the grandmother asked Altele what the people of the town could do to bring peace to her soul. The girl began to answer, but the old woman woke up suddenly before she could understand what Altele was saying.

Only in the third dream did the girl speak clearly, saying it was her wish that on the last night of Hanukkah all the people of Bilgoray, together with the rabbi and the elders, should come to her grave and light the Hanukkah candles there. They should bring all the children with them, eat pancakes, and play dreidel on the frozen snow.

"When the rabbi heard these words, he began to tremble, and he said, 'It's all my fault. I didn't pray enough for that child.' He told the old woman to wait, poured some tea for her, and looked in the books to see if what the girl asked was in accordance with the law. Though he couldn't find a similar case in all the volumes of his library, the rabbi decided on his own that the wish of that grieved spirit should be granted. He told the old woman that on a cold and windy night there is very little chance for lights to burn outdoors. However, if the ghost of the girl could extinguish all the lights indoors, she might also have the power to do the opposite. The rabbi promised the old woman to pray with all his heart for success.

"Early in the morning, when the beadle came to the rabbi, he asked him to take his wooden hammer and go from house to house, knock on shutters, and tell the people what they must do. Even though Hanukkah is a holiday, the rabbi had ordered the older people to fast until noon and ask forgiveness of the girl's sacred soul—and also pray that there should be no wind in the evening.

"All day long a fierce wind blew. Chimneys were blown off some roofs. The sky was overcast with dark clouds. Not only the unbelievers, but even some of the God-fearing men, doubted lights could stay lit in a storm like this. There were those who suspected that the old woman invented the dream, or that a demon came to her disguised as her late grandchild in order to scoff at the faithful and lead them astray. The town's healer, Nissan, who trimmed his beard and came to the synagogue only on the Sabbath, called the old woman a liar and warned that the little ones might catch terrible colds at the graveyard and get inflammation of the lungs. The blizzard seemed to become wilder from minute to minute. But suddenly, while the people were reciting the evening prayer, a change took place. The sky cleared, the wind subsided, and warm breezes wafted from the surrounding fields and forests. It was already the beginning of the month of Teveth and a new moon was seen surrounded with myriads of stars.

"Some of the unbelievers were so stunned they couldn't utter a word. Nissan the healer promised the rabbi that scissors would never touch his beard again and that he would come to pray every day of the week. Not only older children, but even the younger ones, were taken to the graveyard. Lights were kindled, blessings were recited, the women served the pancakes with jam that they had prepared. The children played dreidel on the frozen snow, which was as smooth as ice. A golden light shone over the little girl's grave, a sign that her soul enjoyed the Hanukkah celebration. Never before or after did the graveyard seem so festive as on that eighth night of Hanukkah. All the unbelievers did penance. Even the Gentiles heard of the miracle and acknowledged that God had not forsaken the Jews.

"The next day Mendel the scribe wrote down the

whole event in the parchment Community Book, but the book was burned years later in the time of the First Fire."

"When did this happen?" one of the children asked.

Reb Berish clutched his beard, which had once been red, then turned white, and finally became yellowish from the snuff he used. He pondered for a while and said, "Not less than eighty years ago."

"And you remember it so clearly?"

"As if it took place yesterday."

The light in Reb Berish's Hanukkah lamp began to sputter and smoke. The studyhouse became full of shadows. With his bare fingers the old man pulled three potatoes out of the stove, broke off some pieces, and offered them to the children. He said, "The body dies, but the soul goes up to God and lives forever."

"What do all the souls do when they are with God?" one of the boys asked.

"They sit in Paradise on golden chairs with crowns on their heads and God teaches them the secrets of the Torah."

"God is a teacher?"

"Yes, God is a teacher, and all the good souls are His pupils," Reb Berish replied.

"How long will the souls go on learning?" a boy asked.

"Until the Messiah comes, and then there will be the resurrection of the dead," Reb Berish said. "But even then God will continue to teach in His eternal yeshiva, because the secrets of the Torah are deeper than the ocean, higher than heaven, and more delightful than all the pleasures the body could ever enjoy."

Mazel & Shlimazel

OR THE MILK OF A LIONESS

In a faraway land, on a sunny spring day, the sky was as blue as the sea, and the sea was as blue as the sky, and the earth was green and in love with them both. Two spirits were passing through a village. One was called Mazel, which means good luck, and the other, Shlimazel, bad luck.

Spirits are not seen by man, but they can see one another.

Mazel was young, tall, slim. His cheeks were pink and he had sand-colored hair. He was dressed in a green jacket, red riding breeches, and wore a hat with a feather in it. There were silver spurs on his high boots. Mazel seldom walked. Usually he rode his horse, which was also a spirit. On this particular day, he felt like strolling through the village on foot.

Shlimazel limped along beside him with the help of a

knotty-wood cane—an old man with a wan face and angry eyes under his bushy brows. His nose was crooked and red from drinking. His beard was as gray as spiderwebs. He was attired in a long black coat and on his head sat a peaked hat.

Mazel spoke and Shlimazel listened. Mazel was in a boasting mood. "Everybody wants me, everybody loves me," he said. "Wherever I go, I bring joy. Naturally the people cannot see me because I am a spirit, but they all long for me just the same: merchants and sailors, doctors and shoemakers, lovers and card players. All over the world they call, 'Mazel, come to me.' Nobody calls for you, Shlimazel. You'll have to admit that what I say is true."

Shlimazel pursed his lips and clutched his beard. "Yes, I must agree that you're a charmer," he said. "But the world is ruled by the strong and not by the charming. What can take you a year to accomplish, I can destroy in one second."

Shlimazel had made a point and now Mazel bit his lip in annoyance. "We all know you can destroy," he replied. "But you always do it in the same way—either you kill, or you burn, or you send sickness or famine, war or poverty. I, on the other hand, am always full of fresh ideas. I know millions of ways to make people happy."

"I have billions of ways of making them unhappy."

"That's not true. You always use the same old tricks," Mazel insisted. "I'll bet that you can't even find a single new way of spoiling something nice that I've done."

"Is that so? What will you wager?" Shlimazel countered.

"If you win," Mazel said, "I will give you a barrel of the precious wine of forgetfulness. If you lose, you keep your red nose out of my business for fifty years."

"Agreed," Shlimazel replied. "Well, what will you do that's so nice?"

"I will go to the poorest hut in this village and bring happiness to whoever lives there. I will remain with that person for an entire year. The moment the year is at an end, you may take over, but only on condition that you will neither kill him through a mishap nor make him sick nor impoverish him. And on no account are you to use any of your old and tired games. Now, how much time will you need to undo what I have done?"

"One second," Shlimazel replied.

"It's a bet."

Mazel stretched out his hand. The green gem of hope sparkled from a ring on his third finger. He grasped Shlimazel's gaunt and wrinkled hand, which had crooked fingers with horny nails. The day was warm, but Shlimazel's hand was as cold as ice.

Soon after they parted, Mazel came to a hut which he knew must be the poorest in the village. The logs from which it had been built were rotted and covered with moss. Its thatched roof had turned black with time. There was no chimney and the smoke from the stove escaped through a hole in the roof. The glass panes had long since disappeared from the windows, which were boarded over.

Mazel had to bend his head to get through the door. Inside, toadstools sprouted from the unplastered walls.

On a broken-down cot which was covered with straw

sat a young peasant lad. He was barefoot and half naked. Mazel asked him his name.

"Tam," he replied.

"Why are you so down and out?" Mazel inquired.

Tam could not see Mazel, but nevertheless he spoke to him, thinking that he was talking to himself. Tam said, "I once had parents, but they were unlucky. My father died of consumption. My mother went to the forest to gather mushrooms and was bitten by a poisonous snake. The small piece of land they left me is so full of rocks that I can hardly farm it. And last year there was a drought and a locust plague. This year I won't even have a harvest because I had nothing to sow."

"Still, one shouldn't lose hope," Mazel said.

"What can I hope for?" Tam asked. "If you don't sow, you don't reap. My clothes are in tatters and the girls of the village laugh at me. A man without luck is worse than dead."

"Something good may still happen," suggested Mazel.

"When?"

"Soon."

"How?"

Before Mazel could reply, there was a sound of trumpets and galloping hooves. Twenty-four royal guards on horseback preceded the king's carriage drawn by six white stallions. The horsemen were uniformed in red pantaloons, yellow tunics, and plumed white helmets. A company of courtiers, also mounted, followed the carriage.

All the villagers had come out to admire the royal travelers. Whoever was wearing a hat removed it. Some of the villagers kneeled. The girls curtsied.

At first it looked as if the carriage would pass through the village without stopping and the people would hardly be able to catch a glimpse of their king. But Mazel had already figured things out. As the carriage reached Tam's hut, one of its wheels rolled off and the vehicle almost turned over. The riders reined in their horses and the entire company came to a standstill.

The door of the carriage opened and the king came out, followed by the seventeen-year-old Crown Princess Nesika, his only child. Nesika was famous for her beauty both at home and abroad. The royal party was returning from a ball given in her honor by the king of a neighboring land. The princess's golden hair fell to her shoulders, her eyes were blue, her skin white, her neck long, and her waist narrow. She was gowned in a white dress reaching to the tips of her slippers. The king had always spoiled her because her mother had died when Nesika was small. But today he was angry at his lovely daughter.

The purpose of the ball had been to introduce Nesika to Crown Prince Typpish and a match was to be arranged between them. However, Nesika had not liked the prince, and he was the seventh prince in a row that she had rejected. Of the first, she had said that he laughed too loud and too often. The second spoke of nothing but his skill at hunting foxes. She had seen the third beating his dog. The fourth had the most irritating habit of beginning each sentence with "I." The fifth had been a practical joker. The sixth had the habit of telling the same stories over and over again. As for Typpish, Nesika had simply announced that she would not have him because his boots were foolish.

"How can boots be foolish?" her father asked.

"If the feet are foolish, the boots are foolish," Nesika replied.

"How can feet be foolish?" her father insisted.

"If the head is foolish, the feet are foolish," Nesika retorted.

Each time Nesika had found a reason not to be married. The king was beginning to be afraid she would turn into an old maid.

According to the law of the land, Nesika could become queen on her father's death only if she had a husband to help her rule. If she failed to marry, the prime minister, whose name was Kamstan, would ascend the throne in her place. Kamstan was well known for being an intriguer, a coward, and a miser. He was so extremely stingy that for their golden wedding anniversary, when it is customary to present an object of gold, he gave his beloved wife a tin thimble wrapped in gold paper.

When the wheel fell off his carriage, the already angry king flew into a rage. He rebuked his attendants for endangering his life and demanded to know which one of them could set the wheel back in place the fastest.

Tam knew little about fixing a wheel and nothing about fancy carriages. But since Mazel stood behind him, he was filled with courage and called out, "I can do it, Your Majesty."

The king looked with curiosity at the half-naked lad. After some hesitation, and a nudge from Mazel, he said, "If you can do it—do it—and quickly."

The villagers, who knew Tam as a ne'er-do-well and a

bungler, watched in fear. They were sure that he would fail and that the king would vent his anger on the entire village.

When Mazel stands behind a man, that man succeeds in everything, and so it was with Tam. As a young boy he had worked for a short time in a smithy, but he was sure that he remembered nothing of what he had learned there. However, no sooner had he picked up the wheel than everything came back to him. The king looked on in amazement at how deftly the young lad worked. When the job was finished, the king asked Tam how it happened that such an able young man was going around in tatters and lived in a ruin.

"Because I'm unlucky," Tam replied.

"Luck sometimes changes very quickly," the king said. "Come along to court, and we'll find something there for you to do."

It all happened so suddenly that the villagers could not believe their eyes. The king simply opened the door of his carriage and told Tam to get in. Then he gave the command to drive on.

Tam was in constant fear that the wheel would come off again, but even though the horses galloped along at full speed, the wheel remained in place.

The king and Nesika questioned Tam about his life in the village. The lad replied in a humble manner and his answers were brief and clever. Mazel was talking through him. The king turned to Nesika and spoke in a foreign language which Tam didn't understand but Mazel did: "See what bright young men there are among our peasants." And Nesika replied in the same language, "Many a prince could learn from him." After a while she added thoughtfully, "He is handsome, too. All he needs are some decent clothes."

Since Mazel had only a year's time to work in, things began to happen at once. That very day, as soon as they arrived at the palace, the king gave orders that a bath be prepared for Tam and he be given fresh linen and new clothes. He was put to work in the royal smithy.

Tam very soon began to show unusual skill. He could mend carriages that were considered beyond repair. He could shoe horses so wild that no one else dared go near them. He also turned out to be a great horseman. In less than a month he was appointed master of the king's stables.

Once each year the royal races were held at court. Tam was permitted to take part and he managed almost immediately to enchant the courtiers, visiting dignitaries, the king's wise men, and, as a matter of fact, the entire country.

Tam had chosen to ride an unknown horse, but with Mazel's help it became the fleetest horse in the history of the land. With Tam as rider it easily cleared the broadest ditches, the highest fences, and won all the purses. He cut such an elegant figure that all the ladies of the court fell in love with him.

Needless to say, Nesika had been in love with him from the very start. As always with those who are deeply in love, Nesika thought that her feelings for Tam were her secret. Actually, the entire court knew about it, even her father, the king. He also knew that lovers can be very stubborn. And since the proud king did not want to marry his daughter to the son of peasants, he decided to give Tam a task so challenging that he was bound to fail. He sent him with a small group of retainers into the depths of the kingdom to demand the allegiance of a wild and rebellious tribe that no lord of the king had been able to win over. With Mazel's help Tam not only succeeded but returned with magnificent gifts for the king and Princess Nesika.

Tam's fame continued to grow. Bards and minstrels sang of his deeds. High officials came to him for advice. He became the most admired and best-loved man in the kingdom. When the humble achieve success, they often become haughty and forget those among whom they grew up. Tam always found time to help the peasants and the poor.

It is known that the greater a man becomes, the more powerful are his enemies. Prime Minister Kamtsan, who wanted the throne, intrigued against Tam. He and his henchmen spread the word that Tam was a sorcerer. How else could a lowly peasant have managed to succeed where lords had failed? They said Tam had sold his soul to the Devil. When that year, night after night, a strange comet with a long tail was seen in the sky, Tam's enemies insisted it was an omen that Tam would bring misfortune on the king and lead the country to ruin.

Shlimazel had promised Mazel to leave Tam in peace for a full year, but this did not prevent him from quietly preparing to trap Tam the moment the time was up. Shlimazel could not wait to win his bet and get hold of the barrel of the wine of forgetfulness. It was known that one sip of this wine gave more enjoyment than all other pleasurable things on earth. Shlimazel had for ages been suffering from sleeplessness and nightmares. He knew that the wine of forgetfulness would at last bring him sleep and sweet dreams of silver seas, golden rivers, gardens of crystal trees, and women of heavenly beauty. He also wanted to show his followers, the demons, goblins, hobgoblins, imps, and other evil spirits, that he was more powerful than Mazel and could outwit him.

Suddenly the king became ill. There were great doctors in the court but they could not discover what was wrong with him. At last, after long consultation, they decided that the king suffered from a rare disease for which the only cure was the milk of a lioness. Where does one get the milk of a lioness? There was a zoo in the capital, but at that moment it had no lioness with nursing cubs. The king's faith in Tam was so great that he sent for him and asked him to fetch the milk of a lioness. Anyone else in Tam's place would have been frightened out of his wits on hearing such a request. Since Mazel stood behind him, Tam replied simply, "Yes, my king, I will find a lioness, milk her, and bring her milk to you."

The king was so touched by Tam's brave reply that he called out to his courtiers, "You are my witnesses. The day Tam returns with the milk of a lioness, I will give him the hand of my daughter in marriage."

Prime Minister Kamtsan, standing among the courtiers, could contain himself no longer. "Your Majesty," he said, "no man can milk a lioness and live. Tam has made a promise that he cannot keep."

"And if he does bring milk, what guarantee is there that it will really be a lioness's milk?" added one of Kamtsan's followers.

"Your Majesty, I will find a lioness and milk her," Tam repeated with confidence.

"Go, and success be with you," the king said. "But I warn you: do not fool me by bringing me the milk of any other animal."

"If I deceive Your Majesty, I will deserve to die," Tam replied.

Everybody expected that Tam would arm himself with weapons and a net with which to ensnare the beast, or perhaps take along herbs with which to put the lioness to sleep. They could not believe he would travel without servants to help him. But he left alone and unarmed, riding his horse and carrying only a stone jug for the milk.

When the courtiers saw this, even those who had had confidence in Tam began to doubt. He had departed in such haste that he had not even stopped to bid farewell to anxious Nesika. Kamtsan's friends immediately spread the rumor that Tam had been so frightened by the difficult mission given him by the king that he had simply run away. All the wise men agreed that no lioness would let herself be milked by a human.

Of course, what nobody knew was that Mazel cantered along beside Tam. Tam had hardly ridden an hour's time when on a low hill he saw a large lioness. Her two cubs were standing nearby.

With the courage of those who are protected by Mazel, Tam approached the lioness, knelt down, and began to milk her as if she were a cow. He filled the jug with the lioness's warm milk, sealed it carefully, rose, and patted her on the head. Only then did the lioness seem to realize what had happened. Her yellow eyes seemed to say, "What have I permitted! Have I forgotten that I am queen of all the beasts? Where is my pride? My dignity?" And suddenly she let out a terrible roar. Luckily, Tam had already mounted his horse, for it bolted in fear and raced away in the direction of the capital.

When Tam returned so soon, everyone was convinced that the milk he brought back could not be that of a lioness. Lions lived in the desert, in a part of the kingdom that lay weeks away from the capital. It was clear to all that Tam intended to deceive the sick king so that when the king died Tam would rule through Nesika.

The king himself was as suspicious as the rest. Nevertheless, he summoned Tam to appear before him. Tam entered the royal chamber carrying the jug of milk in both hands.

Kneeling before the king, he said, "Your Majesty, I have brought what you sent me for—the milk of a dog."

A dead silence followed his words. The king's eyes filled with anger.

"You dare laugh at my misfortune. Milk of a dog you have brought me. You will pay for this with your life."

Why had Tam said that he had brought the milk of a dog?

It so happened that the very second that Tam approached the king's sickbed Mazel's year had come to an end and Shlimazel had taken his place. It was Shlimazel who made Tam say "dog" instead of "lioness."

Shlimazel had indeed in one second destroyed what had taken Mazel a year to do. And, as had been agreed between them, Shlimazel had not used any of his old tricks.

Tam tried to correct his mistake, but his voice had gone with his luck and he stood there speechless. At the king's signal, Kamtsan ordered two guards to seize Tam and place him in chains. They brought him to the dungeon where those condemned to death were kept.

When Nesika heard what had happened, she fell into despair. She ran to her father's chambers to beg him to save Tam. For the first time, the sick king refused to permit her into his presence.

That night the palace, indeed the whole capital, was dark and quiet. Only Kamtsan and his henchmen secretly celebrated Tam's downfall. They knew the king would soon die, and since Nesika was unmarried, Kamtsan would inherit the kingdom. The prime minister offered his guests bread and beer. Miser that he was, it was his custom to make his guests pay for their food and drink. On this occasion, however, he charged them only for their beer.

And in the deepest cellar of the palace, which was known to be haunted, Mazel and Shlimazel held their meeting. Shlimazel had expected Mazel to look disappointed and angry, as do those who have lost a bet. But Mazel was not a sore loser. As usual, he was calm and composed.

"Shlimazel, you've won, and I congratulate you," he said.

"Do you realize that your lucky Tam will be hanged at dawn?" Shlimazel asked.

"Yes, I do."

"Have you forgotten my wine of forgetfulness?"

"No, I haven't."

Mazel went out and soon returned, rolling a barrel covered with dust and cobwebs. He set it upright, handed Shlimazel a goblet, and said, "Drink, Shlimazel, as much as your heart desires." Shlimazel placed his goblet under the spigot, filled it, and drank greedily. A broad smirk spread over his devilish face. "For one who is the master of the unlucky"—he grinned—"I sure am lucky."

He took another long drink, and beginning to sound tipsy, he said, "Listen to me, Mazel. Instead of fighting me, why don't you join me? Together we'd make a great team."

"You mean together we could ruin the world," Mazel said.

"Absolutely."

"And what then? After a while we'd have nothing left to do."

"As long as we can drink the wine of forgetfulness, why worry?"

"To get wine, someone has to plant the vineyard," Mazel reminded him. "Someone has to pick the grapes, press them, and prepare the wine. Nothing produces nothing—not even the wine of forgetfulness."

"If this wine works, I don't care about the future."

"It will work soon," Mazel said. "Drink and forget yourself."

"Have a drink too, Mazel, my friend."

"No, Shlimazel, forgetfulness is not for me."

Shlimazel drank one goblet after another. His wrinkled face half laughed, half cried, and he began to speak about himself in the way drunkards sometimes do.

"I wasn't born Shlimazel," he said. "My father was poor, but he was a good spirit. He was a water carrier in Paradise. My mother was a servant of a saint. My parents sent me to Reb Zeinvel's school. They wanted me to become a seraph, or at least an angel. But I hated my parents because they forced me to study. To spite them, I joined a gang of imps. We did all kinds of mischief. We stole manna. We stuffed ourselves with pilfered stardust, moon milk, and other forbidden delicacies. At night we descended to earth, got into stables, and frightened horses. We broke into larders and left devil's dung in the food. We disguised ourselves as wolves and chased sheep. What didn't we do? Once, I turned myself into a frog and hid in Reb Zeinvel's snuffbox. When he opened it to take a pinch, I jumped out and bit his nose. I rose slowly but steadily in the ranks of the evil host until I became what I am today—Shlimazel, Master of Bad Luck." Shlimazel filled another goblet and began to sing in a hoarse voice:

You may plot and you may scheme,
Mazel is an empty dream.
Now Shlimazel's taken over,
Tam will never be in clover.
Mazel talks, Shlimazel acts,
turning curses into facts.
Mazel wins a round or two,
Shlimazel sees the battle through.

On Mazel no one can depend,
Shlimazel's victor in the end.

Shlimazel uttered a snort and fell down like a log.

That was what Mazel had been waiting for. There was little time, because dawn was approaching and in the palace courtyard the dignitaries were already gathering for Tam's hanging. The guards appeared with Tam in chains. Kamtsan, surrounded by his flatterers, was conspicuous among the lords. He had already taken bribes and promised the highest positions to those who paid the most.

At a signal from Kamtsan, the drummers began their drumming. The masked executioner, dressed half in red and half in black, prepared to place the noose around Tam's neck. At that moment Mazel appeared. No one saw him but everybody felt his presence. The sun suddenly rose and covered everything with a purple light.

Now that Shlimazel lay in a drunken stupor and Mazel stood near the prisoner, Tam was again filled with courage. He called out in a clear voice, "My lords, it is the custom, before the condemned dies, to give him one last wish. My wish is to see the king."

The drummers, in confusion, interrupted their drumming. Though Kamtsan protested, the other lords overruled him and commanded that Tam be led to the king, who lay on his sickbed.

Tam knelt before the king and spoke: "Your Majesty, allow me to explain why I said that I had brought you the milk of a dog. It is known that the lion is the king of

[37]

the animals, yet in comparison with you, my lord, a lion is no more than a dog. And so I called the lioness a dog as an expression of my respect and admiration for Your Majesty. I did bring you the milk of a lioness. I beg you, drink it and it will make you well. I swear on my love for Nesika that I am telling the truth."

Since Mazel again stood at Tam's side, the king believed Tam.

"But the milk has been poured out," Kamtsan interrupted.

Nesika, who had not slept all night, praying and hoping that Tam would somehow be saved, had heard what had taken place and had rushed to her father's room. When Kamtsan said that the milk had been thrown away, she cried out, "No, Kamtsan, I have kept it. I requested the servants to give it to me because I believed in Tam."

She herself ran to bring the milk to her father. The amazement of all present grew as they watched the king drink the milk to the last drop. It worked so quickly that he became well before their very eyes. His cheeks lost their pallor, his dim eyes regained their former brightness, and his strength returned. The entire court rejoiced, except, naturally, Kamtsan and those to whom he had sold high positions in the kingdom. Nesika was the happiest of all.

She fell at her father's feet and said, "Father, Tam saved your life. Every word he spoke was true. Now keep your promise and let us be married."

The king immediately ordered that a wedding fit for a future queen be prepared. Royalty and dignitaries were invited from all the surrounding countries. Kings, queens, princes, and princesses came to the wedding accompanied by their royal entourages. They brought the most precious gifts.

Nesika was a splendid sight in her wedding dress, which had a train ten yards long that was carried by twenty pages. On her head she wore a dazzling coronet set with the diamond image of a lioness. On his uniform Tam wore the Order of Selfless Devotion, the country's highest honor.

Tam and Nesika were the happiest couple in the land. Nesika bore her husband seven children—four princes and three princesses, all handsome, healthy, and courageous.

Nobody lives forever. A day came when the king died. Nesika became queen, and Tam her prince consort. Nesika never decided any matters of state without the advice of her husband, because whatever Tam concerned himself with turned out well.

As for Kamtsan, he felt so sorry for himself that he took to drinking. Since he remained stingy as ever, he spent his time hanging around taverns, waiting for someone to treat him. Those who had once flattered him were the first to turn away.

Even though after some time Shlimazel awoke from his sleep, he never went near Tam again. For such was the power of the wine of forgetfulness that Shlimazel didn't even remember that Tam existed. As Shlimazel had always been fond of drink and drunkards, he now attached himself to Kamtsan. Mazel, of course, continued to help Tam. Actually, Tam no longer needed Mazel, except once in a while. Tam had learned that good luck follows those who are diligent, honest, sincere, and helpful to others. The man who has these qualities is indeed lucky forever.

Translated by the author and Elizabeth Shub

Why Noah Chose the Dove

When the people sinned and God decided to punish them by sending the flood, all the animals gathered around Noah's ark. Noah was a righteous man, and God had told him how to save himself and his family by building an ark that would float and shelter them when the waters rose.

The animals had heard a rumor that Noah was to take with him on the ark only the best of all the living creatures. So the animals came and vied with one another, each boasting about its own virtues and whenever possible belittling the merits of others.

The lion roared: "I am the strongest of all the beasts, and I surely must be saved."

The elephant blared: "I am the largest. I have the longest trunk, the biggest ears, and the heaviest feet."

"To be big and heavy is not so important," yapped the fox. "I, the fox, am the cleverest of all."

"What about me?" brayed the donkey. "I thought I was the cleverest."

"It seems anyone can be clever," yipped the skunk. "I smell the best of all the animals. My perfume is famous."

"All of you scramble over the earth, but I'm the only one that can climb trees," shrieked the monkey.

"The only one!" growled the bear. "What do you think I do?"

"And how about me?" chattered the squirrel indignantly.

"I belong to the tiger family," purred the cat.

"I'm a cousin of the elephant," squeaked the mouse.

"I'm just as strong as the lion," snarled the tiger. "And I have the most beautiful fur."

"My spots are more admired then your stripes," the leopard spat back.

"I am man's closest friend," yelped the dog.

"You're no friend. You're just a fawning flatterer," bayed the wolf. "I am proud. I'm a lone wolf and flatter no one."

"Baa!" blatted the sheep. "That's why you're always hungry. Give nothing, get nothing. I give man my wool, and he takes care of me."

"You give man wool, but I give him sweet honey," droned the bee. "Besides, I have venom to protect me from my enemies."

"What is your venom compared with mine?" rattled the snake. "And I am closer to Mother Earth than any of you."

"Not as close as I am," protested the earthworm, sticking its head out of the ground.

"I lay eggs," clucked the hen.

"I give milk," mooed the cow.

"I help man plow the earth," bellowed the ox.

"I carry man," neighed the horse. "And I have the largest eyes of all of you."

"You have the largest eyes, but you have only two, while I have many," the housefly buzzed right into the horse's ear.

"Compared with me, you're all midgets." The giraffe's words came from a distance as he nibbled the leaves off the top of a tree.

"I'm almost as tall as you are," chortled the camel. "And I can travel in the desert for days without food or water."

"You two are tall, but I'm fat," snorted the hippopotamus. "And I'm pretty sure that my mouth is bigger than anybody's."

"Don't be so sure," snapped the crocodile, and yawned.

"I can speak like a human," squawked the parrot.

"You don't really speak—you just imitate," the rooster crowed. "I know only one word, 'cock-a-doodle-doo,' but it is my own."

"I see with my ears; I fly by hearing," piped the bat.

"I sing with my wing," chirped the cricket.

There were many more creatures who were eager to praise themselves. But Noah had noticed that the dove was perched alone on a branch and did not try to speak and compete with the other animals.

"Why are you silent?" Noah asked the dove. "Don't you have anything to boast about?"

"I don't think of myself as better or wiser or more attractive than the other animals," cooed the dove. "Each one of us has something the other doesn't have, given us by God who created us all."

"The dove is right," Noah said. "There is no need to boast and compete with one another. God has ordered me to take creatures of all kinds into the ark, cattle and beast, bird and insect."

The animals were overjoyed when they heard these words, and all their grudges were forgotten.

Before Noah opened the door of the ark, he said, "I love all of you, but because the dove remained modest and silent while the rest of you bragged and argued, I choose it to be my messenger."

Noah kept his word. When the rains stopped, he sent the dove to fly over the world and bring back news of how things were. At last she returned with an olive leaf in her beak, and Noah knew that the waters had receded. When the land finally became dry, Noah and his family and all the animals left the ark.

After the flood God promised that never again would he destroy the earth because of man's sins, and that seed time and harvest, cold and heat, summer and winter, day and night would never cease.

The truth is that there are in the world more doves than there are tigers, leopards, wolves, vultures, and other ferocious beasts. The dove lives happily without fighting. It is the bird of peace.

Translated by Elizabeth Shub

Zlateh the Goat

At Hanukkah time the road from the village to the town is usually covered with snow, but this year the winter had been a mild one. Hanukkah had almost come, yet little snow had fallen. The sun shone most of the time. The peasants complained that because of the dry weather there would be a poor harvest of winter grain. New grass sprouted, and the peasants sent their cattle out to pasture.

For Reuven the furrier it was a bad year, and after long hesitation he decided to sell Zlateh the goat. She was old and gave little milk. Feivel the town butcher had offered eight gulden for her. Such a sum would buy Hanukkah candles, potatoes and oil for pancakes, gifts for the children, and other holiday necessaries for the house. Reuven told his oldest boy Aaron to take the goat to town.

Aaron understood what taking the goat to Feivel

meant, but had to obey his father. Leah, his mother, wiped the tears from her eyes when she heard the news. Aaron's younger sisters, Anna and Miriam, cried loudly. Aaron put on his quilted jacket and a cap with earmuffs, bound a rope around Zlateh's neck, and took along two slices of bread with cheese to eat on the road. Aaron was supposed to deliver the goat by evening, spend the night at the butcher's, and return the next day with the money.

While the family said goodbye to the goat, and Aaron placed the rope around her neck, Zlateh stood as patiently and good-naturedly as ever. She licked Reuven's hand. She shook her small white beard. Zlateh trusted human beings. She knew that they always fed her and never did her any harm.

When Aaron brought her out on the road to town, she seemed somewhat astonished. She'd never been led in that direction before. She looked back at him questioningly, as if to say, "Where are you taking me?" But after a while she seemed to come to the conclusion that a goat shouldn't ask questions. Still, the road was different. They passed new fields, pastures, and huts with thatched roofs. Here and there a dog barked and came running after them, but Aaron chased it away with his stick.

The sun was shining when Aaron left the village. Suddenly the weather changed. A large black cloud with a bluish center appeared in the east and spread itself rapidly over the sky. A cold wind blew in with it. The crows flew low, croaking. At first it looked as if it would rain, but instead it began to hail as in summer. It was early in the day, but it became dark as dusk. After a while the hail turned to snow.

In his twelve years Aaron had seen all kinds of weather, but he had never experienced a snow like this one. It was so dense it shut out the light of the day. In a short time their path was completely covered. The wind became as cold as ice. The road to town was narrow and winding. Aaron no longer knew where he was. He could not see through the snow. The cold soon penetrated his quilted jacket.

At first Zlateh didn't seem to mind the change in weather. She, too, was twelve years old and knew what winter meant. But when her legs sank deeper and deeper into the snow, she began to turn her head and look at Aaron in wonderment. Her mild eyes seemed to ask, "Why are we out in such a storm?" Aaron hoped that a peasant would come along with his cart, but no one passed by.

The snow grew thicker, falling to the ground in large, whirling flakes. Beneath it Aaron's boots touched the softness of a plowed field. He realized that he was no longer on the road. He had gone astray. He could no longer figure out which was east or west, which way was the village, the town. The wind whistled, howled, whirled the snow about in eddies. It looked as if white imps were playing tag on the fields. A white dust rose above the ground. Zlateh stopped. She could walk no longer. Stubbornly she anchored her cleft hooves in the earth and bleated as if pleading to be taken home. Icicles hung from her white beard, and her horns were glazed with frost.

Aaron did not want to admit the danger, but he knew just the same that if they did not find shelter they would freeze to death. This was no ordinary storm. It was a mighty blizzard. The snowfall had reached his knees. His hands were numb, and he could no longer feel his toes. He choked when he breathed. His nose felt like wood, and he rubbed it with snow. Zlateh's bleating began to sound like crying. Those humans in whom she had so much confidence had dragged her into a trap. Aaron began to pray to God for himself and for the innocent animal.

Suddenly he made out the shape of a hill. He wondered what it could be. Who had piled snow into such a huge heap? He moved toward it, dragging Zlateh after him. When he came near it, he realized that it was a large haystack which the snow had blanketed.

Aaron realized immediately that they were saved. With great effort he dug his way through the snow. He was a village boy and knew what to do. When he reached the hay, he hollowed out a nest for himself and the goat. No matter how cold it may be outside, in the hay it is always warm. And hay was food for Zlateh. The moment she smelled it she became contented and began to eat. Outside, the snow continued to fall. It quickly covered the passageway Aaron had dug. But a boy and an animal need to breathe, and there was hardly any air in their hideout. Aaron bored a kind of a window through the hay and snow and carefully kept the passage clear.

Zlateh, having eaten her fill, sat down on her hind legs and seemed to have regained her confidence in man. Aaron ate his two slices of bread and cheese, but after the difficult journey he was still hungry. He looked at Zlateh and noticed her udders were full. He lay down next to her, placing himself so that when he milked her he could squirt the milk into his mouth. It was rich and sweet. Zlateh was not accustomed to being milked that way, but she did not resist. On the contrary, she seemed eager to reward Aaron for bringing her to a shelter whose very walls, floor, and ceiling were made of food.

Through the window Aaron could catch a glimpse of the chaos outside. The wind carried before it whole drifts of snow. It was completely dark, and he did not know whether night had already come or whether it was the darkness of the storm. Thank God that in the hay it was not cold. The dried hay, grass, and field flowers exuded the warmth of the summer sun. Zlateh ate frequently; she nibbled from above, below, from the left and right. Her body gave forth an animal warmth, and Aaron cuddled up to her. He had always loved Zlateh, but now she was like a sister. He was alone, cut off from his family, and wanted to talk. He began to talk to Zlateh. "Zlateh, what do you think about what has happened to us?" he asked.

"Maaaa," Zlateh answered.

"If we hadn't found this stack of hay, we would both be frozen stiff by now," Aaron said.

"Maaaa," was the goat's reply.

"If the snow keeps on falling like this, we may have to stay here for days," Aaron explained.

"Maaaa," Zlateh bleated.

"What does 'maaaa' mean?" Aaron asked. "You'd better speak up clearly."

"Maaaa, maaaa," Zlateh tried.

"Well, let it be 'maaaa' then," Aaron said patiently. "You can't speak, but I know you understand. I need you and you need me. Isn't that right?"

"Maaaa."

Aaron became sleepy. He made a pillow out of some hay, leaned his head on it, and dozed off. Zlateh, too, fell asleep.

When Aaron opened his eyes, he didn't know whether it was morning or night. The snow had blocked up his window. He tried to clear it, but when he had bored through to the length of his arm, he still hadn't reached the outside. Luckily he had his stick with him and was able to break through to the open air. It was still dark outside. The snow continued to fall and the wind wailed, first with one voice and then with many. Sometimes it had the sound of devilish laughter. Zlateh, too, awoke, and when Aaron greeted her, she answered, "Maaaa." Yes, Zlateh's language consisted of only one word, but it meant many things. Now she was saying, "We must accept all that God gives us—heat, cold, hunger, satisfaction, light, and darkness."

Aaron had awakened hungry. He had eaten up his food, but Zlateh had plenty of milk.

For three days Aaron and Zlateh stayed in the haystack. Aaron had always loved Zlateh, but in these three days he loved her more and more. She fed him with her milk and helped him keep warm. She comforted him with her patience. He told her many stories, and she always cocked her ears and listened. When he patted her, she licked his hand and his face. Then she said, "Maaaa," and he knew it meant, I love you, too.

The snow fell for three days, though after the first day it was not as thick and the wind quieted down. Sometimes Aaron felt that there could never have been a summer, that the snow had always fallen, ever since he could remember. He, Aaron, never had a father or mother or sisters. He was a snow child, born of the snow, and so was Zlateh. It was so quiet in the hay that his ears rang in the stillness. Aaron and Zlateh slept all night and a good part of the day. As for Aaron's dreams, they were all about warm weather. He dreamed of green fields, trees covered with blossoms, clear brooks, and singing birds. By the third night the snow had stopped, but Aaron did not dare to find his way home in the darkness. The sky became clear and the moon shone, casting silvery nets on the snow. Aaron dug his way out and looked at the world. It was all white, quiet, dreaming dreams of heavenly splendor. The stars were large and close. The moon swam in the sky as in a sea.

On the morning of the fourth day Aaron heard the ringing of sleigh bells. The haystack was not far from the road. The peasant who drove the sleigh pointed out the way to him—not to the town and Feivel the butcher, but home to the village. Aaron had decided in the haystack that he would never part with Zlateh.

Aaron's family and their neighbors had searched for the boy and the goat but had found no trace of them during the storm. They feared they were lost. Aaron's mother and sisters cried for him; his father remained silent and gloomy. Suddenly one of the neighbors came running to their house with the news that Aaron and Zlateh were coming up the road.

There was great joy in the family. Aaron told them how he had found the stack of hay and how Zlateh had fed him with her milk. Aaron's sisters kissed and hugged Zlateh and gave her a special treat of chopped carrots and potato peels, which Zlateh gobbled up hungrily.

Nobody ever again thought of selling Zlateh, and now that the cold weather had finally set in, the villagers needed the services of Reuven the furrier once more. When Hanukkah came, Aaron's mother was able to fry pancakes every evening, and Zlateh got her portion, too. Even though Zlateh had her own pen, she often came to the kitchen, knocking on the door with her horns to indicate that she was ready to visit, and she was always admitted. In the evening Aaron, Miriam, and Anna played dreidel. Zlateh sat near the stove watching the children and the flickering of the Hanukkah candles.

Once in a while Aaron would ask her, "Zlateh, do you remember the three days we spent together?"

And Zlateh would scratch her neck with a horn, shake her white bearded head, and come out with the single sound which expressed all her thoughts, and all her love.

Translated by the author and Elizabeth Shub

A Hanukkah Eve
in Warsaw

I

For two weeks now Warsaw—and perhaps all Poland—had lain in the grip of a cold spell the likes of
which hadn't been seen in years. But I, a child not yet
seven, kept going to cheder early each morning. We—my
parents, my older brother Joshua, my sister Hindele, my
younger brother Moshe, and I—lived at 10 Krochmalna
Street and the cheder was located at 5 Grzybowska
Street. In the mornings, an assistant to the teacher came
to take me to cheder, and he brought me home again in
the evenings. To keep me from freezing on the way,
Mother wrapped me in two woolen vests, two pairs of
socks, and gloves. She stuck a hood on my head which
covered my red hair and earlocks; when I looked in the
mirror I couldn't recognize myself and stuck my tongue
out at the stranger.

The long winter night passed full of dreams. Now I
dreamed I was an emperor, and now a beggar. An old

crone of a gypsy snatched me and locked me in a cellar. I also dreamed that it was summer and that I was strolling with Shosha, the daughter of our neighbor Bashele, in a garden full of blooming flowers and singing birds. I sailed a boat on the Vistula but soon pirates captured me and spirited me off to Madagascar to be sold into slavery. My dreams blended with my fantasies and with the tales I had heard from my mother or read in storybooks.

That winter morning was a cold but sunny one. The sky above the rooftops loomed a light blue. Although our oven was heated with wood and coal, frost patterns had formed on our windows overnight. They resembled trees, not those common to Poland, but rather the date palms and fig and carob trees the Bible said grew in the Land of Israel.

Normally, I stayed at the cheder until nightfall, but that day was the eve of Hanukkah and I was scheduled to come home earlier than usual. I liked Hanukkah—the only holiday that came in the winter. In the evening, right after services, Father would bless the Hanukkah candles, Mother would fry potato pancakes, I would get a tin dreidel and money for the holiday. I could hardly wait to get home.

Before I left the house, Mother gave me a paper bag containing bread and butter, cheese, and an apple. This was to be my second breakfast. The assistant teacher took my hand and led me down the stairs into the street. Mother warned him not to let go of me. In such a large city a child could easily get lost. The streets were filled with sleighs and I was liable to be run over, God forbid. I was ashamed that my mother was such a worrier. She came from a small town and provincial people imagined all kinds of dangers in the big city. I had come to Warsaw when I was three and I considered myself a city boy. I could have gone to cheder by myself; I didn't have to be escorted there. I envied the other children my age who went to cheder alone. It seemed to me they laughed at me for being escorted like a baby.

God in heaven, how different the street looked today, all covered by the fresh snow that had fallen overnight! The sleighs and pedestrians hadn't yet managed to trample it, and it glared beneath the sun, reflecting dazzling crystals of every color of the rainbow. One solitary tree grew on our street and its naked branches were covered with frost. They reminded me of the arms of a huge Hanukkah candelabrum. Sleighs rode by with bells on horses' collars jingling. The animals' nostrils exuded steam. Cushions of snow lay on roofs and balconies. The whole world had turned white, rich, and dreamlike.

2

Coming to cheder was for me a daily trial. The other pupils quickly made friends with one another. They conducted all kinds of secret business transactions among themselves. One boy gave another a silver button and got a gold button in exchange. Quietly, so that the teacher wouldn't see, they traded pencils, pens, and sometimes chocolates and cookies they brought from home. Most of the students were sons of storekeepers or factory owners and were already little businessmen themselves. Their parents lived in the wealthier streets. Some of the

students brought a different toy to cheder each day—
lead soldiers, whistles, trumpets. One boy had a pen with
a peephole. When you looked into it you saw Cracow.
Another boy had a music box. When you turned the key
it played a tune. One boy had a real watch. Most of them
had black hair, and some were blond, but no one in the
cheder besides me had hair as red as fire. Nor did anyone
else wear such long earlocks. I was a rabbi's son and my
parents dressed me in the old-fashioned style. I had been
raised in Warsaw, but I looked like a yokel. The boys
laughed at me and my small-town costumes. They even
mocked the way I pronounced some words in Yiddish.
Besides, they couldn't do any trading with me. I brought
nothing to cheder except my Pentateuch.

I always felt ashamed when I came to cheder, and I
often prayed to God to let me grow up faster so that I
could be through with being a child. But I had some
satisfaction, too. All children love to hear stories and I
had acquired the reputation of a storyteller. I was also
able to add my own fantasies to the stories we read in the
Pentateuch. At Hanukkah time the teacher studied with
us the section that dealt with Joseph and his brothers. I
retained the meaning of the Hebrew words better than
many of the other children, and I repeated the tale as if
I had been there in person. Joseph's dreams became my
dreams. The brothers envied me and sold me into slavery
to the Ishmaelites, who in turn sold me to the Egyptians.
Potiphar had me imprisoned, and later I became viceroy
to Pharaoh. Jacob, Joseph, the other tribes, Laban,
Rachel, Leah, Bilhah, Zilpah were all as close and familiar to me as my own mother and father, as our neigh-

bor Bashele and her daughter, Shosha, with whom I carried on an unspoken love affair. As I sat in cheder over the Pentateuch, I yearned for her and her childish words, which held a thousand delights for me . . .

By three o'clock we had concluded our portion and the teacher, Reb Moshe Yitzchok, a patriarch of eighty, put down the pointer and the hare's leg with the thong that he used to whip bad pupils, and told us to go home.

The assistant teacher came up to me and began, with hesitation, "You always say that you could find your way home by yourself. Is this true?"

"Yes, it's true."

"You wouldn't get lost?"

"Lost? I could get home in the middle of the night!"

"I've got something to do and I don't have the time to take you home. Can I trust you to get home by yourself?"

"Yes, yes . . ."

"You won't tell your parents?"

"Tell? No, never!"

"Is that a promise?"

"I swear it on my ritual fringes."

"You don't have to swear on your ritual fringes."

"I wouldn't say anything even if they should kill me."

"Well, all right. Go straight home and don't stop along the way. You'll tell them I took you to the gate of your house."

"Yes."

The assistant teacher helped me put on my overcoat, the hood, the gloves, the galoshes. The other boys laughed and made fun of me. They called me a sissy, a mama's boy, a little rabbi, a spoiled brat. One of them showed me his tongue, another made the sign of the fig. A third said, "He is Joseph from the Bible. His father will make him a coat of many colors . . ."

3

I wanted to boast to the boys that I was going home all by myself, but the assistant teacher apparently guessed my intentions, for he put his finger to his lips.

I went out into the street, and for the first time I felt like a grownup. How short the days were in winter! It was just a quarter past three but the sky was already a dusky blue. Several cheder boys were sliding on the frozen gutter, trying to make the figure called "little shoemaker." When they saw me walking alone, they began to yell and make faces as if about to chase me. One of them threw a snowball at me. I moved away from them quickly. They only waited for a chance to start a fight and show off their strength. On Gnoyna Street I stopped in front of a shop window. Although the store belonged to a Jew, it sold the globes, bells, lights, and spangles Gentiles drape on Christmas trees. A man holding a long pole lit the gas streetlights. Women sat in doorways, on boxes and on footstools, hawking their wares—potato cakes, hot chick-peas, hot lima beans, bagels, oil cakes. The smells these delicacies sent out were delicious. I began to fantasize what I would do if I had a million rubles. I would buy all these goodies and make a feast for Shosha. We would munch on chocolate, halvah, tangerines, and take a ride in a sleigh. I would stop going to cheder and have a rabbi tutor me at home.

I was so preoccupied with my reveries I didn't notice that it had started snowing. A dense snow began to fall, dry and grainy as salt. My eyes crusted over. The street gaslights became covered with snow and their shine turned orange, blue, green, violet. This wasn't merely snow but snow mixed with sleet. Chunks of ice fell from the sky and a strong wind began to blow. Maybe the world was coming to an end? It seemed to me that there was thunder and lightning.

I started to run and I fell several times. I picked myself up, and to my alarm I saw that I had strayed into some other street. Here, the streetlights weren't gas but electric. I saw a trolley that wasn't drawn by horses. The rod extending from its roof to the wires overhead sprayed bluish sparks. A fear came over me—I was lost! I stopped passersby and asked them directions, but they ignored me. One person did answer me, but in Polish, a language I had never learned. I could barely keep from crying. I wanted to turn back to where I had come from, but apparently I only strayed farther away. I passed brightly illuminated stores and a building with balconies and columns like some royal palace. Music was playing upstairs, and below, merchants were clearing away their goods from the stalls. The wind scattered kerchiefs, handkerchiefs, shirts, and blouses, and they whirled in the air like imps. That which I had always feared had apparently happened—the evil spirits had turned their wrath on me.

Now the wind thrust me forward, now it dragged me back. It blew up the skirt of my coat and tried to lift me in the air. I knew where the gale sought to carry me—to

Sodom, to beyond the Mountains of Darkness, to As-modeus's castle, to Mt. Sair, where the ground is copper and the sky is iron. I wanted to cry out to God, to utter some prayer or incantation, but my mouth had gone numb and my nose was stiff as wood. The cold pene-trated through my coat, and through both vests. My eye-lids became swollen and I could no longer see in the white maelstrom.

Suddenly I heard a shrill clanging and shouts. Some-one sprang and, seizing me from behind, half dragged, half carried me off. Was this a demon, a wraith? A man in a long coat and a black beard turned white from the snow and frost shouted at me in rage, "Where are you running? Where do you creep to? You just missed being run over by the trolley car."

I wanted to thank him but I couldn't utter a word.

The man asked, "Who lets a child out in such a bliz-zard? You have no parents?"

I still don't know why, but I said, "No, I'm an orphan."

"An orphan, eh? Who do you live with?"

"My grandfather."

"Where does your grandfather live?"

I gave a false address—13 Krochmalna Street.

"What are you doing here if you live at 13 Kroch-malna? Got lost, eh?"

"No."

"Where were you going?"

"I wanted to say the mourner's prayer," I replied, astounded by my own lie.

"No synagogues or prayerhouses on Krochmalna? I see that you're lost. Come, I'll take you back."

He took my hand and led me along.

He asked, "What does your grandfather do? How does he make a living?"

"A porter," I said. The words issued from my mouth as if on their own.

"An old man a porter? He's still got the strength to carry? You hungry?"

"No. Yes."

"Wait, I'll get you something."

We walked only a few minutes. I had assumed I had strayed far from Krochmalna, but suddenly I saw it again. I wanted to get away from the man and my lies, but he held me firmly by the hand. He said, "Don't try to run away, boy. Poverty is no disgrace."

He led me into a restaurant. I had passed this restaurant earlier that day. Summer and winter a cloud of steam hovered inside it, and it always smelled of fried onions, garlic, meat, soup, beer. At night music was played there. I once heard my mother say that they served food that wasn't strictly kosher and that it was patronized by gangsters, thieves, the rabble. One boor there had bet that he could eat a whole roast goose. He was about to swallow the last bite when he got sick and had to be taken to the hospital. Now I was there myself. The floor was tiled in white and black like a checkerboard. Burly men and fat women sat at tables covered in red. Some ate boiled beef, others drank beer from mugs. Many gaslights were flashing. Waiters in white aprons carried huge trays with dishes above the diners' heads. There were other rooms here; from one came the sounds of singing, an accordion, hands clapping.

The man with me couldn't find a table. He stood with me in the crush and spoke to everyone and to no one: "An orphan. Nearly got run over. Hungry, poor thing. Half frozen. Give him something to eat. It's a good deed!"

He begged in my behalf. Again I tried to slip away from him, but he held me fast. The walls here were covered with red tapestries and hung with mirrors, so that I saw myself many times over.

A stout woman came up and asked my benefactor, "Why are you holding this boy? Has he done something?"

"Done something? He's done nothing. A poor orphan and hungry."

"An orphan? He's our rabbi's son. His parents are living. I saw his mother this very day at the butcher's."

"Eh? But he told me he was an orphan and that his grandfather is a porter—"

"A porter? Has he gone mad?"

The man apparently grew so confused that he let go of my hand. I dashed off. In a moment I was outside again.

4

I barely recognized the street. My brother Joshua had often spoken of the North Pole and the fact that the nights there lasted six months. Krochmalna Street now appeared to me like the North Pole. Huge mounds of snow had fallen. Whole towers and mountains had formed on the gutter. The pedestrians sank into the snowy depths. Misty trails extended from the street lamps. The sky hung low, reflecting a violet tinge with no moon or stars showing. I tried to run, fearing the man would catch me and punish me for my lies. I had committed so many sins! My parents would soon discover that I had deceived the man and posed as an orphan. They would also learn that the assistant teacher had let me walk home alone and that I had gotten lost. The boys at the cheder would have something to mock at and would make up new nicknames for me. The assistant teacher would become my enemy.

Suddenly I recalled a story my brother Joshua had told me about a boy who had been sent on a Passover night to open the door for the prophet Elijah and had vanished. Years later he came home a grown man and a professor. He had walked from the town where his parents lived to Warsaw, and then on to Berlin. Rich people there had helped him obtain an education. That's what I would have to do, too—run away from home! I would read all the books about the sun, the moon, the stars. I would learn how mountains, rivers, oceans, and the North Pole had formed. My father had one answer for everything—God had created it all. He wanted me to study only religious books. But the worldly books obviously had many other explanations.

Joshua often spoke about science. He said that a cheder education left one ignorant. He spoke of a telescope through which you could see the mountains and craters of the moon. Since we lived in Warsaw, I could proceed straight to Berlin. I knew that a train left for Germany from the Vienna depot. I would simply follow the tracks till I came to Berlin. But what would my parents do if I didn't come home? And what about Shosha? I would miss her terribly. A strange notion came to me: maybe Shosha would run away with me. In storybooks I often read of boys and girls who left home together on account of love. True, these were grownups, but I loved Shosha. I thought of her during the day and I dreamed about her at night. We would study together in Berlin, and when I became a professor, we would marry and come back to Warsaw. Everyone on Krochmalna Street would come out to greet us. My mother and Shosha's mother would weep and embrace. By then, everyone would have forgotten the silly things I had done today. The cheder boys who now pushed me around and called me names would come to me to teach them science and philosophy . . .

I had reached the gate of 10 Krochmalna Street, but instead of going home I went to Shosha's. I had to talk to her! In my mind I prayed to God that she would be home alone. Her father worked in a store and her mother often went to shop at the bazaar or to gossip with her sister. This time luck was with me. I knocked and Shosha opened. She seemed frightened by me and she said, "Oh, just look at you! White as a snowman."

It was warm in Shosha's kitchen and I promptly began telling her of my plans. She sat down on a footstool. She was blond, blue-eyed, and wore her hair in braids. She was exceptionally pale. Although she was my age, she was like a child of five. She played with dolls and got poor grades at the Polish school she attended. She couldn't read or figure properly. I now suggested that she accompany me to Berlin. Shosha heard me out calmly, then asked, "What will we eat?"

I was dumbfounded. I had completely forgotten that a person had to eat.

After a while I said, "We'll take food from home."

"And where will we sleep?"

I didn't know what to say. The trip to Berlin would undoubtedly take weeks. In the summer you could sleep outdoors, but in the winter it would be too cold. For a moment I wondered at my own stupidity and at Shosha's wisdom. Suddenly the door opened and my mother came in with my sister, Hindele, close behind her.

Hindele exclaimed, "There he is, Mama! What did I tell you?"

Mother stared at me in confusion. "So there you are . . . We've been searching for you two hours. I thought, who knows *what* happened . . ." And all at once she erupted, "Unfaithful child!"

I knew full well the meaning of this expression—a faithless son and a rebellious one. According to the law of the Pentateuch, I should be turned over by my parents to the town elders, who would condemn me to be stoned. An interrogation was forthcoming and I had no excuses ready.

My sister said, "We were waiting for you for the blessing of the Hanukkah candles."

"Where were you all this time? Didn't the assistant teacher bring you?" Mother asked.

"Yes, he brought me."

"When? You've been sitting here two hours?"

"He just came in this second," Shosha said.

"Why were you running around in such a storm? Why did you come here instead of home?"

"He wants us to follow the train tracks . . ." Shosha said, not intending to inform, but simply because she didn't understand the significance of it all.

My sister began to laugh. "He wants to run away with little Shosha! He's carrying on a love affair with her!"

"Don't laugh, Hindele, don't laugh!" Mother said. "The boy is making me sick!"

"Look at him! White as chalk!" my sister observed.

"Come!" Mother said.

She grabbed me by the collar and led me away. I anticipated a severe punishment, but when Father saw me, he only smiled and said, "I'm waiting for you with Hanukkah candles. I have a gift for you, too."

"He's got no gifts coming," Mother exclaimed. "He was outside in the cold the whole time. You didn't even ask where I found him!" she reproached Father. "At our neighbor's, at Bashele's!"

"Who is this Bashele?" Father asked.

"Abraham Kaufman's wife."

"What was he doing there?"

"They have a girl, some little fool, and he wants to run away with her."

Father arched his brows. "Oh, so? Well, it's Hanukkah. I don't want to spoil the holiday."

In honor of the holiday Father had donned his velvet housecoat. Our ceiling lamp was lit. The Hanukkah candelabrum stood ready. A red candle—the so-called sexton—rested in its holder. Father poured in olive oil and fussed with the wick. He made the benediction and lit a candle with the "sexton." Father's red beard glowed like fire. He took a prayer book with wooden covers from his pocket. It had a carving of the Western Wall on the front cover and one of the Cave of Machpelah on the back.

He said, "This prayer book comes from the Land of Israel."

"From the Land of Israel?"

I took the prayer book with joy and trepidation. I had never before held an object that stemmed from this distant and sacred land. It seemed to me that this prayer book exuded the scent of figs, dates, carob beans, cloves, cedar. All the stories from the Scriptures suddenly came to mind: of Sodom, of the Dead Sea, of Rachel's Tomb, of Joseph's dreams, of the ladder the angels climbed up to and down from heaven, as well as of King David, King Solomon, the Queen of Sheba.

My sister, Hindele, said, "Why does he get a gift?" And she added, "The worst dog gets the best bone."

"You'll see that the boy will cause us shame and disgrace!" Mother complained. "I don't believe that the assistant teacher brought him here at all. He always brings him into the house."

"Well, it's a holiday, a holiday!" Father said half to us, half to himself.

"You'll spoil him so, he'll become completely wild," Mother warned.

"With the Almighty's help, he'll grow up a decent man," Father said. He turned to me. "Pray from this book. Everything that comes from the Land of Israel is holy. This Wall is a remnant of the Holy Temple, which the evildoers demolished. The Divine Presence reigns there forever. Jews sinned; that's why the Temple was destroyed. But the Almighty is all-merciful. He is our Father and we are His children. God willing, the Messiah will come and we'll all go back to our homeland. A fiery Temple will descend upon Jerusalem. The dead will be resurrected. Our grandfathers, grandmothers, great-grandfathers, and all the generations will live again. The light of the sun will be seven times brighter than now. The saints will sit with crowns upon their heads and study the secrets of the Torah."

"Mama, the potato pancakes are getting cold," Hindele said.

"Oh, yes!"

And my mother and sister went back to the kitchen.

"Where did you go?" Father asked. "It's freezing outside. You might have caught cold, God forbid. You'd be better off glancing into a holy book."

"Papa, I'd like to study science," I said, astounded at my own words.

"Science? What kind of science?"

"Why summer is warm and winter is cold. How high is the moon and what happens up on the stars. How deep is the earth and how tall is the sky. Everything . . . everything . . ."

"All knowledge is contained in the Torah," Father replied. "Every letter of the Torah conceals countless secrets and infinite depth. Those who study the cabala acquire more truth than all the philosophers."

"Papa, teach me the cabala."

"Cabala isn't for boys. You may not study the cabala until you're thirty."

"I want it now!"

"Wait. You're still a child. What do you do there at the neighbors'? Who is that little girl? Since she's a fool, what do you need with her?"

"She is *not* a fool."

"Eh? Then what is she?"

"She is good. The boys at cheder call me names, but she is nice to me. When we grow up, I want to marry her," I said, baffled by my own words. It was as if a dybbuk had spoken out of me and I was overcome with fear.

Father smiled, but he promptly grew earnest. "Everything comes from heaven. It's said that forty days before a person is born, an angel in heaven calls out: 'This one's daughter will marry that one's son.' What's this girl's name?"

"Shosha."

"Shosha? I had an Aunt Shosha. She was my aunt and your great-aunt."

"Where does she live?"

"Aunt Shosha? In heaven, in Paradise. She was a saint. She would go to the Belz rabbi and he would place her in a seat of honor. In her old age she went to the Land of Israel and there she died. Oh, I have another gift for you, a dreidel."

The door opened and Mother and Hindele brought in the potato pancakes. During the brief time Mother had been in the kitchen her face had relaxed. My sister was smiling. I showed Mother the shining new dreidel and she gave me a sharp glance.

"You got lost, eh?"

I wanted to deny it, but I could not speak from too

much happiness. Besides, she knew everything, just like a prophetess. She often read my mind. Her big gray eyes seemed to say, "I know all your antics but I love you anyhow."

Translated by Joseph Singer

The Fools of Chelm & the Stupid Carp

In Chelm, a city of fools, every housewife bought fish for the Sabbath. The rich bought large fish, the poor small ones. They were bought on Thursday, cut up, chopped, and made into gefilte fish on Friday, and eaten on the Sabbath.

One Thursday morning the door opened at the house of the community leader of Chelm, Gronam Ox, and Zeinvel Ninny entered, carrying a trough full of water. Inside was a large, live carp.

"What is this?" Gronam asked.

"A gift to you from the wise men of Chelm," Zeinvel said. "This is the largest carp ever caught in the Lake of Chelm, and we all decided to give it to you as a token of appreciation for your great wisdom."

"Thank you very much," Gronam Ox replied. "My wife, Yente Pesha, will be delighted. She and I both love carp. I read in a book that eating the brain of a carp increases wisdom, and even though we in Chelm are immensely clever, a little improvement never hurts. But let me have a close look at him. I was told that a carp's tail shows the size of his brain."

Gronam Ox was known to be nearsighted, and when he bent down to the trough to better observe the carp's tail, the carp did something that proved he was not as wise as Gronam thought. He lifted his tail and smacked Gronam across the face.

Gronam Ox was flabbergasted. "Something like this never happened to me before," he exclaimed. "I cannot believe this carp was caught in the Chelm lake. A Chelm carp would know better."

"He's the meanest fish I ever saw in my life," agreed Zeinvel Ninny.

Even though Chelm is a big city, news traveled quickly there. In no time at all the other wise men of Chelm arrived at the house of their leader, Gronam Ox. Treitel Fool came, and Sender Donkey, Shmendrick Numskull, and Dopey Lekisch. Gronam Ox was saying, "I'm not going to eat this fish on the Sabbath. This carp is a fool, and malicious to boot. If I eat him, I could become foolish instead of cleverer."

"Then what shall I do with him?" asked Zeinvel Ninny.

Gronam Ox put a finger to his head as a sign that he was thinking hard. After a while he cried out, "No man or animal in Chelm should slap Gronam Ox. This fish should be punished."

"What kind of punishment shall we give him?" asked

Treitel Fool. "All fish are killed anyhow, and one cannot kill a fish twice."

"He shouldn't be killed like other fish," Sender Donkey said. "He should die in a different way to show that no one can smack our beloved sage, Gronam Ox, and get away with it."

"What kind of death?" wondered Shmendrick Numskull. "Shall we perhaps just imprison him?"

"There is no prison in Chelm for fish," said Zeinvel Ninny. "And to build such a prison would take too long."

"Maybe he should be hanged," suggested Dopey Lekisch.

"How do you hang a carp?" Sender Donkey wanted to know. "A creature can be hanged only by its neck, but since a carp has no neck, how will you hang him?"

"My advice is that he should be thrown to the dogs alive," said Treitel Fool.

"It's no good," Gronam Ox answered. "Our Chelm dogs are both smart and modest, but if they eat this carp, they may become as stupid and mean as he is."

"So what should we do?" all the wise men asked.

"This case needs lengthy consideration," Gronam Ox decided. "Let's leave the carp in the trough and ponder the matter as long as is necessary. Being the wisest man in Chelm, I cannot afford to pass a sentence that will not be admired by all the Chelmites."

"If the carp stays in the trough a long time, he may die," Zeinvel Ninny, a former fish dealer, explained. "To keep him alive we must put him into a large tub, and the water has to be changed often. He must also be fed properly."

"You are right, Zeinvel," Gronam Ox told him. "Go and find the largest tub in Chelm and see to it that the carp is kept alive and healthy until the day of judgment. When I reach a decision, you will hear about it."

Of course Gronam's words were the law in Chelm. The five wise men went and found a large tub, filled it with fresh water, and put the criminal carp in it, together with some crumbs of bread, challah, and other tidbits a carp might like to eat. Shlemiel, Gronam's bodyguard, was stationed at the tub to make sure that no greedy Chelmite wife would use the imprisoned carp for gefilte fish.

It just so happened that Gronam Ox had many other decisions to make and he kept postponing the sentence. The carp seemed not to be impatient. He ate, swam in the tub, became even fatter than he had been, not realizing that a severe sentence hung over his head. Shlemiel changed the water frequently, because he was told that if the carp died, this would be an act of contempt for Gronam Ox and for the Chelm Court of Justice. Yukel the water carrier made a few extra pennies every day by bringing water for the carp. Some of the Chelmites who were in opposition to Gronam Ox spread the gossip that Gronam just couldn't find the right type of punishment for the carp and that he was waiting for the carp to die a natural death. But, as always, a great disappointment awaited them. One morning about half a year later, the sentence became known, and when it was known, Chelm was stunned. The carp had to be drowned.

Gronam Ox had thought up many clever sentences before, but never one as brilliant as this one. Even his enemies were amazed at this shrewd verdict. Drowning is just the kind of death suited to a spiteful carp with a large tail and a small brain.

That day the entire Chelm community gathered at the lake to see the sentence executed. The carp, which had become almost twice as big as he had been before, was brought to the lake in the wagon that carried the worst criminals to their death. The drummers drummed. Trumpets blared. The Chelmite executioner raised the heavy carp and threw it into the lake with a mighty splash.

A great cry rose from the Chelmites: "Down with the treacherous carp! Long live Gronam Ox! Hurrah!"

Gronam was lifted by his admirers and carried home with songs of praise. Some Chelmite girls showered him with flowers. Even Yente Pesha, his wife, who was often critical of Gronam and dared to call him fool, seemed impressed by Gronam's high intelligence.

In Chelm, as everywhere else, there were envious people who found fault with everyone, and they began to say that there was no proof whatsoever that the carp really drowned. Why should a carp drown in lake water? they asked. While hundreds of innocent fish were killed every Friday, they said, that stupid carp lived in comfort for months on the taxpayers' money and then was returned sound and healthy to the lake, where he is laughing at Chelm justice.

But only a few listened to these malicious words. They pointed out that months passed and the carp was never caught again, a sure sign that he was dead. It is true that the carp just might have decided to be careful and to avoid the fisherman's net. But how can a foolish carp who slaps Gronam Ox have such wisdom?

Just the same, to be on the safe side, the wise men of Chelm published a decree that if the nasty carp had refused to be drowned and was caught again, a special jail should be built for him, a pool where he would be kept prisoner for the rest of his life.

The decree was printed in capital letters in the official gazette of Chelm and signed by Gronam Ox and his five sages—Treitel Fool, Sender Donkey, Shmendrick Numskull, Zeinvel Ninny, and Dopey Lekisch.

Translated by the author and Ruth Schachner Finkel

The Wicked City

When God commanded Abraham to leave the
land of Haran, his nephew Lot decided to go with him.
Lot was a lawyer in Haran, well known for his defense of
criminals. In such matters he was very shrewd, though
he had little feeling for justice. He instructed his clients
to lie, hired false witnesses, and bribed the judges.

Lot had grown rich and powerful. He had a large
house, a pretty wife, and two lively daughters, Bechirah
and Tsirah. Nevertheless, his wife was not content. She
wanted more gold, more pearls, and more slaves. She had
heard that Sodom was an immensely rich city where
there were many criminals who would need a lawyer,
and she persuaded Lot that they should move there.

Abraham was a holy man, a servant of God, who knew
nothing about the way his nephew conducted his affairs.
God told Abraham to leave his country and he obeyed.
When Lot suggested to him that they travel together in

the direction of Canaan, which was near Sodom, his uncle readily agreed.

Before he left Haran, Lot sold his house, his cows, his oxen, his horses, his donkeys, and his camels. He and his family rode on Abraham's donkeys, ate his bread, and at night covered themselves with his animal hides.

Sarah, Abraham's wife, said to him, "Why does Lot use your belongings? He is not a poor man."

"He is my brother's son," Abraham replied. "Besides, we have no children and after our death he will inherit all we have. Why shouldn't he use now what will one day be his?"

When they approached the land of Canaan, God told Abraham that he was to settle there. But Lot said, "Uncle, I do not wish to remain a burden on you. I will go on to Sodom. I was told that there is a great need for lawyers there, and I surely will be able to earn my bread."

"Go, and may God bless you," Abraham replied.

Lot left for Sodom with his wife and daughters. When they arrived at the gates of the city, however, they were stopped. Strangers were banned from Sodom by law. The people were even forbidden to sell food to travelers. In those rare cases where a foreigner was allowed inside, he was usually killed during the night. Such was the custom of this sinful city.

Lot was about to turn back, but his wife addressed the gatekeepers: "My husband is a lawyer and a famous defender of criminals. In Haran there was a man who had murdered both his parents, but my husband got him off scot-free."

"How did he manage that?" asked one of the gate-keepers.

"He pointed out to the judge that the killer was an orphan and an orphan deserves mercy. The murderer was not only freed but inherited his parents' fortune as well and is now one of the richest men in Haran."

When the gatekeepers heard this story, they sent a messenger to the elders of Sodom. The elders were so impressed to hear of Lot's defense of the orphan that they not only decided to allow Lot to enter the city but invited him to remain and become a citizen of Sodom.

Lot quickly got used to Sodom and its customs. True, he spoke the local language with an accent, but otherwise he behaved like a born Sodomite.

His wife accustomed herself to Sodom's way of life even more readily. Once, when a beggar came to ask for bread, she replied, "I give only stale bread."

"I'm so hungry," the beggar said, "that even stale bread will satisfy me."

"But, alas, we baked today and the bread is still fresh. Come back in a few days. The bread will then be stale and I will give you some," Lot's wife said, although she knew very well that the beggar would die of hunger if he had to wait so long for food.

On another occasion, a peddler came to her and said, "I have two sacks of apples for which the usual price is a silver shekel per sack. But I am in need of cash, and so you may have both sacks of apples and I will only charge you for one. That gives you one sack free."

Lot's wife took one sack of apples but did not pay the peddler a penny.

"Why don't you pay me?" the peddler asked.

"I took the free sack," she replied. When he tried to argue, she set her dogs on him and he barely escaped with his life.

The neighbors who heard about these incidents were filled with admiration for Lot's wife. It wasn't long before she forbade her daughters to speak either Hebrew or Aramaic, the language of Haran. "In Sodom, behave like a Sodomite," she instructed them. She also told them never to mention their Great-uncle Abraham and their Great-aunt Sarah. "It is below our dignity as honorable citizens of Sodom to have an old fool in our family who believes in God and obeys his word," she said.

One day Lot's wife hired a drummer to walk the streets of Sodom and sing the praises of Lot. The drummer stood in the marketplace and called out, "My lord Lot in his wisdom is able to save from prison or death thieves, murderers, vandals, swindlers, and robbers. There has not been so great a defender of criminals as my employer since the days of the flood."

The number of Lot's clients immediately increased. He became one of the most popular men in the city and was appointed Chief Justice of the Supreme Court of Sodom. His daughters, Bechirah and Tsirah, married two young Sodomites who were studying law under Lot.

One thing annoyed Lot. He could not rid himself of his foreign accent, and sometimes he forgot himself and used Hebrew and Aramaic expressions. His wife and daughters were embarrassed by the fact that Lot could not hide his Hebrew origin. This was especially true when he drank too much. In Sodom it was the custom to drink excessively. Lot often drank, and at such times he used whole phrases of Hebrew and shamed his family.

One day a messenger arrived with the news that Abraham of Canaan was coming to visit Lot.

Lot was beside himself. In Sodom all men shaved, but Abraham wore a long white beard. He spoke only Hebrew or Aramaic, and what was worse, he did not believe in idols. He served a God who was said to have created heaven and earth and whom none had ever seen. Lot knew in advance that the visit from his old-fashioned uncle could bring him only shame and disgrace.

His wife and daughters were even more upset. Bechirah and Tsirah announced that if that old Hebrew uncle came to the house, they would leave. But Lot argued, "How can I not receive him? He is my father's brother. Besides, I am his heir. His wife, Sarah, is old and will certainly never bear a child."

"You've been talking about that inheritance for years," Lot's wife said. "Abraham is almost a hundred years old. It's time for him to die."

"What do you want me to do—kill him?" Lot asked.

"Why not?" his wife replied. "If Sarah dies and he marries a young woman, he may still have an heir and we won't get a shekel of his money."

Lot could scarcely persuade his wife to let the old man come.

Before long, Abraham arrived in Sodom. As a relative of the illustrious Lot, he was allowed to enter the city. But Abraham brought his nephew even more embarrassment than Lot had feared. His beard seemed even longer than before, and he carried a staff and sack like a beggar. He was accompanied by two servants, Gabriel and Raphael, who were as outlandish in appearance as he.

The very first day Abraham did something that grieved Lot immensely. He stood in the marketplace and in a hoarse voice called out, "People of Sodom, repent. Stop your thieving, swindling, murdering; desist from abusing strangers, dishonoring your parents, and eating the flesh of animals while they still live. If you do not forsake your evil ways, God will destroy Sodom!"

The people who heard Abraham's words laughed at him and mocked him. "What god is that, you old fool?" one of them asked.

"The God who created heaven and earth," Abraham replied, "a God who hates bloodshed and falsehood, cruelty and injustice."

"Where is this god of yours? Of what is he made? Stone? Gold? Copper? Ivory?"

"Neither stone nor gold nor copper nor ivory. No one carved or cast Him," Abraham answered. "He cannot be seen, He has created the oceans, the mountains, the deserts, the people and animals. He is all-merciful and provides for all that lives."

"Why did Lot allow his crazy uncle to come here?" one of the bystanders asked. Others pelted Abraham and his two companions with the dung of asses.

"This is what happens when one admits strangers," said another. "Sooner or later they bring other foreigners with them."

"He should be deported," cried a man in the crowd.

"No need to deport me," Abraham replied. "I do not want to stay. But I warn you for the last time: Repent!"

But no one showed any sign of repentance.

That evening in Lot's house Abraham repeated his warning: "Sodom will be destroyed." He said to Lot, "If you want to remain alive, rise at dawn, take your family, and leave the city behind. Soon after the sunrise, there will be nothing left of Sodom but sulphur and ashes."

"The old man is insane," screamed Lot's wife, no longer able to contain her anger.

Lot had ordered his servants to prepare a feast for Abraham and his companions. They had roasted a suckling pig, stewed beef in blood, and boiled a baby goat in its mother's milk. These were the delicacies of Sodom. But Abraham, Gabriel, and Raphael refused to eat, saying that such food was an abomination before God. Abraham asked that some unleavened bread be prepared for him.

Lot's wife was mortified before her slaves. Bechirah and Tsirah felt shamed before their husbands.

Outside Lot's house a crowd had gathered. They threw stones at the windows, demanding that Abraham and his companions be brought out so they could make sport and torture them according to the customs of Sodom. With great difficulty Lot persuaded the rabble to leave.

It was very late when Lot and his family went to bed, but Abraham and his companions did not retire. Lot, who could not sleep, overheard Abraham pleading with his God:

"Wilt Thou destroy the just with the wicked? If there

be fifty just men in the city, wilt Thou also destroy and not spare the place for the fifty just that are therein? That be far from Thee to do after this manner . . . Shall not the judge of all the earth do right?

"What if there be five less than fifty just persons?

"What if there be forty found there?

"What if there be thirty found there?

"What if there be twenty found there?

"What if ten shall be found there?"

Lot's wife, too, had awakened. "The old man is certainly not in his right mind," she said to Lot. "If you do not get rid of him tomorrow, I will leave you, and the court will make you turn over your entire fortune to me. You will have to pay me a thousand shekels a week or go to jail."

"I implore you to be quiet," Lot pleaded. "Is it my fault that I have a silly old uncle?"

"It is certainly not my fault," Lot's wife hissed. "Nor is it the fault of our daughters and sons-in-law. They won't be able to show their faces in the street. Even so, they call us 'the Hebrews.' Whenever there is a disagreement, they yell, 'Dirty Hebrews,' and tell us to go back to Haran."

Finally Lot and his wife dozed off. The night was hot. A burning wind rose from the desert and blew fine hot sand through the cracks of the shutters. Jackals wailed in the distance.

At dawn, when Lot got out of bed and looked out the window, he grew afraid. The sky was unusually red. The air was heavy and smelled of scorch and sulphur. The rising sun was the color of blood.

Lot said to his wife, "Who knows, perhaps my Uncle

Abraham is right and a catastrophe is about to befall us. Sometimes the insane have a sixth sense."

"What should we do?"

"Let us get out of the city," urged Lot. "That can't hurt. We'll accompany the old fool a short distance and then turn back."

His wife disagreed. "If the neighbors see us leave, they'll think we've taken the old man's threats about the destruction of the city seriously. They'll accuse us of believing in Abraham's God, and if the elders hear about it, they'll make us leave for good."

"We'll say we're going on a picnic," Lot said. "Let's take a hamper of food and wine along."

Lot's wife and daughters were finally persuaded, but Lot's sons-in-law wanted nothing to do with the picnic. They whispered to each other that it was high time to get rid of their father-in-law and his family.

After much squabbling and haggling, Lot loaded a hamper of pork and a keg of wine on a donkey. Lot's wife did not lock the house because in Sodom a lock was of little value; lock-breaking was even studied by children in school. But the thieves' admiration for Lot would prevent them from robbing their beloved judge.

Now the sun had disappeared. The sky was overcast with yellowish clouds. The air became heavier and the smell of ashes and sulphur stronger. Flocks of crows flew about, croaking. Vultures appeared. The camels and donkeys brayed. The oxen bellowed. Dogs barked. Cats meowed. The earth burned the soles of people's feet. The animals stampeded from the city. Even the rats and mice departed from Sodom in droves.

The people of Sodom hurried to prostrate themselves

before their clay, stone, silver, and gold idols in the temples. They promised sacrifices of cattle and human beings to placate what they believed was the wrath of their gods.

Abraham and his companions, Lot and his family, had scarcely left the city, on the road toward Zoar, when a raging fire descended from the sky and turned Sodom into a furnace of smoke and flame. Abraham called to Lot and his family, "Don't look back! Run with all your might!"

"My house, my furniture! My clothes! My rugs! My furs, my jewelry!" wailed Lot's wife. She looked back, perhaps debating whether to return, and in that very instant became a pillar of salt.

"Woe, woe, see what has happened to our mother," Lot's daughters screamed. Lot tried to take his wife by the arm, and when he saw that she did not move, he put his hand to his mouth in fright. It tasted of salt. "Salt! My wife has turned into salt!" he wailed.

Abraham, however, urged them on, and only after they had covered a good distance did he permit them to stop and look back. What had been a teeming city only a short while before was now a mountain of smoldering ashes.

"Lot," Abraham said, "know you that my companions Gabriel and Raphael are angels. Now that you see the truth, repent and turn to God."

"What truth? I believe neither in God nor in angels," Lot said.

"But you see what has happened to Sodom," Abraham insisted.

"The volcano erupted. It has nothing to do with your God and His angels."

Turning to the angels, Abraham said, "He will remain as he is until he dies. Let us go on our way."

"Uncle Abraham," Lot said, "will you first give me part of my inheritance? You will soon die and I have no money left."

"I cannot give you part of your inheritance," Abraham answered, "because my wife, Sarah, is to give birth to a son. Thus have the angels promised. Is that not so, Gabriel and Raphael?"

"Yes, it is true. Sarah, thy wife, shall bear thee a son."

"Are you saying that in her old age Sarah will give birth to a son?" Lot asked in astonishment and began to laugh. His daughters laughed with him.

"Why do you laugh, Lot?" Gabriel said. "Is there anything the Lord cannot do?"

"Nonsense, superstition," Lot said. "Tell your fairy tales to the fools of Canaan, not to me. I'm too clever to believe such idiocy."

Abraham and the angels continued on their way, leaving Lot and his daughters behind.

"Father, what are we to do now?" Lot's daughters asked.

"I have lost my wife, and you have no more husbands," Lot replied, "but we do have a keg of wine." They uncorked the wine keg and were soon completely drunk.

After a while they found a cave, where they settled down and lived like savages. Except for defending criminals, there was nothing Lot knew how to do. His pampered daughters, who had learned little except how to eat, drink, and give orders to slaves and servants, and how to mock the poor, the beaten, and the sick, now lived in filth and sin.

The evil city of Sodom was never rebuilt. It remained a desert where not even wild animals ventured.

In time Lot again settled in some corrupt city and again became the champion of murderers, thieves, and swindlers. He never heard from Abraham again, but he no longer cared, because he learned from wandering peddlers that the angels had spoken the truth; there would be no inheritance for him.

Abraham did not again visit his faithless nephew, Lot, and Lot's sinful daughters. Sarah bore Abraham a son just as the angels had predicted.

He was called Isaac. He, in turn, sired Jacob, from whom stem the Twelve Tribes of Israel.

Translated by the author and Elizabeth Shub

Rabbi Leib &
the Witch Cunegunde

Rabbi Leib, the son of Sarah, and the witch Cunegunde were both miracle workers. The difference between them was that Rabbi Leib performed his wonders with the aid of divine power and Cunegunde used the power of the Devil. Cunegunde had a son, the famous brigand Bolvan, who robbed merchants on the roads. He had collected a fortune in stolen goods, which he hoarded in a cave. Although Bolvan did the actual hijacking, it was Cunegunde who made all the plans. By her witchcraft she was able to make invisible the entrance to the cave where their loot was kept, so that the police could never find it. At sixty, Cunegunde still had pitch-black hair and a smooth, fresh skin. It was said that she possessed a potion that kept her looking young.

For years Rabbi Leib and Cunegunde waged silent warfare. Whenever Rabbi Leib gave a merchant an amulet to guard him against evil, Bolvan could neither rob nor harm him. This resulted in many losses for the brigand. Cunegunde tried to outwit Rabbi Leib, but his prayers usually proved stronger than her witchcraft.

Rabbi Leib was so often the winner that finally Cunegunde could not help admiring him. And from admiration to love is but one step. However, Cunegunde could only love as a witch does. Here is the letter she wrote to Rabbi Leib:

You, Leib, are the strongest man on earth and I, Cunegunde, am the strongest woman. If we got married, we could rule the world. We could rob the greatest banks, empty the richest mints, and the mightiest rulers would tremble before us.

And Rabbi Leib's reply:

I don't want to rob banks or empty mints. I want to serve God and not the Devil. I'd rather live with a snake than with you.

When Cunegunde received Rabbi Leib's letter, her love for him became mixed with hatred. She vowed she would force him to marry her and then revenge herself on him. She wrote to him again.

You can't escape. You will fall into my clutches. You will marry me whether you like it or not, and you will have the same bitter end as my five husbands before you.

It was known that Cunegunde, five times a widow, had in each case destroyed her husband.

Rabbi Leib and Cunegunde both lived in the same huge forest. She had a luxurious underground house with a secret entrance through the hollow of a tree. He owned a small hut by a stream in which he immersed himself each morning before prayers. He liked to pray among the trees. From time to time, he went to the village nearby to purchase food. Rabbi Leib ate neither meat nor fish, nor anything else that came from a living creature. He bought his scant provisions and always laid in a large supply of seeds for the birds of the forest. Every day hundreds of them came to feed in the clearing in front of his hut. As he prayed, the birds sang and twittered and their voices lifted his spirit and strengthened his faith.

Suddenly strange things began to happen and Rabbi Leib recognized them as the work of Cunegunde. Venomous snakes appeared near his hut and attacked the birds. At night the howling of wild dogs disturbed him in his studies. One dawn as he bathed in the stream, a strange little beast not unlike a hedgehog bit into his leg with its sharp teeth. Rabbi Leib uttered a holy incantation and the beast let go. But the marks of its teeth remained behind.

Rabbi Leib bought loaves of bread fresh from the oven in the village, but when he arrived home the bread was moldy. Worms, mice, and rats invaded his hut. Rabbi Leib kept some fowl which he never slaughtered; he loved the sound of roosters crowing and chickens cackling. One night a weasel stole into his yard and killed them all.

The water of his stream, which had always been crystal clear, suddenly became muddy and began to smell.

One evening when Rabbi Leib went into the forest to pray, he noticed a man, covered with soot like a chimney sweep, on the roof of his hut. The man carried a broom as long as a sapling and a coil of thick rope. He had the wild eyes of a beast and pointed white teeth. Rabbi Leib called out to him:

Creature of darkness lurking here,
to the wastes of Sodom disappear.

For a moment the demon hesitated. Then he called back: "I will not move until you listen to what I have to say."

"Who are you? What do you want?"

"My name is Hurmizah. I am the devoted servant of my mistress, Cunegunde. She sent me to tell you that she is pining away for love of you. If you do not consent to marry her, she will avenge herself on all your friends and family. She has not the power to harm you, but she can do as she pleases with the others. However, if you agree to become her husband, she will give you half her treasures, bags full of gold, diamonds, and other precious things. She will also build you a palace on Mt. Seir, near Asmodeus's own castle, and have you appointed one of his seven councilors. A thousand he-demons and she-demons will do your bidding. Instead of immersing yourself in your muddy little stream, you will bathe in a pool of balsam. Naamah herself will dance for you, together with her maids. You will drink five-thousand-year-old wine from the cellars of Malkizedek." Hurmizah would have continued but Rabbi Leib intoned a holy name that he used only in cases of utmost need and Cunegunde's messenger was forced to leave. As he spread out a pair of batlike wings, he called, "Leib, think it over. I'll be back tomorrow. In the end Cunegunde's witchcraft will conquer your incantations."

He flew off, leaving behind him the smell of pitch, sulphur, and devil's dung.

That night Rabbi Leib could not sleep. He lit a candle, but the wind blew it out. From his chimney came the sound of whistling and laughter. Although he knew that Cunegunde could not harm him, he worried about his friends and relatives and about his beloved birds. He had to get rid of the witch once and for all. But how?

The following night when the demon chimney sweep appeared again on Rabbi Leib's roof, the rabbi said to him, "Hurmizah, last night I could not sleep a wink and I thought everything over. I came to the conclusion that Cunegunde is right. She and I together would be the mightiest pair in the world. Fly to your mistress and tell her that I am prepared to marry her."

When Hurmizah heard these words, he said, "It's a good thing you've come to your senses, my lord. My mistress Cunegunde planned to destroy your house, burn down the forest, dry up the stream, and that just as a start. Nobody is mightier or more beautiful. Together you will rule over man and beast." Hurmizah departed at once to carry the good news to Cunegunde.

Cunegunde wasted no time. She dressed in her best clothes, placed a diamond tiara on her head, and adorned herself with many precious bracelets and anklets. She mounted a broom with silver whisks and flew to Rabbi Leib's hut. Behind her came her retinue: creatures with pointed noses, twisted horns, long tails, and ears reaching down to their shoulders. A giant with a nose like a ram's horn carried a fat midget as round as a pot on his back. As they traveled along, they screamed, laughed, hooted, blasphemed.

Rabbi Leib, dressed in a white robe, stepped out of his hut to greet the bridal party. The entire company landed before him. Cunegunde said, "Leib, I forgive all the injustices you committed against me. You are about to become my husband, and I, your wife. As soon as we are married, the forces of good will lose their power, and you and I, with the help of Satan, will be the lords of heaven and earth."

"Cunegunde," Rabbi Leib replied, "I tried to resist your charms, but I could not. Do with me as you wish."

"My children, put up the wedding canopy," Cunegunde ordered.

Four goblins at once brought forth a black canopy. Instead of four posts, it was supported by four snakes. From somewhere the sound of caterwauling music started up. Hurmizah gave away the bride. Another giant devil played best man to Rabbi Leib. The wedding ceremony began at dawn, just before the sun rose. Cunegunde laughed to herself. She had already figured out how to destroy Rabbi Leib. But first she had to learn his holy incantations so as to deprive him of divine power. Gloatingly she thought to herself, With all your wisdom, Leib, you're just a fool.

One of the devils took out a black wedding ring and handed it to Rabbi Leib, who was to place it on Cunegunde's first finger. If he had done so, they would actually have become man and wife and he would have been a slave of the netherworld forever. But instead of putting the ring on her finger, Rabbi Leib said, "Cunegunde, my dear, before you become my wife, I want to give you a present."

"What kind of present?"

"A golden locket that will endow you with powers in both the upper and the nether world. Allow me to hang it around your lovely neck."

Cunegunde smiled smugly and said, "Very well, Leib. Hang your locket around my neck." And she lowered her head to help him. That was all Rabbi Leib needed. The locket held a charm blessed by the saintly Rabbi Michael of Zlotchev. Rabbi Leib placed the locket around Cunegunde's neck. Cunegunde turned to Hurmizah to show off the precious gift and to gloat over Rabbi Leib's faith in her. But suddenly she let out a terrifying scream. The locket was burning into her flesh like a fire of hell. She tried to tear it from her neck, but her hands were powerless.

Rabbi Leib had again managed to outwit the witch Cunegunde.

When the devils and hobgoblins saw that their mistress was powerless, they fled in fear. The evil ones are cowards at heart. Cunegunde remained alone. She fell on her knees and begged Rabbi Leib to remove the locket, promising him all the treasures in her possession. But Rabbi Leib had learned that there can be no compassion for the creatures of the netherworld. He knew what had happened in olden times to Joseph della Reina, the famous saint, who had captured Satan and bound him in chains. Satan had begged for some snuff and when Rabbi Joseph took pity and gave it to him, Satan turned the snuff into a fire that melted his chains and enabled him to escape.

"Cunegunde, although I now have the power to destroy you, I have decided not to kill you but to send you to a place from which you will never be able to return." Then he incanted:

Cunegunde, Keteff's daughter,
to the land of Admah fly
and remain there till you die.

Admah was one of the towns destroyed in biblical times together with Sodom and Gomorrah.

In vain Cunegunde wept, implored, and made all kinds of promises. A strong wind swept her up in the air and carried her away as swiftly as an arrow flies from a bow. The locket fell from her neck and she lost her power for all time. She lived out her life in the wasteland of Admah, not far from the place where Lot's wife had been turned into a pillar of salt.

Without the protection of his mother, Cunegunde's son, Bolvan, became an ordinary thief. The police soon found the hidden cave where his loot was stored and arrested him. All the gold, precious stones, and stolen goods were returned to their rightful owners, or to their heirs. Bolvan, bound in chains, died in prison while still waiting for his trial.

From then on, Rabbi Leib lived in peace. The stream in which he immersed himself each morning was again crystal clear and the birds gathered in front of his hut to be fed. He supported the poor, cured the sick, and helped those who were possessed by evil spirits.

As long as he lived, the black host stayed away from the forest. It was only after his death that they dared to return to try their old tricks. Soon after, a new saint appeared, the famous miracle worker Reb Baruch, and the ancient war between good and evil started all over again.

Translated by the author and Elizabeth Shub

The Parakeet
Named Dreidel

It happened about ten years ago in Brooklyn, New York. All day long a heavy snow was falling. Toward evening the sky cleared and a few stars appeared. A frost set in. It was the eighth day of Hanukkah, and my silver Hanukkah lamp stood on the windowsill with all candles burning. It was mirrored in the windowpane, and I imagined another lamp outside.

My wife, Esther, was frying potato pancakes. I sat with my son, David, at a table and played dreidel with him. Suddenly David cried out, "Papa, look!" And he pointed to the window.

I looked up and saw something that seemed unbelievable. Outside on the windowsill stood a yellow-green bird watching the candles. In a moment I understood what had happened. A parakeet had escaped from its home somewhere, had flown out into the cold street and landed on my windowsill, perhaps attracted by the light.

A parakeet is native to a warm climate, and it cannot stand the cold and frost for very long. I immediately took steps to save the bird from freezing. First I carried away the Hanukkah lamp so that the bird would not burn itself when entering. Then I opened the window and with a quick wave of my hand shooed the parakeet inside. The whole thing took only a few seconds.

In the beginning the frightened bird flew from wall to wall. It hit itself against the ceiling and for a while hung from a crystal prism on the chandelier. David tried to calm it: "Don't be afraid, little bird, we are your friends." Presently the bird flew toward David and landed on his head, as though it had been trained and was accustomed to people. David began to dance and laugh with joy. My wife, in the kitchen, heard the noise and came out to see what had happened. When she saw the bird on David's head, she asked, "Where did you get a bird all of a sudden?"

"Mama, it just came to our window."

"To the window in the middle of the winter?"

"Papa saved its life."

The bird was not afraid of us. David lifted his hand to his forehead and the bird settled on his finger. Esther placed a saucer of millet and a dish of water on the table, and the parakeet ate and drank. It saw the dreidel and began to push it with its beak. David exclaimed, "Look, the bird plays dreidel."

David soon began to talk about buying a cage for the bird and also about giving it a name, but Esther and I reminded him that the bird was not ours. We would try to find the owners, who probably missed their pet and were worried about what had happened to it in the icy weather. David said, "Meanwhile, let's call it Dreidel."

That night Dreidel slept on a picture frame and woke us in the morning with its singing. The bird stood on the frame, its plumage brilliant in the purple light of the rising sun, shaking as in prayer, whistling, twittering, and talking all at the same time. The parakeet must have belonged to a house where Yiddish was spoken, because we heard it say *"Zeldele, geh schlofen"* (Zeldele, go to sleep), and these simple words uttered by the tiny creature filled us with wonder and delight.

The next day I posted a notice in the elevators of the neighborhood houses. It said that we had found a Yiddish-speaking parakeet. When a few days passed and no one called, I advertised in the newspaper for which I wrote, but a week went by and no one claimed the bird. Only then did Dreidel become ours. We bought a large cage with all the fittings and toys that a bird might want, but because Hanukkah is a festival of freedom, we resolved never to lock the cage. Dreidel was free to fly around the house whenever he pleased. (The man at the pet shop had told us that the bird was a male.)

Nine years passed and Dreidel remained with us. We became more attached to him from day to day. In our house Dreidel learned scores of Yiddish, English, and Hebrew words. David taught him to sing a Hanukkah song, and there was always a wooden dreidel in the cage for him to play with. When I wrote on my Yiddish typewriter, Dreidel would cling to the index finger of either my right or my left hand, jumping acrobatically with every letter I wrote. Esther often joked that Dreidel was helping me write and that he was entitled to half my earnings.

Our son, David, grew up and entered college. One winter night he went to a Hanukkah party. He told us that he would be home late, and Esther and I went to bed early. We had just fallen asleep when the telephone rang. It was David. As a rule he is a quiet and composed young man. This time he spoke so excitedly that we could barely understand what he was saying. It seemed that David had told the story of our parakeet to his fellow students at the party, and a girl named Zelda Rosen had exclaimed, "I am this Zeldele! We lost our parakeet nine years ago." Zelda and her parents lived not far from us, but they had never seen the notice in the newspaper or the ones posted in elevators. Zelda was now a student and a friend of David's. She had never visited us before, although our son often spoke about her to his mother.

We slept little that night. The next day Zelda and her parents came to see their long-lost pet. Zelda was a beautiful and gifted girl. David often took her to the theater and to museums. Not only did the Rosens recognize their bird, but the bird seemed to recognize his former owners. The Rosens used to call him Tsip-Tsip, and when the parakeet heard them say "Tsip-Tsip," he became flustered and started to fly from one member of the family to the other, screeching and flapping his wings. Both Zelda and her mother cried when they saw their beloved bird alive. The father stared silently. Then he said, "We have never forgotten our Tsip-Tsip."

I was ready to return the parakeet to his original owners, but Esther and David argued that they could never part with Dreidel. It was also not necessary, because that day David and Zelda decided to get married after their graduation from college. So Dreidel is still with us, always eager to learn new words and new games. When David and Zelda marry, they will take Dreidel to their new home. Zelda has often said, "Dreidel was our matchmaker."

On Hanukkah he always gets a gift—a mirror, a ladder, a bathtub, a swing, or a jingle bell. He has even developed a taste for potato pancakes, as befits a parakeet named Dreidel.

Lemel & Tzipa

This story was told me by my mother, and I'm retelling it here word for word, as closely as possible.

Once there was a well-to-do countryman named Tobias, and he and his wife, Leah, had a daughter, Tzipa, who was a fool the likes of which you couldn't find in the entire region. When Tzipa grew up, marriage brokers began to propose matches for her, but as soon as a prospective groom came to look her over and she began to spout her nonsense, he would flee from her. It appeared that Tzipa would be left an old maid.

The husband and wife went to ask advice of a rabbi, who told them, "Marriages are made in heaven. Since Tzipa is a fool, heaven will surely provide a foolish groom for her. Just ask around about a youth who's a bigger fool than your daughter, and when the two fools marry, they'll be happy together."

The parents were pleased by this advice. They went to

a matchmaker and told him to find the biggest fool in the Lublin province for their daughter. They promised the matchmaker double the fee usually paid for arranging a match. The matchmaker knew that no city contained so many fools as Chelm, so that was where he headed.

He came to a house and saw a youth sitting in front of it and crying. The matchmaker asked, "Young fellow, why are you crying?"

And the youth said, "My mother baked a whole dish of blintzes for Shevuoth. When she went out to buy sour cream for the blintzes, she warned me, 'Lemel, don't eat the blintzes until Shevuoth.' I promised her that I wouldn't, but the moment she left the house I got a great urge for a blintz and I ate one, and after the first I got the urge for another, and a third, and a fourth, and before you know it, I finished the whole dish of blintzes. I was so busy eating blintzes I didn't see the cat watching me. Now I'm very much afraid that when Mother comes back the cat will tell her what I've done and Mother will pinch me and call me what she calls me anyhow—fool, oaf, dummy, ninny, simp, clod, donkey."

This Lemel is made for Tzipa, the matchmaker thought.

Aloud he said, "I know how to speak the cat language. I'll tell the cat to say nothing, and when I give a cat an order he listens, for I am the King of the Cats."

Hearing these words, Lemel commenced to dance with joy. The matchmaker began to utter fabricated words to the cat—whatever came to his lips: "Petche-metche-ketche-letche."

Then he asked, "Lemel, do you want a bride?"

"Certainly!"

"I have just the bride for you—no one like her in the whole world. Tzipa is her name."

"Does she have red cheeks?" Lemel asked. "I like a girl with red cheeks and long braids."

"She has everything you want."

Lemel began to dance anew and clap his hands. At that moment his mother came in with the pot of sour cream. When she saw her son dancing, she asked, "Lemel, what's the big celebration about?"

And Lemel replied, "I ate up all the blintzes and I was afraid the cat would tell, but this man ordered the cat not to talk."

"Dummox! Dolt!" the mother screamed. "What will I do with you? What girl would want to marry such a dunderhead?"

"Mama, I have a bride already!" Lemel exclaimed. "Her name is Tzipa and she has long cheeks and red braids."

A few days later Lemel and Tzipa drew up their articles of engagement. They could not write their names and Lemel signed with three dots and Tzipa with three dashes. Lemel got a dowry of two hundred gulden. Since Lemel didn't understand about money and didn't know the difference between one banknote and another, Tzipa's father wrapped the five-gulden notes in white paper and the ten-gulden notes in blue paper. Lemel also got a silver watch, but since he couldn't read figures, when he wanted to know the time he stopped a person in the street and asked, "What time is it?" At the same time he added, "I can't see because I've lost my glasses." This was what his mother had told him to use as an excuse.

When the day of the wedding came, Tzipa began to weep bitterly.

Her mother asked, "Tzipa, why are you crying?"

And Tzipa replied, "I'm ashamed to marry a stranger."

The mother said, "I married a stranger, too. After the wedding, the husband and wife become close and are no longer strangers."

But Tzipa countered, "You, Mama, married Papa, but I have to marry a complete stranger."

The mother said, "Tzipa, you're a big fool but your groom is a fool, too, and together you'll be, God willing, two happy fools."

After lengthy discussions, Tzipa allowed herself to be escorted to the wedding canopy.

Some time after the wedding, Tzipa's father said to his son-in-law, "Lemel, your father is a merchant, I'm a merchant, and I want you to be a merchant, too. I've given you a dowry. Use it to go into business."

"What's a merchant?" Lemel asked, and his father-in-law said, "A merchant is someone who buys cheap and sells dear. That's how he makes a profit. Take the dowry, go to Lublin, and if you spot a bargain there, buy it as cheaply as possible, then come back here and sell it at a high price."

Lemel did as his father-in-law ordered. Tzipa gave him a chicken wrapped in cabbage leaves for the road. In the wagon, Lemel got hungry and wanted to eat the chicken, but it was raw. Tzipa's mother had told her to give her husband a chicken, but since she didn't say anything about cooking it, Tzipa had given Lemel a raw chicken.

Lemel stopped at an inn. He was very hungry. They

asked him what he wanted to eat and he said, "Give me everything you have and I'll eat until I'm full."

Said and done. First they gave him a glass of wine, then another; then an appetizer of tripe with calf's foot. Lemel ate this with lots of bread and horseradish. Then they served him a bowl of noodle soup. After Lemel had finished one bowl of soup, he asked for another. Then they served Lemel a huge portion of meat with groats, cabbage, potatoes, and carrots. Lemel finished everything and was still hungry. Then they served him a compote of prunes, apples, pears, and raisins. Lemel gulped it all down and yet his hunger was still not sated. Finally, they served him tea with sponge cake and honey cake. Lemel drank the tea and ate the cake, but somehow the hunger still gnawed at him. The innkeeper said, "I hope that by now you are full."

But Lemel replied, "No, I'm still hungry."

The innkeeper took a cookie out of the cabinet and said, "Try this."

Lemel ate the cookie and immediately felt sated. He said, "Now I'm full. Had I known that you can get full from a cookie, I needn't have ordered all those other dishes."

The innkeeper promptly saw that he was dealing with a dolt. He himself was a swindler and he said, "Now it's too late. But if you ever come here again, I'll give you such a cookie right off the bat and you won't have to order the other dishes. Now, be so good as to pay for the meal."

Lemel took from his purse the banknotes rolled in white paper and those rolled in blue paper and he said, "One paper contains the five-gulden bills and the other the ten-gulden bills, but I don't remember which is which."

The innkeeper unrolled the two stacks, and as befits a swindler, he told Lemel that a ten-gulden was a five-gulden bill. He also swindled Lemel with the change.

In Lublin, Lemel went from store to store seeking bargains, but somehow there were no bargains to be found. Lying in bed at night, Lemel began to think about the miraculous cookie which made you instantly full. "If I knew how to bake such cookies I'd be rich," Lemel said to himself. "There isn't enough food in Chelm, the people are hungry, and everyone would welcome such cookies."

He himself had felt sated for nearly twenty hours after eating this cookie.

The next day Lemel headed home and he stopped at the same inn. He ordered the miraculous cookie, but the innkeeper said, "I just now served the last of them to a guest. But I can sell you the recipe. Believe me, when you bake these cookies in Chelm you'll sell them for a big profit and you'll become as rich as Rothschild."

"What does this recipe cost?"

The innkeeper named a high price, but Lemel decided that by baking such cookies he could get back all the money he would pay, with a huge profit besides. So he bought the recipe. Having already seen that Lemel couldn't read, write, or even determine the value of a coin, the innkeeper composed the following recipe:

Take three quarts of duck's milk, five pounds of flour ground from iron, two pounds of cheese made from snow, one pound of fat from a flintstone, a half pound of feath-

ers from a red crow, and a quarter pound of juice squeezed from copper. Throw it all in a pot made of wax and let it cook three days and three nights over the fire of a potato tree. After three days, knead a dough out of the mixture, cut out the cookies with a knife made of butter, and bake them in an oven made of ice till they turn red, brown, and yellow. Then dig a pit, throw in the whole mess, and put up a board with a sign over it reading: WHEN YOU SEND A FOOL TO MARKET, THE MERCHANTS REJOICE.

After Lemel finished paying for the meal and the recipe, he barely had enough left for the fare home. But he was pleased with the bargain he had made.

When he came home and told Tzipa about the miraculous cookie, she began to clap her hands and dance. But the joy didn't last long. When Lemel's father-in-law came home and read the recipe, he became furious and screamed, "Lemel, you've been swindled!"

Tzipa promptly began to cry. Tzipa's mother cried along with her.

After a while, Lemel said, "All my troubles stem from the fact that I can't read. I must learn to read, and the quicker the better."

"Yes, my son," Tzipa's father said. "A merchant must be able to read and write."

Since there were no teachers in the village, Lemel resolved to go to Lublin to learn to read. Again, the father-in-law gave him money for the fare and to pay for the lessons. In Lublin, Lemel went to Lewartow Street to seek out a teacher. He walked past a store displaying eyeglasses in the window. He looked inside and saw a customer put on a pair of glasses and glance into a book while the proprietor asked, "Now can you read?"

"Yes, now I can read well," the customer said.

Lemel thought to himself, Since putting on glasses enables you to read, what do I need with a teacher?

Lemel had no urge to study. He yearned to go home to Tzipa.

He went into the store and said to the proprietor, "Give me a pair of glasses so that I can read."

The proprietor asked what strength glasses he had worn before and Lemel said, "I don't know anything about it. Let me test them."

The proprietor handed him a pair of glasses and opened a book before him.

Lemel looked into the book and said, "I can't read."

"I'll give you stronger glasses," the proprietor said.

Lemel tested the second pair and said, "I still can't read."

The proprietor offered him many different glasses to try, but Lemel kept giving the same answer—he still couldn't read.

After a while, the proprietor said, "Forgive me, but maybe you can't read at all?"

"If I could read, I wouldn't have come to you in the first place," Lemel said.

"In that case, you must first go to a teacher and learn to read. You can't learn to read from putting on a pair of glasses," the storekeeper said.

Lemel grew depressed by the answer. He had been prepared to put on the glasses and go back home. After a while Lemel decided that he couldn't go on without

Tzipa. He missed her terribly. He went to seek out a teacher not so much to learn how to read as to have the teacher write a letter home for him. He soon found one. When Lemel asked how long it would take for him to learn to read, the teacher said, "It could take a year, but not less than a half year."

Lemel grew very sad. He said to the teacher, "Could you write a letter for me? I want to send a letter to my Tzipa."

"Yes, I could write a letter for you. Tell me what to write."

Lemel began to dictate:

Dear Tzipa,
I'm already in Lublin. I thought that if you put on glasses you could read, but the proprietor of the store said that glasses don't help. The teacher says it would take a half year or a whole year to teach me to read and that I would have to stay here in Lublin the whole time. Dear Tzipele, I love you so much that when I'm away from you one day I must die of longing. If I am without you for a half year, I'll have to die maybe a hundred times or even more. Therefore, I've decided to come home, if my father-in-law, your father, will agree. I hope to find some kind of work for which you don't have to read or write.

Longingly,
Your Lemel

When Tzipa received this letter and her father read it to her, she burst into tears and dictated a letter to Lemel which read as follows:

Dear Lemel,
When you don't see me for a day you must die, but when
I don't see you for a minute, I go crazy. Yes, my dear
Lemel, come back. I don't need a writer but a good hus-
band and, later, a houseful of children—six boys and six
girls. Father will find some kind of work for you. Don't
wait but come straight home, because if you come back
dead and find me crazy, it wouldn't be so good for either
of us.

Your devoted Tzipa

When the teacher read Tzipa's letter to Lemel he burst out crying. That very same day he started for home. Before getting into the wagon in Lublin, he went to the market to buy a present for Tzipa. He went into a mirror store with the intention of buying her a mirror. At the same time he told the storekeeper everything that had happened to him—how he had been swindled with the cookie and how he had been unable to learn to read with the glasses.

The storekeeper was a prankster and dishonest as well. He said, "Such people as you, Lemel, and your wife, Tzipa, should be many. I have a potion which, when you drink it, will make you become double, triple, quadruple. How would you like there to be ten Lemels and ten Tzipas who would all love each other? One Lemel and one Tzipa could stay home all day, another set could go to market to buy goods, a third set could take a walk, a fourth set could eat blintzes with sour cream, and the fifth set could go to Lublin and learn to read and write."

"How is this possible?" Lemel asked.

"Drink the potion and you'll see for yourself."

The storekeeper gave Lemel a glass of plain water and told him to drink merely one drop of it. Then he led Lemel into a room where two mirrors hung facing each other, one of which was tilted slightly to the side. When Lemel came into the room he saw not one Lemel in the mirror but a whole row of Lemels. He walked over to the other mirror and there were many Lemels there, too.

The storekeeper stood by the door and said, "Well, did I deceive you?"

"Oh, I can't believe my own eyes!" Lemel exclaimed. "How much is this potion?"

"It's very expensive," the storekeeper said, "but for you, I'll make it cheap. Give me all the money you have except for your fare home. You've snagged a terrific bargain."

Lemel paid on the spot and the storekeeper gave him a big bottle filled with water. He told him, "You and your Tzipa need drink only one drop a day. This bottle will last you for years. If it gets used up, you can always come back to Lublin and I'll refill it for you for free. Wait, I'll give you a written guarantee."

The storekeeper took out a sheet of paper and wrote on it: "God loves fools. That's why He made so many of them."

When Lemel came home and his father-in-law saw the bottle of water and read the note, he realized that Lemel had been swindled again.

But when Lemel saw Tzipa his joy was so intense he forgot all his troubles. He kissed and hugged her and cried, "I don't need many Tzipas. One Tzipa is enough for me, even if I should live to be a thousand!"

"And I don't need many Lemels. One Lemel is enough

for me, even if I should live to be a million!" Tzipa exclaimed.

Yes, Lemel and Tzipa were both fools, but they possessed more love than all the sages. After a while, Lemel bought a horse and wagon and became a coachman. For this he didn't have to know how to read or write. He drove passengers to and from Chelm and everyone liked him for his punctuality, his friendliness, and for the love he showed his horse. Tzipa began to have children and bore Lemel six boys and six girls. The boys took after Tzipa and the girls after Lemel, but they were all good-natured fools and they all found mates in Chelm. Lemel and Tzipa lived happily to a ripe old age, long enough to enjoy a whole tribe of grandchildren, great-grandchildren, and great-great-grandchildren.

Translated by Joseph Singer

The Day I Got Lost

It is easy to recognize me. See a man in the street wearing a too long coat, too large shoes, a crumpled hat with a wide brim, spectacles with one lens missing, and carrying an umbrella though the sun is shining, and that man will be me, Professor Shlemiel. There are other unmistakable clues to my identity. My pockets are always bulging with newspapers, magazines, and just papers. I carry an overstuffed briefcase, and I'm forever making mistakes. I've been living in New York City for over forty years, yet whenever I want to go uptown, I find myself walking downtown, and when I want to go east, I go west. I'm always late and I never recognize anybody.

I'm always misplacing things. A hundred times a day I ask myself, Where is my pen? Where is my money?

Where is my handkerchief? Where is my address book? I am what is known as an absentminded professor.

For many years I have been teaching philosophy in the same university, and I still have difficulty in locating my classrooms. Elevators play strange tricks on me. I want to go to the top floor and I land in the basement. Hardly a day passes when an elevator door doesn't close on me. Elevator doors are my worst enemies.

In addition to my constant blundering and losing things, I'm forgetful. I enter a coffee shop, hang up my coat, and leave without it. By the time I remember to go back for it, I've forgotten where I've been. I lose hats, books, umbrellas, rubbers, and above all manuscripts. Sometimes I even forget my own address. One evening I took a taxi because I was in a hurry to get home. The taxi driver said, "Where to?" And I could not remember where I lived.

"Home!" I said.

"Where is home?" he asked in astonishment.

"I don't remember," I replied.

"What is your name?"

"Professor Shlemiel."

"Professor," the driver said, "I'll get you to a telephone booth. Look in the telephone book and you'll find your address."

He drove me to the nearest drugstore with a telephone booth in it, but he refused to wait. I was about to enter the store when I realized I had left my briefcase behind. I ran after the taxi, shouting, "My briefcase, my briefcase!" But the taxi was already out of earshot.

In the drugstore, I found a telephone book, but when I

looked under S, I saw to my horror that though there were a number of Shlemiels listed, I was not among them. At that moment I recalled that several months before, Mrs. Shlemiel had decided that we should have an unlisted telephone number. The reason was that my students thought nothing of calling me in the middle of the night and waking me up. It also happened quite frequently that someone wanted to call another Shlemiel and got me by mistake. That was all very well—but how was I going to get home?

I usually had some letters addressed to me in my breast pocket. But just that day I had decided to clean out my pockets. It was my birthday and my wife had invited friends in for the evening. She had baked a huge cake and decorated it with birthday candles. I could see my friends sitting in our living room, waiting to wish me a happy birthday. And here I stood in some drugstore, for the life of me not able to remember where I lived.

Then I recalled the telephone number of a friend of mine, Dr. Motherhead, and I decided to call him for help. I dialed and a young girl's voice answered.

"Is Dr. Motherhead at home?"

"No," she replied.

"Is his wife at home?"

"They're both out," the girl said.

"Perhaps you can tell me where they can be reached?" I said.

"I'm only the babysitter, but I think they went to a party at Professor Shlemiel's. Would you like to leave a message?" she said. "Who shall I say called, please?"

"Professor Shlemiel," I said.

"They left for your house about an hour ago," the girl said.

"Can you tell me where they went?" I asked.

"I've just told you," she said. "They went to your house."

"But where do I live?"

"You must be kidding!" the girl said, and hung up.

I tried to call a number of friends (those whose telephone numbers I happened to think of), but wherever I called, I got the same reply: "They've gone to a party at Professor Shlemiel's."

As I stood in the street wondering what to do, it began to rain. "Where's my umbrella?" I said to myself. And I knew the answer at once. I'd left it—somewhere. I got under a nearby canopy. It was now raining cats and dogs. It lightninged and thundered. All day it had been sunny and warm, but now that I was lost and my umbrella was lost, it had to storm. And it looked as if it would go on for the rest of the night.

To distract myself, I began to ponder the ancient philosophical problem. A mother chicken lays an egg, I thought to myself, and when it hatches, there is a chicken. That's how it has always been. Every chicken comes from an egg and every egg comes from a chicken. But was there a chicken first? Or an egg first? No philosopher has ever been able to solve this eternal question. Just the same, there must be an answer. Perhaps I, Shlemiel, am destined to stumble on it.

It continued to pour buckets. My feet were getting wet and I was chilled. I began to sneeze and I wanted to wipe my nose, but my handkerchief, too, was gone.

At that moment I saw a big black dog. He was standing in the rain getting soaked and looking at me with sad eyes. I knew immediately what the trouble was. The dog was lost. He, too, had forgotten his address. I felt a great love for that innocent animal. I called to him and he came running to me. I talked to him as if he were human. "Fellow, we're in the same boat," I said. "I'm a man shlemiel and you're a dog shlemiel. Perhaps it's also your birthday, and there's a party for you, too. And here you stand shivering and forsaken in the rain, while your loving master is searching for you everywhere. You're probably just as hungry as I am."

I patted the dog on his wet head and he wagged his tail. "Whatever happens to me will happen to you," I said. "I'll keep you with me until we both find our homes. If we don't find your master, you'll stay with me. Give me your paw," I said. The dog lifted his right paw. There was no question that he understood.

A taxi drove by and splattered us both. Suddenly it stopped and I heard someone shouting, "Shlemiel! Shlemiel!" I looked up and saw the taxi door open, and the head of a friend of mine appeared. "Shlemiel," he called. "What are you doing here? Who are you waiting for?"

"Where are you going?" I asked.

"To your house, of course. I'm sorry I'm late, but I was detained. Anyhow, better late than never. But why aren't you at home? And whose dog is that?"

"Only God could have sent you!" I exclaimed. "What a night! I've forgotten my address, I've left my briefcase in a taxi, I've lost my umbrella, and I don't know where my rubbers are."

"Shlemiel," my friend said, "if there was ever an absentminded professor, you're it!"

When I rang the bell of my apartment, my wife opened the door. "Shlemiel!" she shrieked. "Everybody is waiting for you. Where have you been? Where is your briefcase? Your umbrella? Your rubbers? And who is this dog?"

Our friends surrounded me. "Where have you been?" they cried. "We were so worried. We thought surely something had happened to you!"

"Who is this dog?" my wife kept repeating.

"I don't know," I said finally. "I found him in the street. Let's just call him Bow Wow for the time being."

"Bow Wow, indeed!" my wife scolded. "You know our cat hates dogs. And what about the parakeets? He'll scare them to death."

"He's a quiet dog," I said. "He'll make friends with the cat. I'm sure he loves parakeets. I could not leave him shivering in the rain. He's a good soul."

The moment I said this the dog let out a bloodcurdling howl. The cat ran into the room. When she saw the dog, she arched her back and spat at him, ready to scratch out his eyes. The parakeets in their cage began flapping their wings and screeching. Everybody started talking at once. There was pandemonium.

Would you like to know how it all ended?

Bow Wow still lives with us. He and the cat are great friends. The parakeets have learned to ride on his back as if he were a horse. As for my wife, she loves Bow Wow even more than I do. Whenever I take the dog out, she says, "Now, don't forget your address, both of you."

I never did find my briefcase, or my umbrella, or my rubbers. Like many philosophers before me, I've given up trying to solve the riddle of which came first, the chicken or the egg. Instead, I've started writing a book called *The Memoirs of Shlemiel*. If I don't forget the manuscript in a taxi, or a restaurant, or on a bench in the park, you may read them someday. In the meantime, here is a sample chapter.

Translated by the author and Elizabeth Shub

Menashe & Rachel

The poorhouse in Lublin had a special room for children—orphans, sick ones, and cripples. Menashe and Rachel were brought up there. Both of them were orphans and blind. Rachel was born blind and Menashe became blind from smallpox when he was three years old. Every day a tutor came to teach the children prayers, as well as a chapter of the five books of Moses. The older ones also learned passages of the Talmud. Menashe was now barely nine years old, but already he was known as a prodigy. He knew twenty chapters of the Holy Book by heart. Rachel, who was eight years old, could recite "I Thank Thee" in the morning, the Shema before going to sleep, make benedictions over food, and she also remembered a few supplications in Yiddish.

On Hanukkah the tutor blessed the Hanukkah lights for the children, and every child got Hanukkah money and a dreidel from the poorhouse warden. Rich women brought them pancakes sprinkled with sugar and cinnamon.

Some of the charity women maintained that the two blind children should not spend too much time together. First of all, Menashe was already a half-grown boy and a scholar, and there was no sense in his playing around with a little girl. Second, it's better for blind children to associate with seeing ones, who can help them find their way in the eternal darkness in which they live. But Menashe and Rachel were so very deeply attached to each other that no one could keep them apart.

Menashe was not only good at studying the Torah but also talented with his hands. All the other children got tin dreidels for Hanukkah, but Menashe carved two wooden ones for Rachel and himself. When Menashe was telling stories, even the grownups came to listen. Not only Rachel, but all the children in the poorhouse were eager to hear his stories. Some his mother had told him when she was still alive. Others he invented. He was unusually deft. In the summer he went with the other children to the river and did handstands and somersaults in the water. In the winter when a lot of snow fell, Menashe, together with other children, built a snowman with two coals for eyes.

Menashe had black hair. His eyes used to be black, too, but now they had whitish cataracts. Rachel was known as a beauty. She had golden hair and eyes as blue as cornflowers. Those who knew her could not believe that such shining eyes could be blind.

The love between Menashe and Rachel was spoken of not only in the poorhouse but in the whole neighborhood. Both children said openly that when they grew up they would marry. Some of the inmates in the poorhouse called them bride and groom. There were some do-gooders who believed the two children should be parted by force, but Rachel said that if she was taken away from Menashe she would drown herself in a well. Menashe warned that he would bite the hand that tried to separate him from Rachel. The poorhouse warden went to ask the advice of the Lublin rabbi, and the rabbi said that the children should be left in peace.

One Hanukkah evening the children got their Hanukkah money and ate the tasty pancakes; then they sat down and played dreidel. It was the sixth night of Hanukkah. Six lights burned in the brass lamp in the window. Until tonight Menashe and Rachel had played together with the other children. But tonight Menashe said to Rachel, "Rachel, I have no desire to play."

"Neither have I," Rachel answered. "But what shall we do?"

"Let's sit down near the Hanukkah lamp and just be together."

Menashe led Rachel to the Hanukkah lamp. They followed the sweet smell of the oil in which the wicks were burning. They sat down on a bench. For a while both of them were silently enjoying each other's company as well as the warmth that radiated from the little flames. Then Rachel said, "Menashe, tell me a story."

"Again? I have told you all my stories already."

"Make up a new one," Rachel said.

"If I tell you all my stories now, what will I do when we marry and become husband and wife? I must save some stories for our future."

"Don't worry. By then you will have many new stories."

"Do you know what?" Menashe proposed. "You tell me a story this time."

"I have no story," Rachel said.

"How do you know that you don't have any? Just say whatever comes to your mind. This is what I do. When I'm asked to tell a story I begin to talk, not knowing what will come out. But somehow a story crops up by itself."

"With me nothing will crop up."

"Try."

"You will laugh at me."

"No, Rachel, I won't laugh."

It grew quiet. One could hear the wood burning in the clay stove. Rachel seemed to hesitate. She wet her lips with the tip of her tongue. Then she began, "Once there was a boy and a girl—"

"Aha."

"He was called Menashe and she Rachel."

"Yes."

"Everyone thought that Menashe and Rachel were blind, but they saw. I know for sure that Rachel saw."

"What did she see?" Menashe asked in astonishment.

"Other children see from the outside, but Rachel saw from the inside. Because of this people called her blind. It wasn't true. When people sleep, their eyes are closed, but in their dreams they can see boys, girls, horses, trees, goats, birds. So it was with Rachel. She saw everything deep in her head, many beautiful things."

"Could she see colors?" Menashe asked.

"Yes, green, blue, yellow, and other colors, I don't know what to call them. Sometimes they jumped around and formed little figures, dolls, flowers. Once, she saw an angel with six wings. He flew up high and the sky opened its golden doors for him."

"Could she see the Hanukkah lights?" Menashe asked.

"Not the ones from the outside, but those in her head. Don't you see anything, Menashe?"

"I, too, see things inside me," Menashe said after a long pause. "I see my father and my mother and also my grandparents. I never told you this, but I remember things from the time I could still see."

"What do you remember?" Rachel asked.

"Oh, I was sick and the room was full of sunshine. A doctor came, a tall man in a high hat. He told Mother to pull down the curtain because he thought I was sick with the measles and it is not good when there is too much light in the room if you have measles."

"Why didn't you tell me this before?" Rachel asked.

"I thought you wouldn't understand."

"Menashe, I understand everything. Sometimes when I lie in bed at night and cannot fall asleep, I see faces and animals and children dancing in a circle. I see mountains, fields, rivers, gardens, and the moon shining over them."

"How does the moon look?"

"Like a face with eyes and a nose and a mouth."

"True. I remember the moon," Menashe said. "Sometimes at night when I lie awake I see many, many things and I don't know whether they are real or I'm only imagining. Once, I saw a giant so tall his head reached the clouds. He had huge horns and a nose as big as the trunk of an elephant. He walked in the sea but the water only reached to his knees. I tried to tell the warden what I saw and he said I was lying. But I was telling the truth."

For some time both children were silent. Then Menashe said, "Rachel, as long as we are small we should never tell these secrets to anybody. People wouldn't believe us. They might think we were making them up. But when we grow up we will tell. It is written in the Bible: 'For the Lord seeth not as man seeth; for man looketh on the outward appearance but the Lord looketh on the heart.'"

"Who said this?"

"The prophet Samuel."

"Oh, Menashe, I wish we could grow up quickly and become husband and wife," Rachel said. "We will have children that see both from the outside and from the inside. You will kindle Hanukkah lights and I will fry pancakes. You will carve dreidels for our children to play with, and when they go to bed we will tell them stories. Later, when they fall asleep, they will dream about these stories."

"We will dream also," Menashe said. "I about you and you about me."

"Oh, I dream about you all the time. I see you in my dreams so clearly—your white skin, chiseled nose, black hair, beautiful eyes."

"I see you, too—a golden girl."

Again there was a silence. Then Rachel said, "I'd like to ask you something, but I am ashamed to say it."

"What is it?"

"Give me a kiss."

"Are you crazy? It's not allowed. Besides, when a boy kisses a girl they call him a sissy."

"No one will see."

"God sees," Menashe said.

"You said before that God looks into the heart. In my heart we are already grown up and I am your wife."

"The other children are going to laugh at us."

"They are busy with the dreidels. Kiss me! Just once."

Menashe took Rachel's hand and kissed her quickly. His heart was beating like a little hammer. She kissed him back and both of their faces were hot. After a while Menashe said, "It cannot be such a terrible sin, because it is written in the Book of Genesis that Jacob loved Rachel and he kissed her when they met. Your name is Rachel, too."

The poorhouse warden came over. "Children, why are you sitting alone?"

"Menashe has just told me a story," Rachel answered.

"It's not true, she told me a story," Menashe said.

"Was it a nice story?" the warden asked.

"The most beautiful story in the whole world," Rachel said.

"What was it about?" the warden asked, and Menashe said, "About an island far away in the ocean full of lions, leopards, monkeys, as well as eagles and pheasants with golden feathers and silver beaks. There were many trees on the island—fig trees, date trees, pomegranate trees, and a stream with fresh water. There was a boy and a girl there who saved themselves from a shipwreck by clinging to a log. They were like Adam and Eve in Paradise, but there was no serpent and—"

"The children are fighting over the dreidel. Let me see what's going on," the warden said. "You can tell me the rest of the story tomorrow." He rushed to the table.

"Oh, you made up a new story," Rachel said. "What happened next?"

"They loved one another and got married," Menashe said.

"Alone on the island forever?" Rachel asked.

"Why alone?" Menashe said. "They had many children, six boys and six girls. Besides, one day a sailboat landed there and the whole family was rescued and taken to the Land of Israel."

Shlemiel the Businessman

Shlemiel, who lived in Chelm, was not always a stay-at-home and there was a time when his wife did not sell vegetables in the marketplace. Mrs. Shlemiel's father was a man of means, and when his daughter married Shlemiel, he gave her a dowry.

Shortly after the wedding, Shlemiel decided to use the dowry to go into business. He had heard that in Lublin goats could be bought cheaply and he went there to buy one. He wanted a milk goat so that he could make cheese to sell. The goat dealer offered him a goat whose large udders were filled with milk. Shlemiel paid him the five gulden he asked for the goat, tied a string around its neck, and led it back toward Chelm.

On the way home, Shlemiel stopped in the village of Piask, known for its thieves and swindlers, although Shlemiel was not aware of this. He went into an inn to eat and left the goat tethered to a tree in the courtyard.

He ordered some sweet brandy, an appetizer of chopped liver with onions, a plate of chicken soup with noodles, and, as befits a successful businessman, some tea and honey cake for dessert. Before long he began to feel the effects of the brandy. He boasted to the innkeeper about the wonderful animal he had picked up in Lublin. "What a bargain I got," he announced. "A young, healthy goat, and what a great milker she promises to be."

The innkeeper, who happened to be a typical Piask swindler, owned an old billy goat that was blind in one eye and had a long white beard and a broken horn. Only the fact that it was so emaciated saved it from the butcher. After listening to Shlemiel praise his new goat, the innkeeper went into the courtyard and replaced Shlemiel's young animal with his old one. Shlemiel was so preoccupied with his business plans that he hardly looked at the goat when he untied it and so didn't notice that he was leading back to Chelm a different goat from the one he had bought.

Since it was Shlemiel's first business venture, the entire family was waiting impatiently to see the animal he was bringing back from the big city. They were all gathered in Shlemiel's house—his father-in-law, his brothers- and sisters-in-law, as well as friends and neighbors. When Shlemiel finally arrived, they ran out to the yard to greet him. Even before he opened the gate, he began to extol the virtues of his purchase—the goat's strength, its full udders.

When the old billy goat followed Shlemiel through the gate, there was consternation. His father-in-law clutched at his beard, dumbfounded. His mother-in-law spread her arms in a gesture of bewilderment. The young men laughed and the young women giggled. His father-in-law was the first one to speak up: "Is this what you call a young goat? It's a half-dead billy."

At first Shlemiel protested violently, but then for the first time he took a good look at the animal he had brought home. When he saw the old billy goat, he beat his head with his fists. He was convinced that the goat dealer had cheated him, although he could not figure out when he could have managed to do so. Shlemiel was so furious that after a sleepless night he set out for Lublin to return the goat and give the dealer a piece of his mind.

On the way he again stopped in Piask, at the same inn. He told the innkeeper that he had been swindled in Lublin and that he was on his way to get the right goat or his money back. If the merchant did not give him satisfaction, he intended to call the police. The innkeeper had more than once been in trouble with the authorities. He realized that an investigation might lead to him and that was the last thing he wanted.

As Shlemiel poured out his complaints against the Lublin goat dealer, the innkeeper clicked his tongue in sympathy and said, "It's well known that the merchants of Lublin are cheaters. Be watchful or you will be swindled a second time." Soon thereafter, as Shlemiel was busy eating his lunch, the innkeeper went out into the courtyard and again exchanged the goats. When Shlemiel was ready to leave, he was so preoccupied with imagining what he would say to the dealer that he again paid little attention to the animal he was leading.

Shlemiel arrived at the goat dealer's and began to threaten and upbraid him. The astonished dealer pointed out that the goat Shlemiel was returning was indeed young and had milk-filled udders. Shlemiel took one look at the goat and was left speechless. When at last he found his tongue, he exclaimed, "All I can say is that I must have been seeing things." He apologized profusely, took the goat, and again started back to Chelm. When he reached Piask, he as usual stopped at the inn for some refreshment. He ordered chicken and dumplings and, to celebrate the fact that he had made a good bargain after all, some sweet brandy. The innkeeper, born thief that he was, couldn't resist swindling such an easy victim. Offering Shlemiel a second brandy on the house, he went out into the yard and again exchanged the goats.

When Shlemiel left the inn, night was falling. By this time he was a bit tipsy and hardly glanced at the goat as he untied it and started for home.

When Shlemiel returned to Chelm for the second time leading an old billy goat instead of a young female, there was pandemonium. Word spread quickly and the whole town went wild. The matter was immediately brought before the elders, who deliberated seven days and seven nights and came to the conclusion that when a nanny goat is take from Lublin to Chelm it turns into a billy goat on the way. They therefore proclaimed a law prohibiting the import of goats from Lublin by any resident of Chelm. The old goat soon died and Shlemiel had lost one-third of his wife's dowry.

Shlemiel, having failed in his business dealings with Lublin, decided to try his luck in Lemberg. He had no sooner arrived in that city and settled himself in his room at the inn than the street on which it was located was filled with the screams of people and the continuous loud blast of a trumpet. Shlemiel had slept little on his way to Lemberg and had gone to bed on his arrival. He called for a servant to ask what the commotion was all about and was told that a house across the road was on fire and that the fire wagons had arrived. Shlemiel might have gone out to look at the fire, but he was exhausted from his long journey. After being assured that there was no danger to the inn and that the fire was being extinguished, he dozed off.

On awakening, he went to the lobby and asked one of the guests how the fire had started and how long it had taken to put it out. "Was it done merely by blowing a trumpet?" he wanted to know.

The man Shlemiel addressed happened to be one of Lemberg's most cunning thieves and Shlemiel's question immediately gave him an idea. "Yes," he replied. "Here in Lemberg we have a trumpet that extinguishes fires. It has only to be blown and the fire goes out."

Shlemiel could hardly express his amazement. He had heard of the many wonders of Lemberg, but never of a fire-fighting trumpet. It immediately occurred to him what a great source of profit such a trumpet could be in a town like Chelm, where all the houses were made of wood and most of the roofs of straw.

"How much does such a trumpet cost?" Shlemiel inquired.

"Two hundred gulden," the man replied.

Two hundred gulden was a large sum of money. It amounted to almost the entire remainder of Mrs.

Shlemiel's dowry. But when Shlemiel thought it over, he came to the conclusion that such a trumpet was more than worth the money. In Chelm there were many fires each year, especially in summertime. Houses and entire streets burned down. Although there were several firemen in Chelm, their equipment consisted of a single wagon drawn by an ancient nag. By the time the wagon arrived with its one barrel of water, everything had usually burned down. Shlemiel hadn't the slightest doubt that the owner of a fire-fighting trumpet could make a fortune. He told the man that he would like to buy such a trumpet and the other was more than willing to supply one. It was not long before he delivered a huge brass trumpet and a written guarantee that when blown it would extinguish all fires.

Shlemiel was overjoyed. This time he was sure he was on his way to becoming a rich man.

Back in Chelm, Shlemiel displayed to his family and neighbors the amazing instrument he had brought back from Lemberg. The word spread quickly and soon the people of Chelm were divided: some believed in the trumpet's powers and others maintained that Shlemiel had again been swindled. The matter would most certainly have come before the elders, but it was summertime and they were not in session.

Shlemiel's father-in-law was one of those with no faith in the trumpet. "It's another billy goat," he said. Shlemiel was so eager to demonstrate what the trumpet could do that he decided to set his father-in-law's house on fire, intending, of course, to blow out the fire with the trumpet before any real damage was done.

His father-in-law's house was old and dry and it was soon enveloped in flames. Shlemiel blew his trumpet until he could blow no more, but alas, the house continued to burn. The family was able to escape, but all their possessions were lost.

Despite the season, an emergency session of the elders was called immediately. The elders pondered the event for seven days and seven nights, and came to the conclusion that a trumpet able to extinguish fires in Lemberg lost its power, for some unknown reason, in Chelm. Gronam Ox proposed a law prohibiting the import of fire-fighting trumpets from Lemberg to Chelm. It was unanimously passed and duly recorded by Feivel Thickwit.

Shlemiel had lost his wife's dowry and had burned down his father-in-law's house; nevertheless, he refused to give up the idea of going into business. Having failed in Lublin and Lemberg, Shlemiel decided to do business with some local product in Chelm itself.

Chelm produced a sweet brandy that was Shlemiel's favorite drink. He decided to buy a keg of it and sell it in the market for three groschen a glass. He had figured out that if he could sell the whole kegful each day, he would make three-gulden profit a day. This time Mrs. Shlemiel made up her mind to help her husband. Shlemiel had no money left to pay the vintner, but his wife pawned a pin and they bought the brandy.

The following day they set up a small stand in the marketplace, placed the keg and a few glasses on it, and began hawking their drink to passersby: "Sweet brandy, a refreshing and invigorating drink for all, three groschen a glass."

Sweet brandy was a popular drink in Chelm, but three groschen a glass was too high a price. Only one customer bought a glass, quite early in the day, and he paid for it with a three-groschen coin. When an hour had passed and there were no more buyers, Shlemiel began to lose heart. He became so restless that he needed a drink. He held the three-groschen coin in his hand and said to his wife, "In what way is my money inferior to another man's? Here is three groschen and sell me a drink."

Mrs. Shlemiel thought the matter over and said, "You are right, Shlemiel. Your coin is as good as anyone else's." And she gave him a glass of brandy. Shlemiel drank it up and licked his lips. Most delicious! After a while Mrs. Shlemiel got thirsty, too. And she said to Shlemiel, "In what way is my three-groschen piece worse than another's? Here is my money and let me have a drink."

To make a long story short, Shlemiel and Mrs. Shlemiel continued drinking and passing the coin between them all day long. When evening came, the best part of the keg's contents was consumed and all they had to show for the day's work was a single three-groschen coin.

Shlemiel and his wife tried in vain to figure out where they had made a mistake this time; no matter how they puzzled over the problem, they could not find the solution. They had sold almost an entire keg of sweet brandy for cash, but the cash was not to be seen. Shlemiel believed that not even the elders of Chelm could explain what had happened to the money he and his wife had paid to each other.

This ended Shlemiel's attempts to go into business, and it was from that time on that Mrs. Shlemiel began to sell vegetables in the market. As for Shlemiel, he stayed at home and when the children were born took care of them. He also fed the chickens Mrs. Shlemiel kept under the stove.

Shlemiel's father-in-law was so disgusted with his son-in-law that he moved to Lublin. It was the first time in the history of Chelm that one of its citizens left the village for good. Nevertheless, Mrs. Shlemiel, though she chided him, continued to admire her husband. Shlemiel would often say to her, "If the Lublin nanny goat had not turned into a billy goat, and if the trumpet had been able to extinguish fires in Chelm, I would now be the richest man in town."

To which Mrs. Shlemiel would reply, "You may be poor, Shlemiel, but you are certainly wise. Wisdom such as yours is rare even in Chelm."

Translated by the author and Elizabeth Shub

Joseph & Koza

It happened long, long ago in the land which is now Poland. The country was covered with thick forests and swamps and the people were divided into many tribes that waged bloody battles among themselves. They fought with bows and arrows, swords and spears, because in those days they had neither rifles nor guns.

The roads were dangerous. Highwaymen lay in wait for merchants to rob and murder them. Often, travelers were attacked by wolves, bears, boars, and other wild beasts. And there were the many warlocks and witches who had sworn allegiance to Baba Yaga the Terrible and other evil powers. No one in all of Poland could read or write. The people worshipped idols of stone, clay, and wood, to whom they sacrificed not only animals but human beings as well.

The most powerful tribe in Poland inhabited Mazovia, a huge tract of land near the river Vistula. Mazovia was ruled by a chieftain called Wilk, who had a wife named Wilkova. Wilk was a tall man with a ruddy face and flaxen hair. He had a mustache whose tips reached down to his shoulders. Other chieftains in the land possessed crowns made of gold, silver, and precious stones, but Wilk's crown was a hollow gourd with notches cut in its rim to hold beeswax candles. The candles were lit when Wilk wore the crown.

Wilk kept a witch and stargazer called Zla, and the chieftain never made a move without consulting her. It was said that Zla could perform miracles. She rode in a carriage drawn by wolves and used a living snake as a whip.

Once each year it was the custom of the Mazovians to sacrifice their most beautiful maiden to the river Vistula. The people gathered at the river's shore. They drank wine, beer, mead, killed and roasted pigs, sang and danced all day long. Late in the day, when the sun was about to sink below the horizon, they brought forth the maiden. She was carried to a high cliff overlooking the river and thrown in. The Mazovians believed that this sacrifice would pacify the evil spirits of the Vistula.

It was the witch Zla who each year chose the most beautiful maiden of the land. First she read the stars for signs and then she consulted with the Devil. No one ever questioned Zla's choice.

Wilk had seven sons but only one daughter, Koza. Koza had golden hair and blue eyes, and the chieftain and his wife loved her above all else. When Koza was seventeen, and the time had come for her to marry, many kings' sons came to Mazovia to woo her. They competed in feats of prowess to see who would win her hand. One young suitor tore a wolf in half with his bare hands. Another strangled an ox. A third tore up a tree by the roots. Finally the young men fought each other with swords. They were as cruel to one another as they had been to the animals.

Koza was forced to witness these wild tournaments, but none of the young princes pleased her. She was kind-hearted by nature and hated bloodshed.

Every year on the first night of the month of Kwiecien (our April, more or less), the witch Zla studied the stars to determine who was the prettiest girl in Mazovia. That spring as she searched the heavens on the appointed night, she suddenly moaned out loud. It was Koza whom the stars had revealed to her.

When Wilk heard that he must sacrifice his daughter, he was grief-stricken. His wife fainted away. But Koza tried to comfort her parents. She said to her father, "If by giving my life to the Vistula, I can satisfy the evil spirits and serve our people, I will gladly do so."

The sacrificial ceremony always took place at the beginning of summer, on the first day of the month of Lipiec, or July. During the ninety days of waiting, the chosen maiden lived in a large tent erected in an apple orchard not far from the riverbank. The highborn young ladies of Mazovia came to keep Koza company. They sang and danced for her, wove wreaths of flowers, and brought her gifts to sweeten the long vigil.

One day a wanderer appeared at the gate of Wilk's palace. He was tall, had a black beard, long black hair, and black eyes. He carried a pouch on his back and a

large scroll under his arm. The Mazovians had never be-
fore seen a scroll and they looked at it in amazement.
The stranger told the guards that he had come to see
Chieftain Wilk.

"Who are you? Where do you come from?" he was
asked.

"From Jerusalem."

The guards informed Wilk, who sent for the stranger.

"What is your name?" Wilk asked.

"Joseph."

"Joseph? I've never heard of such a name. Who are
you? And what do you want?"

Joseph replied, "I'm a Jew and I come from the city of
Jerusalem. I am a goldsmith by profession. I make bracelets, brooches, and rings. I am on my way from Cracow,
where I made a crown with golden horns for the king. I
spent over a year in his palace, and there I learned to
speak your language."

"What are you carrying under your arm?" Wilk asked.

"A scroll."

"What is a scroll?"

"This one bears God's commandments."

"Which god's commandments? Is he made of bone?
Wood? Stone? Copper?"

"My God cannot be made by human hands," Joseph
replied. "He has always lived. He is the creator of the
earth, the sky, the sea, of all livings things, men and
animals. Many, many ages ago, He revealed Himself to
Moses on Mt. Sinai and gave him His commandments."

Wilk did not know what to make of all this. Finally
he said to Joseph, "I would order a crown like the one

you made for the King of Cracow, but this year is a time of mourning for me. Return next year and I will have you make a crown for me."

"Why are you in mourning?" Joseph asked.

"In sixty days my daughter Koza is to be sacrificed to the Vistula."

"The God of Israel has forbidden human sacrifice!" Joseph protested.

"How can that be?" Wilk asked. "If we fail to present the river with our most beautiful maiden, the evil powers will see that we get neither rain nor sunshine, and so our fields will give no harvest. If we do not bring this sacrifice to the Vistula, the river will overflow. It will be cold in the summertime and our crops will perish."

"Nonsense!" Joseph exclaimed. "It is God who makes the crops grow. God does not demand that a young maiden be drowned. It is a sin!"

Wilk pondered Joseph's words, and then he said, "It is true that I am the ruler of my people, but I know little about such matters. The wisest person in my country is the witch Zla. I will order my servants to provide you with food and a tent to sleep in, and tomorrow you will speak to Zla. But remember, she reads the stars and serves Baba Yaga and other powers of evil. Should you anger her, she can destroy you or turn you into a hedgehog, a rat, or a frog. We all fear her, because the Devil and the abyss are the sources of her strength."

"I do not fear her," Joseph replied. "The word of God is stronger than all witches and devils."

When Wilk's headmen and councilors learned about Joseph and what he had said, there was fear and confusion among them. Some insisted that the stranger was a messenger of doom and should be executed at once. Others thought that his words should be put to the test. After long arguing, it was decided that a debate should be held between Joseph and Zla in the presence of the entire court, presided over by Chieftain Wilk himself. Joseph immediately consented. At first Zla insisted that it was beneath her dignity to debate with an unknown intruder. But Wilk ordered her to appear.

The debate was fierce and lasted from morning till night. Zla denied the existence of one god and pointed out how vengeful the spirits of the Vistula were, particularly Topiel, whose palace was at the bottom of the river. She claimed that the maidens sacrificed to the Vistula did not really die but became the wives and concubines of Topiel. They danced, sang, and played music to keep him entertained. As proof of Topiel's power, she related how, at the winter and summer solstices, Baba Yaga herself visited the king of the river. She came flying to the Vistula in a huge mortar, holding a pestle the size of a pine tree in one hand and, in the other, a giant broom with which she swept away the light of the world. Who could dare rebel against such power?

Zla warned that unless Koza was given to the river on the first day of the month of Lipiec, there would be a storm, floods, thunder and lightning such as never before. Hailstones as large as rocks would destroy the crops. And should any grain survive the storm, it would be consumed by locusts, worms, and field mice.

Joseph unrolled the scroll he had brought with him. He explained what it said in the language of the land.

"God created the world in six days. God does not demand human sacrifices. He instructs man not to kill, steal, or bear false witness, but to honor his father and mother, and to be just and help those in need." Turning to Zla, he said, "No matter how strong the devils are, it is God who rules the world, not they. And the maidens you throw into the Vistula—they drown and rot. No devil can keep them alive under the water. The Vistula is not deep. Look carefully and you will see their bones."

The sun was moving toward the west, but the debate continued. Wilk's followers were divided into two camps. The older ones sided with Zla; the younger ones were with Joseph. When Joseph saw that his arguments could not convince them all, he said, "My lords, I can prove to you that the truth is on my side."

"How can you prove it?" asked Chieftain Wilk.

"The grain is harvested in the month of Sierpien. Wait until the end of Sierpien before you sacrifice the maiden. If the plagues Zla has prophesied occur, you will throw Koza into the Vistula and I myself will accept death at your hands because I misled you. But should these catastrophes not take place, you will have proof that I am right and that the words I read to you are the words of the true God."

Upon hearing this, Zla flew into a rage and began threatening Mazovia with even greater misfortunes. But Wilk lifted his scepter, which was made of amber, and announced: "It will be as Joseph has said. The sacrifice of Koza is postponed until the end of Sierpien. Until that time, Joseph is to be imprisoned in the dungeon."

It was the law that once the chieftain lifted his scepter

and spoke, nothing further must be said. All were silent. Only Zla could not contain her anger, and she screamed, "By the end of the month of Sierpien, Mazovia will be a desert!"

The Princess Koza and her ladies-in-waiting had not been present at the debate, but they soon learned what had taken place. Koza was prepared to give her life, but nevertheless, deep in her heart, she was afraid. She wanted neither to die nor to become one of Topiel's many wives and live in his underwater palace. When Joseph's words were repeated to her, she was filled with gratitude and love for him. She prayed to the gods of Mazovia that what he had said be true. Her ladies prayed with her.

Meanwhile, the days were mild and sunny. The sky was blue. It rained several times, but there was no flood. Each time clouds gathered, Zla insisted that the storm was beginning, but the rain always stopped and the sky became clear again.

The month of Sierpien, our August, approached and the grain fields of Mazovia grew dense, golden, and ripe. The peasants had already begun to harvest the fields. They followed their usual rituals to ensure a good crop. Each village had its wooden rooster, decorated with green stalks of wheat and rye and tender twigs from fruit trees. The peasant girls, dancing around the rooster, sprayed water on it through a sieve. The Mazovians believed that in addition to Baba Yaga there were many lesser *babas*, as well as little imps called *dziads*, who lived in the furrows of the fields and who could do terrible damage unless they were exorcised through incantations and special ceremonies.

Although the time Joseph had set was almost at an end, Zla did not give up. She continued to prophesy that before Sierpien was out, the Vistula would overflow. She warned that day would become dark as night and that from the forest would come *babuks* riding vipers. They would destroy the sheaves of grain, the peasants' huts, the haystacks, and the granaries. Topiel himself, his face red, his beard white, with the wings of an eagle and the feet of a bear, would emerge from the Vistula. He would strangle children and kill the cattle. The river would spread itself over all the land.

On the twentieth day of Sierpien, Koza asked to be taken to her father. She begged him for permission to visit Joseph in his dungeon. Wilk agreed and sent two of her ladies with her. When Koza was shown into Joseph's cell, she found him sitting and writing on parchment with a quill. Koza had never seen a quill, ink, or parchment. She fell on her knees before him, and both ladies knelt beside her. "Joseph," she said, "you are the greatest god of all." She began to weep and kiss his sandals.

Joseph made her rise. "I am not a god. There are no gods. One God creates us all," he said.

"Do you have a wife?" Koza asked.

"No, Koza, I am not married."

"Then I wish to be your wife."

"As it is destined, so will it be," Joseph replied.

He took three golden bracelets from his pack. One of them was set with a jeweled Star of David. He placed it on Koza's wrist and presented each of her companions with one of the remaining bracelets.

Since Joseph was convinced that Koza would not be

drowned, that there would be no reason for Wilk to be in mourning, he had spent his time in prison making a golden crown for Mazovia's ruler. The Mazovians had no alphabet of their own, so Joseph had engraved the crown with Wilk's name in Hebrew letters, as well as the figure of a wolf, because Wilk means wolf.

Excitement grew in Mazovia as the end of Sierpien approached. Those who no longer believed in Zla—mostly the young—sang, danced, and were confident of Joseph's final victory. The harvest, an especially plentiful one, had been gathered by now. The women began to grind the grain into flour. As always after harvest time, the evenings were devoted to games and festivity. Riddles were asked, stories were told. It was the custom that the girl who had harvested the last furrow became a *baba*. She blackened her face with soot, braided thistles into her hair, and carried a large witch's hoop. One of the boys impersonated a rooster. He attached wings to his shoulders, put a comb on his head, and tied spurs to his heels. He crowed and flapped, and made believe he was about to attack the girl *baba*, while she cackled like a hen and plucked feathers from his fake wings. Later the harvesters and threshers built a huge bonfire on which they roasted sides of pork and chestnuts. They drank mead and beer. The nights were as dark as the days were bright, and falling stars were frequently seen. The frogs croaked with human voices. Despite Zla's prophecy that any day the evil spirits of the Vistula would emerge to bring havoc, the young people went bathing in the river at night.

The older people who still believed in Zla warned that

Sierpien was not yet over. They were certain the catastrophe would come. Many of them left their valley
homes and camped on the hilltops to save themselves
from the deluge. Others pointed out that it was not yet
too late to choose another fair maiden to throw to the
Vistula.

Zla continued to shower her curses on Joseph. She
foretold that on the last day of Sierpien the sun would be
extinguished, the moon would fall out of the sky, the
trees would wither, and everything alive would perish.
The waters of the Vistula would turn yellow and hot as
boiling sulphur, and cover the entire earth.

The last day of Sierpien was the most beautiful of all.
Not a single cloud marred the blue sky. The birds sang
endlessly. The air was sweet as honey. Yet, until night
fell, Zla was sure the flood would come. When the golden
sun set behind the Vistula, she tore her hair, wailed,
screamed, and whirled about in frenzy, but the world did
not come to an end. Throughout Mazovia the news
spread of Joseph's victory and of his coming marriage to
Koza. Zla was so humiliated that she hid in a deep
cave.

Now that Joseph had been proven right, his freedom
was restored and Wilk was prepared to give him his
daughter in marriage. But there were many obstacles.
Some of the older courtiers and their wives remained on
the side of Zla, and the witch sent word from her cave
that Joseph was a warlock who would bring a curse on
the land. In addition, Joseph followed strange customs
that the people of Mazovia could not understand. He
refused to eat pork. When he prayed, he wrapped him-

self in a shawl striped black and white and trimmed with fringes, and turned his face toward the east. At the entrance to his hut he had fastened a piece of parchment that he called a mezuzah. On the Sabbath he neither kindled a fire nor did his goldsmith's work. He also refused to bow before the idols of Mazovia—and he did not like to hunt. Chieftain Wilk soon came to realize that if Joseph remained among them, there would be a rebellion in Mazovia.

Wilk now tried to persuade his daughter that the stranger was not the right husband for her. But Koza, who had always obeyed her father, suddenly became stubborn. She fell at his feet and said, "I will never love anyone but Joseph. If I cannot be his wife, I will throw myself in the Vistula and the river will have its sacrifice."

"But Joseph cannot remain in Mazovia," Wilk said. "Because of him, the people are divided. If he stays, all will suffer."

"Then I will go with him to Jerusalem," said Koza.

Wilk called his councilors together to seek their advice. Most of them were of the opinion that a young woman's love must be respected. Others argued that it would be an insult to the chieftain's honor if he gave his daughter in marriage to a stranger who refused to worship the gods of Mazovia. Zla, who did not give up easily, sent a message to the council room announcing that the stars were against the match. However, faith in the stars and Zla's prophecies was no longer strong. The men whose daughters had been sacrificed to the Vistula now accused Zla of being a murderess who had sent to their deaths the most beautiful girls of Mazovia.

When Zla learned that Wilk had agreed to the marriage of Joseph and Koza despite her threats and warnings, she decided to make one final effort to interfere. There were magic powers that could be used only once. If she failed, her power would be destroyed forever. First she fasted three days and three nights, then she lit seven candles made of human fat. When this was done, she shaved off her elflocks and clipped her long, claw-like nails, kneaded these into a lump of dough, and burned it before an image of Baba Yaga, all the while invoking the evil powers.

On the fourth night she made her way to a thick forest, and using the most potent incantations and spells, she summoned Baba Yaga and her retinue of devils.

The night was hot and dark. Suddenly a wind arose and a scarlet light appeared. Baba Yaga arrived in her mortar, carrying her pestle in one hand and her tree broom in the other. Her face was like pitch, but her nose was red, turned up, with broad, flaring nostrils. Her eyes burned like live coals. Instead of hair, thistles grew out of her skull, and though she was a woman, she had a beard like a man. Her companions rode on brooms, canes, and shovels. Even Topiel, King of the Vistula, came—foaming with rage. The beasts of the forest, frightened by these apparitions, howled and screeched and hid themselves in ditches and tree hollows.

Zla bowed seven times to Baba Yaga. "Mighty Baba! As you already know, a man has come from the faraway city of Jerusalem and his name is Joseph. With cunning words, he has conquered the heart of Chieftain Wilk and won the love of Koza. Because of him, there was no sacrifice to the Vistula this year. Now he is about to marry Koza. If their marriage takes place, it will mean that we who worship you have lost our right to rule over human fate. I implore you, therefore, not to let this wedding take place."

"There will be no wedding!" Baba Yaga cried in a voice as hoarse as a saw. "I'll sweep it away with my broom and crush it with my pestle."

"There will be no wedding!" Topiel roared. "I will drown it with my waters."

"There will be no wedding!" chorused all the goblins, hobgoblins, sprites, and imps, each in his own shrill voice.

That night Zla went to bed assured that the evil spirits would emerge victorious, after all. It might have been impossible for them to destroy the crops and bring a flood, but surely they could stop a marriage. But Zla did not know that Joseph possessed the sacred powers of a soothsayer and could see what was happening long distances away. He knew that Zla had summoned the evil forces. He also knew how to overcome them. He prayed to God, and his prayer was heard. On the day of the wedding, Baba Yaga, Topiel, and all the evil creatures were suddenly overcome by a deep sleep. Zla tried desperately to summon them, but they did not wake up.

Since the wedding ceremony could not be performed in the temple of the idols, it took place in the palace garden. Koza's parents and her ladies-in-waiting were the only guests. Joseph placed a golden ring on her first finger and intoned the words of the marriage vow himself.

The following day, Joseph and Koza mounted two magnificent stallions, given to them by Wilk, and started on their long journey to the Holy Land. Although the gift of the horses was a very generous one, it did not compare with the crown Joseph had made for Wilk.

It was very difficult for Wilk and Wilkova to part with their only daughter. Koza, too, suffered at leaving her parents. But so it has always been—a wife must go with her husband, especially one who has saved her life. A huge throng accompanied them to the very edge of Mazovia. Trumpets were blown, drums and bells played; at night, torches were lit.

If one left one's country in those days, there was no way to send messages back. One was never heard from again. But somehow the Mazovians learned that Joseph and Koza were living happily in Jerusalem. Joseph's fame as a goldsmith spread far and wide. Koza bore him sons and daughters, who were brought up in the faith that there is only one God.

In Mazovia, from that time on, human sacrifice was forbidden. And later, when Mazovia and the surrounding tribal lands were united into one kingdom, called Poland, the Poles became Christians. Human sacrifice was then abolished throughout the country.

Zla had long since died; and Baba Yaga, Topiel, and all their evil band were heard about mainly in stories that grandmothers told their grandchildren as they churned butter or wove flax. But for many centuries it was the custom on the first day of summer for the girls of Mazovia to assemble on the shores of the Vistula. They would throw a straw dummy into the river in memory of the maidens sacrificed to Topiel. While the straw girl was bobbing up and down in the current, drifting toward the open sea, they would sing, dance, and celebrate Joseph's rescue of the beautiful Koza.

Translated by the author and Elizabeth Shub

A Hanukkah Evening
in My Parents' House

All year round my father, a rabbi in Warsaw, did not allow his children to play any games. Even when I wanted to play cat's cradle with my younger brother, Moshe, Father would say, "Why lose time on such nonsense? Better to recite psalms."

Often when I got two pennies from my father and I told him that I wanted to buy chocolate, ice cream, or colored pencils he would say, "You would do a lot better to find a poor man and give your pennies to him, because charity is a great deed."

But on Hanukkah, after Father lit the Hanukkah candles, he allowed us to play dreidel for half an hour. I remember one such night especially. It was the eighth night and in our Hanukkah lamp eight wicks were burning. Outside, a heavy snow had fallen. Even though our stove was hot, frost trees were forming on the window-panes. My brother Joshua, who was eleven years older than I, already a grownup, was saying to my sister, Hindele, "Do you see the snow? Each flake is a hexagon; it has six sides with fancy little designs and decorations—every one a perfect jewel and slightly different from all the others."

My brother Joshua read scientific books. He also painted landscapes—peasants' huts, fields, forests, animals, sometimes a sunset. He was tall and blond. Father wanted him to become a rabbi, but Joshua's ambition was to be an artist. My sister, Hindele, was even older than Joshua and already engaged to be married. She had dark hair and blue eyes. The idea that Hindele was going to be the wife of some strange young man and even going to change her surname seemed to me so peculiar that I refused to think about it.

When Father heard what Joshua had said about the snow, he promptly said, "It's all the work of God Almighty, who bestows beauty on everything He creates."

"Why must each flake of snow be so beautiful, since people step on it or it turns to water?" Hindele asked.

"Everything comes easily to nature," Joshua answered. "The crystals arrange themselves in certain patterns. Take the frost trees—every winter they are the same. They actually look like fig trees and date trees."

"Such trees don't grow here in Poland but in the Holy Land," Father added. "When the Messiah comes, all God-fearing people will return to the Land of Israel. There will be the resurrection of the dead. The Holy Temple will be rebuilt. The world will be as full of wisdom as the sea of water."

The door opened and Mother came in from the kitchen.

She was frying the Hanukkah pancakes. Her lean face was flushed. For a while she stood there and listened. Although Mother was the daughter of a rabbi herself, she always pleaded with Father to be lenient and not to preach to us all the time as she felt he did. I heard her say, "Let the children have some fun. Who is winning?"

"It's little Moshe's lucky day," Hindele said. "He's cleaned us all out, the darling."

"Don't forget to give a few pennies to the poor," Father said to him. "In olden times one had to give tithe to the priests, but now the tithe should be given to the needy."

Mother nodded, smiled, and returned to the kitchen, and we continued our game. The tin dreidel, which I had bought before Hanukkah, had four Hebrew letters engraved on its sides: *nun*, *gimel*, *he*, and *shin*. According to Father, these letters were the initials of words which meant: a great miracle happened there—an allusion to the war between the Maccabees and the Greeks in 170 B.C. and the victory of the Maccabees. It is for this victory and the purification of the Holy Temple in Jerusalem from idols that Hanukkah is celebrated. But for us children *gimel* meant winning, *nun* losing, *he* half winning, and *shin* another chance for the player. Moshe and I took the game seriously, but Joshua and Hindele played only to keep us company. They always let us, the younger ones, win.

As for me, I was interested both in the game and in the conversation of the adults. As if he read my mind, I heard Joshua ask, "Why did God work miracles in ancient times, and why doesn't He work miracles in our times?"

Father pulled at his red beard. His eyes expressed indignation.

"What are you saying, my son? God works miracles in all generations even though we are not always aware of them. Hanukkah especially is a feast of miracles. My grandmother Hindele—you, my daughter, are named after her—told me the following story: In the village of Tishewitz there was a child named Zaddock. He was a prodigy. When he was three years old, he could already read the Bible. At five he studied the Talmud. He was very goodhearted both to human beings and to animals. There was a mouse where his family lived and every day little Zaddock used to put a piece of cheese at the hole in the wall where the creature was hiding. At night he put a saucer of milk there. One day—it happened to be the third day of Hanukkah—little Zaddock overheard a neighbor tell of a sick tailor in the village who was so poor that he could not afford to buy wood to heat his hut. Little Zaddock had heard that in the forest near the village there were a lot of fallen branches to be picked up for nothing, and he decided to gather as much wood as he could carry and bring it to the sick man. The child was so eager to help that he immediately set out for the forest without telling his mother where he was going.

"It was already late in the day when he left the house, and by the time he reached the forest it was dark. Little Zaddock had lost his way and he would surely have died from the cold, when suddenly he saw in the darkness three Hanukkah lights. For a while they lingered before his eyes, and then they began to move slowly. Little Zaddock went after them, and they brought him back to the village, to the hut where the sick man lived with his family. When the lights reached the door of the sick man's hut, they fell, turning into gold coins. The sick man was able to buy bread for his family and himself, fuel to heat the oven, as well as oil for the Hanukkah lights. It wasn't long before he got well and was again able to earn a living."

"Daddy, what happened to Zaddock when he grew up?" I asked.

"He became a famous rabbi," Father said. "He was known as the saintly Rabbi Zaddock."

It became so quiet that I could hear the spluttering of the Hanukkah candles and the chirping of our house cricket. Mother came in from the kitchen with two full plates of pancakes. They smelled delicious.

"Why is it so quiet—is the game over?" she asked.

My brother Moshe, who had seemed to be half asleep when Father told his story, suddenly opened his big blue eyes wide and said, "Daddy, I want to give the money I won to a sick tailor."

"You were preaching to them, huh?" Mother asked half reproachfully.

"I didn't preach, I told them a story," Father said. "I want them to know that what God could do two thousand years ago He can also do in our time."

Tsirtsur & Peziza

In a dark space between the stove and the wall, where the housewife stored her brooms, mops, and baking paddles, there lived an orphan imp called Peziza. She had only one friend in the world, Tsirtsur, a cricket. He, too, made his home behind the stove in a crevice between two bricks. An imp doesn't have to eat at all, but how Tsirtsur managed to survive is a riddle. Perhaps just the smell of fresh bread baking, a speck of flour that a house breeze swept back there, a drop of moisture in the air were enough for him. In any case, Tsirtsur never complained to Peziza about the lack of food. He dozed all day long. When evening came, he was wide awake and began chirping stories that often continued through the night.

Peziza had never known her father, Lantuch the imp. Her mother, Pashtida, who came from a wealthy family,

had fallen in love with Lantuch. She had often told
Peziza about the world that existed beyond the stove and
about their relatives, the devils, gnomes, and hobgoblins,
each with his own tricks and deviltries. Even so, if one
has spent one's entire life behind a stove, one knows little
of what is going on in the world, and Peziza had a strong
curiosity, a trait no doubt inherited from her parents.
While Tsirtsur chirped out his endless tales, Peziza
dreamed of impish adventures.

Sometimes Peziza would ask Tsirtsur to tell her how it
was outside and he would reply, "My mother said there's
only trouble. Cold winds blow, cruel creatures devour
one another."

"Nevertheless," Peziza would say thoughtfully, "I'd
like to have a look myself at what the devils out there are
doing."

And that is exactly what Fate had in mind.

One day there was a loud pounding and hammering.
The stove shook, bricks fell. Peziza flew up and down in
fright. The houseowners had decided to rebuild the
stove. The racket continued all day long and both creatures huddled together until evening. When a piece of
wall fell away, Tsirtsur cried, "If we don't get out of here,
we'll be killed." There was a break which reached to the
outside. They crept through it and found themselves in
the back yard of the house. They stood on grass among
shrubs and trees. It was the first time Peziza and Tsirtsur
had breathed fresh air.

How beautiful the outside was! A huge sky, a moon,
stars. Dew was forming. There was the whirring of
myriads of crickets. They sounded just like Tsirtsur.

"I will dig myself a hole," Tsirtsur said, "because when the sun rises I must not stay in the open."

"My mother, too, warned me against the sun," Peziza agreed. "But a hole in the earth is not a proper hiding place for me. There is a hollow in that tree. I will spend the day there."

"The most important thing is that we don't lose each other," Tsirtsur declared. "I'll dig my hole near the roots of your tree."

Tsirtsur immediately began digging. He spoke to Peziza as he worked. "As long as it is summer, the outdoors is not so dangerous. But winter is a bitter time for crickets. It gets cold and something called snow covers the ground. Few crickets survive in such weather."

"Do you mind if I take a look around while you're busy?" Peziza asked.

"You may get lost."

"I won't fly far. I'll recognize this tree. It is taller than the others."

Tsirtsur urged Peziza not to wander away. But curious Peziza was not yet ready to settle down in her hollow. Her desire to see all the new things around her was too strong. She flew off and came to rest on a roof. I never knew I could fly so well, she thought. Suddenly she heard someone calling to her. She looked in the direction of the voice and saw an imp perched on a weather vane. Although the only other imp Peziza had ever seen was her mother, she knew at once that this imp was a young man. He had two pairs of wings and his horns were transparent. "What is your name?" he asked.

Peziza was so surprised that for a moment she remained speechless. Then she said, "Peziza."

"Peziza? My name is Paziz."

"Is that true or are you joking?"

"Why should I joke? That is my name. Maybe we're related. Let's fly."

Paziz jumped down from the weather vane and somersaulted over the roof to Peziza. He took off and she flew after him, amazed that she was not afraid. The night was full of shadowy creatures: imps, shades, goblins. One danced on a chimney, another slid down a drainpipe, a third whirled around using a weather vane as a carousel, a fourth clambered up a lamppost. Paziz flew so quickly that it made Peziza dizzy, but she managed to keep up with him. They passed over fields, forests, rivers, lakes, hamlets, and towns. As they flew along, Paziz entertained Peziza with stories of ruined castles, broken windmills, and forsaken houses. How large the world was! How strange the night! How endless the roads! Peziza could have flown on forever, but she knew that when the cock crows and the sun rises, an imp must hide. She also missed Tsirtsur.

"Where are we?" she asked. "I hope I will recognize my tree."

"There is no lack of trees here," Paziz remarked.

"Yes, but my friend Tsirtsur the cricket is waiting for me."

"What kind of a friendship is that? An imp and a cricket?"

"We've always been together. I could never live without him," Peziza replied.

"Very well, then. I will bring you back to where we started from."

They had been flying swiftly, but homeward bound

they traveled even more quickly than before. In her dreams Peziza had never imagined an imp as clever and brave as Paziz was. He had not spent his life, as she had, in a dark space between a stove and a wall. Each day he found a different resting place. At night he wandered wherever he pleased. He made many friends.

At last the roof where Paziz and Peziza had met came into view and Peziza recognized her tree nearby. To her amazement, when they landed she saw that Tsirtsur was not alone. There was another cricket with him. Tsirtsur, too, had found a friend, and the new cricket was helping him dig his home.

"Where have you been?" Tsirtsur called when he saw Peziza. "I was afraid you were lost."

"I never would have found my way back had it not been for Paziz," she replied, and introduced the imp to Tsirtsur.

Tsirtsur cricked politely: "As you see, I too have found a friend. Her name is Grillida."

Fate always has surprises up its sleeve. When Peziza and Tsirtsur were forced to leave their home behind the stove, they were sure their end was near. But the powers that be had their own plans. Instead of misfortune, Peziza found Paziz and Tsirtsur, Grillida. The couples soon became so attached to each other that they were inseparable and before long were married according to the customs of imps and crickets.

As long as summer lasted, they all enjoyed the outdoors. Paziz and Peziza spent their nights flying about and traveled as far as the big city of Lublin. Tsirtsur and Grillida amused themselves by telling each other stories.

When day came, the crickets rested in the nest they had dug and the imps slept in their tree hollow.

Little by little the nights began to get cool. A mist rose from the river. The frogs croaked less frequently. One seldom heard the whirring of crickets. Tsirtsur and Grillida kept close together for warmth. Sometimes it rained, lightninged, and thundered at night. Paziz and Peziza did not suffer from the cold, but they, too, had their troubles. First, they felt sorry for their friends, the crickets. Second, the tree in which they lived stood not far from the synagogue and every day they were disturbed by the blowing of a ram's horn. It is known that imps are afraid of the sound of a ram's horn. Whenever Peziza heard the horn's blast, she began to tremble and cry.

One evening Peziza noticed that the chimney leading to the stove behind which she and Tsirtsur used to live had smoke coming out of it. It had been rebuilt and was again in use. All four friends took counsel and decided to try to get behind the stove for the winter. Peziza and Paziz would have no difficulty getting there. They could fly into the house through an open window or through the chimney when the stove was cold. But for Tsirtsur and Grillida it would be a long and difficult journey. However, with the imps helping the crickets along, they all made their way to the old space between the stove and the wall.

The days became shorter, the nights longer. Outdoors it rained and snowed. The frosts came, but behind the stove it was dark, warm, and smelled of bread, cakes, and Sabbath pudding. The owners often toasted noodles and baked apples. In the kitchen, the housewife and her daughters plucked chickens and told stories about ghosts, hobgoblins, and imps. After having spent so much time listening to the people of the house, Peziza and Tsirtsur had learned to understand the language of humans. They had long since discovered that like crickets and imps, humans, too, dream of love and happiness.

Tsirtsur and Grillida never again left their nest, but Paziz and Peziza would often go out through the chimney to air their wings and revel in the adventures of the netherworld. Each time they returned they brought back new stories for the stay-at-homes. Some were gay and mischievous, others devilish and frightening, but all delighted the crickets and gave Tsirtsur much to chirp about with Grillida in the long winter nights.

Translated by the author and Elizabeth Shub

Naftali the Storyteller & His Horse, Sus

I

The father, Zelig, and the mother, Bryna, both complained that their son, Naftali, loved stories too much. He could never go to sleep unless his mother first told him a story. At times she had to tell him two or three stories before he would close his eyes. He always demanded: "Mama, more, more! . . ."

Fortunately, Bryna had heard many stories from her mother and grandmother. Zelig himself, a coachman, had many things to tell—about spirits who posed as passengers and imps who stole into stables at night and wove braids into the horses' tails and elflocks into their manes. The nicest story was about when Zelig had still been a young coachman.

One summer night Zelig was coming home from Lublin with an empty wagon. It just so happened that he hadn't picked up any passengers from Lublin to his hometown, Janów. He drove along a road that ran through a forest. There was a full moon. It cast silvery nets over the pine branches and strings of pearls over the bark of the tree trunks. Night birds cried. From time to time a wolf's howl was heard. In those days the Polish woods still swarmed with bears, wolves, foxes, martens, and many other wild beasts. That night Zelig was despondent. When his wagon was empty of passengers, his wallet was empty of money, and there wouldn't be enough for Bryna to prepare for the Sabbath.

Suddenly Zelig saw lying in the road a sack that appeared to be full of flour or ground sugar. Zelig stopped his horse and got down to take a look. A sack of flour or sugar would come in handy in a household.

Zelig untied the sack, opened it, took a lick, and decided that it was ground sugar. He lifted the sack, which was unusually heavy. Zelig was accustomed to carrying his passengers' baggage and he wondered why a sack of sugar should feel so heavy.

It seems I didn't have enough to eat at the inn, Zelig thought. And when you don't eat enough, you lose your strength.

He loaded the sack into the wagon. It was so heavy that he nearly strained himself.

He sat down on the driver's box and pulled on the reins, but the horse didn't move.

Zelig tugged harder and cried out, "*Wyszta!*" which in Polish means "Giddap!"

But even though the horse pulled with all his might, the wagon still wouldn't move forward.

What's going on here, Zelig wondered. Can the sack be so heavy that the horse cannot pull it?

This made no sense, for the horse had often drawn a wagonful of passengers along with their baggage.

"There is something here that's not as it should be," Zelig said to himself. He got down again, untied the sack, and took another lick. God in heaven, the sack was full of salt, not sugar!

Zelig stood there dumbfounded. How could he have made such a mistake? He licked again, and again, and it was salt.

"Well, it's one of those nights!" Zelig mumbled to himself.

He decided to heave the sack off the wagon, since it was clear that evil spirits were toying with him. But by now the sack had become as heavy as if it were filled with lead. The horse turned his head backward and stared, as if curious as to what was going on.

Suddenly Zelig heard laughter coming from inside the sack. Soon afterward the sack crumbled and out popped a creature with the eyes of a calf, the horns of a goat, and the wings of a bat. The creature said in a human voice, "You didn't lick sugar or salt but an imp's tail."

And with these words the imp burst into wild laughter and flew away.

Dozens of times Zelig the coachman told this same story to Naftali but Naftali never grew tired of hearing it. He could picture it all—the forest, the night, the silver moon, the curious eye of the horse, and the imp. Naftali asked all kinds of questions: Did the imp have a beard? Did it have feet? How did its tail look? Where did it fly off to?

Zelig couldn't answer all the questions. He had been

too frightened at the time to notice the details. But to the last question Zelig replied, "He probably flew to beyond the Dark Regions, where people don't go and cattle don't stray, where the sky is copper, the earth iron, and where the evil forces live under roofs of petrified toadstools and in tunnels abandoned by moles."

2

Like all the children in town, Naftali rose early to go to cheder. He studied more diligently than the other children. Why? Because Naftali was eager to learn to read. He had seen older boys reading storybooks and he had been envious of them. How happy was one who could read a story from a book!

At six, Naftali was already able to read a book in Yiddish, and from then on he read every storybook he could get his hands on. Twice a year a bookseller named Reb Zebulun visited Janów, and among the other books in the sack he carried over his shoulder were some storybooks. They cost two groschen a copy, and although Naftali got only two groschen a week allowance from his father, he saved up enough to buy a number of storybooks each season. He also read the stories in his mother's Yiddish Pentateuch and in her books of morals.

When Naftali grew older, his father began to teach him how to handle horses. It was the custom in those days for a son to take over his father's livelihood. Naftali loved horses very much but he wasn't anxious to become a coachman driving passengers from Janów to Lublin and from Lublin to Janów. He wanted to become a bookseller with a sackful of storybooks.

His mother said to him, "What's so good about being a bookseller? From toting the sack day in day out, your back becomes bent, and from all the walking, your legs swell."

Naftali knew that his mother was right and he thought a lot about what he would do when he grew up. Suddenly he came up with a plan that seemed to him both wise and simple. He would get himself a horse and wagon, and instead of carrying the books on his back, he would carry them in the wagon.

His father, Zelig, said, "A bookseller doesn't make enough to support himself, his family, and a horse besides."

"For me it will be enough."

One time when Reb Zebulun the bookseller came to town, Naftali had a talk with him. He asked him where he got the storybooks and who wrote them. The bookseller told him that in Lublin there was a printer who printed these books, and in Warsaw and Vilna there were writers who wrote them. Reb Zebulun said that he could sell many more storybooks, but he lacked the strength to walk to all the towns and villages, and it didn't pay him to do so.

Reb Zebulun said, "I'm liable to come to a town where there are only two or three children who want to read storybooks. It doesn't pay me to walk there for the few groschen I might earn nor does it pay me to keep a horse or hire a wagon."

"What do these children do without storybooks?" Naftali asked. And Reb Zebulun replied, "They have to make do. Storybooks aren't bread. You can live without them."

"I couldn't live without them," Naftali said.

During this conversation Naftali also asked where the writers got all these stories and Reb Zebulun said, "First of all, many unusual things happen in the world. A day doesn't go by without some rare event happening. Besides, there are writers who make up such stories."

"They make them up?" Naftali asked in amazement. "If that is so, then they are liars."

"They are not liars," Reb Zebulun replied. "The human brain really can't make up a thing. At times I read a story that seems to me completely unbelievable, but I come to some place and I hear that such a thing actually happened. The brain is created by God, and human thoughts and fantasies are also God's works. Even dreams come from God. If a thing doesn't happen today, it might easily happen tomorrow. If not in one country, then in another. There are endless worlds and what doesn't happen on earth can happen in another world. Whoever has eyes that see and ears that hear absorbs enough stories to last a lifetime and to tell to his children and grandchildren."

That's what old Reb Zebulun said, and Naftali listened to his words agape.

Finally, Naftali said, "When I grow up, I'll travel to all the cities, towns, and villages, and I'll sell storybooks everywhere, whether it pays me or not."

Naftali had decided on something else, too—to become a writer of storybooks. He knew full well that for this you had to study, and with all his heart he determined to learn. He also began to listen more closely to what people said, to what stories they told, and to how they told them. Each person had his or her own manner of speaking. Reb Zebulun told Naftali, "When a day passes, it is no longer there. What remains of it? Nothing more than a story. If stories weren't told or books weren't written, man would live like the beasts, only for the day."

Reb Zebulun said, "Today we live, but by tomorrow today will be a story. The whole world, all human life, is one long story."

3

Ten years went by. Naftali was now a young man. He grew up tall, slim, fair-skinned, with black hair and blue eyes. He had learned a lot at the studyhouse and in the yeshiva and he was also an expert horseman. Zelig's mare had borne a colt and Naftali pastured and raised it. He called him Sus. Sus was a playful colt. In the summer he liked to roll in the grass. He whinnied like the tinkling sound of a bell. Sometimes, when Naftali washed and curried him and tickled his neck, Sus burst out in a sound that resembled laughter. Naftali rode him bareback like a Cossack. When Naftali passed the marketplace astride Sus, the town girls ran to the windows to look out.

After a while Naftali built himself a wagon. He ordered the wheels from Leib the blacksmith. Naftali loaded the wagon with all the storybooks he had collected during the years and he rode with his horse and his goods to the nearby towns. Naftali bought a whip, but he swore solemnly to himself that he would never use it. Sus didn't need to be whipped or even to have the whip waved at him. He pulled the light wagonful of books eagerly and easily. Naftali seldom sat on the box but walked alongside his horse and told him stories. Sus cocked his ears when Naftali spoke to him and Naftali was sure that Sus understood him. At times, when Naftali asked Sus whether he had liked a story, Sus whinnied, stomped his foot on the ground, or licked Naftali's ear with his tongue as if he meant to say, "Yes, I understand . . ."

Reb Zebulun had told him that animals live only for the day, but Naftali was convinced that animals have a memory, too. Sus often remembered the road better than he, Naftali, did. Naftali had heard the story of a dog whose masters had lost him on a distant journey and months after they had come home without their beloved pet, he showed up. The dog crossed half of Poland to come back to his owners. Naftali had heard a similar story about a cat. The fact that pigeons fly back to their coops from very far away was known throughout the world. In those days, they were often used to deliver letters. Some people said this was memory, others called it instinct. But what did it matter what it was called? Animals didn't live for the day only.

Naftali rode from town to town; he often stopped in villages and sold his storybooks. The children everywhere loved Naftali and his horse, Sus. They brought all kinds of good things from home for Sus—potato peels, turnips, and pieces of sugar—and each time Sus got something to eat he waved his tail and shook his head, which meant "Thank you."

Not all the children were able to study and learn to read, and Naftali would gather a number of young children, seat them in the wagon, and tell them a story, sometimes a real one and sometimes a made-up one.

Wherever he went, Naftali heard all kinds of tales—of demons, hobgoblins, windmills, giants, dwarfs, kings, princes, and princesses. He would tell a story nicely, with all the details, and the children never grew tired of listening to him. Even grownups came to listen. Often the grownups invited Naftali home for a meal or a place to sleep. They also liked to feed Sus.

When a person does his work not only for money but out of love, he brings out the love in others. When a child couldn't afford a book, Naftali gave it to him free. Soon Naftali became well known throughout the region. Eventually, he came to Lublin.

In Lublin, Naftali heard many astonishing stories. He met a giant seven feet tall who traveled with a circus and a troupe of midgets. At the circus Naftali saw horses who danced to music, as well as dancing bears. One trickster swallowed a knife and spat it out again, another did a somersault on a high wire, a third flew in the air from one trapeze to another. A girl stood on a horse's back while it raced round and round the circus ring. Naftali struck up an easy friendship with the circus people and he listened to their many interesting stories. They told of fakirs in India who could walk barefoot over burning coals. Others let themselves be buried alive, and after they were dug out several days later, they were healthy and well. Naftali heard astounding stories about sorcerers and miracle workers who could read minds and predict the future. He met an old man who had walked from Lublin to the Land of Israel, then back again. The old man told

Naftali about cabalists who lived in caves behind Jerusalem, fasted from one Sabbath to the next, and learned the secrets of God, the angels, the seraphim, the cherubim, and the holy beasts.

The world was full of wonders and Naftali had the urge to write them down and spread them far and wide over all the cities, towns, and villages.

In Lublin, Naftali went to the bookstores and bought storybooks, but he soon saw that there weren't enough storybooks to be had. The storekeepers said that it didn't pay the printers to print them since they brought in so little money. But could everything be measured by money? There were children and even grownups everywhere who yearned to hear stories and Naftali decided to tell all that he had heard. He himself hungered for stories and could never get enough of them.

4

More years passed. Naftali's parents were no longer living. Many girls had fallen in love with Naftali and wanted to marry him, but he knew that from telling stories and selling storybooks he could not support a family. Besides, he had become used to wandering. How many stories could he hear or tell living in one town? He therefore decided to stay on the road. Horses normally live some twenty-odd years, but Sus was one of those rare horses who live a long time. However, no one lives forever. At forty Sus began to show signs of old age. He seldom galloped now, nor were his eyes as good as they once were. Naftali was already gray himself and the children called him Grandpa.

One time Naftali was told that on the road between Lublin and Warsaw lay an estate where all booksellers came, since the owner was very fond of reading and hearing stories. Naftali asked the way and he was given directions to get there. One spring day he came to the estate. Everything that had been said turned out to be true. The owner of the estate, Reb Falik, gave him a warm welcome and bought many books from him. The children in the nearby town had already heard about Naftali the storyteller and they snatched up all the storybooks he had brought with him. Reb Falik had many horses grazing and when they saw Sus they accepted him as one of their own. Sus promptly began to chew the grass where many yellow flowers grew and Naftali told Reb Falik one story after another. The weather was warm, birds sang, twittered, and trilled, each in its own voice.

The estate contained a tract of forest where old oaks grew. Some of the oaks were so thick they had to be hundreds of years old. Naftali was particularly taken by one oak standing in the center of a meadow. It was the thickest oak Naftali had ever seen in his life. Its roots were spread over a wide area and you could tell that they ran deep. The crown of the oak spread far and wide, and it cast a huge shadow. When Naftali saw this giant oak, which had to be older than all the oaks in the region, it occurred to him: "What a shame an oak hasn't a mouth to tell stories with!"

This oak had lived through many generations. It may have gone back to the times when idol worshippers still lived in Poland. It surely knew the time when the Jews had come to Poland from the German states where they had been persecuted and the Polish king Kazimierz I had opened the gates of the land to them. Naftali suddenly realized that he was tired of wandering. He now envied the oak for standing so long in one place, deeply rooted in God's earth. For the first time in his life Naftali got the urge to settle down in one place. He also thought of his horse. Sus was undoubtedly tired of trekking over the roads. It would do him good to get some rest in the few years left him.

Just as Naftali stood there thinking these thoughts, the owner of the estate, Reb Falik, came along in a buggy. He stopped the buggy near Naftali and said, "I see you're completely lost in thought. Tell me what you're thinking."

At first Naftali wanted to tell Reb Falik that many kinds of foolish notions ran through the human mind and that not all of them could be described. But after a while he thought, Why not tell him the truth?

Reb Falik seemed a kindhearted man. He had a silver-white beard and eyes that expressed the wisdom and goodness that sometimes come with age. Naftali said, "If you have the patience, I'll tell you."

"Yes, I have the patience. Take a seat in the buggy. I'm going for a drive and I want to hear what a man who is famous for his storytelling thinks about."

Naftali sat down in the buggy. The horses hitched to the buggy walked slowly and Naftali told Reb Falik the story of his life, as well as what his thoughts were when he saw the giant oak. He told him everything, kept nothing back.

When Naftali finished, Reb Falik said, "My dear Naftali, I can easily fulfill all your wishes and fantasies. I am, as you know, an old man. My wife died some time ago. My children live in the big cities. I love to hear stories and I also have lots of stories to tell. If you like, I'll let you build a house in the shade of the oak and you can stay there as long as I live and as long as you live. I'll have a stable built for your horse near the house and you'll both live out your lives in peace. Yes, you are right. You cannot wander forever. There comes a time when every person wants to settle in one place and drink in all the charms that the place has to offer."

When Naftali heard these words, a great joy came over him. He thanked Reb Falik again and again, but Reb Falik said, "You need not thank me so much. I have many peasants and servants here, but I don't have a single person I can talk to. We'll be friends and we'll tell each other lots of stories. What's life, after all? The future isn't here yet and you cannot foresee what it will bring. The present is only a moment and the past is one long story. Those who don't tell stories and don't hear stories live only for that moment, and that isn't enough."

5

Reb Falik's promise wasn't merely words. The very next day he ordered his people to build a house for Naftali the storyteller. There was no shortage of lumber or of craftsmen on the estate. When Naftali saw the plans for the house, he grew disturbed. He needed only a small house for himself and a stable for Sus. But the plans called for a big house with many rooms. Naftali asked Reb Falik why such a big house was being built for him, and Reb Falik replied, "You will need it."

"What for?" Naftali asked.

Gradually, the secret came out. During his lifetime Reb Falik had accumulated many books, so many that he couldn't find room for them in his own big house and many books had to be stored in the cellar and in the attic. Besides, in his talks with Reb Falik, Naftali had said that he had many of his own stories and stories told him by others written down on paper and that he had collected a chestful of manuscripts, but he hadn't been able to have these stories printed, for the printers in Lublin and in the other big cities demanded a lot of money to print them and the number of buyers of storybooks in Poland wasn't large enough to cover such expenses.

Alongside Naftali's house, Reb Falik had a print shop built. He ordered crates of type from Lublin (in those days there was no such thing as a typesetting machine) as well as a hand press. From now on Naftali would have the opportunity to set and print his own storybooks. When he learned what Reb Falik was doing for him, Naftali couldn't believe his ears. He said, "Of all the stories I have ever heard or told, for me this will be by far the nicest."

That very summer everything was ready—the house, the library, the print shop. Winter came early. Right after Succoth the rains began, followed by snow. In winter there is little to do on an estate. The peasants sat in their huts and warmed themselves by their stoves or they went to the tavern. Reb Falik and Naftali spent lots of time together. Reb Falik himself was a treasure trove of stories. He had met many famous squires. In his time he had visited the fairs in Danzig, Leipzig, and Amsterdam. He had even made a trip to the Holy Land and had seen the Western Wall, the Cave of Machpelah, and Rachel's Tomb. Reb Falik told many tales and Naftali wrote them down.

Sus's stable was too big for one horse. Reb Falik had a number of old horses on his estate that could no longer work so Sus wasn't alone. At times, when Naftali came into the stable to visit his beloved Sus, he saw him bowing his head against the horse on his left or his right, and it seemed to Naftali that Sus was listening to stories told him by the other horses or silently telling his own horsy story. It's true that horses cannot speak, but God's creatures can make themselves understood without words.

That winter Naftali wrote many stories—his own and those he heard from Reb Falik. He set them in type and printed them on his hand press. At times, when the sun shone over the silvery snow, Naftali hitched Sus and another horse to a sleigh and made a trip through the nearby towns to sell his storybooks or give them away to those who couldn't afford to buy them. Sometimes Reb Falik went along with him. They slept at inns and spent time with merchants, landowners, and Hasidim on their way to visit their rabbis' courts. Each one had a story to tell and Naftali either wrote them down or fixed them in his memory.

The winter passed and Naftali couldn't remember how. On Passover, Reb Falik's sons, daughters, and grandchildren came to celebrate the holiday at the estate, and again Naftali heard wondrous tales of Warsaw, Cracow, and even of Berlin, Paris, and London. The kings waged wars, but scientists made all kinds of discoveries and inventions. Astronomers discovered stars, planets, comets. Archaeologists dug out ruins of ancient cities. Chemists found new elements. In all the countries, tracks were being laid for railroad trains. Museums, libraries, and theaters were being built. Historians uncovered writings from generations past. The writers in every land described the life and the people among whom they dwelled. Mankind could not and would not forget its past. The history of the world grew ever richer in detail.

That spring something happened that Naftali had been expecting and, therefore, dreading. Sus became sick and stopped grazing. The sun shone outside, and Naftali led Sus out to pasture, where the fresh green grass and many flowers sprouted. Sus sat down in the sunshine, looked at the grass and the flowers, but no longer grazed. A stillness shone out from his eyes, the tranquillity of a creature that has lived out its years and is ready to end its story on earth.

One afternoon, when Naftali went out to check on his beloved Sus, he saw that Sus was dead. Naftali couldn't hold back his tears. Sus had been a part of his life.

Naftali dug a grave for Sus not far from the old oak where Sus had died, and he buried him there. As a marker over the grave, he thrust into the ground the whip that he had never used. Its handle was made of oak.

Oddly enough, several weeks later Naftali noticed that the whip had turned into a sapling. The handle had put down roots into the earth where Sus lay and it began to sprout leaves. A tree grew over Sus, a new oak which drew sustenance from Sus's body. In time young branches grew out of the tree and birds sang upon them and built their nests there. Naftali could hardly bring himself to believe that this old dried-out stick had possessed enough life within it to grow and blossom. Naftali considered it a miracle. When the tree grew thicker, Naftali carved Sus's name into the bark along with the dates of his birth and death.

Yes, individual creatures die, but this doesn't end the story of the world. The whole earth, all the stars, all the planets, all the comets represent within them one divine history, one source of life, one endless and wondrous story that only God knows in its entirety.

A few years afterward, Reb Falik died, and years later, Naftali the storyteller died. By then he was famous for his storybooks not only throughout Poland but in other countries as well. Before his death Naftali asked that he be buried beneath the young oak that had grown over Sus's grave and whose branches touched the old oak. On Naftali's tombstone were carved these words from the Scriptures:

LOVELY AND PLEASANT IN THEIR LIVES,

AND IN THEIR DEATH

THEY ARE NOT DIVIDED

Translated by Joseph Singer

Hershele & Hanukkah

Three lights burned in old Reb Berish's menorah. It was so quiet in the studyhouse one could hear the wick in the ceiling lamp sucking kerosene. Reb Berish was saying:

"Children, when one lives as long as I do, one sees many things and has many stories to tell. What I am going to tell you now happened in the village of Gorshkow.

"Gorshkow is small even today. But when I was a boy the marketplace was the entire village. They used to joke, 'Whenever a peasant comes with his cart to Gorshkow, the head of the horse is at one end of the village and the rear wheels of the cart at the other end.' Fields and forests surrounded Gorshkow on all sides. A man by the name of Isaac Seldes who lived there managed a huge estate owned by a Polish squire. The squire, a count, spent all his time abroad and came to Poland only when his money was exhausted. He borrowed more money from Reb Isaac Seldes on mortgage and gradually his whole estate became Isaac's property. Officially, it still belonged to the squire because a Jew was not allowed to own land in the part of Poland which belonged to Russia.

"Reb Isaac managed the property with skill. The squire used to flog the peasants when they did something wrong or if the mood struck him. But Reb Isaac spoke to the peasants as if they were his equals and they were loyal to him. When there was a wedding among them or when a woman gave birth, he attended the celebration. When a peasant fell sick, Reb Isaac's wife, Kreindl, rolled up her sleeves and applied cups or leeches or rubbed the patient with turpentine. Reb Isaac Seldes owned a britska with two horses, and he rode alongside the fields and advised the peasants when to plow, what to sow, or what vegetables to plant. He had a special dairy house on the estate for churning butter and making cheese. He had a large stable of cows, hundreds of chickens that laid eggs, as well as beehives and a water mill.

"He had everything except children. It caused Reb Isaac and his wife grief. The medications that the doctors of Lublin prescribed for Kreindl never did any good.

"Even though they were only two people, Reb Isaac and his wife lived in a large house that had once be-longed to the present squire's grandfather. But what use is a big house for just a husband and a wife? However, they both had poor relatives whose children came to live on the estate. Reb Isaac hired a teacher to instruct the boys in the Bible and the Talmud. Kreindl taught the girls sewing, knitting, and needlepoint. They stitched biblical scenes onto canvas with colored thread, like the story of Abraham attempting to sacrifice his only son on an altar and the angel preventing him from doing so, or Jacob meeting Rachel at the well and rolling the stone away so she could water the sheep.

"Hanukkah was always a gay occasion in Reb Isaac's house. After blessing the candles, he gave Hanukkah money to all the children and they all played dreidel. Kreindl and her maids fried potato pancakes in the kitchen and they were served with jam and tea. Often poor people turned up at the estate, and whoever came hungry, in tattered clothes and bare feet, left with a full belly, warm clothing, and proper footwear.

"One Hanukkah evening when the children were playing dreidel and Reb Isaac was playing chess with the teacher, who was not only a Talmud scholar but also well versed in mathematics and language, Reb Isaac heard a scratching at the door. A deep snow had fallen outside. If guests visited the estate in the winter, they came during the day, not in the evening. Reb Isaac opened the door himself, and to his amazement, on the other side of the threshold stood a fawn, still without antlers. Normally, an animal keeps away from human beings, but this fawn seemed hungry, cold, and emaciated. Perhaps it had lost its mother. For a while Reb Isaac stared in wonder. Then he took the young animal by its throat and brought it into the house. When the children saw the fawn, they forgot about the dreidel and the Hanukkah gifts. They were all thrilled with the charming animal. When she saw the fawn, Kreindl almost dropped the tray of pancakes she was holding. Reb Isaac wanted to give a pancake to the fawn, but Kreindl called out, 'Don't do it. It's too young. It needs milk, not pancakes.' The maids came in and one of them went to bring a bowl of milk. The fawn drank all of it and lifted up its head as if to say, 'I want more.' This little creature brought much joy to everybody in the house. All agreed that the fawn should not be let out again in the woods, which teemed with wolves, foxes, martens, and even bears. A servant brought in some hay and made a bed for the fawn in one of the rooms. Soon, it fell asleep.

"Reb Isaac thought that soon the children would return to their games, but all they could talk about was the fawn, and Reb Isaac and Kreindl had to give them a solemn promise to keep it safe in the house until after Passover.

"Now that the children had extracted this promise, a new debate began—what name to give the fawn? Almost everyone wanted to call it Hershele, which is the Yiddish word for fawn, but for some strange reason Kreindl said, 'You are not going to give this name to the animal.'

" 'Why not?' the children and even the grownups asked in astonishment.

" 'I have a reason.'

"When Kreindl said no, it remained no. The children had to come up with another name, and then Kreindl said, 'Children, I have it.'

" 'What is it?' the children asked in unison. And Kreindl said, 'Hanukkah.'

"No one had ever heard of an animal called Hanukkah, but they liked it. Only now did the children start to eat the pancakes, and they washed them down with tea with lemon and jam. Then they began to play dreidel again and they did not finish the games until midnight.

"Late at night, when Reb Isaac and Kreindl went to bed, Reb Isaac asked Kreindl, 'Why didn't you like the name Hershele for the fawn?' and Kreindl replied, 'That is a secret.'

" 'A secret from me?' Isaac asked. 'Since we married you've never had any secrets from me.'

"And Kreindl answered, 'This time I cannot tell you.'

" 'When will you tell me?' Isaac asked, and Kreindl said, 'The secret will reveal itself.'

"Reb Isaac had never heard his wife speak in riddles but it was not in his nature to insist or to probe.

"Now, dear children, I am going to tell you the secret even before Kreindl told it to her husband," old Reb Berish said.

"A few weeks earlier an old man came to the estate with a sack on his back and a cane in his hand. He had a white beard and white sidelocks. When Kreindl gave him food to eat he took a large volume out of his sack, and while he ate, he read it. Kreindl had never seen a beggar behave like a rabbi and a scholar. She asked him, 'Why do you carry books on your back? Aren't they heavy?' And the old man replied, 'The Torah is never heavy.' His words impressed Kreindl, so she began to talk to him and she told him how grieved she was at not having children. Suddenly she heard herself say, 'I see that you are a holy man. Please, pray to God for me and give me your blessing. I promise you that if your blessing is answered in heaven, I will give you a sack full of silver guldens when you return and you will never need to beg for alms.'

" 'I promise you that in about a year's time you will have a child.'

" 'Please, holy man,' Kreindl said. 'Give me a token or a sign that your promise will come true.' And the old man said, 'Some time before your child is conceived an animal will enter your house. When the child is born, call it by the name of this animal. Please remember my words.'

"Before the old man left, Kreindl wanted to give him clothes and food, but he said, 'God will provide all this for me. I don't need to prepare it in advance. Besides, my sack is filled with sacred books and there is no place for anything else.' He lifted his hands over Kreindl's head and blessed her. Then he left as quietly as he had come. Kreindl pondered the words of this strange old man for many weeks. Reb Isaac happened not to be at home when he came and Kreindl did not tell her husband about his visit. She had received many wishes and benedictions from gypsies, fortune-tellers, and wanderers, and she did not want to arouse hopes in Isaac that might never materialize.

"That night when the fawn came into the house Kreindl understood that this was the animal the beggar had mentioned. Since a fawn is called Hershele in Yiddish, she would give birth to a male child and call him Hershele. Kreindl's words that the secret would reveal

itself soon came true. She became pregnant and Reb
Isaac understood that the coming of the fawn was an
omen of this hoped-for event. He said, 'When our child is
born, if it is a male we will call it Hershele,' and Kreindl
answered, 'As you wish, my beloved, so it will be.'

"Winter had passed, spring had come. Hanukkah had
been growing in the cold winter months and he sprouted
antlers. Everyone could see that the animal was no
longer happy indoors. His beautiful eyes expressed a
yearning to go back to the forest. One morning Kreindl
gave Hanukkah a tasty meal of hay mixed with chopped
potatoes and carrots and then opened the gate to the
fields and forests. Hanukkah gave his mistress a look that
said 'Thank you,' and he ran to the green pastures and
the woods.

"Kreindl predicted that in the winter Hanukkah would
turn up again, but Reb Isaac said such things cannot be
foretold. 'Hanukkah has grown up and an adult deer can
find its own food even in the winter.'

"Not long after, Kreindl gave birth to a healthy little
boy with dark hair and brown eyes, and there was great
joy in the house. The happy father and mother had prepared a special repast for the poor on the day of the
circumcision ceremony. Reb Isaac and Kreindl both
hoped that the old beggar might hear about it and come
to the feast. But he never came. However, other poor
people heard about it and they came. A large table was
placed on the lawn and the needy men and women were
served challah, gefilte fish, chicken, fruit, as well as wine
and honey cake. Some of the younger crowd danced a
scissor dance, a good-morning dance, an angry dance, a

kazatske. Before they left, all the poor got gifts of money, food, and clothes.

"The summer drew to a close and it became cool again. After the Succoth holiday the rains, the snowfall, and the frosts began. The feast of Hanukkah approached, and although everyone wondered what had happened to the fawn in the cold weather, nobody spoke about it, so as not to worry Kreindl. This winter was even more severe than the former one. The whole estate was buried in snow. On the first night of Hanukkah, Kreindl and the maids were busy frying pancakes. After Reb Isaac blessed the first light and gave coins to the children, they sat down to play dreidel. The baby, Hershele, slept in his cradle. The children of the house had prepared a gift for him—a fawn made of sugar, and on its belly was the inscription *Hanukkah*. When it was given to Hershele, he immediately began to suck on it. But the fawn didn't come that night. Reb Isaac comforted Kreindl by quoting the Gemara: 'Miracles don't happen every day.'

"Kreindl shook her head. 'I hope to God that Hanukkah is not hungry and cold.'

"On the second night of Hanukkah, while all the children were playing dreidel, Reb Isaac was about to checkmate the teacher, and Kreindl, along with the maids, was preparing to clean the table, they heard a scratching on the door. Kreindl ran to open it and cried out with joy. At the door stood Hanukkah, already a half-grown deer, his body silvery with frost. He had not forgotten his benefactors. He had come to stay for the winter. Hershele woke up from the noise, and when he was shown the animal, he stretched out his little hand toward him. Hanukkah licked the hand with his tongue, as if he knew that Hershele was his namesake.

"From then on, the deer came to the estate every year and always about the time of Hanukkah. He had become a big stag with large antlers. Hershele grew, too, although not as fast. The third winter the deer brought a doe with him. It seemed that he had fought for his mate with another stag because a part of his antler was broken. Hanukkah and his mate were taken in. There was much discussion among the children what to name Hanukkah's wife. This time the teacher made a proposal. She was named Zot Hanukkah. This is how the section of the Bible that is read on the Sabbath of Hanukkah begins. The word 'zot,' which means 'this,' indicates the feminine gender. This name pleased everyone."

Reb Berish paused for a long while. The lights in the brass lamp were still burning. The children felt that the little flames were also listening to the story. Then a boy asked, "Did the old beggar ever come back?"

"No, I never heard that he did, but you can be sure that this man was not just an ordinary beggar."

"What was he?" another boy asked.

"The prophet Elijah," Reb Berish said. "It is known that Elijah is the angel of good tidings. He never comes in the image of an angel. People would go blind if they looked into the dazzling light of an angel. He always comes disguised as a poor man. Even the Messiah, according to the Talmud, will come in the disguise of a poor man, riding on a donkey."

Old Reb Berish closed his eyes and it was hard to know whether he was dozing or contemplating the coming of the Messiah. He opened them again and said, "Now you can go home and play dreidel."

"Will you tell us another story tomorrow?" another boy asked, and old Reb Berish replied, "With God's help. I have lived long and I have more stories to tell than you have hair in your sidelocks."

When Shlemiel Went to Warsaw

Though Shlemiel was a lazybones and a sleepyhead and hated to move, he always daydreamed of taking a trip. He had heard many stories about faraway countries, huge deserts, deep oceans, and high mountains, and often discussed with Mrs. Shlemiel his great wish to go on a long journey. Mrs. Shlemiel would reply, "Long journeys are not for a Shlemiel. You better stay home and mind the children while I go to market to sell my vegetables." Yet Shlemiel could not bring himself to give up his dream of seeing the world and its wonders.

A recent visitor to Chelm had told Shlemiel marvelous things about the city of Warsaw. How beautiful the streets were, how high the buildings and luxurious the stores. Shlemiel decided once and for all that he must see this great city for himself. He knew that one had to prepare for a journey. But what was there for him to take? He had nothing but the old clothes he wore. One morning, after Mrs. Shlemiel left for the market, he told the older boys to stay home from cheder and mind the younger children. Then he took a few slices of bread, an onion, and a clove of garlic, put them in a kerchief, tied it into a bundle, and started for Warsaw on foot.

There was a street in Chelm called Warsaw Street and Shlemiel believed that it led directly to Warsaw. While still in the village, he was stopped by several neighbors who asked him where he was going. Shlemiel told them that he was on his way to Warsaw.

"What will you do in Warsaw?" they asked him.

Shlemiel replied, "What do I do in Chelm? Nothing."

He soon reached the outskirts of town. He walked slowly because the soles of his boots were worn through. Soon the houses and stores gave way to pastures and fields. He passed a peasant driving an ox-drawn plow. After several hours of walking, Shlemiel grew tired. He was so weary that he wasn't even hungry. He lay down on the grass near the roadside for a nap, but before he fell asleep he thought, When I wake up, I may not remember which is the way to Warsaw and which leads back to Chelm. After pondering a moment, he removed his boots and set them down beside him with the toes pointing toward Warsaw and the heels toward Chelm. He soon fell asleep and dreamed that he was a baker baking onion rolls with poppy seeds. Customers came to buy them and Shlemiel said, "These onion rolls are not for sale."

"Then why do you bake them?"

"They are for my wife, for my children, and for me."

Later he dreamed that he was the King of Chelm.

Once a year, instead of taxes, each citizen brought him a pot of strawberry jam. Shlemiel sat on a golden throne and nearby sat Mrs. Shlemiel, the queen, and his children, the princes and princesses. They were all eating onion rolls and spooning up big portions of strawberry jam. A carriage arrived and took the royal family to Warsaw, America, and to the river Sambation, which spurts out stones the week long and rests on the Sabbath.

Near the road, a short distance from where Shlemiel slept, was a smithy. The blacksmith happened to come out just in time to see Shlemiel carefully placing his boots at his side with the toes facing in the direction of Warsaw. The blacksmith was a prankster, and as soon as Shlemiel was sound asleep he tiptoed over and turned the boots around. When Shlemiel awoke, he felt rested but hungry. He got out a slice of bread, rubbed it with garlic, and took a bite of onion. Then he pulled his boots on and continued on his way.

He walked along and everything looked strangely familiar. He recognized houses that he had seen before. It seemed to him that he knew the people he met. Could it be that he had already reached another town, Shlemiel wondered. And why was it so similar to Chelm? He stopped a passerby and asked the name of the town. "Chelm," the man replied.

Shlemiel was astonished. How was this possible? He had walked away from Chelm. How could he have arrived back there? He began to rub his forehead and soon found the answer to the riddle. There were two Chelms and he had reached the second one.

Still, it seemed very odd that the streets, the houses,

the people were so similar to those in the Chelm he had left behind. Shlemiel puzzled over this fact until he suddenly remembered something he had learned in cheder: "The earth is the same everywhere." And so why shouldn't the second Chelm be exactly like the first one? This discovery gave Shlemiel great satisfaction. He wondered if there was a street here like his street and a house on it like the one he lived in. And indeed, he soon arrived at an identical street and house. Evening had fallen. He opened the door and to his amazement saw a second Mrs. Shlemiel with children just like his. Everything was exactly the same as in his own household. Even the cat seemed the same. Mrs. Shlemiel at once began to scold him.

"Shlemiel, where did you go? You left the house alone. And what have you there in that bundle?"

The children all ran to him and cried, "Papa, where have you been?"

Shlemiel paused a moment and then he said, "Mrs. Shlemiel, I'm not your husband. Children, I'm not your papa."

"Have you lost your mind?" Mrs. Shlemiel screamed.

"I am Shlemiel of Chelm One and this is Chelm Two."

Mrs. Shlemiel clapped her hands so hard that the chickens sleeping under the stove awoke in fright and flew out all over the room.

"Children, your father has gone crazy," she wailed. She immediately sent one of the boys for Gimpel the healer. All the neighbors came crowding in. Shlemiel stood in the middle of the room and proclaimed, "It's true, you all look like the people in my town, but you are not the same. I came from Chelm One and you live in Chelm Two."

"Shlemiel, what's the matter with you?" someone cried. "You're in your own house, with your own wife and children, your own neighbors and friends."

"No, you don't understand. I come from Chelm One. I was on my way to Warsaw, and between Chelm One and Warsaw there is a Chelm Two. And that is where I am."

"What are you talking about. We all know you and you know all of us. Don't you recognize your chickens?"

"No, I'm not in my town," Shlemiel insisted. "But," he continued, "Chelm Two does have the same people and the same houses as Chelm One, and that is why you are mistaken. Tomorrow I will continue on to Warsaw."

"In that case, where is my husband?" Mrs. Shlemiel inquired in a rage, and she proceeded to berate Shlemiel with all the curses she could think of.

"How should I know where your husband is?" Shlemiel replied.

Some of the neighbors could not help laughing; others pitied the family. Gimpel the healer announced that he knew of no remedy for such an illness. After some time, everybody went home.

Mrs. Shlemiel had cooked noodles and beans that evening, a dish that Shlemiel liked especially. She said to him, "You may be mad, but even a madman has to eat."

"Why should you feed a stranger?" Shlemiel asked.

"As a matter of fact, an ox like you should eat straw, not noodles and beans. Sit down and be quiet. Maybe some food and rest will bring you back to your senses."

"Mrs. Shlemiel, you're a good woman. My wife

wouldn't feed a stranger. It would seem that there is some small difference between the two Chelms."

The noodles and beans smelled so good that Shlemiel needed no further coaxing. He sat down, and as he ate he spoke to the children:

"My dear children, I live in a house that looks exactly like this one. I have a wife and she is as like your mother as two peas are like each other. My children resemble you as drops of water resemble one another."

The younger children laughed; the older ones began to cry. Mrs. Shlemiel said, "As if being a Shlemiel wasn't enough, he had to go crazy in addition. What am I going to do now? I won't be able to leave the children with him when I go to market. Who knows what a madman may do?" She clasped her head in her hands and cried out, "God in heaven, What have I done to deserve this?"

Nevertheless, she made up a fresh bed for Shlemiel; and even though he had napped during the day, near the smithy, the moment his head touched the pillow he fell fast asleep and was soon snoring loudly. He again dreamed that he was the King of Chelm and that his wife, the queen, had fried for him a huge panful of blintzes. Some were filled with cheese, others with blueberries or cherries, and all were sprinkled with sugar and cinnamon and were drowning in sour cream. Shlemiel ate twenty blintzes all at once and hid the remainder in his crown for later.

In the morning, when Shlemiel awoke, the house was filled with townspeople. Mrs. Shlemiel stood in their midst, her eyes red with weeping. Shlemiel was about to scold his wife for letting so many strangers into the house, but then he remembered that he himself was a stranger here. At home he would have gotten up, washed, and dressed. Now in front of all these people he was at a loss as to what to do. As always when he was embarrassed, he began to scratch his head and pull at his beard. Finally, overcoming his bashfulness, he decided to get up. He threw off the covers and put his bare feet on the floor. "Don't let him run away," Mrs. Shlemiel screamed. "He'll disappear and I'll be a deserted wife, without a Shlemiel."

At this point Baruch the baker interrupted. "Let's take him to the elders. They'll know what to do."

"That's right! Let's take him to the elders," everybody agreed.

Although Shlemiel insisted that since he lived in Chelm One, the local elders had no power over him, several of the strong young men helped him into his pants, his boots, his coat and cap and escorted him to the house of Gronam Ox. The elders, who had already heard of the matter, had gathered early in the morning to consider what was to be done.

As the crowd came in, one of the elders, Dopey Lekisch, was saying, "Maybe there really are two Chelms."

"If there are two, then why can't there be three, four, or even a hundred Chelms?" Sender Donkey interrupted.

"And even if there are a hundred Chelms, must there be a Shlemiel in each one of them?" argued Shmendrick Numskull.

Gronam Ox, the head elder, listened to all the arguments but was not yet prepared to express an opinion. However, his wrinkled, bulging forehead indicated that he was deep in thought. It was Gronam Ox who questioned Shlemiel. Shlemiel related everything that had happened to him, and when he finished, Gronam asked, "Do you recognize me?"

"Surely. You are wise Gronam Ox."

"And in your Chelm is there also a Gronam Ox?"

"Yes, there is a Gronam Ox and he looks exactly like you."

"Isn't it possible that you turned around and came back to Chelm?" Gronam inquired.

"Why should I turn around? I'm not a windmill," Shlemiel replied.

"In that case, you are not this Mrs. Shlemiel's husband."

"No, I'm not."

"Then Mrs. Shlemiel's husband, the real Shlemiel, must have left the day you came."

"It would seem so."

"Then he'll probably come back."

"Probably."

"In that case, you must wait until he returns. Then we'll know who is who."

"Dear elders, my Shlemiel has come back," screamed Mrs. Shlemiel. "I don't need two Shlemiels. One is more than enough."

"Whoever he is, he may not live in your house until everything is made clear," Gronam insisted.

"Where shall I live?" Shlemiel asked.

"In the poorhouse."

"What will I do in the poorhouse?"

"What do you do at home?"

"Good God, who will take care of my children when I go to market?" moaned Mrs. Shlemiel. "Besides, I want a husband. Even a Shlemiel is better than no husband at all."

"Are we to blame that your husband left you and went to Warsaw?" Gronam asked. "Wait until he comes home."

Mrs. Shlemiel wept bitterly and the children cried, too. Shlemiel said, "How strange. My own wife always scolded me. My children talked back to me. And here a strange woman and strange children want me to live with them. It looks to me as if Chelm Two is actually better than Chelm One."

"Just a moment. I think I have an idea," interrupted Gronam.

"What is your idea?" Zeinvel Ninny inquired.

"Since we decided to send Shlemiel to the poorhouse, the town will have to hire someone to take care of Mrs. Shlemiel's children so she can go to market. Why not hire Shlemiel for that? It's true, he is not Mrs. Shlemiel's husband or the children's father. But he is so much like the real Shlemiel that the children will feel at home with him."

"What a wonderful idea!" cried Feivel Thickwit.

"Only King Solomon could have thought of such a wise solution," agreed Treitel Fool.

"Such a clever way out of this dilemma could only have been thought of in our Chelm," chimed in Shmendrick Numskull.

"How much do you want to be paid to take care of Mrs. Shlemiel's children?" asked Gronam.

For a moment Shlemiel stood there completely bewildered. Then he said, "Three groschen a day."

"Idiot, moron, ass?" screamed Mrs. Shlemiel. "What are three groschen nowadays? You shouldn't do it for less than six a day." She ran over to Shlemiel and pinched him on the arm. Shlemiel winced and cried out, "She pinches just like my wife."

The elders held a consultation among themselves. The town budget was very limited. Finally Gronam announced: "Three groschen may be too little, but six groschen a day is definitely too much, especially for a stranger. We will compromise and pay you five groschen a day. Shlemiel, do you accept?"

"Yes, but how long am I to keep this job?"

"Until the real Shlemiel comes home."

Gronam's decision was soon known throughout Chelm, and the town admired his great wisdom and that of all the elders of Chelm.

At first, Shlemiel tried to keep the five groschen that the town paid him for himself. "If I'm not your husband, I don't have to support you," he told Mrs. Shlemiel.

"In that case, since I'm not your wife, I don't have to cook for you, darn your socks, or patch your clothes."

And so, of course, Shlemiel turned over his pay to her. It was the first time that Mrs. Shlemiel had ever gotten any money for the household from Shlemiel. Now when she was in a good mood, she would say to him, "What a pity you didn't decide to go to Warsaw ten years ago."

"Don't you ever miss your husband?" Shlemiel would ask.

"And what about you? Don't you miss your wife?" Mrs. Shlemiel would ask.

And both would admit that they were quite happy with matters as they stood.

Years passed and no Shlemiel returned to Chelm. The elders had many explanations for this. Zeinvel Ninny believed that Shlemiel had crossed the black mountains and had been eaten alive by the cannibals who live there. Dopey Lekisch thought that Shlemiel most probably had come to the Castle of Asmodeus, where he had been forced to marry a demon princess. Shmendrick Numskull came to the conclusion that Shlemiel had reached the edge of the world and had fallen off. There were many other theories; for example, that the real Shlemiel had lost his memory and had simply forgotten that he was Shlemiel. Such things do happen.

Gronam did not like to impose his theories on other people; however, he was convinced that Shlemiel had gone to the other Chelm, where he had had exactly the same experience as the Shlemiel in this Chelm. He had been hired by the local community and was taking care of the other Mrs. Shlemiel's children for a wage of five groschen a day.

As for Shlemiel himself, he no longer knew what to think. The children were growing up and soon would be able to take care of themselves. Sometimes Shlemiel would sit and ponder: Where is the other Shlemiel? When will he come home? What is my real wife doing? Is she waiting for me, or has she got herself another

Shlemiel? These were questions that he could not answer.

Every now and then Shlemiel would still get the desire to go traveling, but he could not bring himself to start out. What was the point of going on a trip if it led nowhere? Often, as he sat alone puzzling over the strange ways of the world, he would become more and more confused and begin humming to himself:

> *Those who leave Chelm*
> *end up in Chelm.*
> *Those who remain in Chelm*
> *are certainly in Chelm.*
> *All roads lead to Chelm.*
> *All the world is one big Chelm.*

Translated by the author and Elizabeth Shub

Elijah the Slave

In ancient times, in a distant land, there was a large
city where many rich men lived. It had magnificent
palaces, broad avenues, parks, and gardens.

In their midst was a tiny street of broken-down houses.
They had narrow windows and doorways, and their roofs
leaked. In the humblest of these, there lived a holy man.
Tobias was his name, and his wife was called Peninah.
They had five children, three sons and two daughters.

Tobias was a scribe who copied the sacred scrolls. In
this way he was able to earn a meager living.

But suddenly he was taken ill and lost the use of his
right hand. Soon there was no bread in the house. The
larder was so empty that even the mice ran away. There
was nothing for the cat to catch. The boys could not go
to school because they had no shoes. Tobias's clothes
were in rags and tatters.

When the neighbors saw the family's need, they tried

to help. But Tobias refused their offers, saying, "There is a God and He will help us."

One day Tobias's wife said to him, "If God intends to help us, it better be soon. But whatever He might do, for you to just sit at home doesn't improve matters. You must go out into the city. Even while waiting for a miracle, it's good to do something. Man must begin and God will help him."

"How can I show my face among people when I have no clothes to wear?"

"Wait, my husband, and I will take care of that."

Peninah went to a neighbor and borrowed a coat, a hat, and shoes. She helped Tobias dress, and truly he looked like a new man. "Now, go," Peninah said, "and luck be with you." When he left, she told the children to pray that their father would not come home with empty hands.

As Tobias approached the center of the city, a stranger stopped him. He was tall and had a white beard. He wore a long coat and carried a staff. "Peace be with you, Tobias," he said, and held out his hand. Tobias, forgetting he could not move his right hand, clasped the stranger's with it. He was baffled by this miraculous recovery.

"Who do I have the honor of greeting?" Tobias asked.

"My name is Elijah and I am your slave."

"My slave?" Tobias said in astonishment.

"Yes, your slave, sent from heaven. Take me to the marketplace and sell me to the highest bidder."

"If you come from heaven, I am *your* slave," Tobias answered. "How can a slave sell his master?"

"Do as I say," Elijah replied.

Since Elijah was a messenger from God, Tobias had no choice but to obey.

In the marketplace, many rich merchants gathered around Tobias and Elijah. Never before had a slave who looked so noble and wise been offered for sale.

The richest and most forward of the merchants addressed him. "What can you do, slave?"

"Anything you wish," Elijah said.

"Can you build a palace?"

"The most magnificent you have ever seen."

"Even more splendid than the king's?"

"More splendid—and bigger."

"Why should we believe you?" asked one of the merchants.

Elijah took a sack of wooden blocks from his pocket and with them built a miniature palace. He did it with such speed and the palace's beauty was so unusual that the merchants were dazzled.

"Can you build a real palace like this one?" the richest merchant asked.

"A better one," said Elijah.

The merchants, sensing that this slave had supernatural powers, began the bidding at once. "Ten thousand gulden," one shouted.

"Fifty thousand," called another.

"One hundred thousand," offered a third.

The highest price—800,000 gulden—was finally offered by the richest merchant, and he paid the money to Tobias.

Turning to Elijah, the merchant said, "If the real palace

is as beautiful as you promise, I will make you a free man."

"Very well," Elijah replied. And to Tobias he said, "Go home and rejoice with your wife and children. Your days of poverty are over."

After giving praise to God and thanking Elijah for his goodness, Tobias returned home.

The joy of his wife and children was great.

As always, Tobias gave a tenth part of his money to the poor; and even though he was now a rich man, he decided to go back to his beloved work as a scribe.

Night came and Elijah spoke to God: "I sold myself as a slave to save your servant Tobias. I pray you now to help me build the palace."

Immediately a band of angels descended from heaven. They worked all night long. When the sun rose, the palace was finished.

The rich merchant came and gazed in awe. Never had an edifice of such splendor been seen by human eyes.

"Here is your palace," Elijah said. "Keep your word and give me my freedom."

"You are free, my lord," replied the merchant, and he bowed low before God's messenger.

The angels laughed.

God looked down from his seventh heaven and smiled.

The angels spread their wings and, together with Elijah, flew upward into the sky.

Translated by the author and Elizabeth Shub

The Power of Light

During World War II, after the Nazis had bombed and bombed the Warsaw ghetto, a boy and a girl were hiding in one of the ruins—David, fourteen years old, and Rebecca, thirteen.

It was winter and bitter cold outside. For weeks Rebecca had not left the dark, partially collapsed cellar that was their hiding place, but every few days David would go out to search for food. All the stores had been destroyed in the bombing, and David sometimes found stale bread, cans of food, or whatever else had been buried. Making his way through the ruins was dangerous. Sometimes bricks and mortar would fall down, and he could easily lose his way. But if he and Rebecca did not want to die from hunger, he had to take the risk.

That day was one of the coldest. Rebecca sat on the ground wrapped in all the garments she possessed; still, she could not get warm. David had left many hours before, and Rebecca listened in the darkness for the sound of his return, knowing that if he did not come back nothing remained to her but death.

Suddenly she heard heavy breathing and the sound of a bundle being dropped. David had made his way home. Rebecca could not help but cry "David!"

"Rebecca!"

In the darkness they embraced and kissed. Then David said, "Rebecca, I found a treasure."

"What kind of treasure?"

"Cheese, potatoes, dried mushrooms, and a package of candy—and I have another surprise for you."

"What surprise?"

"Later."

Both were too hungry for a long talk. Ravenously they ate the frozen potatoes, the mushrooms, and part of the cheese. They each had one piece of candy. Then Rebecca asked, "What is it now, day or night?"

"I think night has fallen," David replied. He had a wristwatch and kept track of day and night and also of the days of the week and the month. After a while Rebecca asked again, "What is the surprise?"

"Rebecca, today is the first day of Hanukkah, and I found a candle and some matches."

"Hanukkah tonight?"

"Yes."

"Oh, my God!"

"I am going to bless the Hanukkah candle," David said.

He lit a match and there was light. Rebecca and David stared at their hiding place—bricks, pipes, and the uneven ground. He lighted the candle. Rebecca blinked her eyes. For the first time in weeks she really saw David. His hair was matted and his face streaked with dirt, but his eyes shone with joy. In spite of the starvation and persecution David had grown taller, and he seemed older than his age and manly. Young as they both were, they had decided to marry if they could manage to escape from war-ridden Warsaw. As a token of their engagement, David had given Rebecca a shiny groschen he found in his pocket on the day when the building where both of them lived was bombed.

Now David pronounced the benediction over the Hanukkah candle, and Rebecca said, "Amen." They had both lost their families, and they had good reason to be angry with God for sending them so many afflictions, but the light of the candle brought peace into their souls. That glimmer of light, surrounded by so many shadows, seemed to say without words: Evil has not yet taken complete dominion. A spark of hope is still left.

For some time David and Rebecca had thought about escaping from Warsaw. But how? The ghetto was watched by the Nazis day and night. Each step was dangerous. Rebecca kept delaying their departure. It would be easier in the summer, she often said, but David knew that in their predicament they had little chance of lasting until then. Somewhere in the forest there were young men and women called partisans who fought the Nazi invaders. David wanted to reach them. Now, by the light of the Hanukkah candle, Rebecca suddenly felt renewed courage. She said, "David, let's leave."

"When?"

"When you think it's the right time," she answered.

"The right time is now," David said. "I have a plan."

For a long time David explained the details of his plan to Rebecca. It was more than risky. The Nazis had enclosed the ghetto with barbed wire and posted guards armed with machine guns on the surrounding roofs. At night searchlights lit up all possible exits from the destroyed ghetto. But in his wanderings through the ruins, David had found an opening to a sewer which he thought might lead to the other side. David told Rebecca that their chances of remaining alive were slim. They could drown in the dirty water or freeze to death. Also, the sewers were full of hungry rats. But Rebecca agreed to take the risk; to remain in the cellar for the winter would mean certain death.

When the Hanukkah light began to sputter and flicker before going out, David and Rebecca gathered their few belongings. She packed the remaining food in a kerchief, and David took his matches and a piece of lead pipe for a weapon.

In moments of great danger people become unusually courageous. David and Rebecca were soon on their way through the ruins. They came to passages so narrow they had to crawl on hands and knees. But the food they had eaten, and the joy the Hanukkah candle had awakened in them, gave them the courage to continue. After some time David found the entrance to the sewer. Luckily the sewage had frozen, and it seemed that the rats had left because of the extreme cold. From time to time David and Rebecca stopped to rest and to listen. After a while they crawled on, slowly and carefully. Suddenly they stopped in their tracks. From above they could hear the clanging of a trolley car. They had reached the other side of the ghetto. All they needed now was to find a way to get out of the sewer and to leave the city as quickly as possible.

Many miracles seemed to happen that Hanukkah night. Because the Nazis were afraid of enemy planes, they had ordered a complete blackout. Because of the bitter cold, there were fewer Gestapo guards. David and Rebecca managed to leave the sewer and steal out of the city without being caught. At dawn they reached a forest where they were able to rest and have a bite to eat.

Even though the partisans were not very far from Warsaw, it took David and Rebecca a week to reach them. They walked at night and hid during the days—sometimes in granaries and sometimes in barns. Some peasants stealthily helped the partisans and those who were running away from the Nazis. From time to time David and Rebecca got a piece of bread, a few potatoes, a radish, or whatever the peasants could spare. In one village they encountered a Jewish partisan who had come to get food for his group. He belonged to the Haganah, an organization that sent men from Israel to rescue Jewish refugees from the Nazis in occupied Poland. This young man brought David and Rebecca to the other partisans who roamed the forest. It was the last day of Hanukkah, and that evening the partisans lit eight candles. Some of them played dreidel on the stump of an oak tree while others kept watch.

From the day David and Rebecca met the partisans, their life became like a tale in a storybook. They joined more and more refugees who all had but one desire—to settle in the Land of Israel. They did not always travel by train or bus. They walked. They slept in stables, in burned-out houses, and wherever they could hide from the enemy. To reach their destination, they had to cross Czechoslovakia, Hungary, and Yugoslavia. Somewhere at the seashore in Yugoslavia, in the middle of the night, a small boat manned by a Haganah crew waited for them, and all the refugees with their meager belongings were packed into it. This all happened silently and in great secrecy, because the Nazis occupied Yugoslavia.

But their dangers were far from over. Even though it was spring, the sea was stormy and the boat was too small for such a long trip. Nazi planes spied the boat and tried without success to sink it with bombs. They also feared the Nazi submarines which were lurking in the depths. There was nothing the refugees could do besides pray to God, and this time God seemed to hear their prayers, because they managed to land safely.

The Jews of Israel greeted them with a love that made them forget their suffering. They were the first refugees who had reached the Holy Land, and they were offered all the help and comfort that could be given. Rebecca and David found relatives in Israel who accepted them with open arms, and although they had become quite emaciated, they were basically healthy and recovered quickly. After some rest they were sent to a special school where foreigners were taught modern Hebrew. Both David and Rebecca were diligent students. After finishing high school, David was able to enter the academy of engineering in Haifa, and Rebecca, who excelled in languages and literature, studied in Tel

Aviv—but they always met on weekends. When Rebecca was eighteen, she and David were married. They found a small house with a garden in Ramat Gan, a suburb of Tel Aviv.

I know all this because David and Rebecca told me their story on a Hanukkah evening in their house in Ramat Gan about eight years later. The Hanukkah candles were burning, and Rebecca was frying potato pancakes served with applesauce for all of us. David and I were playing dreidel with their little son, Menahem Eliezer, named after both of his grandfathers. David told me that this large wooden dreidel was the same one the partisans had played with on that Hanukkah evening in the forest in Poland. Rebecca said to me, "If it had not been for that little candle David brought to our hiding place, we wouldn't be sitting here today. That glimmer of light awakened in us a hope and strength we didn't know we possessed. We'll give the dreidel to Menahem Eliezer when he is old enough to understand what we went through and how miraculously we were saved."

Growing Up

I

The whole night I kept dreaming. What I dreamed, I couldn't recall later, but they must have been fantastic dreams full of youthful valor, for I awoke feeling strong and cheerful. Everything was pleasurable—washing with the cold water at the sink, putting on the gabardine and fringed garment, even praying from the new prayer book with the large type. At the age of eleven I already understood the meaning of the Hebrew words—"How goodly are thy tents, Jacob, thy tabernacles, O Israel. As for me, in the abundance of thy loving kindness will I come into thy house."

In my fantasy I envisioned the city of Jerusalem and the Holy Temple. The Messiah had come and the Resurrection had taken place. I donned the robes of a priest about to offer a sacrifice. I saw the altar, the table with the shewbread, the ark, the cherubim—all in gold. And beyond stretched Mt. Zion and the mighty city of Jerusalem, with its walls, gates, and flat-roofed houses. King David again occupied his royal throne, and his son Solomon learned the language of lions, tigers, eagles, and the woodcock. The light of the sun was seven times brighter than ever. A day was as long as a year. Everything that had ever been existed once again. All my ancestors, going back to Adam and Eve, had risen from their graves. There was no more death or injustice, only happiness and divine revelation.

At the same time I knew full well that all this was just in my head. Actually, I was in Warsaw, my father was a poor neighborhood rabbi, the Land of Israel belonged to the Turks, the Temple lay in ruins. David, Solomon, Bathsheba, and the Queen of Sheba were all dead. My friend was not a prince of the Kingdom of Israel but Black Feivel, whose father was a porter in Janash's bazaar and whose mother sold crockery in the market-place. Until just a few weeks ago I had attended cheder on Twarda Street, but I had stopped going because my father couldn't afford the two rubles a month tuition.

I rushed through my prayers and breakfast. For weeks Feivel and I had been formulating a secret, outlandish plan. This was the day I was to become a writer and Feivel a printer. I would soon publish my first book—all of sixteen pages long. Its price would be two kopeks. Feivel and I had figured it all out with precision. There were at least fifty thousand boys and girls in Warsaw who liked to read storybooks. If every boy and girl bought my book, we would take in a hundred thousand kopeks, or a thousand rubles. With this sum we could buy our own printing shop and publish additional books.

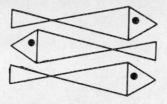

Farrar, Straus & Giroux, Inc.

*takes pleasure
in sending you this copy
for review*

STORIES FOR CHILDREN

Isaac Bashevis Singer

Publication Date: November 5, 1984

Price: $13.95

Two clippings of your review will be greatly appreciated

We would accumulate so much money that we would be able to take a ship to the Land of Israel.

This trip was vital not only for us but for all the Jews in the world. Someone had told me that in Jerusalem there was a cave where cabalists sat seeking a hidden name of God that would bring the Messiah. This name had come in a dream to me, Isaac, son of Pinhos Mena-hem. An angel with six wings had shown himself to me and uttered the name, which consisted of twenty-four letters. The angel had warned me not to utter this name in any other city except Jerusalem. If my lips let it slip in Warsaw, the sky would turn red and the whole world would be consumed by fire.

For a while I had kept this secret to myself, but one day I blurted it out to Feivel. It happened while we were walking on Senators Street to see the courtyard of the Warsaw firemen, its huge fire bell and the tower with the circular balcony where a fireman walked round and round on the lookout for fires. This tower was so tall that the fireman, a fully grown man, looked like a toy from below. When the sunlight struck his brass helmet, it glowed as if it were on fire.

The situation was this—sometime before, Black Feivel had found a silver forty-kopek piece and had confided to me his delight over this windfall. Feivel was a year older than I, but he listened to me as if I were his senior. He loved to hear my stories. Not a day went by that I didn't make up some tale about kings, demons, savages, giants, dwarfs, treasures, villains. I had boasted to him that I was versed in the cabala. Feivel's faith in me was like that of a Hasid in his rabbi. I had told him that I was possessed by the spirit of Joseph della Reina, a saint who centuries before had captured Satan and put him in chains. Had Satan remained so confined, Rabbi Joseph could have brought the Messiah at that time, but he had taken pity on Satan, who had cried and bemoaned his fate and pleaded with Rabbi Joseph for something to eat or drink, or at least for a pinch of snuff. When Rabbi Joseph gave him the snuff, Satan broke into hellish laughter and two sparks shot from his nostrils. Right after that, the chains crumpled from his body and he flew away along with ten thousand demons to Mt. Sair near Sodom, where the dark powers hold sway.

I told Feivel that Rabbi Joseph's soul had entered my body and that I was destined to carry out what he had commenced.

2

The practical plan was this: Black Feivel had found an incredible bargain for a gulden—a case of rubber type, a pad for ink, and a kind of composing stick into which to set the rubber type to form words. There was even a brush with which to pull proofs. Feivel would serve as the typesetter and printer, and I would be the author. Until we launched ourselves on a grander scale, I would get the paper from Father's notebooks, into which he wrote his interpretations of the Talmud. All we lacked was a place to do our work. But after an intense search, Feivel found what he was after—a Hasidic studyhouse that stood empty all day. It was used only in the mornings and evenings for services. I knew full well that what we were doing was fraught with danger. The beadle or someone else was liable to drop in and catch us at it. Nor would it be easy to go around selling these books, but Feivel and I had grown so enthused about the writing, the publishing, and the big profits that we had become bedazzled by it all. Feivel had already set my name as well as the title page of my first book, *Into the Wild Forest.*

This was to be the story of a boy, Haiml, whose mother had died and whose father had been remarried to a wicked woman. The stepmother caused the boy so much grief that he ran away from home and went to live in the woods. He found a hollow in a big tree, a thousand-year-old oak, and he settled there. He lived on berries, mushrooms, and the other foodstuffs found in a forest. Everything would have been fine, but one night Haiml heard the soft moaning of a girl. It soon turned out that this hollow was the entrance to an underground cave where a monster by the name of Mordush lived. This monster had kidnapped a girl, Rebecca, the daughter of a wealthy man, and was trying to force her to become his wife. But Rebecca was engaged already to a young man named Ben Zion, a rabbi's son, and she didn't want to trade him for an old villain who had only one eye in the middle of his forehead and who ate human flesh. Mordush even tried to make a cannibal out of her, but Rebecca swore that she would sooner starve to death than eat the flesh of a human being who had just recently lived, hoped, and loved . . .

I was supposed to plan out this story to its end this very night. Ben Zion had to rescue Rebecca and take revenge upon Mordush, and Haiml also had to receive some sort of reward for uncovering the crime. But somehow my creative juices dried up at this point and I couldn't continue the thread of the story. In the process of writing I had grown so attached to Rebecca that I desired her for myself. Actually, in this story, Haiml (who was really myself) was only eleven years old and Rebecca was sixteen, and this would hardly have been a suitable match, but what prevented me from adding a few years to Haiml? I had to find some way to dispose of Ben Zion. Should he die of longing? Should he become a hermit? Should he forget Rebecca and marry the daughter of some magnate? I had just launched my writing career and already I had fallen into a literary dilemma.

When I went down later to meet Feivel, I envied the boys playing tag, hide-and-seek, cops-and-robbers, and nuts, who didn't have to worry about plots and stories. I had prematurely assumed the duties of a writer and publisher, a printer already awaited my efforts, and I knew somehow that I would bear this burden as long as I lived . . .

3

The plan to publish a book had fallen through. First of all, Feivel had lost several of the rubber characters. Second, I couldn't find the right paper in my father's desk drawer. Third, each time we went to the studyhouse we encountered several youths swaying over open volumes. Fourth, I hadn't found a way of getting rid of Ben Zion and the whole story would have to be rewritten. Feivel said it couldn't be otherwise but that Satan had gotten wind of our plan and had arranged it that I couldn't go to Jerusalem and bring the Messiah.

We roved the streets of Warsaw with the impetus of those against whom all the evils have combined to conspire. My velvet cap was pushed back onto my nape, my red earlocks were drenched with sweat, the wide fringed garment peeped out from my unbuttoned gabardine. Despite my youth, my parents dressed me in rabbinical fashion. They wanted me to become a rabbi. Each time I passed a mirror I grew frightened at my own appearance. My hair was as red as fire, my face and neck an unusual white. A frenzied eagerness shone from my blue eyes. I was fully aware that I was too young to probe into the cabala. I had often heard my father say that those who tried to study the cabala before thirty went crazy or slid into heresy. At times it seemed to me that I *was* actually crazy. Wild notions flashed through my brain, fantasies that I could not bridle. Now I was an emperor and now a sorcerer; now I donned a cap that rendered me invisible, and now I flew to the moon and brought back treasures of gold and diamonds and a potion that rendered me wiser than King Solomon and stronger than Samson. Instead of bringing the Messiah, in my imagination I became the Messiah himself. I blew the ram's horn so that its blast resounded around the world. I mounted a cloud and flew to Jerusalem, followed by hordes of angels ready to do my bidding.

Feivel was taller than I. His earlocks were so black they appeared blue. His eyes were just as black and his skin as swarthy as a gypsy's. Feivel's gabardine had perhaps a hundred rents in it revealing the lining beneath.

His toes stuck out of his boots. Feivel was not only taller but much stronger than I. He always carried a heavy stick torn from a bush, ready to protect me. If some boy called me names, like shlemiel, shmagega, and the like, Feivel would chase after him and beat him. Feivel was both my disciple and my bodyguard. He never grew tired of hearing my outlandish words and weird stories. At times, when I flew into a temper, I abused him and I even gave him a shove or a slap, but he never struck back. At the same time he waged a silent war with me— the rebelliousness of a slave against his master seethed within him . . .

I could talk while we walked, but when Feivel wanted to say something he had to stop. Before he could get anything out he first blinked his eyes a few times. Even as he praised me, he implied that I fabricated things that made no sense whatsoever. He would say, "Since you say it, it's probably so . . ." And his gypsy-like eyes flashed with mockery.

Our plan to publish a book had gone awry, but I had a dozen other plans that day: we would establish a yeshiva for the secret study of the cabala. I would be the rabbi and he, Feivel, would be my beadle. I would become a heretic, and while I rode horseback on the Sabbath he, Feivel, would follow behind and listen to my wisdom. I would seal a covenant with Satan while he would bring the daughter of the Grand Vizier to me in my palace.

"What would you do with her?" Feivel asked me.

"Fly with her to the Mountains of Darkness."

"Oh, the things you say!"

"I fear no one . . ."

We crossed the Praga Bridge and our feet brought us of their own volition to the Terespol railroad station. I was drawn to trains. We went out on the platform. A train was about to depart for somewhere deep in Russia. The black locomotive belched smoke, hissed steam, and gushed hot water like some other-world beast. Its mighty driving wheel dripped oil. A hugh gendarme—tall and broad, his face red and pockmarked, his deep chest hung with medals—paced to and fro issuing orders in Russian.

I said, "This train is going to Siberia."

"Where is Siberia?" Feivel asked.

"In the cold regions. The people there eat bear meat. For six months—the whole winter—it's night."

"When is it the Sabbath?" Feivel asked.

"There are no Jews there. It's never the Sabbath . . ."

"What's beyond Siberia?" Feivel asked.

"That's the end of the world. Giants live there who have three eyes in the center of their bellies."

"What do they eat?"

"Each other . . ."

4

In the evening I came home tired and sweaty. I hadn't eaten any lunch. My boots were dusty. My mother angrily brought me a mirror to show me how grimy my face was. She asked me again and again where I had been all day, but I couldn't tell her. In the living room, the ceiling lamp was lit. We had a guest from Bilgoray, a man who traveled around collecting subscriptions for the author of a holy book. His name was Wolf Bear, but he looked like a goat with his narrow white beard and red-rimmed eyes. When he spoke, he moved his gums like a goat chewing its cud. He wore a patched gabardine and a soiled shirt with a wrinkled collar. He had eaten supper at our house and he conversed in a bleating voice. My older brother, Joshua, also sat at the table, as did my sister, Hindele. Mother gave me what was left over from both the meals I had missed—potatoes with rice, dumplings with soup, a roast chicken liver, and a slice of bread.

I was so hungry that I bolted down whole mouthfuls of food, while at the same time I pricked up my ears to hear Wolf Bear's words. I heard him say, "You become depressed when you travel around, but you get to see the world. Every town presents a different face. The people of Zelechow are just as vicious as in the days when they drove out Rabbi Levi Yitzchok in an ox wagon. In other places they gave me the few gulden without any questions, but in Zelechow they wanted to know who the author was and demanded to see the manuscript. They sat me down and began to argue with me just as if I were the author. They also found errors in the text. The women there all use too much salt and pepper. They serve you a tiny morsel of meat and a lot of mustard. They eat rice pudding with horseradish. Everything there is done with sharpness. I go to a cobbler and ask if he can put half-soles on my boots, so what does he say? 'Why half-soles? Why not full soles? And why do you have to mention your boots? Where else would I put the soles, on your skullcap?' His eyes were as piercing as a hedgehog's. They're all like that there, even the rabbi. You'll laugh, but in no other town do so many thorns grow as in Zelechow.

"How far is Zichlin from Zelechow? Not far. But the people there are as soft as silk. I come to the rabbi and show him the manuscript and he says, 'Thank God, holy books are still being written in this world. Jews don't forget the Torah.' In Zichlin the rabbi's wife herself made up a bed for me. They put honey on the table every day of the week. In Zelechow it's hard to arrange a match. All the girls become old maids. The young men go off to America and are never heard from again. I spent eight days in Zichlin and there was a wedding held each day. What's the sense behind this, eh? On the other hand, why did Sodom become Sodom? One leprous sheep infects the whole flock. It starts with one vicious person and it spreads to all. How did Warsaw become Warsaw? First they built one house, then another, and gradually a city emerged. Everything grows. Even stones grow."

"Stones don't grow, Reb Wolf Bear," my brother, Joshua, interjected.

"No? Well, so be it. There is a town in Volhynia called Maciejow where the sand is so deep that, when you fall into it, you can't get out. You sink down slowly. They say that if you put your ear to the sand, you can hear the cries of those trapped below. How can this be? How long can a person live underground, unless it's a doorway to Gehenna? On the road, I met a man from the Land of Israel. He spoke Hebrew. Aramaic, too. He has seen the whole world. At first he said that he didn't know any Yiddish, but as we got to talking I saw that he did know it. He had visited Shushan, the old capital of Persia. He had been to Mt. Ararat and seen Noah's ark. It rests on the tip of the mountain and eagles soar above it. You try to reach it because it seems so close, but when you get to the top, there is no ark. And that's how it is with all things. Illusion or who knows what. In what connection do I say this, eh? Yes, now I remember. The man was riding in the desert and he came to a place that was the gateway to Gehenna. You could hear the cries of the sinners. The earth is hollow there. There are caves underneath and cities and who knows what else."

"The earth isn't hollow," my brother, Joshua, said.

"Why not? Everything is possible. If you sit in one spot you think it's the same all over, but when you travel, you get to see all kinds of wonders. I've been to Wieliczka. They dig for salt there. There is enough salt for the whole world. They made houses out of salt, beds, even a wardrobe. In Czestochowa again, a statue of the Virgin Mary stands on a mountain. She is completely of gold and her eyes are diamonds. One time a man stole one of the eyes and replaced it with a glass one. He was caught in the act and sentenced to hard labor."

"Yes, I know, Macuch," I piped up.

"Eh? How do you know?" Reb Wolf Bear asked me.

"It was in the paper," I replied.

"Oh so? In olden times children knew nothing. Today they know everything. In Lublin there was a wonder child, a Yenuka, and at the age of three he sprouted a beard. At five he gave a sermon in the synagogue and scholars came to debate with him. He was married at seven. When he reached nine, his beard turned as white as snow. He died at ten, an old man."

"Did you see this Yenuka with your own eyes?" Joshua asked.

"See him? No. But the whole world knows about it."

My father arched the brows over his blue eyes and his red beard glowed like gold. "Joshua, don't contradict!"

"It isn't true," Joshua said. He turned pale and his blue eyes reflected scorn.

"Have you been everywhere and do you know the truth?" Father asked. "The world is full of wonders. We only know what goes on down here. Only God the Almighty knows what happens in the other spheres."

I didn't know the reason myself, but an urge to cry came over me. I barely contained my tears. I went to my parents' bedroom and lay down on the bed in the dark. I suddenly realized—without knowing how myself—that I was too young to write a book. My brother, Joshua, often mentioned the word "literature." He told Mother that each nation creates its own literature. That which Reb Wolf Bear now related at the table has to be literature, I thought. But how can a beggar from a small village create literature?

It was all one great mystery. I wasn't asleep yet, but my brain had already begun to weave a dream. Each time I tried to grasp it, its threads dissolved. I lay in bed, and at the same time I rode that train to Siberia. I heard the clacking of the wheels, the whistle of the locomotive. I heard my mother open the door and mumble, "Dozed off, the poor boy."

A few minutes later, I really fell asleep. The fantastic dreams started, the wild adventures. All the fantasies of the day turned into nocturnal visions. That night I dreamed that I was Rabbi Joseph della Reina. I uttered God's name and the daughter of the Grand Vizier came flying to me. She looked like a neighbor's daughter,

Estherel, who lived in our house on the third floor. In the dream, I asked Estherel, "What shall we do?"

And she replied, "I'll become your bride."

I awoke frightened, drenched in sweat. I had often heard my brother and my sister talk of love. Suddenly it became clear to me that I loved Estherel. I had heard that novels were written about love and it occurred to me to name the girl in my book Estherel and that I could become Ben Zion, who saved her from the cannibal and married her. I decided that when I grew up I would write not just a storybook but a whole novel about Estherel and myself.

Translated by Joseph Singer

The Lantuch

In the summers, my Aunt Yentl liked to tell stories
on the Sabbath after the main meal, when my Uncle
Joseph lay down for a nap. My aunt would take a seat on
the bench in front of the house, and the cat, Dvosha,
would join her. On the Sabbaths the cat would be given
the remnants of the Sabbath meal—scraps of meat and
fish. Dvosha would plant herself at my aunt's feet; she
liked to hear my aunt tell stories. From the way she
cocked her ears and narrowed her eyes, green as goose-
berries, it was apparent she understood what my aunt
was saying.

For the Sabbath, my aunt wore a dress sewn with
arabesques and a bonnet with glass beads, festooned with
green, red, and blue ribbons. Presently, my mother came
out, and two of our female neighbors, Riva and Sheindel.
I was the last to emerge and I took a seat on a footstool.
Besides the fact that I liked to listen to my Aunt Yentl's

stories, sooner or later I would get from her the Sabbath fruit—an apple, a pear, plums. Sometimes she would give me a Sabbath cookie baked with cinnamon and raisins. She always said the same thing when she gave it to me, "It'll give you the strength to study."

This time the conversation centered on a house demon or a sprite called a lantuch. Aunt Yentl liked to talk about spirits, demons, and hobgoblins, and I heard her say, "A lantuch? Yes, there is such a spirit as a lantuch. These days people don't believe in such things, but in my time they knew that everything can't be explained away with reason. The world is full of secrets. A lantuch is an imp, but he's not malicious. He causes no harm. On the contrary, he tries to help the members of the household all he can. He is like a part of the family. Usually he is invisible, but it sometimes happens that you can see him. Where do they live? Sometimes in a cellar, sometimes in a woodshed, sometimes behind the stove along with the cricket. Lantuchs love crickets. They bring them food and they understand their language."

"Aunt Yentl, when I grow up I'll learn the language of crickets," I piped up.

Aunt Yentl smiled with every wrinkle in her face. "My child, this isn't a language that can be learned. Only King Solomon knew the language of beasts. He could talk with the lions, the bears, the wolves, and with all the birds, too. But let's get back to the lantuch. There was a lantuch at my parents' house. In the summers he lived in the woodshed, and in the winters behind the stove. We didn't see him, but sometimes we heard him. One time when my sister Keila sneezed, he said, 'God bless you!' We all heard it. The lantuch loved us all, but he loved my sister Keila most of all. When Keila married and went to live in Lublin with her in-laws—I was only a girl of eight then —the lantuch came to her on her last night home to say goodbye. In the middle of the night Keila heard a rustle and the door opened by itself.

"The lantuch came up to Keila's bed and said in rhyme:

> *Wash basin,*
> *soak basin,*
> *meat cleaver,*
> *kugel-eater,*
> *I'll fret*
> *And you won't forget.*

"Keila became so frightened that she lost her tongue. He kissed her forehead, and soon after he left. For a long time Keila lay there in a daze, then she lit a candle. Keila was very fond of almond cake. When my mother, may she rest in peace, baked almond cake for Simchas Torah or Purim, Keila would nibble half of it. Anyway, she lit the candle and on her blanket lay an almond cake still warm from the oven. She started to cry and we all came running in to her. I saw the almond cake with my own eyes. Where the lantuch got it from, I haven't the slightest idea. Maybe some housewife happened to bake almond cakes and he pinched one, or maybe they know how to bake them themselves. Keila didn't eat the cake, but she put it away some place, and it grew hard as a stone.

"In our town of Janów there was a teacher who had a sick wife and an only daughter who had been blind from birth. All of a sudden the teacher died and the two women were left all alone and helpless. There was talk in town of putting the two women in the poorhouse, but who wants to go to a poorhouse? The paupers there lay on straw pallets right on the bare floor and the food wasn't good either. When the attendant came to take the mother and daughter to the poorhouse, they both began to lament: 'Rather than rot away in the poorhouse we'd sooner die!'

"You can't force anyone to go to the poorhouse. The attendant thought, The husband probably left them a few gulden, and so long as they still have some bread, they'll put on airs. When they get hungry enough, they'll thank God there is such a place as the poorhouse.

"Days went by and weeks, and the mother and daughter still didn't give in. The town grew curious—what were they up to? The mother was bedridden and the daughter blind. There are blind people who can get around, but the teacher's daughter—Tzirel was her name —never strayed beyond her own courtyard. I can see her now: reddish hair, a glowing face, trim limbs. Her eyes were blue and appeared healthy but she couldn't see a thing. People began to wonder if maybe the mother and daughter had more money than had been assumed, but that couldn't be. First of all, the teacher had been poor, and second, neither the mother nor the daughter ever left the house. Neither of them was ever seen in any store. Then where did they get the food, even if they did have the money?

"My dear people, there was a lantuch in their house, and when he saw that the breadwinner was gone and the women had been left penniless and without a stitch to their backs, he assumed the burden himself. You're laughing? It's nothing to laugh at. He brought them everything they needed—bread, sugar, herring. He did it all at night. One time a youth walked by their house in the middle of the night and he heard wood being chopped in the yard. He grew suspicious. Who would be chopping wood in the middle of the night? He opened the gate to the courtyard and saw an ax swinging and chips flying, but there was no one there. It was the lantuch chopping wood for the winter. The next day, when the youth revealed what he had seen, people laughed at him. 'You probably dreamed it,' they said. But it was true.

"A few weeks later, a shipping agent came back from Lublin, also in the middle of the night. He walked past a well and he saw the rope descending into the water and a pailful of water coming up. But there was no one around. He promptly realized that this was the work of *that* band —the creatures of the night. But the shipping agent— Meir David was his name—was a strong person and not easily frightened. He took hold of his ritual fringes, quietly recited 'Hear, O Israel,' and stopped to see what would happen next. After the unseen one had drawn one pail of water, he drew a second, and then the two pails began to be borne along as if an invisible water carrier was carrying them on a yoke. Meir David followed the pails of water to where the widow and her blind daughter lived. The next day the shipping agent went to the rabbi and told him what his eyes had seen. This Meir

David was an honest man and not one to make up things. A fuss erupted in town. The rabbi summoned the widow and her daughter to him, but the widow was too sick to walk. She couldn't talk either. Soon after, she died.

"The blind daughter said to the rabbi, 'Someone provides for us, but who it is I do not know. It must be an angel from heaven.'

"No, it wasn't any angel but the lantuch. After the mother died, the daughter sold the house and went to live with relatives in Galicia."

"The lantuch didn't go along?" our neighbor Riva asked.

"Who knows? As a rule, they don't stir from the house," Aunt Yentl said.

"Do they live forever?" Sheindel asked.

"No one lives forever," Aunt Yentl replied.

It grew silent. I looked at the cat; she had fallen asleep.

Aunt Yentl glanced at me. "I'll get you the Sabbath fruit now. If a young man wants to study the Torah, he must keep up his strength."

And she brought me a Sabbath cookie and three plums.

Translated by Joseph Singer

Utzel &
His Daughter, Poverty

Once there was a man named Utzel. He was very poor and even more lazy. Whenever anyone wanted to give him a job to do, his answer was always the same: "Not today."

"Why not today?" he was asked. And he always replied, "Why not tomorrow?"

Utzel lived in a cottage that had been built by his great-grandfather. The thatched roof needed mending, and although the holes let the rain in, they did not let the smoke from the stove out. Toadstools grew on the crooked walls and the floor had rotted away. There had been a time when mice lived there, but now there weren't any because there was nothing for them to eat. Utzel's wife had starved to death, but before she died she had given birth to a baby girl. The name Utzel gave his daughter was very fitting. He called her Poverty.

Utzel loved to sleep and each night he went to bed

with the chickens. In the morning he would complain that he was tired from so much sleeping and so he went to sleep again. When he was not sleeping, he lay on his broken-down cot, yawning and complaining. He would say to his daughter, "Other people are lucky. They have money without working. I am cursed."

Utzel was a small man, but as his daughter, Poverty, grew, she spread out in all directions. She was tall, broad, and heavy. At fifteen she had to lower her head to get through the doorway. Her feet were the size of a man's and puffy with fat. The villagers maintained that the lazier Utzel got, the more Poverty grew.

Utzel loved nobody, was jealous of everybody. He even spoke with envy of cats, dogs, rabbits, and all creatures who didn't have to work for a living. Yes, Utzel hated everybody and everything, but he adored his daughter. He daydreamed that a rich young man would fall in love with her, marry her, and provide for his wife and his father-in-law. But not a young man in the village showed the slightest interest in Poverty. When her father reproached the girl for not making friends and not going out with young men, Poverty would say, "How can I go out in rags and bare feet?"

One day Utzel learned that a certain charitable society in the village loaned poor people money, which they could pay back in small sums over a long period. Lazy as he was, he made a great effort—got up, dressed, and went to the office of the society. "I would like to borrow five gulden," he said to the official in charge.

"What do you intend to do with the money?" he was asked. "We lend money only for useful purposes."

"I want to have a pair of shoes made for my daughter," Utzel explained. "If Poverty has shoes, she will go out with the young people of the village and some wealthy young man will surely fall in love with her. When they get married, I will be able to pay back the five gulden."

The official thought it over. The chances of anyone falling in love with Poverty were very small. Utzel, however, looked so miserable that the official decided to give him the loan. He asked Utzel to sign a promissory note and gave him five gulden.

Utzel had tried to order a pair of shoes for his daughter a few months before. Sandler the shoemaker had gone so far as to take Poverty's measurements, but the shoemaker had wanted his money in advance. From the charitable society Utzel went directly to the shoemaker and asked whether he still had Poverty's measurements.

"And supposing I do?" Sandler replied. "My price is five gulden and I still want my money in advance."

Utzel took out the five gulden and handed them to Sandler. The shoemaker opened a drawer and after some searching brought out the order for Poverty's shoes. He promised to deliver the new shoes in a week, on Friday.

Utzel, who wanted to surprise his daughter, did not tell her about the shoes. The following Friday, as he lay on his cot yawning and complaining, there was a knock on the door and Sandler came in carrying the new shoes. When Poverty saw the shoemaker with a pair of shiny new shoes in his hand, she cried out in joy. The shoemaker handed her the shoes and told her to try them on. But, alas, she could not get them on her puffy feet. In the months since the measurements had been taken, Poverty's feet had become even larger than they were before. Now the girl cried out in grief.

Utzel looked on in consternation. "How is it possible?" he asked. "I thought her feet stopped growing long ago."

For a while Sandler, too, stood there puzzled. Then he inquired, "Tell me, Utzel, where did you get the five gulden?" Utzel explained that he had borrowed the money from the charitable loan society and had given them a promissory note in return.

"So now you have a debt," exclaimed Sandler. "That makes you even poorer than you were a few months ago. Then you had nothing, but today you have five gulden less than nothing. And since you have grown poorer, Poverty has grown bigger, and naturally her feet have grown with her. That is why the shoes don't fit. It is all clear to me now."

"What are we going to do?" Utzel asked in despair.

"There is only one way out for you," Sandler said. "Go to work. From borrowing one gets poorer and from work one gets richer. When you and your daughter work, she will have shoes that fit."

The idea of working did not appeal to either of them, but it was even worse to have new shoes and go around barefoot. Utzel and Poverty both decided that immediately after the Sabbath they would look for work.

Utzel got a job as a water carrier. Poverty became a maid. For the first time in their lives, they worked diligently. They were kept so busy that they did not even think of the new shoes, until one Sabbath morning Poverty decided she'd try them on again. Lo and behold, her feet slipped easily into them. The new shoes fit.

At last Utzel and Poverty understood that all a man possesses he gains through work, and not by lying in bed and being idle. Even animals were industrious. Bees make honey, spiders spin webs, birds build nests, moles dig holes in the earth, squirrels store food for the winter. Before long Utzel got a better job. He rebuilt his house and bought some furniture. Poverty lost more weight. She had new clothes made and dressed prettily like the other girls of the village. Her looks improved, too, and a young man began to court her. His name was Mahir and he was the son of a wealthy merchant. Utzel's dream of a rich son-in-law came true, but by then he no longer needed to be taken care of.

Love for his daughter had saved Utzel. In his later years he became so respected he was elected a warden of that same charitable loan society from which he had borrowed five gulden.

On the wall of his office there hung the string with which Sandler had once measured Poverty's feet, and above it the framed motto: *Whatever you can do today, don't put off till tomorrow.*

Translated by the author and Elizabeth Shub

The Squire

Five Hanukkah lights burned in the Hanukkah lamp in the Trisker Hasidic studyhouse, as well as the large candle called the beadle. In the oven, potatoes were roasting and their smell tickled everyone's nostrils. Old Reb Berish sneezed and the boys around him wished him good health.

He wiped his nose with a large handkerchief and said, "Some people think that in olden times miracles were more frequent than today. That is not true. The truth is that miracles were rare in all times. If too many miracles occurred, people would rely on them too much. Free choice would cease. The Powers on High want men to do things, make an effort, not to be lazy. But there are cases where only a miracle can save a man.

"Something like this happened when I was a boy here in Bilgoray about eighty years ago—and perhaps even a little longer. Our village was much smaller than it is today. Where Zamość Street is now there was still forest. Lublin Street was only an alley. Where we are sitting now there was a pasture for cows. There lived then in Bilgoray a wealthy young man by the name of Falik, a talmudic scholar. He was the owner of a dry-goods store. He had other businesses as well. His wife, Sarah, came from Lublin, from a fine family. Suddenly the couple's good luck changed. Whether it was a punishment for some transgression or just a decree from heaven, I don't know. First, the store burned down. There was no fire insurance in those years. Then Sarah became ill. There was no doctor or druggist in Bilgoray. There were only three remedies for people to apply—leeches, cups, and bleeding. If these three didn't help, nothing more could be done. Sarah died and left three orphans, a boy by the name of Mannes and two younger girls, Pessele and Etele.

"Not long after Sarah's death, Falik himself became mortally sick. He grew pale and emaciated, and after a while he became bedridden and it seemed he would never recover. Lippe the healer recommended chicken broth, barley soup, and goat milk. Nothing changed. First of all, Falik lost his appetite, and second, he was left without any income. Nowadays people are selfish, they don't care about others, but in former times people helped one another when in need. They tried to send bread to Falik, and meat, butter, and cheese, but he refused to accept charity. The community leader came to him and offered him help secretly, so that no one would know, but Falik said, 'I would know.'

"It happened the first night of Hanukkah. As always

there was a great deal of snow, frost, blizzards. Things had reached such a stage in Falik's house that finally there was not even a loaf of bread. In better times Falik had possessed a number of silver objects—candlesticks, a spice box, a Passover plate—but Mannes, the oldest child, had sold them all. There was one precious article still in the house, an antique Hanukkah lamp made by some ancient silversmith. There lived a usurer in town who would pay a pittance for the most costly objects. Mannes wanted to sell him the Hanukkah lamp, too, but Falik said to his son, 'Wait until after Hanukkah.' There were a few pennies left in the house, but instead of buying bread Mannes bought oil and wicks for the Hanukkah lights. The girls complained that they were hungry, and Mannes said to them, 'Let's imagine that it is Yom Kippur.' I know this story, because Mannes told it to me years later.

"Since Falik could not leave his bed anymore, Mannes brought the lamp to his father on the first night of Hanukkah and Falik made the proper benedictions and lit the first light. He also hummed the song 'Rock of Ages,' and kissed his children. Then Mannes took the Hanukkah lamp to the living room and put it on the windowsill, according to the law. The children sat at the table hungry, without having eaten supper. It was cold in the house. Only a year before, Falik had given his children Hanukkah money to play dreidel and Sarah had fried pancakes for the family. Now everything was bathed in gloom. The children looked at each other with eyes that seemed to ask, 'From whence cometh my help?'

"Suddenly someone knocked at the door. 'Who could

this be?' Mannes asked himself. 'Probably someone with a gift.' His father had warned him again and again not to accept any gifts. Mannes decided not to open the door this time, so as to avoid arguing with the good people. But the knocking at the door did not stop. After a while Mannes went to the door, ready to say, 'Father told me not to accept anything.' When he opened it he saw a squire—tall, broad-shouldered, in a long fur coat with tails down to his ankles and a fur hat sprinkled with snow. Mannes became so frightened that he lost his tongue. It almost never happened that a squire came into a Jewish house, especially in the evening. In my day, when a squire visited a village, he came in a carriage harnessed to eight horses, and his valets rode in front to clear a way for him. Often they blew trumpets to announce that the great lord was coming. Bilgoray still belonged to Count Zamojski, who was as rich and mighty as a king. To Mannes the squire said, 'I passed by in my sleigh and I saw a little light in a lamp the likes of which I had never seen in all my life—with goblets, flowers, a lion, a deer, a leopard, an eagle, all beautifully done. Why did you kindle only one light if there are eight holders? Is this some Jewish holiday? And where are your parents?' Mannes knew Polish and how to speak to an important man. He said, 'Come in, your excellency. It is for us a great honor.'

"The squire entered the living room and for a long while he stared at the Hanukkah lamp. He began to question Mannes, and the boy told him the story of Hanukkah—how the Jews fought the Greeks in ancient times in the Land of Israel. He also told him of the miracle that had happened with the oil for lighting the menorah in the temple: how after the war there was barely enough oil left to light the menorah for one day, but a miracle happened and the oil was sufficient for eight days. Then the squire saw a dreidel on the table and asked, 'What is this?'

"Although the children had no money with which to play, they had put a dreidel there just to remember former times. Mannes explained to the squire that Hanukkah is the only holiday when children are allowed to play games. He told him the rules of dreidel. The squire asked, 'Could I play with you? My driver will wait with the sleigh. It's cold outside, but my horses are covered with blankets and the driver has a fur jacket.'

" 'Your excellency,' Mannes said, 'my father is sick. We have no mother and we don't have a penny to our name.' The squire said, 'I intend to offer you a thousand gulden for your magnificent lamp, but I don't have the whole sum with me, so I will give you five hundred gulden in advance and with this money you can play.' As he said this, he took a large bag of gold coins from his coat and threw it on the table. The children were so astounded that they forgot their hunger. The game began and the greatest unbeliever could have seen that the whole event was a wonder from heaven. The children kept winning and the squire kept losing. In one hour the squire lost all his gold and the children won every coin. Then the squire cried out, 'Lost is lost. My driver and my horses must be cold. Good night, happy Hanukkah, and don't worry about your father. With God's help he will soon recover.'

"Only after the squire had left did the children realize what had happened to them. Not only had they gotten five hundred gulden as an advance on the lamp, but the squire had lost additional money. Half the table was covered with coins. The girls, Pessele and Etele, burst out crying. Mannes ran outside to see if the squire, the sleigh, the horses and driver were still there, but they had all vanished without leaving any tracks in the snow. Usually horses harnessed to a sleigh have bells on their necks and one can hear the jingling from far away, but the night was quiet. I will make it short. The moment the squire left, Falik opened his eyes. He had gone to sleep near to death and he woke up a healthy man. Nothing but a miracle could have saved him, and so the miracle occurred."

"Who was the squire? The prophet Elijah?" the boys asked.

"Who knows? He certainly was not a Polish squire."

"Did he ever come to get the lamp?"

"Not as long as I was in Bilgoray," the old man replied.

"If he had been the prophet Elijah, he would have kept his promise," one of the boys remarked.

Old Reb Berish did not answer immediately. He pulled his beard and pondered. Then he said, "They have a lot of time in heaven. He might have come to their children's children or to their grandchildren. I married and moved to another village. As far as I know, the Hanukkah lamp remained with Falik and his children as long as they lived. Some rabbi said that when God works a miracle, He often does it in such a way that it should appear natural. There were some unbelievers in Bilgoray and they said that it was a real squire, a rich spendthrift who was in a mood to squander his money. Those who deny God always try to explain all wonders as normal events or as coincidences—I'm afraid the potatoes are already burning," he added.

Old Reb Berish opened the door of the oven and with his bare fingers began to pull out half-burned potatoes from the glowing coals.

Ole & Trufa

The forest was large and thickly overgrown with all kinds of leaf-bearing trees. It was in the month of November. Usually it's cold this time of year and it even happens that it snows, but this November was relatively warm. The nights were cool and windy, but as soon as the sun came out in the mornings, it turned warm. You might have thought it was summer except that the whole forest was strewn with fallen leaves—some yellow as saffron, some red as wine, some the color of gold, and some of mixed color. The leaves had been torn down by the rain, by the wind, some by day, some at night, and they now formed a deep carpet over the forest floor. Although their juices had run dry, the leaves still exuded a pleasant aroma. The sun shone down on them through the living branches, and worms and flies which had somehow survived the autumn storms crawled over them. The space beneath the leaves provided hiding places for crickets, field mice, and many other creatures who sought protection in the earth. The birds that don't migrate to warmer climates in the winter but stay behind perched on the bare tree limbs. Among them were sparrows—tiny birds, but endowed with much courage and the experience accumulated through thousands of generations. They hopped, twittered, and searched for the food the forest offered this time of year. Many, many insects and worms had perished in recent weeks, but no one mourned their loss. God's creatures know that death is merely a phase of life. With the coming of spring, the forest would again fill with grasses, green leaves, blossoms, and flowers. The migrating birds would return from far-off lands and locate their abandoned nests. Even if the wind or the rain had disturbed a nest, it could be easily repaired.

On the tip of a tree which had lost all its other leaves, two still remained. One leaf was named Ole and the other, Trufa. Ole and Trufa both hung from one twig. Since they were at the very tip of the tree they received lots of sunlight. For some reason unknown to Ole or Trufa, they had survived all the rains, all the cold nights and winds, and still clung to the tip of the twig. Who knows the reason one leaf falls and another remains? But Ole and Trufa believed the answer lay in the great love they bore each other. Ole was slightly bigger than Trufa and a few days older, but Trufa was prettier and more delicate. One leaf can do little for another when the wind blows, the rain pours, or the hail begins to fall. It even happens in summer that a leaf is torn loose—come autumn and winter nothing can be done. Still, Ole encouraged Trufa at every opportunity. During the worst storms, when the thunder clapped, the lightning flashed, and the wind tore off not only leaves but even whole branches, Ole pleaded with Trufa, "Hang on, Trufa! Hang on with all your might!"

At times during cold and stormy nights, Trufa would complain, "My time has come, Ole, but you hang on!"

"What for?" Ole asked. "Without you, my life is senseless. If you fall, I'll fall with you."

"No, Ole, don't do it! So long as a leaf can stay up it mustn't let go . . ."

"It all depends if you stay with me," Ole replied. "By day I look at you and admire your beauty. At night I sense your fragrance. Be the only leaf on a tree? No, never!"

"Ole, your words are so sweet but they're not true," Trufa said. "You know very well that I'm no longer pretty. Look how wrinkled I am! All my juices have dried out and I'm ashamed before the birds. They look at me with such pity. At times it seems to me they're laughing at how shriveled I've become. I've lost everything, but one thing is still left me—my love for you."

"Isn't that enough? Of all our powers love is the highest, the finest," Ole said. "So long as we love each other we remain here, and no wind, rain, or storm can destroy us. I'll tell you something, Trufa—I never loved you as much as I love you now."

"Why, Ole? Why? I'm all yellow."

"Who says green is pretty and yellow is not? All colors are equally handsome."

And just as Ole spoke these words, that which Trufa

had feared all these months happened—a wind came up and tore Ole loose from the twig. Trufa began to tremble and flutter until it seemed that she, too, would soon be torn away, but she held fast. She saw Ole fall and sway in the air, and she called to him in leafy language, "Ole! Come back! Ole! Ole!"

But before she could even finish Ole vanished from sight. He blended in with the other leaves on the ground and Trufa was left all alone on the tree.

So long as it was still day, Trufa managed somehow to endure her grief. But when it grew dark and cold and a piercing rain began to fall, she sank into despair. Somehow she felt that the blame for all the leafy misfortunes lay with the tree, the trunk with all its mighty limbs. Leaves fell but the trunk stood tall, thick, and firmly rooted in the ground. No wind, rain, or hail could upset it. What did it matter to a tree which probably lived forever what became of a leaf? To Trufa, the trunk was a kind of God. It covered itself with leaves for a few months, then it shook them off. It nourished them with its sap for as long as it pleased, then it let them die of thirst. Trufa pleaded with the tree to give her back her Ole and to make it summer again, but the tree didn't heed, or refused to heed, her prayers . . .

Trufa didn't think a night could be so long as this one —so dark, so frosty. She spoke to Ole and hoped for an answer, but Ole was silent and gave no sign of his presence.

Trufa said to the tree, "Since you've taken Ole from me, take me, too."

But the tree didn't acknowledge even this prayer.

After a while, Trufa dozed off. This wasn't sleep but a strange languor. Trufa awoke and to her amazement found that she was no longer hanging on the tree. The wind had blown her down while she was asleep. This was different from the way she used to feel when she awoke on the tree with the sunrise. All her fears and anxieties had now vanished. The awakening also brought with it an awareness she had never felt before. She knew now that she wasn't just a leaf that depended on every whim of the wind, but that she was a part of the universe. She no longer was small or weak or transient, but a part of eternity. Through some mysterious force, Trufa understood the miracle of her molecules, atoms, protons, and electrons—the enormous energy she represented and the divine plan of which she was a part. Next to her lay Ole and they greeted each other with a love they hadn't been aware of before. This wasn't a love that depended on chance or caprice, but a love as mighty and eternal as the universe itself. That which they had feared all the days and nights between April and November turned out to be not death but redemption. A breeze came and lifted Ole and Trufa in the air, and they soared with the bliss known only by those who have freed themselves and have joined with eternity.

Translated by Joseph Singer

Dalfunka, Where the Rich Live Forever

It happened in Chelm, a city of fools. Where else could it have happened? On a winter morning in the community house Gronam Ox, the wisest man of Chelm, and his five sages, Dopey Lekisch, Zeinvel Ninny, Treitel Fool, Sender Donkey, and Shmendrick Numskull sat at a long table. All six looked tired and had red eyes from lack of sleep. For seven days and nights they had been thinking about a problem which they could not solve. The treasury of the city of Chelm was empty. For many weeks Gronam Ox and his sages had not received their salaries.

Even though it was not Hanukkah, Shlemiel the beadle sat at the other end of the table playing dreidel by himself. Suddenly the door opened and Zalman Typpish entered. He was the richest man in Chelm. He had a long white beard. When they saw Zalman Typpish, Gronam and the sages looked up in surprise. Zalman Typpish never paid a visit to the community house because they levied high taxes on him.

"Good morning, Gronam Ox. Good morning, sages," Zalman Typpish greeted them solemnly.

"A good morning to you, Zalman Typpish," all of them answered in accord. "What made you pay such an early visit?"

"I came to ask your advice," Zalman Typpish said. "If it is good I will pay the treasury two thousand gold pieces."

"What sort of advice?" Gronam Ox asked.

"You all know I have just turned eighty. You also know that no man lives forever. But I, Zalman Typpish, wish to live forever. I would like forever to eat blintzes with sour cream, drink tea with jam, coffee with chicory, forever smoke my long pipe. To make it short, I want to live forever."

"Live forever!" exclaimed Gronam Ox and his five sages. "How is this possible?"

"This is the reason I came to you," Zalman said. "If you will tell me how to live forever, you will get what I just promised." Saying these words, Zalman Typpish took out a bag filled with gold coins and poured them on the table.

When Gronam and his sages saw the pile of gold, they began to murmur. Zalman Typpish was known as a miser. Gronam Ox immediately put his index finger on his forehead in order to think hard. The other sages did the same thing. After long thought, Gronam Ox said, "You know well that Chelm is the wisest city in the world and I, Gronam Ox, am the wisest man in Chelm, which means that I am the wisest man in the universe. But just the same, I cannot give you the kind of advice you desire. No man can live forever. Even I, Gronam Ox, won't live forever."

"Even Methuselah did not live forever," Dopey Lekisch chimed in.

"Even King Solomon did not live forever," Zeinvel Ninny added.

"Even our rabbi is not going to live forever," Treitel Fool pronounced.

"Even a lion does not live forever," Sender Donkey remarked.

"Even an elephant does not live forever," Shmendrick Numskull said.

"All this is true, but I, Zalman Typpish, decided that I must live forever. If you won't advise me how to do it, you won't get a penny."

Gronam Ox was about to say that he was sorry, but at that moment Shlemiel the beadle stuck out his tongue and placed his thumb on the tip of his nose as a sign that he wanted to speak.

"What do you want to say, Shlemiel?" Gronam Ox asked.

"I found a way," Shlemiel said.

"You found a way?" Gronam Ox asked in astonishment.

"Yes, my lord. The thing is like this. Last week I had nothing to do all day long and I started to look over the records of our Chelm suburbs. Among others I glanced through the records of our suburb Dalfunka."

"Dalfunka, where all the paupers and beggars of Chelm live?" Gronam Ox asked.

"Yes, Dalfunka," Shlemiel said. "As you know, we have in our books the names of all those who are born and died in the last three hundred years. When I went through the list of all who died in Dalfunka, I realized that no rich man ever died there. This means that the rich in Dalfunka live forever. My advice, therefore, is that Zalman Typpish should buy a house in Dalfunka, settle there, and never die. As simple as that."

Gronam Ox opened his mouth and stared agape. "Shlemiel, you gave the right advice. But how is this possible? Are you cleverer than I am?"

"No one is cleverer than you, Gronam Ox," the five sages sang out in chorus.

"My only explanation is that since you have been sitting so many years near us, a part of our wisdom spilled over on you," said Gronam Ox.

"True," the five sages agreed.

Dopey Lekisch added, "Even a horse would become wise if it stayed with us so long."

"Zalman, you got good advice. Now give us the two thousand gold coins," Gronam Ox suggested.

"Before I give you so much money, I must be sure that the advice is right," Zalman Typpish answered. "I will give you an advance of ten gold coins now, and after I have moved to Dalfunka and have lived forever, I will pay the balance."

"We cannot wait that long," Gronam Ox protested. "We need the payment right now."

"Either take the ten gold coins or you will receive nothing," Zalman Typpish insisted.

For a long while Gronam Ox and his sages haggled

with Zalman Typpish, but as always Zalman Typpish prevailed. He gave Gronam Ox the ten gold coins and left.

For five years Zalman Typpish lived in Dalfunka, ate blintzes with sour cream, drank tea with jam, coffee with chicory, smoked his long pipe, and did not die. Gronam Ox often asked for the balance, but Zalman Typpish always had the same answer: "First let me live forever and then I will pay." It seemed that Zalman Typpish was right in not paying beforehand, because one day in the sixth year he became sick and died.

When Gronam Ox heard the bad news he immediately called for the sages and they pondered seven days and seven nights why Zalman Typpish had died. Again Shlemiel found the explanation. For five years Zalman did no business because one could not earn any money in Dalfunka. Instead, he spent a fortune on such luxuries as sour cream, coffee, tobacco, chickory. He most probably became poor and so he died like all the other poor people. "To live forever in Dalfunka one must be as rich as Rothschild," Shlemiel said.

Gronam Ox and the five sages again admired Shlemiel's sharp mind. Gronam Ox promptly dispatched letters to the Rothschilds inviting them to come speedily to Dalfunka and begin to live forever. But months passed and the Rothschilds did not arrive. This time Gronam Ox discovered the reason himself. He said, "The rich are so stingy that they would rather die cheaply in London, Paris, and Vienna than live forever in Dalfunka at a higher cost."

"So what should we do now?" the sages asked.

"We must get rich ourselves."

"How?" the sages asked.

"Of course, by levying taxes on the paupers of Chelm," Gronam Ox replied.

Shlemiel made the usual sign that he wanted to speak. He wanted to say that, according to his latest figures, even the Rothschilds were not rich enough to live forever in Dalfunka, but Gronam Ox said, "Shlemiel, everything is crystal clear. We don't need your advice anymore. Keep quiet."

"Be silent," Dopey Lekisch chimed in.

"You are only a beadle, not a sage," Zeinvel Ninny shouted.

"Not even half a sage," Treitel Fool screamed.

"And you will never live forever," Sender Donkey hollered.

"Not even a half of forever," Shmendrick Numskull yelled.

Since he was forbidden to talk and he had nothing else to do, Shlemiel took out his dreidel and began to play by himself. While the dreidel spun, Shlemiel was muttering, "If it falls to the right, I lose, and if it falls to the left, you win."

Topiel & Tekla

I

The village of Wislowka lay on the very edge of the Vistula. It had belonged to a Squire Warlicki, who committed suicide when he heard that the tsar would free the serfs. Actually, Wislowka had never brought any income. It had been madness to settle peasants on soil that was almost entirely sand. Even in years of plenty the crops grew sparse and meager. The peasants all became fishermen. Since there was no shipbuilder in the area to build proper boats, the men of Wislowka went fishing on rafts made of rotten logs and in boats resembling troughs and washtubs. Thus, Topiel, the spirit of the river, got his victims each year. Besides the fishermen who drowned in times of storms, it often happened that men and women would drown themselves for lack of food, out of sickness or unrequited love. This was referred to in Wislowka as "going on the Vistula." The peasants had a saying: "Topiel called in his victim."

For some reason no one had drowned in the past two years, which everyone considered a bad omen, because it meant that Topiel was angry, not having gotten the sacrifice due to him. In the third year there came a famine the likes of which the eldest couldn't remember. The winter seed froze and the summer seed dried out. Not a drop of rain fell all summer, and in the month of Sierpien (August) the men assembled in the tavern and after lengthy debates agreed that a child would have to be sacrificed to Topiel. The decision was kept from the women, who were softhearted and had a habit of divulging secrets. Besides, the Russians who ruled Poland had forbidden such things.

There was a peasant in Wislowka by the name of Maciek Kowadlo, whose daughter Tekla, aged sixteen, was pregnant with a child whose father, a tramp, had run away and was never heard from again. Maciek and his wife, Zocha, were the parents of six girls, there was no bread in the house, and Maciek agreed to offer his first grandchild as the sacrifice to Topiel. For this, Maciek would be presented by the peasant community with a young hog to raise until Christmas. The villagers would supply Maciek with enough potato peels, turnips, and cabbage heads to fatten the porker. On the day before Christmas Maciek would slaughter the hog, which would provide him with enough ham and bacon for the whole year. The child would be offered to Topiel as soon as it was born, which, according to Maciek and Zocha's reckonings, would occur during the month of Listopad (November) or, at the very latest, the month of Styczen (January).

[*261*]

The peasants deceived themselves about keeping the matter a secret. All the villagers quickly learned of the decision, even the magistrate. When Tekla heard what would be demanded of her, her mouth twisted as if she was about to cry, but she didn't shed a tear. All her tears dried up within her. Maciek had warned his daughter to keep away from this vagabond by the name of Stefan. But Tekla felt sorry for him. He spoke like a city man and told her he was studying for the priesthood. He promised that she would become his housekeeper and gave her a box of matches for a present, which was a rarity in the village because the peasants made fires by rubbing two sticks together.

Tekla was small for her age. She had watery blue eyes set too far apart, high cheekbones, a snub nose, a round forehead, hair white as flax, and lots of freckles. Because she had grown up during years of famine, she was frail. Her younger sisters were gay and talkative, but Tekla was a silent one. She liked to listen to the stories old women told as they spun flax: tales of demons, evil spirits, werewolves, wizards, witches, and wild beasts. For some reason unknown to herself, she foresaw that she would die young. She even confessed this to the priest, Pawel Domb, who told her, "Everything is in God's hands."

The others in the family never discussed their dreams. But Tekla remembered her dreams and probed them for interpretation. One dream was repeated often—she was sick, cupping glasses were being applied to her as well as leeches, and the undertaker came to measure her for a coffin. Years before, Maciek had owned a goat, and when

Tekla grazed the animal in the pasture she fantasized all kinds of things: that the gypsies abducted her and sold her to cannibals, who cooked her in a pot and ate her like a goose; that she got lost in the forest and a she-wolf raised her and taught her the lupine language; that a robber with one eye in the middle of his forehead caught her in a sack and forced her to bear a monster. The peasant women in Wislowka said that Stefan might have been a devil in disguise. Before Tekla even found out that she would have to give up her child to Topiel, an old crone warned her that she might give birth to a child with fangs and horns and that it was dangerous to nurse such a creature since it could bite off a nipple.

The hog was still small when Maciek brought him home, but grew fatter from day to day. The women of the village kept bringing him garbage and leftovers. The hog had no name and was simply called Wieprz, the Polish word for a male pig. Wieprz could eat from morning to night. He loved to wallow in the mud, and as he did he grunted with pleasure. A childish joy shone out of his little eyes. He is happy, Tekla thought. He doesn't know what awaits him.

Tekla's spirit lagged from day to day. She had allowed herself to be deceived by a tramp, and her father had sold his grandson for a pig. She grew even more silent. She could no longer love her father, her mother, her sisters. She compared herself to the hog the community had chosen for a sacrifice. She no longer went to church on Sundays and no one urged her to go. In the evenings her sisters talked, laughed, and braided one another's hair, but Tekla just sat in a corner and didn't hear their chatter. A bed was made up for her on a bench, but Tekla could no longer stand the house and went to sleep in the hay in the attic. Her belly kept getting higher. The child within her jerked and pushed. In the nights the wind barked and wailed like a pack of wolves.

2

How fast the time flew! Only yesterday, it seemed to Tekla, it was autumn and gossamers floated in the air. Now the rains came along with the cold. The Vistula spilled over its banks and threatened to inundate the village. Since Maciek had no pigsty, the animal was kept inside the hut. He grew so fat that his thin legs could barely support him, and he sat and lay more than he stood. At times his eyes—the color of hazelnuts—reflected a porcine sadness. Does the beast know its end is near, Tekla wondered. She was by nature inclined to ponder things: How high is the sky? How deep is the earth? Why do people live and die? What are dreams? Why are some babies born male and others female? And why are the days in Wislowka so dreary?

Everyone in the house allegedly loved the hog. The girls kissed him and played with him, but soon he would be butchered. Maciek had already honed his ax in anticipation, and Zocha had prepared the vat where the animal's skin would be scorched. She even spoke about the pork cutlets they would fry on the holidays. The neighbors proposed that Zocha lend them some bacon for Christmas which they would repay later. "How can this be?" Tekla asked herself. "How does merciful God allow such wrongs to happen?" On Sundays the priest, Pawel Domb, often preached from the pulpit that God was love and that He had sent down His only begotten son to redeem the world. But why had this son to be crucified? Tekla wanted to ask someone about this, but whom might she ask?

Before the holiday a lot of snow fell, which lent hope that the drought would not be repeated the following year. The Vistula grew ever wilder. In other years by this time the river was covered with ice and one could cross it on sleds, but this year the water was too stormy to freeze over. News came that whole communities had been flooded, bridges had collapsed, and men had drowned. There were witnesses who had seen tables, chairs, noodle boards, and cribs driven by the turbulent current. Tekla was well aware of the reason why Topiel was mad. He foamed with rage at the delay in delivering to him his sacrifice. Tekla once heard the old women say that Topiel had a palace in the depths of the Vistula where he reigned like a king, and that he had many wives and concubines. He had crystal horns, a silver beard, and a fish tail. In the summer he enticed his victims with song, and the naiads helped him lure young lads and maidens. In the winter he roared like a lion. "Is Topiel a man-eater?" Tekla asked herself. But at least he didn't eat his own wives, who sang in chorus with him.

A weird notion flashed through Tekla's mind—maybe she should become one of Topiel's wives and thus bring up her child together with him. She daydreamed of how she would throw herself into the river and Topiel would seize her in his mighty arms and carry her off to his castle. He would sit her down on his lap, kiss her, fondle her, and call her his most beloved Rusalka. She would kneel before him, kiss his feet, and he would promise not to devour her baby, but to bring it up as a son.

The closer it came to Christmas, the more indulgent Zocha and the girls grew toward the hog. They kept on bringing him tidbits and made believe they were angry with Maciek, who would do away with Wieprz.

Zocha grumbled, "Oh, men are so heartless! How can you kill our lovely Wieprz? You glutton!"

The girls, too, complained: "Why kill him? Let him live a while longer. He is still so young."

But Maciek replied, "You'll eat his flesh and you'll lick your fingers."

On the morning of Wieprz's killing, Tekla didn't get out of bed at all. It was too cold now to sleep in the attic, and she lay on a straw pallet near the stove. Her belly was as hard as a drum, her face yellow and bloated. A few feet away Wieprz snored. Maciek, who usually moved slowly and spoke quietly, suddenly grew loud and angry. He tied a rope around Wieprz and dragged him out into the yard. Wieprz erupted into frantic shrieks. Soon Tekla heard a ghastly scream. It seemed to Tekla that Wieprz yelled, "Murderers! Help! Save me! . . ."

Tekla covered herself with the mat and stuffed her ears with her fingers so as not to hear the screams. She was filled with rage toward her father, her mother, her sisters. "I don't want to live in this false world anymore!" a voice within her cried. "I'll go on the Vistula . . ."

It suddenly became clear to her that she had foreseen this end a long time ago, possibly from childhood.

3

The church in Wislowka was small, but when its bell tolled, even the deaf could hear. It called the people of Wislowka to Christmas Eve Mass, but Tekla told her mother that she couldn't go to God's house because she had cramps. The family left her at home. On the stove sat a huge pot containing chunks of Wieprz. A tiny oil lamp glimmered. Shadows danced over the walls and low ceiling.

"I must do it this very minute!" Tekla told herself. She possessed a holiday dress, but now it would be too narrow for her loins, so she put on her everyday skirt, a sheepskin, and a pair of rag shoes with soles of oak bark. Outside, the moon wasn't shining, but the sky teemed with stars. Tekla stood a moment, staring up at the sky. What were stars? Why did they flicker so?

From the church came the sound of singing. Poor as the people of Wislowka were, they had cooked and baked for the holiday, and the smells of meat and fat cakes were carried in the air. The few young men left behind in the village were supposed to disguise themselves in masks with beards, take long staffs in hand, and go from hut to hut singing carols, but Tekla could no longer listen to the songs. She had an urge to say good-bye to someone, but to whom? She headed for the Vistula. The wind slapped her face and the cold pierced her sheepskin. Soon she reached the river. It wasn't completely frozen, but icy floes rushed downstream. The sky swayed on the waves. Tekla's hair tried to tear loose from her skull. She wanted to recite the Lord's Prayer but couldn't remember the words. Suddenly she saw Wieprz. What's Wieprz doing here, she wondered. The hog stood looking up at her with his hazel eyes and raised his snout as if to speak. What happened, did he run away from the hut, Tekla wondered. Oh, this will make a commotion in the village.

She leaned down as if about to pet him, and at that moment she remembered that he was dead. At once Wieprz turned into emptiness and Tekla's breath caught in grief. Nothing was left of Wieprz's body except bones and bristles, but his spirit lived and had come to say goodbye to her. "Goodbye to you, Wieprz," Tekla murmured, and a great love came over her for the tortured creature who, rather than take revenge, showed attachment for the daughter of his murderer.

It was too cold to wait and brood. Tekla walked into the turbulent water. She came to a deep spot and threw herself facedown to Topiel, the King of the Vistula, who emerged from the depths, embraced her in his icy arms, and sunk with her to his glittering castle.

4

Maciek swore that his daughter had drowned herself—he had found one of her rag shoes on the bank—but the people of Wislowka insisted that Maciek had spirited Tekla away somewhere in order to save his grandchild. The peasants burst into Maciek's hut and took away all the meat and tripe that remained of Wieprz. The women even carried off the pot of soup simmering on the stove.

That Christmas no one sang carols in Wislowka. It was clear that Maciek and Zocha had lied, for instead of Topiel's rage being assuaged, it became wilder. He thundered into the gale and laughed a mad laughter. He tore the straw roof off the huts and sent them flying over the village like some otherworldly birds. Topiel was heard to hurl curses of cholera, of lightning, of the fires of hell, and of Baba Yaga, who would come riding astride a mortar and pestle and with her long broom sweep away the light of the world.

Topiel's curses immediately came true. In the middle of the night cries were heard. A spark escaped the chimney of a hut and set the thatched roof on fire. Soon the hut blazed up like a paper lantern. Neighbors watching the flames saw a fiery hobgoblin and three she-devils in the flames. Before morning the storm toppled the chapel with the statue of God's mother, an omen that Satan reigned over the village. The dogs barked all night, and several of them howled so violently that they dropped dead. The dawn broke dark and dismal. A thick fog mixed with smoke and soot hovered over Wislowka. The few roosters still living seemed to forget to crow.

From then on one misfortune followed another. Someone had apparently told the Russians that the peasants in Wislowka had sacrificed a pregnant woman and her unborn child to Topiel, for in the morning when the priest, Pawel Domb, sighing and coughing, preached that the Devil had chosen the day of Christ's birth to snare the faithful, the Russians came and arrested Maciek and his wife, along with some other householders. The prisoners were shackled in chains. True, the tsar had freed the Polish serfs, but the officials still bore a grudge against the former slaves and only sought to frame charges against them. They were sent to Siberia without a trial.

The following summer the crops around Wislowka were scantier than ever. The ears of rye were half empty and those kernels still left were thrashed by hail and wind. Swarms of locusts fell over the fields. They must have been disguised imps, because one heard them chatter in human tongue. In the famine the peasants abandoned their huts and roamed to wherever their feet carried them. Their daughters went into service in the cities. The old people perished of hunger and sickness.

It seemed that Topiel desired the whole of Wislowka for himself. He strewed dunes of sand over the village so deep that in time they covered the roofs and only the chimneys thrust out. The last inhabitants swore that in the night their huts crawled toward the river like snakes. The huts had twisted so that where before there had been a door now there was a window. In the nearby hamlets the peasants said that Topiel came out at night onto the dunes and danced in a whirl with Tekla—she in a shawl of pearls over her naked body, with a child in her arms, and he with a beard of foam-sparkling curls, and a crown of ice.

Translated by Joseph Singer

Hanukkah
in the Poorhouse

Outside there was snow and frost, but in the poorhouse it was warm. Those who were mortally ill or paralyzed lay in beds. The others were sitting around a large Hanukkah lamp with eight burning wicks. Goodhearted citizens had sent pancakes sprinkled with sugar and cinnamon to the inmates. They conversed about olden times, unusual frost, packs of wolves invading the villages during the icy nights, as well as encounters with demons, imps, and sprites. Among the paupers sat an old man, a stranger who had arrived only two days before. He was tall, straight, and had a milk-white beard. He didn't look older than seventy, but when the warden of the poorhouse asked him his age, he pondered a while, counted on his fingers, and said, "On Passover I will be ninety-two."

"No evil eye should befall you," the others called out in unison.

"When you live, you get older not younger," the old man said.

One could hear from his pronunciation that he was not from Poland but from Russia. For an hour or so he listened to the stories which the other people told, while looking intensely at the Hanukkah lights. The conversation turned to the harsh decrees against the Jews and the old man said, "What do you people in Poland know about harsh decrees? In comparison to Russia, Poland is Paradise."

"Are you from Russia?" someone asked him.

"Yes, from Vitebsk."

"What are you doing here?" another one asked.

"When you wander, you come to all kinds of places," the old man replied.

"You seem to speak in riddles," an old woman said.

"My life was one great riddle."

The warden of the poorhouse, who stood nearby, said, "I can see that this man has a story to tell."

"If you have the patience to listen," the old man said.

"Here we *must* have patience," the warden replied.

"It is a story about Hanukkah," said the old man. "Come closer, because I like to talk, not shout."

They all moved their stools closer and the old man began.

"First let me tell you my name. It is Jacob, but my parents called me Yankele. The Russians turned Yankele into Yasha. I mention the Russians because I am one of those who are called the captured ones. When I was a child Tsar Nicholas I, an enemy of the Jews, decreed that Jewish boys should be captured and brought up to be soldiers. The decree was aimed at Russian Jews, not at Polish ones. It created turmoil. The child catchers would barge into a house or into a cheder, where the boys studied, catch a boy as if he were some animal, and send him away deep into Russia, sometimes as far as Siberia. He was not drafted immediately. First he was given to a peasant in a village where he would grow up, and then, when he was of age, he was taken into the army. He had to learn Russian and forget his Jewishness. Often he was forced to convert to the Greek Orthodox faith. The peasant made him work on the Sabbath and eat pork. Many boys died from the bad treatment and from yearning for their parents.

"Since the law stipulated that no one who was married could be drafted for military service, the Jews often married little boys to little girls to save the youngsters from being captured. The married little boy continued to go to cheder. The little girl put on a matron's bonnet, but she remained a child. It often happened that the young wife went out in the street to play with pebbles or to make mud cakes. Sometimes she would take off her bonnet and put her toys in it.

"What happened to me was of a different nature. The young girl whom I was about to marry was the daughter of a neighbor. Her name was Reizel. When we were children of four or five, we played together. I was supposed to be her husband and she my wife. I made believe that I went to the synagogue and she prepared supper for me, a shard with sand or mud. I loved Reizel and we promised ourselves that when we grew up we really would become husband and wife. She was fair, with red hair and blue eyes. Some years later, when my parents brought me the good tidings that Reizel was to marry me, I became mad with joy. We would have married immediately; however, Reizel's mother insisted on preparing a trousseau for the eight-year-old bride, even though she would grow out of it in no time.

"Three days before our wedding, two Cossacks broke into our house in the middle of the night, tore me from my bed, and forced me to follow them. My mother fainted. My father tried to save me, but they slapped him so hard he lost two teeth. It was on the second night of Hanukkah. The next day the captured boys were led into the synagogue to take an oath that they would serve the tsar faithfully. Half the townspeople gathered before the synagogue. Men and women were crying, and in the crowd I saw Reizel. In all misery I managed to call out, 'Reizel, I will come back to you.' And she called back, 'Yankele, I will wait for you.'

"If I wanted to tell you what I went through, I could write a book of a thousand pages. They drove me some-where deep into Russia. The trip lasted many weeks. They took me to a hamlet and put me in the custody of a peasant by the name of Ivan. Ivan had a wife and six children, and the whole family tried to make a Russian out of me. They all slept in one large bed. In the winter they put their pigs in their hut. The place was swarming with roaches. I knew only a few Russian words. My fringed garment was taken away and my sidelocks were cut off. I had no choice but to eat unkosher food. In the first days I spat out the pig meat, but how long can a boy fast? For hundreds of miles around there was not a single

Jew. They could force my body to do all kinds of things, but they could not make my soul forsake the faith of my fathers. I remembered a few prayers and benedictions by heart and kept on repeating them. I often spoke to myself when nobody was around so as not to forget the Yiddish language. In the summer Ivan sent me to pasture his goats. In later years I took care of his cows and horse. I would sit in the grass and talk to my parents, to my sister Leah, and to my brother Chaim, both younger than I, and also to Reizel. Though I was far away from them, I imagined that they heard me and answered me.

"Since I was captured on Hanukkah, I decided to celebrate this feast even if it cost me my life. I had no Jewish calendar, but I recalled that Hanukkah comes about the time of Christmas—a little earlier or later. I would wake up and go outside in the middle of the night. Not far from the granary grew an old oak. Lightning had burned a large hole in its trunk. I crept inside, lit some kindling wood, and made the benediction. If the peasant had caught me, he would have beaten me. But he slept like a bear.

"Years passed and I became a soldier. There was no old oak tree near the barracks, and you would be whipped for leaving the bunk bed and going outside without permission. But on some winter nights they sent me to guard an ammunition warehouse, and I always found an opportunity to light a candle and recite a prayer. Once, a Jewish soldier came to our barracks and brought with him a small prayer book. My joy at seeing the old familiar Hebrew letters cannot be described. I hid somewhere and recited all the prayers, those of the weekdays, the Sabbath, and the holidays. That soldier had already served out his term, and before he went home, he left me the prayer book as a gift. It was the greatest treasure of my life. I still carry it in my sack.

"Twenty-two years had passed since I was captured. The soldiers were supposed to have the right to send letters to their parents once a month, but since I wrote mine in Yiddish, they were never delivered, and I never received anything from them.

"One winter night, when it was my turn to stand watch at the warehouse, I lit two candles, and since there was no wind, I stuck them into the snow. According to my calculation it was Hanukkah. A soldier who stands watch is not allowed to sit down, and certainly not to fall asleep, but it was the middle of the night and nobody was there, so I squatted on the threshold of the warehouse to observe the two little flames burning brightly. I was tired after a difficult day of service and my eyelids closed. Soon I fell asleep. I was committing three sins against the tsar at once. Suddenly I felt someone shaking my shoulder. I opened my eyes and saw my enemy, a vicious corporal by the name of Kapustin—tall, with broad shoulders, a curled mustache, and a thick red nose with purple veins from drinking. Usually he slept the whole night, but that night some demon made him come outside. When I saw that rascal by the light of the still-burning Hanukkah candles, I knew that this was my end. I would be court-martialed and sent to Siberia. I jumped up, grabbed my gun, and hit him over the head. He fell down and I started running. I ran until sunrise. I didn't know where my feet were carrying me. I had entered a thick forest and it seemed to have no end.

"For three days I ate nothing, and drank only melted snow. Then I came to a hamlet. In all these years I had saved some fifteen rubles from the few kopeks that a soldier receives as pay. I carried it in a little pouch on my chest. I bought myself a cotton-lined jacket, a pair of pants, and a cap. My soldier's uniform and the gun I threw into a stream. After weeks of wandering on foot, I came to railroad tracks. A freight train carrying logs and moving slowly was heading south. It had almost a hundred cars. I jumped on one of them. When the train approached a station, I jumped off in order not to be seen by the stationmaster. I could tell from the signs along the way that we were heading toward St. Petersburg, then the capital of Russia. At some stations the train stood for many hours, and I went into the town or village and begged for a slice of bread. The Russians had robbed me of my best years and I had the right to take some food from them. And so I arrived in Petersburg.

"There I found rich Jews, and when I told them of my predicament, they let me rest a few weeks and provided me with warm clothes and the fare to return to my hometown, Vitebsk. I had grown a beard and no one would have recognized me. Still, to come home to my family using my real name was dangerous because I would be arrested as a deserter.

The train arrived in Vitebsk at dawn. The winter was about to end. The smell of spring was in the air. A few stations before Vitebsk, Jewish passengers entered my car, and from their talk I learned that it was Purim. I remembered that on this holiday it was the custom for poor young men to put on masks and to disguise themselves as the silly King Ahasuerus, the righteous Mordecai, the cruel Haman, or his vicious wife, Zeresh. Toward evening they went from house to house singing songs and performing scenes from the Book of Esther, and the people gave them a few groschen. I remained at the railroad station until late in the morning, and then I went into town and bought myself a mask of Haman with a high red triangular hat made of paper, as well as a paper sword. I was afraid that I might be recognized by some townspeople after all, and I did not want to shock my old parents with my sudden appearance. Since I was tired, I went to the poorhouse. The poorhouse warden asked me where I came from and I gave him the name of some faraway city. The poor and the sick had gotten chicken soup and challah from wealthy citizens. I ate a delicious meal—even a slice of cake—washed down by a glass of tea.

"After sunset I put on the mask of the wicked Haman, hung my paper sword at my side, and walked toward our old house. I opened the door and saw my parents. My father's beard had turned white over the years. My mother's face was shrunken. My brother, Chaim, and my sister, Leah, were not there. They must have gotten married and moved away.

"From my boyhood I remembered a song which the disguised Haman used to sing and I began to chant the words:

> *I am wicked Haman, the hero great,*
> *And Zeresh is my spiteful mate,*
> *On the king's horse ride I will,*
> *And all the Jews shall I kill.*

"I tried to continue, but a lump stuck in my throat and I could not utter another word. I heard my mother say, 'Here is Haman. Why didn't you bring Zeresh the shrew with you?' I made an effort to sing with a hoarse voice, and my father remarked, 'A great voice he has not, but he will get his two groschen anyhow.'

" 'Do you know what, Haman,' my mother said, 'take off your mask, sit down at the table, and eat the Purim repast with us.'

"I glanced at the table. Two thick candles were lit in silver candlesticks as in my young days. Everything looked familiar to me—the embroidered tablecloth, the carafe of wine. I had forgotten in cold Russia that oranges existed. But on the table there were some oranges, as well as mandelbread, a tray of sweet and sour fish, a double-braided challah, and a dish of poppy cakes. After some hesitation I took off my mask and sat down at the table. My mother looked at me and said, 'You must be from another town. Where do you come from?'

"I named a faraway city. 'What are you doing here in Vitebsk?' my father asked. 'Oh, I wander all over the world,' I answered. 'You still look like a young man. What is the purpose of becoming a wanderer at your age?' my father asked me. 'Don't ask him so many questions,' my mother said. 'Let him eat in peace. Go wash your hands.'

"I washed my hands with water from the copper pitcher of olden days, and my mother handed me a towel and a knife to cut the challah. The handle was made of mother-of-pearl and embossed with the words 'Holy Sabbath.' Then she brought me a plate of kreplach filled with mincemeat. I asked my parents if they had children and my mother began to talk about my brother, Chaim, and my sister, Leah. Both lived in other towns with their families. My parents didn't mention my name, but I could see my mother's upper lip trembling. Then she burst out crying, and my father reproached her, 'You are crying again? Today is a holiday.' 'I won't cry anymore,' my mother apologized. My father handed her his handkerchief and said to me, 'We had another son and he got lost like a stone in water.'

"In cheder I had studied the Book of Genesis and the story of Joseph and his brothers. I wanted to cry out to my parents, 'I am your son.' But I was afraid that the surprise would cause my frail mother to faint. My father also looked exhausted. Gradually he began to tell me what happened on that Hanukkah night when the Cossacks captured his son Yankele. I asked, 'What happened to his bride-to-be?' and my father said, 'For years she refused to marry, hoping that our Yankele would return. Finally her parents persuaded her to get engaged again. She was about to be married when she caught typhoid fever and died.'

" 'She died from yearning for our Yankele,' my mother interjected. 'The day the murderous Cossacks captured him she began to pine away. She died with Yankele's name on her lips.'

"My mother again burst out crying, and my father said, 'Enough. According to the law, we should praise God for our misfortunes as well as for our good fortunes.'

"That night I gradually revealed to my parents who I was. First I told my father, and then he prepared my mother for the good news. After all the sobbing and kissing and embraces were over, we began to speak about my future. I could not stay at home under my real name. The police would have found out about me and arrested me. We decided that I could stay and live in the house only as a relative from some distant place. My parents were to introduce me as a nephew—a widower without children who came to live in their house after the loss of his wife. In a sense it was true. I had always thought of Reizel as my wife. I knew even then that I could never marry another woman. I assumed the name of Leibele instead of Yankele.

"And so it was. When the matchmakers heard that I was without a wife, they became busy with marriage propositions. However, I told them all that I loved my wife too much to exchange her for another woman. My parents were old and weak and they needed my care. For almost six years I remained at home. After four years my father died. My mother lived another two years, and then she also died and was buried beside him. A few times my brother and sister came to visit. Of course they learned who I really was, but they kept it a secret. These were the happiest years of my adult life. Every night when I went to sleep in a bed at home instead of a bunk bed in the barracks and every day when I went to pray in the synagogue, I thanked God for being rescued from the hands of the tyrants.

"After my parents' deaths I had no reason to remain in Vitebsk. I was thinking of learning a trade and settling down somewhere, but it made no sense to stay in one place all by myself. I began to wander from town to town. Wherever I went I stopped at the poorhouse and helped the poor and the sick. All my possessions are in this sack. As I told you, I still carry the prayer book that the soldier gave me some sixty-odd years ago, as well as my parents' Hanukkah lamp. Sometimes when I am on the road and feel especially downhearted, I hide in a forest and light Hanukkah candles, even though it is not Hanukkah.

"At night, the moment I close my eyes, Reizel is with me. She is young and she wears the white silk bridal gown her parents had prepared for her trousseau. She pours oil into a magnificent Hanukkah lamp and I light the candles with a long torch. Sometimes the whole sky turns into an otherworldly Hanukkah lamp, with the stars as its lights. I told my dreams to a rabbi and he said, 'Love comes from the soul and souls radiate light.' I know that when my times comes, Reizel's soul will wait for me in heaven. Well, it's time to go to sleep. Good night, a happy Hanukkah."

Shrewd Todie
& Lyzer the Miser

In a village somewhere in the Ukraine there lived a poor man called Todie. Todie had a wife, Sheindel, and seven children, but he could never earn enough to feed them properly. He tried many trades, failing in all of them. It was said of Todie that if he decided to deal in candles the sun would never set. He was nicknamed Shrewd Todie because whenever he managed to make some money, it was always by trickery.

This winter was an especially cold one. The snowfall was heavy and Todie had no money to buy wood for the stove. His seven children stayed in bed all day to keep warm. When the frost burns outside, hunger is stronger than ever, but Sheindel's larder was empty. She reproached Todie bitterly, wailing, "If you can't feed your wife and children, I will go to the rabbi and get a divorce."

"And what will you do with it, eat it?" Todie retorted.

In the same village there lived a rich man called Lyzer.

Because of his stinginess he was known as Lyzer the miser. He permitted his wife to bake bread only once in four weeks because he had discovered that fresh bread is eaten up more quickly than stale.

Todie had more than once gone to Lyzer for a loan of a few gulden, but Lyzer had always replied, "I sleep better when the money lies in my strongbox rather than in your pocket."

Lyzer had a goat, but he never fed her. The goat had learned to visit the houses of the neighbors, who pitied her and gave her potato peelings. Sometimes, when there were not enough peelings, she would gnaw on the old straw of the thatched roofs. She also had a liking for tree bark. Nevertheless, each year the goat gave birth to a kid. Lyzer milked her but, miser that he was, did not drink the milk himself. Instead, he sold it to others.

Todie decided that he would take revenge on Lyzer and at the same time make some much-needed money for himself.

One day, as Lyzer was sitting on a box eating borscht and dry bread (he used his chairs only on holidays so that the upholstery would not wear out), the door opened and Todie came in.

"Reb Lyzer," he said, "I would like to ask you a favor. My oldest daughter, Basha, is already fifteen and she's about to become engaged. A young man is coming from Janev to look her over. My cutlery is tin, and my wife is ashamed to ask the young man to eat soup with a tin spoon. Would you lend me one of your silver spoons? I give you my holy word that I will return it to you tomorrow."

Lyzer knew that Todie would not dare to break a holy oath and he lent him the spoon.

No young man came to see Basha that evening. As usual, the girl walked around barefoot and in rags, and the silver spoon lay hidden under Todie's shirt. In the early years of his marriage Todie had possessed a set of silver tableware himself. He had, however, long since sold it all, with the exception of three silver teaspoons that were used only on Passover.

The following day, as Lyzer, his feet bare (in order to save his shoes), sat on his box eating borscht and dry bread, Todie returned.

"Here is the spoon I borrowed yesterday," he said, placing it on the table together with one of his own teaspoons.

"What is the teaspoon for?" Lyzer asked.

And Todie said, "Your tablespoon gave birth to a teaspoon. It is her child. Since I am an honest man, I'm returning both mother and child to you."

Lyzer looked at Todie in astonishment. He had never heard of a silver spoon giving birth to another. Nevertheless, his greed overcame his doubt and he happily accepted both spoons. Such an unexpected piece of good fortune! He was overjoyed that he had loaned Todie the spoon.

A few days later, as Lyzer (without his coat, to save it) was again sitting on his box eating borscht with dry bread, the door opened and Todie appeared.

"The young man from Janev did not please Basha, because he had donkey ears, but this evening another young man is coming to look her over. Sheindel is cooking soup for him, but she's ashamed to serve him with a tin spoon. Would you lend me . . ."

Even before Todie could finish the sentence, Lyzer interrupted. "You want to borrow a silver spoon? Take it with pleasure."

The following day Todie once more returned the spoon and with it one of his own silver teaspoons. He again explained that during the night the large spoon had given birth to a small one and in all good conscience he was bringing back the mother and the newborn baby. As for the young man who had come to look Basha over, she hadn't liked him either, because his nose was so long that it reached to his chin. Needless to say that Lyzer the miser was overjoyed.

Exactly the same thing happened a third time. Todie related that this time his daughter had rejected her suitor because he stammered. He also reported that Lyzer's silver spoon had again given birth to a baby spoon.

"Does it ever happen that a spoon has twins?" Lyzer inquired.

Todie thought it over for a moment. "Why not? I've even heard of a case where a spoon had triplets."

Almost a week passed by and Todie did not go to see Lyzer. But on Friday morning, as Lyzer (in his underdrawers, to save his pants) sat on his box eating borscht and dry bread, Todie came in and said, "Good day to you, Reb Lyzer."

"A good morning and many more to you," Lyzer replied in his friendliest manner. "What good fortune brings you here? Did you perhaps come to borrow a silver spoon? If so, help yourself."

"Today I have a very special favor to ask. This evening

a young man from the big city of Lublin is coming to look Basha over. He is the son of a rich man, and I'm told he is clever and handsome as well. Not only do I need a silver spoon, but since he will remain with us over the Sabbath, I need a pair of silver candlesticks, because mine are brass and my wife is ashamed to place them on the Sabbath table. Would you lend me your candlesticks? Immediately after the Sabbath, I will return them to you."

Silver candlesticks are of great value and Lyzer the miser hesitated, but only for a moment.

Remembering his good fortune with the spoons, he said, "I have eight silver candlesticks in my house. Take them all. I know you will return them to me just as you say. And if it should happen that any of them give birth, I have no doubt that you will be as honest as you have been in the past."

"Certainly," Todie said. "Let's hope for the best."

The silver spoon, Todie hid beneath his shirt as usual. But taking the candlesticks, he went directly to a merchant, sold them for a considerable sum, and brought the money to Sheindel. When Sheindel saw so much money, she demanded to know where he had gotten such a treasure.

"When I went out, a cow flew over our roof and dropped a dozen silver eggs," Todie replied. "I sold them and here is the money."

"I have never heard of a cow flying over a roof and laying silver eggs," Sheindel said doubtingly.

"There is always a first time," Todie answered. "If you don't want the money, give it back to me."

"There'll be no talk about giving it back," Sheindel

said. She knew that her husband was full of cunning and tricks—but when the children are hungry and the larder is empty, it is better not to ask too many questions. Sheindel went to the marketplace and bought meat, fish, white flour, and even some nuts and raisins for a pudding. And since a lot of money still remained, she bought shoes and clothes for the children.

It was a very gay Sabbath in Todie's house. The boys sang and the girls danced. When the children asked their father where he had gotten the money, he replied, "It is forbidden to mention money during the Sabbath."

Sunday, as Lyzer (barefoot and almost naked, to save his clothes) sat on his box finishing up a dry crust of bread with borscht, Todie arrived and, handing him his silver spoon, said, "It's too bad. This time your spoon did not give birth to a baby."

"What about the candlesticks?" Lyzer inquired anxiously.

Todie sighed deeply. "The candlesticks died."

Lyzer got up from his box so hastily that he overturned his plate of borscht.

"You fool! How can candlesticks die?" he screamed.

"If spoons can give birth, candlesticks can die."

Lyzer raised a great hue and cry and had Todie called before the rabbi. When the rabbi heard both sides of the story, he burst out laughing. "It serves you right," he said to Lyzer. "If you hadn't chosen to believe that spoons give birth, now you would not be forced to believe that your candlesticks died."

"But it's all nonsense," Lyzer objected.

"Did you not expect the candlesticks to give birth to

other candlesticks?'' the rabbi said admonishingly. "If you accept nonsense when it brings you profit, you must also accept nonsense when it brings you loss." And he dismissed the case.

The following day, when Lyzer the miser's wife brought him his borscht and dry bread, Lyzer said to her, "I will eat only the bread. Borscht is too expensive a food, even without sour cream."

The story of the silver spoons that gave birth and the candlesticks that died spread quickly through the town. All the people enjoyed Todie's victory and Lyzer the miser's defeat. The shoemaker's and tailor's apprentices, as was their custom whenever there was an important happening, made up a song about it:

> *Lyzer, put your grief aside.*
> *What if your candlesticks have died?*
> *You're the richest man on earth*
> *with silver spoons that can give birth*
> *and silver eggs as living proof*
> *of flying cows above your roof.*
> *Don't sit there eating crusts of bread—*
> *To silver grandsons look ahead.*

However, time passed and Lyzer's silver spoons never gave birth again.

Translated by the author and Elizabeth Shub

The Fearsome Inn

It was as if the snow treasures of heaven had been opened. The snow fell day and night, sometimes straight down and sometimes slanting. Now and then it swirled in the air like a dog chasing its tail. All the roads were covered. The branches of the trees, glazed with ice, resembled the arms of crystal candelabra. In the middle of a field stood what was left of a scarecrow. It shook in the wind, flapping its rags and laughing madly.

On a hill overgrown with thistles, by a windmill with a broken vane and a smithy whose forge had long been cold, stood the inn that belonged to Doboshova the witch. She was the widow of Dobosh, the famous highwayman. For forty years Dobosh had preyed on the roads of Poland, robbing merchants on the way to Warsaw, Cracow, Danzig, Leipzig, and had amassed a huge fortune. When he was finally caught and hanged, Doboshova married Lapitut, her present husband, who was half man, half devil. They settled in the inn and kept themselves busy plying their witchcraft on travelers who stumbled their way.

Doboshova held captive three girls who were her servants. One was called Reitze, one Leitze, and the third Neitze. Reitze had black hair and black eyes; Leitze, blond hair and blue eyes; and Neitze, red hair and green eyes. The girls slaved all day long. At night they slept in the hayloft with the rats and field mice. Many times they tried to escape, but Doboshova and Lapitut had cast a spell on the road so that it led nowhere. Each time a girl tried to run away, she wandered around in circles and returned to the inn completely exhausted. When this happened, Doboshova soaked a reed whip in slops to make it supple. Lapitut gave the girl thirty-nine lashes.

In the summertime wayfarers seldom came to the inn. But in the winter, when blizzards wiped out the roads, travelers often lost their way, and victims were plentiful. This particular morning three young men had strayed to the inn. One was called Herschel. He was on his way on foot to the yeshiva of Lublin and had taken a wrong turn in the storm. The second, Velvel, had been traveling by sleigh to the city of Lemberg to buy merchandise for his father's store. He had fallen asleep and had slipped off the sleigh. The howling wind had prevented the coachmen from hearing him call. Velvel wandered about looking for shelter and finally found himself at Doboshova's inn. The third, Leibel, was returning home from a faraway city where he had been studying the cabala, the ancient Hebrew books that reveal the mysteries of heaven and earth. As a parting gift, his master had given him a piece of chalk, saying, "If you draw a line around man or beast with this piece of chalk, it will imprison them in a circle. Not only will they be unable to escape, but no one will be able to get into the magic ring." But the chalk was of no help in a snowstorm, and Leibel, too, arrived at the inn.

When Doboshova and Lapitut saw the three young guests, they were overjoyed. Doboshova looked like any other innkeeper. But like all witches she had an elflock, which she kept well hidden under a cap. Lapitut had a stumpy horn on his forehead. However, he carefully combed his matted hair down to cover it. The three young men were wet through and frozen. Doboshova led them to the stove so their clothes could dry out and gave orders to the girls to prepare the oven for baking.

"You must be hungry," she said to the young men. "Be kind enough to wait just a bit. I always serve my guests hot rolls fresh from the oven." To Lapitut she said, "Go to the well and fetch water for the barrel so that our visitors can wash their hands and make the benediction before their meal."

The three girls, Reitze, Leitze, and Neitze, knew what was in store for the young men, but they dared not give even a word of warning. First of all, if Lapitut was to catch them, he would whip them to death. Secondly, they knew only too well that all roads led back to the inn.

Everybody went to work at once. Reitze added wood to the oven. Leitze put flour in a bowl and mixed some dough. Neitze kneaded it and shaped it into rolls. Doboshova herself sprinkled the rolls with something that resembled caraway seed. Actually, it was an herb, the very smell of which, when baked, gave nightmares to those Doboshova wanted to ensnare. When the rolls were baked and about to be removed from the oven, Doboshova said to the young men, "You'll find three dippers and three towels by the barrel. Go and wash your hands. The moment you are ready, the rolls will be taken out, and they will be hot and crisp. You can smell them now."

"You are a good housekeeper," Herschel said.

"I wish I could find a wife like you," added Velvel.

"It brings good luck to treat wayfarers well," stated Leibel, the cabala student.

Each took hold of a dipper and bent over the barrel. In that very instant the spicy smell of the herb-covered rolls took effect. All three young men suddenly felt dizzy and began to dream.

Herschel dreamed that he was a slave in a strange land. He had become a trainer of wild beasts. His master, a prince, had ordered him to teach a huge lion, called Arieh, the most dangerous of tricks. Herschel was to make the lion keep its jaws open while he placed his head in the beast's mouth. Then the animal was to close its jaw just enough so as not to harm Herschel and release him on command. At last the trick was learned, and the day came when Herschel was to perform for the first time before the prince and his court. Herschel was in the lion's cage making one last test before the performance. He placed his head in the lion's mouth, patted him on the neck, and after a minute called, "Arieh, enough!" But Arieh did not loosen his jaws. Herschel patted him again and coaxed, "Arieh, enough! Open your mouth!"

But the lion did not move. Instead, he began to roar so terrifyingly that Herschel felt his blood freezing in his veins. The roaring continued, louder and louder, until Herschel could hardly breathe. "God save me," he prayed.

This was Herschel's nightmare.

Velvel also dreamed he was in a strange land. He knew no one. He looked for work but couldn't find any. Finally, he had to beg to eat. One late afternoon he found himself on a street with many buildings. He walked through a gate into a courtyard. He turned to leave, but it had become dark, and he couldn't find his way. He called out, but no one heard him. Groping along a wall, he found an opening. He entered it, hoping it would bring him back to the street. Instead, a stairway led him downward. It got darker and darker. Suddenly he came to a large room. In the glow of the single oil lamp he saw bricks of solid gold, barrels filled with coins. He had stumbled into the vault of the king's mint.

Velvel knew that if he was discovered he would be taken for a thief. He searched the room for the opening through which he had come. He soon found it, but at that moment two workmen appeared and began to close it up with bricks. He crouched in a corner so they would not see him, yet he knew that he had to get out before their work was finished or he would remain without bread and water, perhaps even without air to breathe.

Did he dare ask the workmen to let him out? They would believe that he was there to steal the gold. They would summon the guards. He would be put in chains and thrown into a dungeon. They might torture him.

Finally, he decided that it would be better to appeal to the mercy of the workmen than to be buried alive with the king's treasure. Just as he stepped from his corner, the last brick moved into place and the lamp flickered out. "Wait!" he shouted with all his might, but it was too late.

This was Velvel's nightmare.

Leibel dreamed that he was in a desert. He was hungry and thirsty. After long searching, all he found was a dried-out stream, in the middle of which lay snakes, crocodiles, and lizards. They looked as hungry and parched as he. Their mouths were wide open, showing their pointed teeth. The trunk of a tree lay across the bed of the stream. On the other side, Leibel saw a grove of date palms surrounding what looked like a shimmering pool. Leibel realized that one false step could land him among the monsters. But his thirst was so great that he was prepared to take the risk. He stepped onto the tree trunk and spread out his arms to help him keep his balance as he made his way across.

He had reached the middle of the stream when he saw coming toward him a woman whom he recognized immediately as a witch. Her head was covered with elf-locks, and she had the webbed feet of a goose. Even though she did not resemble her, somehow she reminded him of Doboshova.

Leibel stopped in his tracks. To fall into the hands of such a creature was even worse than being devoured by crocodiles. He turned carefully back to retrace his steps, only to see a male devil coming toward him. A short horn, which spun like a top, protruded from his forehead.

Even though he did not resemble him, somehow he reminded Leibel of Lapitut.

"O Holy Powers, what shall I do now?" cried Leibel in terror.

This was Leibel's nightmare.

At the same moment, all three—Herschel, Velvel, and Leibel—awoke. Their nightmares, which had seemed so long, in reality had lasted only a few seconds. All three still stood bent over the barrel as they heard Doboshova saying, "Well, why don't you wash your hands, my dear lads? The girls are taking the rolls out of the oven."

Dazed, all three washed their hands and wiped them. At last they were seated at the table. Herschel and Velvel were about to recite the benediction for bread and begin eating. Had they done this, they would have been lost, because in addition to the diabolic seeds, Doboshova had put a potion into the dough that deprived human beings of all will. But all at once Leibel cried out, "Wait!"

"What's the matter?" asked Herschel.

"Why?" added Velvel.

"Eat, young men," Doboshova urged in a wheedling tone.

"What is this?" Lapitut grumbled.

"While getting the water, I lost my ring in the barrel," Leibel explained quickly. "It was a family heirloom that goes all the way back to King Solomon. It was given to him by the Queen of Sheba. It can show the way to buried riches, locate sunken ships and caravans covered by the sands of the desert. It can also heal the sick and make the old young. I beg of you, help me find my ring."

Despite the many treasures that they already had, the greed of Doboshova and Lapitut could not be satisfied.

Even more important, they had a great desire to be young again. When they heard what the ring could do, they both ran to the barrel and stuck their hands into the water to search for it.

Leibel jumped up, rushed over to Doboshova and Lapitut, and quickly drew a circle around them with his chalk.

When the two could find no ring in the barrel, they straightened up, ready to return to the table, but they could not step beyond the magic line surrounding them.

"What's going on here?" growled Lapitut.

"What's this circle?" screamed Doboshova.

Reitze, Leitze, and Neitze stood openmouthed.

Herschel and Velvel sat without saying a word, as if they had lost their tongues in astonishment.

This is what had happened.

Just as Leibel was about to say the benediction, he had glanced at Doboshova, and it had suddenly struck him that she resembled the witch he had seen in his nightmare. He cast a quick look at Lapitut and recognized the devil in his dream. Leibel, who had studied the cabala and knew something about the tricks of the evil host, realized that there was something wrong here and that he must act immediately. He made up the story about the ring to prevent the other boys from eating.

Held within the magic boundary, Doboshova and Lapitut were captives for the first time in their lives. As soon as Leitze, Reitze, and Neitze were convinced that Doboshova and Lapitut had lost their power, they told the young men about all they had suffered under the wicked couple's spell.

All three had parents, sisters, and brothers who had

surely searched for them, but since the road to the inn was bewitched, their relatives had been unable to find them.

As the girls related how they had been tricked away from their homes, Doboshova shouted and waved her fists. She threatened to turn them all into hedgehogs, rats, and skunks. Lapitut shouted that he would whip them to death. But Leibel assured the girls that they no longer had anything to fear. To prevent any devils from coming to the aid of their kin, Leibel made a chalk line along the inside of the entire house and around all the doors and windows. He also circled the oven and the fireplace to make sure that no evil spirit could get in through the chimney.

It soon became clear that all these precautions were needed. No sooner did Doboshova and Lapitut discover they were trapped than they began to call on the dark forces of the forest to come to their rescue. In no time demons, devils, imps, sprites, and other impure spirits began to arrive. Some appeared as snakes with wings, others as huge bats, and still others looked like rams, weasels, and toads. Had Leibel not protected the house with his magic chalk, they would have swarmed in. Instead, they hovered around the windows screeching and threatening those inside.

"There's no reason to fear them," Leibel again reassured the young people. "They can do us no harm. It's time to prepare some food so that we can eat."

Reitze, Leitze, and Neitze set about making fresh dough without potions and magic caraway seeds. They baked rolls, pretzels, and cookies and made a delicious meal. Reitze was the best baker, Leitze excelled in roasting, and Neitze could fry the crispest food. The good smells filled the house. Doboshova and Lapitut became exceedingly hungry and begged for food. But Leibel said, "We won't give you a bite unless you sign a pledge in your blood that you will leave the inn and return to the Lower Regions."

This Doboshova and Lapitut refused to do. Devils and witches can easily break a promise, but once they have signed in blood, they must keep their word or lose their powers forever.

When the evil pair realized that they were getting nowhere with threats, they tried flattery. They called Leibel a master of the cabala. They complimented Herschel and Velvel, and even had something nice to say about the girls. They promised all kinds of gifts. Reitze, Leitze, and Neitze were to get beautiful dresses, precious jewelry, and silk underclothing embroidered in gold. Lapitut swore he would teach the young men neverheard-of magic tricks.

"We want neither your gifts nor your teachings," Leibel replied.

For hours Doboshova and Lapitut alternated between curses and coaxing. The devils outside continued their racket, pressing against the windows. Inside, the young people knew that they were safe, protected by the magic chalk.

The winter day passed quickly. Night brought new terrors and temptations. The evil ones laughed and cried, imitated the sounds of trumpets and horns, bleated and hopped about, blasphemed and boasted of their ungodly powers. Some of the creatures of darkness decided to tempt the young people by disguising themselves as beautiful girls, handsome noblemen. The night suddenly became day. The snow outside turned into a sunlit, flower-filled meadow, through which a blue stream flowed. A devil called Topiel, who specialized in luring humans into the water so that they would drown, sang one of his most entrancing melodies to get the young people out of the house. But Leibel would not let any of them succumb, explaining that it was all a delusion.

When the black band saw that no one was coming out, they brought back the night. Three black cats with eyes like green fire appeared in a window. Their meowing was like the ringing of bells. After a while the cats, too, vanished. Instead, a whirling wind shook the roof and whistled in the chimney. There was a howling of wolves and a growling of bears. The outdoors turned fiery red as if reflecting a great conflagration. It began to thunder and lightning, and the inn swayed as in an earthquake. The young people could not help being afraid, but they trusted Leibel and ate their supper while the demons raged.

"No matter how strong the Devil is," Leibel said, "God is stronger."

Immediately after supper, the three girls undressed and went to sleep in the same large bed so that they would be less frightened. They put blindfolds on their eyes and cotton in their ears so as not to see the terrifying sights and not to hear the mocking voices of the fiends. Herschel and Velvel made themselves a bed on the top of the large brick oven. They were so exhausted that they soon fell into a deep sleep. Leibel stayed awake to keep watch. He knew that Doboshova and Lapitut could not hold out much longer. He had a parchment scroll and a sharp quill pen in readiness. One by one the monsters outside tired and departed, each for his own lair. Doboshova and Lapitut were left alone.

Leibel overheard Doboshova whispering to Lapitut: "We can't escape. We'll have to sign."

"I wish I'd never known you," Lapitut snarled in reply.

"If you won't sign now," Leibel called out, "I will go to bed, and you'll have to stand on your feet until morning."

"Oh, I cannot stand another minute," Doboshova moaned.

"I'm dying of hunger," Lapitut wailed. "I can't do without a smoke of mandrake root. If only you'd hand me my pipe."

"Sign the oath, and you will have all you need."

The pair had no choice. They each pricked a wrist with the point of the quill and signed their oath in blood.

I, the witch Doboshova, and I, the devil Lapitut, swear by Satan, Lilith, and by all the impure powers to leave this inn, never to return, neither we nor our children, grand-children, and great-grandchildren to the tenth generation. We leave all our possessions to our guests Herschel, Velvel, and Leibel, and to our onetime servants, Reitze, Leitze, and Neitze. Furthermore, the treasure of the late highwayman Dobosh, hidden in the hollow of the old oak in the yard, is from now on also to belong to the afore-mentioned parties. Furthermore, we remove all spells, charms, witchcraft, evil signs, and curses from the inn and its surroundings, and command that everything return to the state it was in before we came. Signed: Lapitut, the son of Briri, the son of Shabriri, the son of Karteigus, and so on back to my ancestor Satan. Doboshova, the daughter of Naamah, the daughter of Igrath, the daughter of Machlath, and so on back to my grandmother Lilith the First.

The haggling had continued for so long that the sky was beginning to gray with the light of dawn. The young people had awakened. They watched as Leibel erased a small section of the circle around Doboshova and Lapitut and another bit under a window. Then, opening the window, he called in Aramaic, "*Pik*, out."

Doboshova and Lapitut turned into shadows and vanished. Off they went to the desert of deserts, to the wastes of the netherworld, behind the Mountains of Darkness, where there is neither day nor night and dusk is eternal.

The girls were so happy they began to cry for joy.

"Why cry?" Leibel said. "Your troubles are over. The road is open and each of us can return home."

But neither the boys nor the girls made a move to go. The truth is that the inn, which only a few minutes before had looked so gloomy, was now cozy and pleasant. The snow shimmered in the sunlight. Ice spears hung from the roof, reflecting the colors of the rainbow. From the nearby woods came the sound of winter birds chirping and trilling. The smell of pine filled the air.

After breakfast, Leibel led the young people outside

to a huge oak tree that was hundreds of years old. There was a great hollow in its trunk. At the back of the hollow they discovered chests full of gold and precious stones. The jewels lit up the darkness. When the girls saw the treasure, they began to scream with delight. But even with so many riches to take home, not one of them thought of leaving.

The reason was that the greatest magic of all had begun to do its work among them.

Of course, all three girls were filled with admiration and love for Leibel. Had he not driven away Doboshova and Lapitut and the other devils? However, they all knew that Leibel could marry only one of them, and Herschel and Velvel, too, were charming fellows. But who should marry whom?

Again they decided to trust to Leibel's wisdom. And Leibel said, "Let each of us write down on a slip of paper the name of the one we love best and the one we love next best. Then we will study our choices, and we will know what to do."

It turned out that each girl's first choice remained Leibel, but when it came to second choice, Reitze chose Herschel and Leitze chose Velvel, but Neitze's second choice was the same as her first. It so happened that Herschel's first choice was Reitze and Velvel's Leitze. As for Leibel, he, too, had made only one choice: Neitze. When the slips were read out, it was quite clear who should marry whom.

At first the girls thought the weddings should be postponed so that they could invite their parents and friends. But all three boys were eager to get married, and Leibel said, "We can arrange the wedding ceremonies right now and later make a big celebration and invite everyone."

Since they had Dobosh's treasure, there was no lack of wedding rings. The girls found a large embroidered shawl that with the aid of four sticks made a perfect bridal canopy. As there were six young people, four of them could hold up the canopy while a pair stood beneath it for the ceremony. The first pair was Herschel and Reitze. They were the oldest. Herschel, the bridegroom, placed the wedding band on Reitze's finger and recited, "With this ring thou art consecrated to me according to the law of Moses and Israel." Bride and bridegroom both sipped wine from the same goblet and the rest called out, "*Mazel tov.*" Then in turn the other two couples stood beneath the canopy. And so they were married, according to the strictest law of the Talmud.

The brides had found beautiful dresses in Doboshova's cupboards, and even though the clothes were long out of fashion, they looked splendid in them. Reitze and Leitze were a little envious of Neitze, because she had been chosen by Leibel, but they wished her luck with all their hearts just the same. And although Leibel had studied the cabala and was generally better educated than the others, Herschel and Velvel were both taller and better-looking. Besides, Herschel, the yeshiva student, was a scholar in his own way. As for Velvel, he was an excellent businessman and clever in practical matters. None of the girls had made a bad bargain.

For the time being, all the couples remained at the inn. They sent word to their relatives and friends to tell them they were safe and to invite them to a great wedding celebration. Because some of the guests had to come from distant places, the celebration was postponed until spring.

Now that the inn was no longer spellbound, its entire surroundings had changed. Doboshova and Lapitut had thrown a curse on all the land for miles around. Suddenly streams, hills, and valleys appeared where there had been nothing but flat wasteland. Rabbits, deer, wild ducks, geese, pheasants, and other animals abounded where before there had been no living creatures. Winter passed. Spring came. The sky was blue and clear. The earth was richly covered with grass, flowers, and shrubbery. Trees that had seemed dead bore leaves and blossoms.

Word had spread about the inn that, like a mirage, had for years appeared only to those unlucky enough to go astray.

On the thirty-third day after the first day of Passover, the celebration took place. In addition to the guests. people came from all over the country to admire the changed inn and the three happy couples. Wedding jesters and musicians arrived from nearby towns to take part in the festivities. Magicians outdid each other to entertain the crowd with their tricks. After many entreaties, Leibel agreed to show his guests how the magic chalk that had saved the young people worked. He fetched the liveliest rooster from the barn, stood him on a table, and drew a circle around him. No matter how strongly the rooster flapped his wings, he could not fly off the table until Leibel wiped away the chalk to free him. Everybody was amazed.

They sang, danced, and made merry for seven days and seven nights. The moon was full and threw a silver light over the entire landscape. Even though there was not room enough in the inn for so many people and many of the guests slept outdoors, no evil intruder dared to disturb or frighten anyone.

After the last guest had left, it was time for Herschel and Velvel to go home with their wives, as had been decided. Leibel and Neitze had made up their minds to remain in the inn. "Because," Leibel said, "people often go astray, especially in the winter, and there should be someone to give them food and shelter." Leibel and Neitze were determined never to take any money from their guests, since Dobosh's treasure had made them rich.

The couples said goodbye to each other, and Leibel returned to his studies of the holy cabala, the wisdom of which can never be learned in full.

As the years went by, Herschel completed his education and became the head of a yeshiva. He used his money to help poor students.

Velvel became a great merchant and was renowned as a man of charity. All three couples lived happily and had many children and grandchildren. It became a custom each year for the couples and their children to gather at the inn and celebrate the day they had been set free.

Since Leibel's ring with the power to make the old young had never existed, Doboshova and Lapitut lived their allotted years and died. However, other devils have taken their place. These still live somewhere far in the desert, in the underground city of Asmodeus, their king. It is said that Asmodeus has a beard that reaches to the ground and two huge horns on his head. He sits on a throne held up by four snakes instead of legs. He has many wives, but his favorite is still Lilith, who dances for him each night to the caterwauling of a devil's band.

In time the once fearsome inn became known as the greatest academy of the cabala. It is believed that the ancient cabalists could, with the power of holy words, create pigeons, sap wine from a wall, and take seven-league steps.

In his old age Leibel was no longer called merely Leibel, but the saintly Reb Leib. His beard became white as silver. He could cure the sick with a touch, know what was happening in faraway cities, and foresee the future. Neitze, even though she was busy with her grandchildren—most of whom had red hair and green eyes—helped her husband and copied his writings with a quill pen.

The inn was a haven for all travelers who lost their way. It was said that no candles or oil lamps were needed there at night, because angels, seraphim, and cherubs descended at dark and lit the inn with heavenly light.

Translated by the author and Elizabeth Shub

The Cat Who Thought She Was a Dog & the Dog Who Thought He Was a Cat

Once there was a poor peasant, Jan Skiba by name. He lived with his wife and three daughters in a one-room hut with a straw roof, far from the village. The house had a bed, a bench bed, and a stove, but no mirror. A mirror was a luxury for a poor peasant. And why would a peasant need a mirror? Peasants aren't curious about their appearance.

But this peasant did have a dog and a cat in his hut. The dog was named Burek and the cat Kot. They had both been born within the same week. As little food as the peasant had for himself and his family, he still wouldn't let his dog and cat go hungry. Since the dog had never seen another dog and the cat had never seen another cat and they saw only each other, the dog thought he was a cat and the cat thought she was a dog. True, they were far from being alike by nature. The dog barked and the cat meowed. The dog chased rabbits and the cat lurked after mice. But must all creatures be exactly like their own kind? The peasant's children weren't exactly alike either. Burek and Kot lived on good terms, often ate from the same dish, and tried to mimic each other. When Burek barked, Kot tried to bark along, and when Kot meowed, Burek tried to meow, too. Kot occasionally chased rabbits and Burek made an effort to catch a mouse.

The peddlers who bought groats, chickens, eggs, honey, calves, and whatever was available from the peasants in the village never came to Jan Skiba's poor hut. They knew that Jan was so poor he had nothing to sell. But one day a peddler happened to stray there. When he came inside and began to lay out his wares, Jan Skiba's wife and daughters were bedazzled by all the pretty doodads. From his sack the peddler drew yellow beads, false pearls, tin earrings, rings, brooches, colored kerchiefs, garters, and other such trinkets. But what enthralled the women of the house most was a mirror set in a wooden frame. They asked the peddler its price and he said a half gulden, which was a lot of money for poor peasants. After a while, Jan Skiba's wife, Marianna, made a proposition to the peddler. She would pay him five groschen a month for the mirror. The peddler hesitated a moment. The mirror took up too much space in his sack and there was always the danger it might break. He therefore decided to go along, took the first payment of five groschen from Marianna, and left the mirror with the family. He visited the region often and he knew the Skibas to be honest people. He would gradually get his money back and a profit besides.

The mirror created a commotion in the hut. Until then Marianna and the children had seldom seen themselves. Before they had the mirror, they had only seen their reflections in the barrel of water that stood by the door. Now they could see themselves clearly and they began to find defects in their faces, defects they had never noticed before. Marianna was pretty but she had a tooth missing in front and she felt that this made her ugly. One daughter discovered that her nose was too snub and too broad; a second that her chin was too narrow and too long; a third that her face was sprinkled with freckles. Jan Skiba, too, caught a glimpse of himself in the mirror and grew displeased by his thick lips and his teeth, which protruded like a buck's. That day, the women of the house became so absorbed in the mirror they didn't cook supper, didn't make up the bed, and neglected all the other household tasks. Marianna had heard of a dentist in the big city who could replace a missing tooth, but such things were expensive. The girls tried to console each other that they were pretty enough and that they would find suitors, but they no longer felt as jolly as before. They had been afflicted with the vanity of city girls. The one with the broad nose kept trying to pinch it together with her fingers to make it narrower; the one with the too long chin pushed it up with her fist to make it shorter; the one with the freckles wondered if there was a salve in the city that could remove freckles. But where would the money come from for the fare to the city? And what about the money to buy this salve? For the first time the Skiba family deeply felt its poverty and envied the rich.

But the human members of the household were not the

only ones affected. The dog and the cat also grew disturbed by the mirror. The hut was low and the mirror had been hung just above a bench. The first time the cat sprang up on the bench and saw her image in the mirror, she became terribly perplexed. She had never before seen such a creature. Kot's whiskers bristled; she began to meow at her reflection and raised a paw to it, but the other creature meowed back and raised her paw, too. Soon the dog jumped up on the bench, and when he saw the other dog he became wild with rage and shock. He barked at the other dog and showed him his teeth, but the other barked back and bared his fangs, too. So great was the distress of Burek and Kot that for the first time in their lives they turned on each other. Burek took a bite out of Kot's throat and Kot hissed and spat at him and clawed his muzzle. They both started to bleed, and the sight of blood aroused them so that they nearly killed or crippled each other. The members of the household barely managed to separate them. Because a dog is stronger than a cat, Burek had to be tied outside, and he howled all day and all night. In their anguish, both the dog and the cat stopped eating.

When Jan Skiba saw the disruption the mirror had created in his household, he decided a mirror wasn't what his family needed. "Why look at yourself," he said, "when you can see and admire the sky, the sun, the moon, the stars, and the earth, with all its forests, meadows, rivers, and plants?" He took the mirror down from the wall and put it away in the woodshed. When the peddler came for his monthly installment, Jan Skiba gave him back the mirror and, in its stead, bought kerchiefs and slippers for the women. After the mirror disappeared, Burek and Kot returned to normal. Again Burek thought he was a cat and Kot was sure she was a dog. Despite all the defects the girls had found in themselves, they made good marriages. The village priest heard what had happened at Jan Skiba's house and he said, "A glass mirror shows only the skin of the body. The real image of a person is in his willingness to help himself and his family and, as far as possible, all those he comes in contact with. This kind of mirror reveals the very soul of the person."

Translated by Joseph Singer

Menaseh's Dream

Menaseh was an orphan. He lived with his Uncle Mendel, who was a poor glazier and couldn't even manage to feed and clothe his own children. Menaseh had already completed his cheder studies and after the fall holidays was to be apprenticed to a bookbinder.

Menaseh had always been a curious child. He had begun to ask questions as soon as he could talk: How high is the sky? How deep is the earth? What is beyond the edge of the world? Why are people born? Why do they die?

It was a hot and humid summer day. A golden haze hovered over the village. The sun was as small as a moon and yellow as brass. Dogs loped along with their tails between their legs. Pigeons rested in the middle of the marketplace. Goats sheltered themselves beneath the eaves of the huts, chewing their cuds and shaking their beards.

Menaseh quarreled with his Aunt Dvosha and left the house without eating lunch. He was about twelve, with a longish face, black eyes, sunken cheeks. He wore a torn jacket and was barefoot. His only possession was a tattered storybook which he had read scores of times. It was called *Alone in the Wild Forest*. The village in which he lived stood in a forest that surrounded it like a sash and was said to stretch as far as Lublin. It was blueberry time, and here and there one might also find wild strawberries. Menaseh made his way through pastures and wheat fields. He was hungry and he tore off a stalk of wheat to chew on the grain. In the meadows, cows were lying down, too hot even to whisk off the flies with their tails. Two horses stood, the head of one near the rump of the other, lost in their horse thoughts. In a field planted in buckwheat the boy was amazed to see a crow perched on the torn hat of a scarecrow.

Once Menaseh entered the forest, it was cooler. The pine trees stood straight as pillars and on their brownish bark hung golden necklaces, the light of the sun shining through the pine needles. The sounds of cuckoo and woodpecker were heard, and an unseen bird kept repeating the same eerie screech.

Menaseh stepped carefully over moss pillows. He crossed a shallow streamlet that purled joyfully over pebbles and stones. The forest was still, and yet full of voices and echoes.

He wandered deeper and deeper into the forest. As a rule, he left stone markers behind, but not today. He was lonely, his head ached, and his knees felt weak. Am I getting sick, he thought. Maybe I'm going to die. Then I will soon be with Daddy and Mama. When he came to a blueberry patch, he sat down, picked one berry after another, and popped them into his mouth. But they did not satisfy his hunger. Flowers with intoxicating odors grew among the blueberries. Without realizing it, Menaseh stretched full length on the forest floor. He fell asleep, but in his dream he continued walking.

The trees became even taller, the smells stronger, huge birds flew from branch to branch. The sun was setting. The forest grew thinner, and he soon came out on a plain with a broad view of the evening sky. Suddenly a castle appeared in the twilight. Menaseh had never seen such a beautiful structure. Its roof was of silver and from it rose a crystal tower. Its many tall windows were as high as the building itself. Menaseh went up to one of the windows and looked in. On the wall opposite him, he saw his own portrait hanging. He was dressed in luxurious clothes such as he had never owned. The huge room was empty.

Why is the castle empty, he wondered. And why is my portrait hanging on the wall? The boy in the picture seemed to be alive and waiting impatiently for someone to come. Then doors opened where there had been none before, and men and women came into the room. They were dressed in white satin and the women wore jewels and held holiday prayer books with gold-embossed covers. Menaseh gazed in astonishment. He recognized his father, his mother, his grandfathers and grandmothers, and other relatives. He wanted to rush over to them, hug and kiss them, but the window glass stood in his way. He began to cry. His paternal grandfather, Tobias the scribe, separated himself from the group and came to the window. The old man's beard was as white as his long coat. He looked both ancient and young. "Why are you crying?" he asked. Despite the glass that separated them, Menaseh heard him clearly.

"Are you my Grandfather Tobias?"

"Yes, my child. I am your grandfather."

"Who does this castle belong to?"

"To all of us."

"To me, too?"

"Of course, to the whole family."

"Grandpa, let me in," Menaseh called. "I want to speak to my father and mother."

His grandfather looked at him lovingly and said, "One day you will live with us here, but the time has not yet come."

"How long do I have to wait?"

"That is a secret. It will not be for many, many years."

"Grandpa, I don't want to wait so long. I'm hungry and thirsty and tired. Please let me in. I miss my father and mother and you and Grandma. I don't want to be an orphan."

"My dear child. We know everything. We think about you and we love you. We are all waiting for the time when we will be together, but you must be patient. You have a long journey to take before you come here to stay."

"Please, just let me in for a few minutes."

Grandfather Tobias left the window and took counsel with other members of the family. When he returned, he said, "You may come in, but only for a little while. We will show you around the castle and let you see some of our treasures, but then you must leave."

A door opened and Menaseh stepped inside. He was no sooner over the threshold than his hunger and weariness left him. He embraced his parents, and they kissed and hugged him. But they didn't utter a word. He felt strangely light. He floated along and his family floated with him. His grandfather opened door after door and each time Menaseh's astonishment grew.

One room was filled with racks of boys' clothing— pants, jackets, shirts, coats. Menaseh realized that these were the clothes he had worn as far back as he could remember. He also recognized his shoes, socks, caps, and nightshirts.

A second door opened and he saw all the toys he had ever owned: the tin soldiers his father had bought him; the jumping clown his mother had brought back from the fair at Lublin; the whistles and harmonicas; the teddy bear Grandfather had given him one Purim; and the wooden horse that was the gift of Grandmother Sprintze on his sixth birthday. The notebooks in which he had practiced writing, his pencils and Bible lay on a table. The Bible was open at the title page, with its familiar engraving of Moses holding the holy tablets and Aaron in his priestly robes, both framed by a border of six-winged angels. He noticed his name in the space allowed for it.

Menaseh could hardly overcome his wonder when a third door opened. This room was filled with soap bubbles. They did not burst as soap bubbles do, but floated serenely about, reflecting all the colors of the rainbow. Some of them mirrored castles, gardens, rivers, windmills, and many other sights. Menaseh knew that these were the bubbles he used to blow from his favorite bubble pipe. Now they seemed to have a life of their own.

A fourth door opened. Menaseh entered a room with no one in it; yet it was full of the sounds of happy talk, song, and laughter. Menaseh heard his own voice and the songs he used to sing when he lived at home with his parents. He also heard the voices of his former playmates, some of whom he had long since forgotten.

The fifth door led to a large hall. It was filled with the characters in the stories his parents had told him at bedtime and with the heroes and heroines of *Alone in the Wild Forest*. They were all there: David the warrior and the Ethiopian princess whom David saved from captivity; the highwayman Bandurek, who robbed the rich and fed the poor; Velikan the giant, who had one eye in the center of his forehead and who carried a fir tree as a staff in his right hand and a snake in his left; the midget Pitzeles, whose beard dragged on the ground and who was jester to the fearsome King Merodach; and the two-headed wizard Malkizedek, who by witchcraft spirited innocent girls into the desert of Sodom and Gomorrah.

Menaseh barely had time to take them all in when a sixth door opened. Here everything was changing constantly. The walls of the room turned like a carousel. Events flashed by. A golden horse became a blue butterfly; a rose as bright as the sun became a goblet out of which flew fiery grasshoppers, purple fauns, and silver bats. On a glittering throne with seven steps leading up to it sat King Solomon, who somehow resembled Menaseh. He wore a crown and at his feet knelt the Queen of Sheba. A peacock spread his tail and addressed

King Solomon in Hebrew. The priestly Levites played their lyres. Giants waved their swords in the air and Ethiopian slaves riding lions served goblets of wine and trays filled with pomegranates. For a moment Menaseh did not understand what it all meant. Then he realized that he was seeing his dreams.

Behind the seventh door, Menaseh glimpsed men and women, animals, and many things that were completely strange to him. The images were not as vivid as they had been in the other rooms. The figures were transparent and surrounded by mist. On the threshold stood a girl Menaseh's own age. She had long golden braids. Although Menaseh could not see her clearly, he liked her at once. For the first time he turned to his grandfather. "What is all this?" he asked. And his grandfather replied, "These are the people and events of your future."

"Where am I?" Menaseh asked.

"You are in a castle that has many names. We like to call it the place where nothing is lost. There are many more wonders here, but now it is time for you to leave."

Menaseh wanted to remain in this strange place forever, together with his parents and grandparents. He looked questioningly at his grandfather, who shook his head. Menaseh's parents seemed to want him both to remain and to leave as quickly as possible. They still did not speak, but signaled to him, and Menaseh understood that he was in grave danger. This must be a forbidden place. His parents silently bade him farewell and his face became wet and hot from their kisses. At that moment everything disappeared—the castle, his parents, his grandparents, the girl.

Menaseh shivered and awoke. It was night in the forest. Dew was falling. High above the crowns of the pine trees the full moon shone and the stars twinkled. Menaseh looked into the face of a girl who was bending over him. She was barefoot and wore a patched skirt; her long, braided hair shone golden in the moonlight. She was shaking him and saying, "Get up, get up. It is late and you can't remain here in the forest."

Menaseh sat up. "Who are you?"

"I was looking for berries and I found you here. I've been trying to wake you."

"What is your name?"

"Channeleh. We moved into the village last week."

She looked familiar, but he could not remember meeting her before. Suddenly he knew. She was the girl he had seen in the seventh room, before he woke up.

"You lay there like dead. I was frightened when I saw you. Were you dreaming? Your face was so pale and your lips were moving."

"Yes, I did have a dream."

"What about?"

"A castle."

"What kind of castle?"

Menaseh did not reply and the girl did not repeat her question. She stretched out her hand to him and helped him get up. Together they started toward home. The moon had never seemed so light or the stars so close. They walked with their shadows behind them. Myriads of crickets chirped. Frogs croaked with human voices.

Menaseh knew that his uncle would be angry at him for coming home late. His aunt would scold him for leaving without his lunch. But these things no longer mattered. In his dream he had visited a mysterious world. He had found a friend. Channeleh and he had already decided to go berry picking the next day.

Among the undergrowth and wild mushrooms, little people in red jackets, gold caps, and green boots emerged. They danced in a circle and sang a song which is heard only by those who know that everything lives and nothing in time is ever lost.

Translated by the author and Elizabeth Shub

Tashlik

Aaron the watchmaker did not live on our street, but when I climbed to the highest branch of the lime tree that grew in our garden, I could see his house clearly; it was the only one in the village that had a small lawn in front of it. The shutters of Aaron's house were painted green; flowerpots stood in the windows; there were sunflowers in the garden. Aaron and his family lived on the ground floor, that is, with the exception of his daughter, Feigele; she had a room in the attic. At night a lamp burned in Feigele's window long after the lights downstairs had been extinguished. Occasionally I caught a glimpse of her shadow passing across the curtain. Mottel, Feigele's younger brother, had built a dovecote on the roof and often stood on the top of the building chasing pigeons with a long stick. Leon, the older boy, who was studying at a polytechnic in Cracow, rode around the village on a horse when he came home on vacation. There was nothing that that emancipated family did not possess: they had a parrot, canaries, a dog. Aaron played the zither; his wife owned a piano—she came from Lublin and didn't wear a wig. Aaron the watchmaker, who was also both goldsmith and jeweler, was the only man in the village with a telephone in his house; he could speak directly to Zamość . . .

I was not a native of that hamlet. I had been brought up in Warsaw, but when the war came, my parents left the city and went to live with my grandfather the rabbi. There we were stuck in a village which was on no railroad and was surrounded by pine forests. My father was appointed assistant rabbi. I never stopped longing for Warsaw, its streets, its trolley cars, its illuminated show windows, and its tall balconied residences. Aaron the watchmaker and his family represented for me a fragment of the metropolis. Aaron had a library containing books written in several languages. In his store one could put on earphones and listen to the radio. He subscribed to two Warsaw newspapers, one in Polish and one in Yiddish, and was always hunting for a chess partner. Feigele had attended the Gymnasium in Lublin, boarding with an aunt while she was away from home, but now having received her diploma, she had returned to her parents.

Aaron the watchmaker had been a student of my grandfather's and had been considered a religious prodigy until he had been caught reading the Bible in German translation, a sure sign of heresy. Like Moses Mendelssohn, Aaron was a hunchback. Although he had not been officially excommunicated, it was almost as if he had been. He had a high forehead, a mangy-looking goatee, and large black eyes. There was something ancient and half forgotten in his gaze for which I knew no name and which made me think of Spinoza and Uriel Acosta. When he sat at the window of his store studying some mechanism through a watch glass, he seemed to be reading the wheels as a fortune-teller does his crystal. All day his sad smile enunciated over and over again, "Vanity of vanities." Feigele had inherited her father's eyes. She kept to herself, was always to be seen strolling alone, a tall, thin girl with a long, pale face and a thin nose and lips. She always carried two books under her arm, one thick and one thin. A strange gentleness emanated from her. By this time the fashionable girls cut their hair *au garçon*, but Feigele wore hers in a bun. She always took the road to the Russian cemetery. Once I saw her reading the inscriptions in the graveyard.

I was too shy to talk to her, wasn't even sure she knew who I was, since she had a way of looking over people's heads. But I knew that, like me, she was living in exile. She didn't seem to ever stop meditating, would pause to examine trees, and would reflectively stare down well shafts. I kept trying to meet her but couldn't think of a plan. Moreover, I was ashamed of my appearance, decked out as I was in a velvet cap, a long gabardine, and red earlocks. I knew that I must seem to her just another Hasidic boy. How could she guess that I was reading Knut Hamsun and Strindberg on the sly and studying Spinoza's *Ethics* in a Hebrew translation? In addition, I owned a work by Flammarion and was dabbling in the cabala. In the evening, when I perched on the highest branch of the lime tree, I gazed up at the moon and the stars like an astronomer. Feigele's window was also visible to me and just as inaccessible as the sky. I had already been matched with the daughter of a rabbi. Every day my father read me a lesson from the Shulhan Arukh on how to become a rabbi. The villagers watched me constantly to make sure that I committed no transgressions. My father complained that my frivolity jeopardized his livelihood. All I needed was to be caught talking to a girl, particularly Aaron the watchmaker's daughter.

But when I sat in my tree at night watching Feigele's window I knew indubitably that my longing for her must someday bring a response. I already believed in telepathy, clairvoyance, mesmerism. I would narrow my eyes until the light from Feigele's lamp became thin, fiery filaments. My psychic messages would speed across the blackness to her, for I was seeking to emulate Joseph della Reina, who by using the powers of Holy Names had brought the Grand Vizier's daughter in a trance to his bed. I called out to Feigele, trying to invade both her waking thoughts and her dreams. I wrapped a phantom net around her like some sorcerer from the *Arabian Nights*. My incantations must inevitably kindle love in her heart and make her desire me passionately. In return I would give her caresses such as no woman had ever received before . . .

I would adorn her with jewels dug from the moon. We would fly together to other planets and she would dwell a queen in supernal palaces. For reasons which I was unable to explain I became convinced that the beginning of our friendship would date from the reading of the tashlik prayer on Rosh Hashanah afternoon. This premonition was totally illogical. Probably an enlightened girl like Feigele would not even attend the ceremony. But the idea had entered into me like a dybbuk. I kept counting the days and hours until the holiday, formulated plans, conceived of the words I would say to her. Two or three times, perching among the leaves and branches, I noticed Feigele standing at the window looking out. I could not see her eyes but knew that she had heard my call and was searching for me in the darkness. It was the month of Elul and every day the ram's horn was blown in the studyhouse to drive away Satan. Spiderwebs drifted through the air; cold winds blew from the Arctic ice cap. So bright was the moon that night and day were nearly indistinguishable. Crows, awakened by the light, croaked. The grasshoppers were singing their final songs; shadows scampered across the fields surrounding the village. The river wound through the meadows like a silver snake.

It was Rosh Hashanah, and I put on the new gabardine and new shoes I had been given and brushed my sidelocks behind my ears. What more could a young Hasid do to look modern? In the late afternoon I started to loiter on Bridge Street, watching the townspeople file by on their way to the tashlik ceremony. The day was sunny, the sky as blue and transparent as it is in midsummer. Cool breezes mingled with the warmth exuded by the earth. First came the Hasidim, marching together as a group, all dressed in fur hats and satin coats. They hurried along as if they were rushing from their womenfolk and temptation. I had been raised among these people, but now I found their disheveled beards, their ill-fitting clothes, and their insistent clannishness odd. They ran from the Evil One like sheep from a wolf.

After the Hasidim came the ordinary Jews, and after them the women and girls. Most of the older women wore capes and gowns which dated from the time of King Sobieski; they had tiaras and bonnets with ribbons on their heads. Their jewelry consisted of gold head chains, long earrings so weighty they almost tore the lobes of their ears, and brooches inherited from grandmothers and great-grandmothers that vibrated as the women walked. My mother had on a gold silk dress and a pelerine decorated with rhinestones. But the younger women had studied the fashion magazines (which always showed up in the village a year or two after they had been issued) and were dressed in what they considered to be the latest style. Some of them wore narrow skirts that scarcely covered their knees and even bobbed their hair. The ladies' tailors stood to one side commenting on the dress of the women. They contrasted their handiwork with that of their competitors and ridiculed not only one another's designs but the clients who wore them. I kept looking in vain for Feigele. My sorcery had failed and I walked with downcast eyes among the stragglers. Some of the townspeople stood on the wooden bridge reciting the tashlik; others lined the riverbanks. Young women took out their handkerchiefs and shook out their sins. Boys playfully emptied their pockets to be sure that no transgression remained. The village wits made the traditional tashlik jokes: "Girls, shake as hard as you want, but a few sins will remain." "The fish will get fat feeding on so many errors."

I made no attempt to say the prayer but stood under a willow watching a huge red sun which was split in half by a wisp of cloud sinking in the west. Flocks of birds dipped toward the water, their wings one instant silver, the next leaden black. The color of the river turned from green to rose. I had lost everything that mattered here on earth, but still found comfort in the sky. Several of the smaller clouds seemed to be on fire and sailed across the heavens like ships with burning sails. I gaped at the sun as if I were seeing it for the first time. I had learned from Flammarion that this star was a million and a half times as large as the earth and had a temperature of six thousand degrees centigrade on its surface and hundreds of thousands in its interior. Everything came from it—light, warmth, the wood for the oven, and the food in the pot. Even life and suffering were impossible without it. But what was the sun? Where did it come from? Whence did it travel, moving in the Milky Way and also with the galaxy?

Suddenly I understood why the pagans had worshipped it as a god. I had a desire to kneel and bow down myself. Well, could one be certain that it lacked consciousness? *The Guide to the Perplexed* said that the heavenly bodies possess souls and are driven in their orbits by Ideas emitting a divine music as they circle. The music of the spheres now seemed to mingle with the twittering of the birds, the sounds of the coursing river, and the murmur of the praying multitude. Then a greenish-blue shimmer appeared on the horizon, the first star, a brilliant miniature sun. I knew that it had taken years for the rays from this fixed star to reach my eyes. But what were rays? I was seized by a sort of cosmic yearning. I wanted to cease existing and return to my sources, to be once again a part of the universe. I muttered a prayer to the sun: "Gather me to you. I am weary of being myself."

Suddenly I felt a tug at my sleeve. I turned and trembled. Feigele stood next to me. So great was my amazement that I forgot to marvel. She wore a black suit, a black beret, and a white collar. Her face lit by the setting sun shone with a Rosh Hashanah purity. "Excuse me," she said. "Can you locate the tashlik for me? I can't seem to find the place." Her smile seemed to be saying, "Well, this was the best pretext available." In her gaze there were both pride and humility. I, like Joseph della Reina, had summoned my beloved from the Grand Vizier's palace.

She held in her hand a prayer book which had covers stamped in gold. I took one cover of the book and she grasped the other. I started to turn the pages. On one side of the page was Hebrew and on the other Polish. I kept turning the leaves but couldn't find the prayer either. The crowd had already begun to disperse and heads kept turning in our direction. I started to thumb through the book more quickly. The tashlik prayer just could not have been omitted. But where was it? Feigele glanced at me in wonder and her eyes seemed to be saying, "Don't get yourself so wrought up. It's nothing but a stratagem." The letters tumbled before my eyes; the prayer book trembled as though it were living. Inadvertently Feigele's elbow and mine touched and we begged each other's pardon. The prayer seemed to have flown from the book. But I knew that it was there and that my eyes had been bewitched. I was just about to give up looking when I saw the word "tashlik" printed in big bold letters. "Here it is," I cried out, and my heart seemed to stop.

"What? Thank you."

"I haven't recited the tashlik myself," I said.

"Well, suppose we say it together."

"Can you read Hebrew script?"

"Of course."

"This prayer symbolizes the casting of one's sins into the ocean."

"Naturally."

We stood muttering the prayer together as the crowd slowly moved off. Boys threw mocking glances at us; women scowled; girls winked. I knew that this encounter was going to get me into a great deal of trouble at home. But for the moment I reveled in my triumph, a sorcerer whose charms and incantations had worked. The look of religious devotion on Feigele's face made her appear even gentler. The sun had already disappeared behind the trees, and in the distance the forest looked blue and like mountains. Suddenly I felt that I had experienced this moment before. Had it been in a dream or in a former life? The air was alive with sound: the croaking of birds, the buzzing of insects, a ringing as if from bells. The frogs began their evening conversation. A herd of cows passed nearby, their hooves pounding the ground. It was a miracle that the animals did not drive us into the river. No longer did the book tremble in our hands. I heard Feigele murmur:

"The Lord looketh from heaven. He beholdeth all the sons of men . . . He fashioneth all their hearts alike. He considereth all their works . . ."

Translated by the author and Cecil Hemley

Are Children the Ultimate Literary Critics?

Children are the best readers of genuine literature. Grownups are hypnotized by big names, exaggerated quotes, and high-pressure advertising. Critics who are more concerned with sociology than with literature have persuaded millions of readers that if a novel doesn't try to bring about a social revolution it is of no value. Hundreds of professors who write commentaries on writers try to convince their students that only writers who require elaborate commentaries and countless footnotes are the true creative geniuses of our time.

But children do not succumb to this kind of belief. They still like clarity, logic, and even such obsolete stuff as punctuation. Even more, the young reader demands a real story, with a beginning, a middle, and an end, the way stories have been told for thousands of years.

In our epoch, when storytelling has become a forgotten art and has been replaced by amateurish sociology and hackneyed psychology, the child is still the independent reader who relies on nothing but his own taste. Names and authorities mean nothing to him. Long after literature for adults has gone to pieces, books for children will constitute the last vestige of storytelling, logic, faith in the family, in God, and in real humanism.

When I sit down to write a story, I must first have a real topic or theme. One cannot write for children what some critics call "a slice of life." The truth is that the so-called slices of life are a bore even for adults.

I must also have a real desire or a passion to write the story. Sometimes I have a topic but somehow no compulsion to deal with it. I've written down hundreds of topics which I will never use because they don't really interest me.

Finally, I must have the conviction—or at least the illusion—that I am the only one who can write this particular story. It has to be my story. It has to express my individuality, my character, my way of looking at the world.

If these three conditions are present, I will write a story. This holds true when I write for children or for adults.

Some bad books lack these three conditions. They have no story to tell, there's no passion in them, and they have no real connection with the writer.

Because children like clarity and logic, you may wonder how I can write about the supernatural, which, by its very definition, is not clear and not logical. Logic and "realism," as a literary method, are two different things. One can be a very illogical realist and a highly logical mystic. Children are by nature inclined to mysticism. They believe in God, in the Devil, in good spirits and bad spirits, and in all kinds of magic. Yet they require true consistency in these stories. There is often great logic in religion and there is little logic in materialism. Those who maintain that the world created itself are often people without any respect for reason.

It is tragic that many writers who look down on stories of the supernatural are writing things for children which are nothing but sheer chaos. There are books for children where one sentence has nothing to do with another. Things happen arbitrarily and haphazardly, without any connection with the child's experience or ideas.

Not only does such writing not amuse a child, but it damages his way of thinking. Sometimes I have a feeling that the so-called avant-garde writers for children are trying to prepare the child for James Joyce's *Finnegans Wake* or other such puzzles which some of the professors love so much to explain. Instead of helping them think, such writing cripples the child's mind. Put it this way— the supernatural, yes; nonsense, no.

Folklore plays a most important role in children's literature. The tragedy of modern adult literature is that it has completely divorced itself from folklore. Many modern writers have lost their roots. They don't belong and they don't want to belong to any special group. They are afraid of being called clannish, nationalistic, or chauvinistic.

Actually there is no literature without roots. One cannot write good fiction just about a man generally. In literature, as in life, everything is specific. Every man has his actual and spiritual address. It is true that in certain fables the address is not necessary or even superfluous, but all literature is not fables. The more a writer is rooted in his environment, the more he is understood by all people; the more national he is, the more international he becomes.

When I began to write the stories of my collection *Zlateh the Goat*, I knew that these stories would be read not only by Jewish children but by Gentile ones as well. I described Jewish children, Jewish sages, Jewish fools, Jewish bridegrooms, Jewish brides. The events I related did not happen in no-man's-land but in the little towns and villages I knew well and where I was brought up. My saints were Jewish saints and the demons Jewish demons. And this book has been translated into many languages.

Many of today's books for children have no local color, no ethnic charm. The writers try so hard to be international—to produce merchandise which appeals to all—that they appeal to no one. (By the way, the Bible, especially the Book of Genesis, teems with stories for children—all of them short, clear, deeply rooted in their time and soil. This is the reason for their universal appeal.)

Without folklore and deep roots in a specific soil, literature must decline and wither away. This is true in all literature of all times. Luckily children's literature is even now more rooted in folklore than the literature for adults. And this alone makes children's literature so important in our generation.

Some writers sit down to write a book, not because

they love the story, but because they are in love with the message it might bring. There is no famine of messages in our time or in any other time. If all the messages disappeared and only the Ten Commandments remained, we would still have enough messages for the present and the future. Our trouble is not that we don't have enough messages but that we refuse to fulfill them and practice them.

The writer who writes a bad novel and whose message is peace and equality and other such virtues does us no great favor. We've heard all this before and will continue to hear about it in newspaper editorials, in sermons, even from diplomats of the most aggressive nations. There are multitudes of writers whose only claim to literature is that they are on the right side and that their messages are righteous.

Literature needs well-constructed and inventive stories, not stale messages, for every good story has a message that, even if it is not obvious, will be discovered by readers or critics sooner or later. I do not yet know the message of Tolstoy's *War and Peace*, but it was a great book just the same. A genuine story can have many interpretations, scores of messages, mountains of commentaries. Events never get stale; commentaries often are stale from the very beginning.

As a child, I was glad that I was told the same stories my father and grandfathers heard. The children of my time didn't read stories about little ducklings which fell into kettles of soup and emerged as clay frogs. We preferred the stories of Adam and Eve, the Flood, the people who built the Tower of Babel, the divine adventures of

Abraham, Isaac, Jacob, Joseph. We were taught never to rely completely on any authority. We tried to find motivation and consistency in God's laws and His commandments. A lot of the evil taking place today, I often feel, is the result of the rotten stuff this modern generation read in its school days.

Since I began to write for children I have spoken to many children, read stories to them (even though my accent is far from perfect), and answered hundreds of their questions. I am always amazed to see that when it comes to asking questions, children possess the same curiosity as adults: How do you get the idea for a book? Is it invented or taken from life? How long does it take you to write a book? Do you use stories that your mother and father told you?

No matter how young they are, children are deeply concerned with so-called eternal questions: Who created the world? Who made the earth, the sky, people, animals? Children cannot imagine the beginning or end of time and space. As a child I asked all the questions I later found discussed in the works of Plato, Aristotle, Spinoza, Leibnitz, Hume, Kant, and Schopenhauer. Children think about and ponder such matters as justice, the purpose of life, the why of suffering. They often find it difficult to make peace with the idea that animals are slaughtered so that man can eat them. They are bewildered and frightened by death. They cannot accept the fact that the strong should rule the weak.

Many grownups have made up their minds that there is no purpose in asking questions and that one should accept the facts as they are. But the child is often a philosopher and a seeker of God. This is one reason I always suggest they read the Bible. It does not answer all the questions, but it does deal with these questions. It tells us that there is a God who created heaven and earth. It condemns Cain's murder of Abel. It tells us that the wicked are punished and that the just, though they may suffer a lot, are rewarded and loved by the Almighty.

If I had my way, I would publish a history of philosophy for children, where I would convey the basic ideas of all philosophers in simple language. Children, who are highly serious people, would read this book with great interest. In our time, when the literature for adults is deteriorating, good books for children are the only hope, the only refuge. Many adults read and enjoy children's books. We write not only for children but also for their parents. They, too, are serious children.